WELCOME to the DARK SIDE

A FALLEN MEN NOVEL
BOOK TWO

giana darling

For everyone whose lives have been affected by cancer. You are strong, you are brave and I am in awe of your courage of conviction and continual hope.

And for my dad, who always encouraged the rebel and the writer in me, and who succumbed to his own battle with cancer in 2011.

"An overflow of good converts to bad."
—*William Shakespeare*, Richard II. Act V. Scene 3.

PLAYLIST

"Bad to the Bone"—George Thorogood & The Destroyers
"Four Five Seconds"—Rihanna, Kayne West & Paul McCartney
"Stay Free"—Black Mountain
"Nobody's Darling"—Lucero
"John the Revelator"—Curtis Stigers & The Forest Rangers
"Sugar Man" —Rodriguez
"Sink the Pink"—AC/DC
"House of the Rising Son"—Battleme & The Forest Rangers
"The Hills"—The Weeknd
"You Are My Sunshine"—Cream
"Stairway to Heaven" —Led Zepplin
"Make It Rain" —Ed Sheeran
"Take Me to Church"—Hozier
"Sing Sing"—The Bones of J.R. Jones
"God's Gonna Cut You Down"—Jonny Cash
"Family" —Noah Gundersen

PROLOGUE

Loulou

I WAS TOO YOUNG TO REALIZE WHAT THE *POP* MEANT.

It sounded to my childish ears like a giant popping a massive wad of bubble gum.

Not like a bullet releasing from a chamber, heralding the sharp burst of pain that would follow when it smacked and then ripped through my shoulder.

Also, I was in the parking lot of First Light Church. It was my haven not only because it was a church and that was the original purpose of such places, but also because my grandpa was the pastor, my grandmother ran the after-school programs and my father was the mayor so it was just as much his stage as his parents'.

A seven-year-old girl just does not expect to be shot in

the parking lot of a church, holding the hand of her mother on one side and her father on the other, her grandparents waving from the open door as parents picked up their young children from after-school care.

Besides, I was unusually mesmerized by the sight of a man driving slowly by the entrance to the church parking lot. He rode a great growling beast that was so enormous it looked to my childish eyes like a silver-and-black backed dragon. Only the man wasn't wearing shining armor the way I thought he should have been. Instead, he wore a tight long-sleeved shirt under a heavy leather vest with a big picture of a fiery skull and tattered wings on the back of it. What kind of knight rode a mechanical dragon in a leather vest?

My little girl brain was too young to comprehend the complexities of the answer but my heart, though small, knew without context what kind of brotherhood that man would be in and it yearned for him.

Even at seven, I harbored a black rebel soul bound in velvet bows and bible verse.

As if sensing my gaze, my thoughts, the biker turned to look at me, his face cruel with anger. I shivered and as his gaze settled on mine those shots rang out in a staccato beat that perfectly matched the cadence of my suddenly over-worked heart.

Pop. Pop. Pop.

Everything from there happened as it did in action movies, with rapid bursts of sound and movement that swirled into a violent cacophony. I remembered only three things from the shooting that would go down in history as one of the worst incidents of gang violence in the town and province's history.

One.

My father flying to the ground quick as a flash, his hand wrenched from mine so that he could cover his own head. My mother screaming like a howler monkey but frozen to the spot, her hand paralyzed over mine.

Useless.

Two.

Men in black leather vests flooded the concrete like a murder of ravens, their hands filled with smoking metal that rattled off round after round of *pop, pop, pop*. Some of them rode bikes like my mystery biker but most of them were on foot, suddenly appearing from behind cars, around buildings.

More of them came roaring down the road behind the man I'd been watching, flying blurs of silver, green and black.

They were everywhere.

But these first two observations were merely vague impressions because I had eyes for only one person.

The third thing I remembered was him, Zeus Garro, locking eyes with me across the parking lot a split second before chaos erupted. Our gazes collided like the meeting of two planets, the ensuing bedlam a natural offshoot of the collision. It was only because I was watching him that I saw the horror distort his features and knew something bad was going to happen.

Someone grabbed me from behind, hauled me into the air with their hands under my pits. They were tall because I remember dangling like an ornament from his hold, small but significant with meaning. He was using me and even then, I knew it.

I twisted to try and kick him in the torso with the hard heel of my Mary Jane's and he must have assumed I'd be frozen in fright because my little shoe connected with a soft place that immediately loosened his grip.

Before I could fully drop to the ground, I was running and I was running toward him. The man on the great silver and black beast who had somehow heralded the massacre going down in blood and smoke all around me.

His bike lay discarded on its side behind him and he was standing straight and so tall he seemed to my young mind like a great giant, a beast from another planet or the deep jungle, something that killed for sport as well as survival. And he was doing it now, killing men like it was nothing but one of those awful, violent video games my cousin Clyde liked to play. In one hand he held a wicked curved blade already lacquered with blood from the two men who lay fallen at his feet while the other held a smoking gun that, under other circumstances, I might have thought was a pretty toy.

I took this in as I ran toward him, focused on him so I wouldn't notice the *pop*, the screams and wet slaps of bodies hitting the pavement. So I wouldn't taste the metallic residue of gun powder on my tongue or feel the splatter of blood that rained down on me as I passed one man being gutted savagely by another.

Somehow, if I could just get to *him*, everything would be okay.

He watched me come to him. Not with his eyes, because he was busy killing bad guys and shouting short, gruff orders to the guys wearing the same uniform as him but there was something in the way his great big body leaned toward me, shifted on his feet so that he was always orientated my way, that made me feel sure he was looking out for me even as I came for him.

He was just a stone's throw away, but it seemed to take forever for my short legs to move me across the asphalt and when I was only halfway there, his expression changed.

I knew without knowing that the man I'd kicked in his soft place was up again and probably angry. The hairs on the back of my neck stood on end and a fierce shiver ripped down my spine like tearing Velcro. I didn't realize it at the time, but I started to scream just as the police sirens started to wail a few blocks away.

My biker man roared, a violent noise that rent the air in two and made some of the people closest to him pause even in the middle of fighting. Then he was moving, and I remember thinking that for such a tall man, he moved *fast* because within the span of a breath, he was in front of me reaching out a hand to pull me closer...

A moment too late.

Because in that second when his tattooed hands clutched me to his chest and he tried to throw us to the ground, spiraling in a desperate attempt to act as human body armor to my tiny form, a *POP* so much louder than the rest exploded on the air and excruciating pain tore through my left shoulder, just inches from my adrenaline-filled heart.

We landed, and the agonizing pain burned brighter as my shoulder hit the pavement and my biker man rolled fully on top of me with a pained grunt.

I blinked through the tears welling up in my eyes, trying to breathe, trying to *live* through the pain radiating like a nuclear blast site through my chest. All I saw was him. His arm covered my head, one hand over my ear as he pulled back just enough to look down into my face.

That was what I remember most, that third thing, Zeus Garro's silver eyes as they stared down at me in a church parking lot filled with blood and smoke, screams and whimpers, but those eyes an oasis of calm that lulled my flagging heart into a steadier beat.

"I got you, little girl," he said in a voice as rough and deep as any monster's, while he held me as if he were a guardian angel. "I got you."

I clutched a tiny fist into his blood-soaked shirt and stared into the eyes of my guardian monster until I lost consciousness.

Sometimes now, I wonder if I would have done anything differently even if I had known how that bullet would tear through my small body, breaking bones and tender young flesh, irrevocably changing the course of my life forever.

Always, the answer is no.

Because it brought me to him.

Or rather, him to me.

CHAPTER ONE

Loulou

"HE'S GOING TO PRISON FOR THIS," MY DADDY YELLED FROM the hallway.

We were in the hospital. I knew this because I woke up in a white bed in a room with white walls and white floors and there were white tubes stuck into my arm. There were no loud noises, no blood or bodies or biker men around so I knew that everything had calmed down and I was safe.

At least, everything had calmed down except for my daddy. I'd never seen him so mad because Lafayettes weren't supposed to let anyone else know what they were thinking or feeling.

Everyone in the kids ward of Saint Katherine's Hospital

knew what my daddy was thinking *and* feeling right now. I woke up to a foggy head, a dull pain in my shoulder and the sound of him saying a lot of *really* bad words. That was five minutes ago and he still hadn't stopped.

"Benjamin, you are making a scene," my mum said.

"I mean it, Phillipa," he shouted just outside my slightly open door. "That piece of scum is going away for this!"

"I understand your sentiments, Mr. Lafayette, and I can assure you that Zeus Garro will go to jail for his crimes." The staff sergeant hesitated. "But he has a solid shot at a reduced sentence and early parole for saving your daughter—"

"HE DID NO SUCH THING," Daddy bellowed. "*He* is the reason that my daughter is drugged up and lying damaged in a fucking hospital bed. *He* is the reason that Entrance is known as the hometown to a violent, drug-trafficking motorcycle gang. We are fucking lucky that water real estate is at a premium in the province and our education ranking is so high or else no one would ever live here. And do you know why that is, Harold? Because of fucking Zeus Garro."

Oh no.

No way.

My daddy was so *not* going to send my biker man to jail. I didn't really know what he was talking about except that drugs were bad and so was violence, but I did know that my biker saviour was not a bad man. Bad men just didn't throw themselves in front of seven-year-old girls to take a bullet for them.

I was young but I wasn't dumb.

"Daddy," I cried out, but my voice was weak in my dry throat.

"If you would listen to what I'm telling you, Benjamin," staff sergeant Danner tried again. "I'm telling you, Garro is going away for this. He killed a man in front of my fucking officers, shot him right in the goddamn head before we could even take stock of the situation. He's *going away*. What I'm also telling you is that the man he shot in the head was the man who put a bullet in your daughter, the same bullet that went *through* Garro's own chest before it landed in hers. You want to talk about the damage that bullet could've done if it hadn't lost speed going through that barrel of a man first?"

My daddy was silent after that.

"Benjamin," my mum said in her special soft voice that made him listen to her. "He deserves to go to prison but think of the silver lining. If Louise wasn't hurt like this we wouldn't know there was something wrong with her."

My ears stung to hear it, but I wasn't surprised. I'd been sick for a long time now even though no one believed me when I said I felt bad because I didn't have a runny nose or anything.

"We don't know anything yet, Phillipa," my daddy told her sternly.

"We do. The doctors are concerned, honey. It took her too long to stop bleeding, she *lost consciousness for two days*. That is not normal. And then there's the fact that she has been complaining about pain for a few months now—"

"She's looking for attention, Phillipa, that's all."

"Whether or not that may be the case, the doctors are running tests and it is not looking good."

"Being stubborn again, are we, son?" The wheezy old voice of my grandpa came through my door and I straightened automatically in my bed. Grandpa was stern, but he was also super nice to me and he always gave me lollipops if I recited Bible passages correctly.

"Even you can't find absolution for Zeus Garro, Dad," my daddy said.

"Maybe not, but I can find it for him in this situation. Without this incident, how long would it have taken you to realize that Louise is seriously ill. I've said it once, I'll say it one hundred times, just because someone is not who you want them to be, it does not mean they are incapable of good."

My daddy snorted. "I will not thank a felon for saving my daughter, not least of all because he did not even save her! She's laying in a hospital bed with a bullet wound through her shoulder! How am I the only rational person here who sees what a *monster* that man is? He shouldn't even be allowed to rest in the same hospital as my daughter after what he and his *gang* have done."

"Benjamin, that is enough," my mum said. "People can hear you. Think what they might say?"

"No, you're right. We need to spin this just right and I'm too furious to think with a level head right now. We'll go home and talk about what to tell the press. Harold, I don't want any of those vultures in here trying to get to my daughter. Lord knows what she'll say to them."

"Benjamin." My grandpa tsked. "She's just a girl."

"A girl who needs to grow up. What in the world she was doing running away from her parents and into the fray, is beyond me."

Their voices faded as they walked down the hall away

from my room. I lay stiff even though it hurt my arm, because whenever my parents made me want to cry, I told myself to be still and be calm. Crying was for babies like my little sister, Bea. Not for me. I was a Lafayette and Lafayettes didn't cry. Not even when they got shot, not even when they got sick and not even when their family left them all alone in the hospital. I lay there for a long time until Nanny came in with Bea to check on me. They both smiled and laughed when they put cartoons on the little TV on the wall but I didn't feel like smiling. The only thing that made me feel better was the Snickers bar that a super nice nurse named Betsy snuck in for me.

Later, Nanny was somewhere talking to the doctors because they never did that kind of stuff in front of me. Our neighbor, Mrs. Brock, already picked up Bea and took her home. I was alone but I was happy because I was mad at Daddy for hating my guardian monster and Nanny wouldn't stop touching me and saying stuff in French that was supposed to be nice, but I didn't understand.

I was supposed to stay in the kid part of the hospital because they were keeping me overnight but I didn't like it there. There were a lot of kids and a lot of them cried. It was sad and it was even sadder that the nurses and staff tried to cover it up with bright colours and lots of toys. It wasn't a happy place and it kind of freaked me out.

If I stayed in my room like I was supposed to, it was even scarier and sadder because grandpa said I had a good imagination and I did, so it was easy to picture all the monsters crawling around outside, just waiting for me to fall asleep, so they could eat me.

Besides, Daddy had mentioned that my guardian

monster was in the hospital too so maybe I could find him and tell him to run away.

My arm really hurt when I moved but it wasn't too big a deal because my body had been hurting for a while, like my blood was on fire and I was a volcano about to erupt. I winced when I pulled the needle out of my hand and saw the really purple bruise there. It didn't scare me though. I bruised really badly really easily.

It wasn't busy that night so no one noticed me when I walked down the halls and checked out what everyone was doing. People don't really notice kids unless they're in the way.

I searched my floor then the one below me and I was super tired by the time I checked the emergency room, but I made myself keep going because the thought of my hero being hurt made me frightened. I didn't like to see all the blood and chaos in the huge room but I was determined to find my biker man.

I was just pulling back yet another curtain to peek inside when a voice said, "Whatcha doin', kid?"

I froze.

"Just 'cause you stopped movin' doesn't mean I don't see you anymore," the same deep voice told me.

It was the voice of a monster, really dark and rumbly like there was something wrong with his throat. He didn't sound mean though, it kind of sounded like he wanted to laugh.

"I'm not supposed to be down here," I told him without turning around.

"Figured as much. What's a little girl doing in the ER all by herself? Not that I'm not stoked to see you walkin' around after what happened. How's the shoulder, kid?"

I turned around to look at him through my hair and took a step away because I'd forgotten how much he *looked* like a monster. He was humungous like a Titan or a giant but in real life. He was lying in a hospital bed, kinda leaning up against the pillow but I thought that if he stood up his head would hit the ceiling. He had a bunch of really long, crazy hair that was blond and brown and his big arms and sides were covered with drawings. There were pictures on his arms that looked like feathers, like those giant arms were really wings like on an angel.

"Are you an angel?" I asked.

I was closer to him than before, but I didn't remember moving closer to his bed. I reached out to touch his skin because the feathers looked so real and I wanted to know what they felt like.

He made a weird noise like he was choking. "No, kid, I'm no angel."

"I thought maybe you were a monster because you're really big, but you have wings and you saved me from all the bad guys," I explained.

My fingers touched the feather curling over his arm. They didn't feel like real feathers except his skin was smooth like when you pet a feather just right.

"Does it hurt?" I asked.

"No but it hurt like a bitch to get 'em."

"A bitch?"

"Damn, sorry, kid. Don't say that, it's a bad word."

"Then why do you use it?" I frowned. Angels didn't say bad words. My grandpa was the pastor, so I knew these things.

His lips twitched like maybe he wanted to smile. "That's a good question."

I crossed my arms. "So, are you going to answer it or what?"

He laughed this time but I didn't think it was in a mean way so I let him.

"Don't have a good answer for ya. My dad cursed, my mum cursed, so I curse. Grew up with that shit."

"My grandpa says that if you do bad stuff like curse, then bad stuff happens to you." I pointed to the white bandage that covered half his chest. "Maybe that's why you got hurt."

"I got hurt savin' a little girl who needed savin'," he reminded me gently.

I bit my lip and scuffed my heel against the floor. "I'm sorry. I didn't know you got hurt because of me. Do you want me to kiss it better?"

He choked again, like he was swallowing laughter. "I'm good, kid, but thanks. I've had worse, trust me."

There was a thick rope of weirdly smooth and mangled skin on the right side of his neck. I pointed at it. "Like that?"

"I did something a lot worse than curse to get that," he told me and then *winked*.

I giggled.

He had really big eyes like a wolf, really pale and grey.

"What did you do?" I leaned heavily against the side of his bed because I was really tired.

He looked at me for a long time before he said, "I found a guy that did some bad stuff to a friend of mine and I did some bad stuff to him. Before I got 'im, he got me with a blunt machete."

He made a chopping motion against the junction of his neck and shoulder where the scar was.

"For real?" I breathed.

He nodded.

"Wow. If you got him because he chopped you, what did you do to the bad guy that shot us?"

"Smart girl." His lips twitched again and he lifted one of his huge hands to show me his bloody knuckles.

I nodded. "You're definitely big enough to kill someone with your bare hands."

He tilted his head. "Don't seem that disturbed about it, kid. You close to death?"

I mimicked his pose and squinted my eyes at him. "You mean do I know him or something?"

"Yeah, somethin'." He grinned.

"I guess so. I'm dying, probably," I told him. It was dramatic but I wanted to see what he would do if he thought I was really dying. He was an angel so I figured he would know if that was true or not. Besides, my mum always said it was a lady's right to be dramatic and it was the only one of her rules I actually liked.

My feet were cold on the plastic floor so I pushed the bedside chair closer to him and climbed onto it.

"Dyin'?" His body got tight. I watched his face screw up and to the left like a twist cap on soda pop.

"Why are you making a funny face?" I asked.

"Don't think any person finds out a little girl is gonna die is going to smile at it," he replied.

"That's a nice thing to say."

He shook his head, studying me really hard. "I got a son

older than you and a little girl 'bout your age. Hope like fuck that they turn out to be as cool as you, kid."

"Are you sure you aren't an angel?" I asked him, because he was being really nice and it made me feel like I was standing in the sun.

I wanted him to be an angel. My grandpa told me that God could save a person from death if they were pious and faithful, and I was a good girl so I was both. He was the town pastor so I think he knew what he was talking about but I never really believed him. What did God care about me?

But if this man was a real angel maybe it meant that I didn't have to die. Maybe this angel man would wrap me up in his winged arms and make my bones stop hurting.

"Nah, kid, I'm no angel."

"That's too bad. I was thinking you could be my guardian angel or something cool like that."

I stared at him while he laughed at me. One of his big hands pressed to his chest just above his heart where the bandage was wrapped, so I could tell laughing hurt him. But he did it anyway, and he wasn't quiet about it.

"I'd be a shit guardian angel. I'm not a good man, kid."

I stared at him, squinting as I looked at his messy hair, all the dark and twisting images on his really tanned skin. At first, I'd thought he looked like a monster, all big and dark and scary because I didn't understand him.

But, "You have nice eyes. My grandpa says that kind eyes don't lie."

His face relaxed in a way that made something flutter in my tummy.

"What's your name, kid?"

"I'm a Lafayette," I told him because that was the important bit of my name.

He frowned. "Yeah, got that kid. Your dad is one of the guys rootin' for a life sentence and it's safe to say he hates my fuck—*freakin'* guts. I wanna know what you call yourself."

I didn't want to tell him so I bit my lip. My name was stupid and I hated it. Louise was an old person name and I wasn't old. It was also a boring name and I really, really didn't want to grow up to be boring like my mum with her parties and my dad with all his work stuff.

So, I said, "Loulou."

No one had ever called me Loulou before even though I'd tried to make it stick. Mum and Dad said it was a common name, which meant they didn't like it, which meant I couldn't have it.

"Cool. I'm Zeus."

"Zeus," I squeaked. "For real?"

His mouth twitched. "I got a name my parents gave me but don't like it much so, yeah, Zeus."

"That's the coolest name I ever heard," I told him, bouncing up and down in my seat. "Do you know who Zeus is? He's like the king of all the gods on Mt, Olympus. He *throws lightning!*"

"Smart girl," Zeus rumbled in his super cool, super god-like voice.

I stared at him, having a moment because mum told me girls are allowed to have moments and I was pretty sure this man was the absolute coolest man on the planet.

"I'm pretty sure you are the absolute coolest man on the planet," I told him.

His eyes danced at me and got all crinkly in the corners. Suddenly, it was harder to breathe.

"I'm damn sure that you are the absolute coolest girl on the planet too."

"Cool," I said, pretending that wasn't the nicest thing anyone had ever said to me *ever*.

He smiled again.

After a minute, it faded and he said, "You should probably head back to bed before someone worries about ya."

He was right but I really didn't want to go. Zeus was big and strong and I was pretty sure he was half angel, half monster, which meant that all the other monsters in the hospital wouldn't hurt me if I stayed with him.

"Will you stay here all night and fight the monsters if they come to get me?" I asked him, looking around his little curtained room. "Do you have your lightning bolts with you?"

"I got the bolts. You don't worry, kid. I'll stand watch."

"Promise?" I asked and my voice was stupid and small like a baby.

Zeus held out his pinky. It was four times the size of mine and for some reason, I thought that was really cool. I linked mine onto it.

"Pinky swear," he swore.

Then he hooked his thumb over our tangled little fingers to shake it against my thumb. I giggled and for the first time in a long time, when I went to sleep, I didn't dream of monsters, I dreamt of him.

THE NEXT MORNING, I ran down to the ER in my hospital gown, clutching my uneaten green Jell-O from the night before in my hand. I wanted to share it with Zeus because he'd kept the monsters away all night.

"Fuck this, Z, you're gonna go to prison for this, ya know," a scary voice growled from behind Zeus's curtain just as I was going to push it aside.

I froze.

"Maybe."

"There's no maybe about it, dipshit. You got kids at home and you're pullin' this crazy-ass stunt without your brothers at your back?"

"I don't know who my brothers are at the fuckin' moment, Bat, otherwise wouldn't be in this fuckin' mess in the first place. You rather Crux put a bullet in you 'fore I put a bullet in him? He killed our brothers and he went through a motherfuckin' *kid* to get to me."

"Gonna lose half the brothers over this and half of 'em are gonna wanna back you as Prez now he's gone."

"A Prez in prison isn't the best call for the club."

There was a really awkward pause, like when I heard my mum and daddy fight.

"Farrah's gonna flip, you go to prison and leave her with the kids," the angry guy said. "She can't handle that shit on her own."

"Yeah," Zeus said, soft sounding like he was sad. "But this is good, Bat. We needed a change in the club and now that rat bastard is gone, we can move forward."

"Hard to change the norm when the fucking leader of our revolution is goin' to prison for manslaughter."

Manslaughter didn't sound good. It sounded like Zeus had probably killed someone with his bare hands *for real*. I shivered but I wasn't actually scared, not of Zeus. I was scared of what kind of monster that man had been that my angel slayer had to kill him. It didn't occur to me to think it could be a man who shot a little girl in the chest.

"The pigs are sniffing around but I'll hold 'em off until you get out of this place. I brought the truck, bring it round front and meet you there in ten, yeah? Won't buy you much time but I figure you can say goodbye to yer kids."

"Yeah, brother. Thanks," Zeus said.

I quickly ducked away from the opening just before a tall, scary-looking tattooed man blew past me. Before the curtain could close, I slipped into Zeus's space.

He was sitting up in his bed, really dark against the white sheets and way too big for such a tiny bed. They hadn't changed the Band-Aid on his chest because I could see blood on it like a pink flower blooming underneath. His thick brown eyebrows hung low over his eyes as he stared into the distance at something that made him unhappy but as soon as he saw me, he smiled really big.

"Hey there, kid. Come to say goodbye?"

"No," I told him primly as I walked over to the chair

beside his bed and climbed onto it. "I don't want to say goodbye."

His lips twisted, and I noticed they were pretty lips, almost like a girl's. "Don't have much of a choice here. I'm goin' away for a while."

"Because you killed that bad man?"

"Yeah, 'cause I killed that bad man."

"So..." I twisted my fingers in my lap and thought really hard about it. "I'm the reason that you have to go away, then. Because you had to save my stupid life?"

"Hey," he barked so suddenly that I jumped a little. His voice softened as he leaned forward to snag my eyes with his. "Don't want to hear you talk like that, yeah? Innocence is always worth protectin'. If a baby needed your help, are you tellin' me you wouldn't help 'em?"

"I'm not a baby," I told him.

"No." He smiled at me and it made me forget to be annoyed at his comparison. "But babies are sweet and innocent like you. They haven't learned about all the bad stuff in the world yet."

I twisted my fingers in my lap again. "I don't want to be like a baby. I want to *know* about the bad stuff. If I don't know, what am I going to do when it happens to me when I grow up? Wait for some stupid prince to come save me now that my guardian monster is going away?"

Zeus laughed a great big laugh. "No need to grow up too fast, kid. You got lots of time and once you lose that innocence, you can't get it back. Trust me."

"I do," I told him eagerly. "That's why I don't want you to go away and never see me again. Can I visit you where you're going?"

"No, absolutely fuckin' not."

I thought about being hurt for a second and then I guessed, "Because bad people go to where you're going?"

"Exactly."

"But I want you to be my friend," I tried to explain, reaching forward to put my little hand on top of his giant one resting on the bed.

He stared at our hands for a moment with gentle eyes and then looked up at me with a nice smile. "We are, kid."

"Hurrah!" I whispered, because I was excited, but it felt like too important a moment to ruin with a shout.

"What are you doing in here?" Nurse Betsy said in a really high voice like the one my mum used when I was doing something gross or stupid.

She pushed back the curtain that separated Zeus's bed from the rest of the big room and ran over to me, checking me over with her hands and glaring at my new friend.

"What is she doing in here with you? You're in enough trouble as it is," she hissed at him.

I tried to pull away from her, but she pressed me close to her chest, tucking my head into her neck as if that meant I couldn't hear what they were saying.

Sometimes, adults are so dumb.

"Relax, Bets, she was wandering around down here and decided that I looked like a fuckin' angel. She took a seat and we shot the shit for a minute. Nothing else."

He didn't seem that concerned about how angry Betsy was and it was kind of weird that they seemed to know each other. Betsy was tiny and pretty and soft. She didn't look like she had it in her to be friends with Zeus.

"You never *think*," she continued to hiss. "If someone else had come in here and seen you talking to a cute little girl, what do you think they would have done? You're already going to freaking prison for manslaughter. Do you need a molestation charge on top of that?"

I couldn't even see him but the air got weird and heavy and I knew without looking that Zeus was mad.

"Don't even fuckin' say that out loud. I'm a father for fuck's sake, Bets. I'd never hurt a kid."

Betsy relaxed a little against me and pet my hair. "Sorry," she mumbled. "I'm protective of this one. They think she's got Hodgkin's Lymphoma. She's been in here a lot and she's curious, likes to roam."

"Fuck," Zeus said, soft and angry at the same time.

I wanted to reach out and pat him like I did when my dog growled. My grandpa had always warned my mum that I was attracted to dark and damaged things. I was just a kid but I was a smart one and I knew Zeus was both of those things.

A fallen angel. A monster, but a good one under all the scary.

I didn't want someone like him to feel sad for me like everyone else.

"Told you I was dying," I grumbled loudly enough that he could hear me even though my lips were up against Betsy's boobies.

Her arms went loose and I pulled away to see Zeus staring at me with that soft face that made my tummy strange.

"You're not gonna die, kid. Let's stay positive, yeah?"

"You don't know. You're not a doctor."

"No, but I'm Zeus. I throw lightning bolts and I'm king of

all the gods. I know you ain't gonna die and now all you gotta do to get better is believe me. Yeah?"

I stared at him. He had really pretty eyes with lashes thick and dark like a lady.

"I don't wanna die," I whispered.

Betsy squeezed me really hard but I didn't take my eyes off Zeus.

He leaned as close to me as he could. Without meaning to, I reached up and put my hand on his fuzzy cheek. He flinched like I'd hurt him but then he said, "Bad things happen to good people, kid. Sucks that you're sick at all. Tellin' you now, you're gonna get through this and even though I won't be around to see it, I promise you, I *know* it. You said you trust me, right?"

I nodded mutely, stuck somewhere in his silver-dollar eyes.

"Then believe me," he ordered.

"I believe you," I whispered.

"Mr. Garro, we've been told you are healthy enough to be transferred to provincial detention," a voice said over my shoulder and I jumped around to see three uniformed police officers come into our small curtained space.

My daddy followed.

"Daddy, no," I cried out as the men came into the room and one of them began to tell Zeus something in police-talk about his rights. "Daddy, NO!"

"Louise, what in the world are you doing out of bed and with this man?" he demanded, jerking forward to grab my arm in a painful grip and tug me toward him. "Jesus, you never *listen*. Why can't you do as you're told?"

"Daddy, he's my guardian monster," I tried to explain.

"You can't take him away to a bad place or else no one will look after me."

"Don't be a baby, Louise. You have Nanny looking after you. Your mother and I pay her a very fine salary to look after you and Beatrice and teach you French."

"*Je deteste le francais!*" I screamed. "And I'll hate you too if you take Zeus away. He saved my life, Daddy!"

"He put it in danger in the first place," my daddy yelled right in my face and I was so shocked that I stumbled backward and fell. Only my daddy's hard grip on my arm kept me hovering over the floor. "I will not hear you defend him. Now, this nurse is going to take you back to your room where you *will stay* until I say otherwise. Do you understand?"

"Please, Daddy," I whimpered because he was hurting my bad shoulder by holding me like that, and especially because I didn't want my guardian monster to go away.

For the first time in my life, I felt like I had a champion.

"You're hurtin' her," Zeus told my daddy from behind me and even though his voice was calm there was something mean in it that made me scared for my daddy.

Daddy sneered at him. "Mind your business. You seem to have more pressing matters at hand. How do those cuffs feel, Garro? You better get used to them."

I gasped as I turned around to see Zeus's big arms behind his back locked up in silver handcuffs.

"Daddy," I cried again. "Please, don't do this."

"S'okay, kid. It's not your dad that's done anythin', it's me. When you do somethin' bad, you have to pay penance for it, like in church, right?" I nodded. "Right. Well it's the same with the law only you pay penance by going to prison."

"Shut your mouth," Daddy ordered him then turned to

25

Betsy. "Take my daughter to bed and do your fucking job. Make sure she stays there."

"I won't forgive you, Daddy," I told him as Betsy gently ushered me toward the curtain. "Ever."

"I can live with that," he said, then he ignored me and stalked right up into Zeus's face. He was a lot smaller because every man was a lot smaller than Zeus, but he still threatened him. "If I ever see you anywhere near my daughter or this family again, I will personally see to it that your life is ruined beyond all hopes of repair. Understood?"

Zeus looked down at my daddy as if he were a bug that landed on his boot, easily crushed but not worth the bother. "You threaten a man like me, Lafayette, be prepared to reap the fuckin' consequences."

Then with his head high and his body at ease despite the handcuffs, Zeus led the officers out of his curtained room and through the emergency room to the waiting police car outside.

Betsy let me watch as they drove away, tucked under her arm and against her breasts so that my tears got caught in her pink scrubs.

That was the last day I called Benjamin Lafayette "Daddy".

CHAPTER TWO

2008-2009

Zeus is 26 and Louise is 7.

Dear Mr. Guardian Monster,

I hope you feel better now. Daddy told me you went away to a place where bad people go. Does that mean you are in hell? Can I visit you there?

I am worried that if you are away no one will look after me. Mum and Daddy are too busy because they are super important people. Nanny doesn't speak English real good. My little sister Bea is okay but she cries a lot because she is still a baby.

I am still really sick. I had a Christmas play last week and I threw up all over the Baby Jesus. Mrs. Peachtree tried to pick me up, but I threw up on her too. I had to go to the hospital again and I hate the hospital. Nanny told me the doctors told her that there is something really wrong with me. When Mummy came to visit, she cried.

Do you think I am going to die? If I do, can I come stay with you in hell?

xoxo,

Louise Margaret Lafayette

LOU,

NOT GONNA DIE, KID. ANYONE EVER TELL YOU, YOU GOT A DARK IMAGINATION? LITTLE KIDS GET SICK ALL THE TIME AND THEN THEY GET BETTER, YEAH? WASN'T GONNA WRITE BACK BUT I HAD TO TELL YOU TO CUT THAT ~~SHIT~~ NEGATIVE STUFF OUT. NOW, DON'T BE SAD OR ANYTHIN', BUT WE CAN'T WRITE TO EACH OTHER. YOU DON'T GET IT NOW BUT I'M A GROWN MAN AND IT'S ~~FUCKIN'~~ FECKIN' WEIRD TO WRITE A SEVEN-YEAR-OLD LITTLE GIRL FROM PRISON. THAT'S WHERE I AM. PRISON. AND YEAH, LOU, IT'S A LOT LIKE HELL, ONLY WORSE 'CAUSE I FIGURE THERE'S WOMEN IN HELL AND A WHOLE LOTTA SINNIN'. ONLY THING I DO HERE IS READ AND DO PRISON LABOR ON A FECKIN' FARM.

YOU'LL GET IT WHEN YOU'RE OLDER, BUT THIS IS GOODBYE. HAVE A GOOD LIFE, KID, AND KEEP OUTTA TROUBLE, YOU HEAR?

I MAY NOT BE THERE TO LOOK OVER YA, BUT I'LL BE ABLE TO
TELL IF YOU STAY GOOD.

Z.

Dear Mr. Guardian Monster,

*I know you said that I couldn't write to you anymore but I
thought I should tell you that I am not going to get better so I will
probably see you in prison in a little bit. See, I got cancer. Nanny
told me it's in my blood so they can't even do an operation or
anything. Daddy got really mad and he said he's gonna get me a
doctor like Super Man to help me get better. Betsy told me that lots
of kids get cancer but she looked scared. I wouldn't tell anyone but
you, because you are my guardian monster, but I'm scared too.*

I hope you write me back but if not, maybe see you soon.

xoxo,
Louise Margaret Lafayette

*P.S. Do you believe in God? I do but I don't know why he made me
sick. I promise, I pray every day.*

LOU,

~~JESUS CHRIST, FUCK ME, GOD FUCKING DAMMIT.~~

No, Lou, I don't believe in God. How can a man believe in an all-powerful nice guy who lives the high life behind pearly gates while the rest of us suffer down here on earth? How can a man believe that a little girl sweeter than sugar freakin' pie deserves to get cancer?

You are gonna get better, kid. I know it. You know how I feckin' know it? 'Cause you are a little warrior. You didn't cry in the face of a huge biker with a gun pointed at your heart and you ain't gonna cry 'cause of this, you hear me? You are strong and you are gonna fight this.

It's still a feckin' stupid idea for me to write to you, but Jesus, how can a guardian monster abandon his girl when she needs him?

Here still. Tell Betsy to write me a letter with more detail about the cancer, yeah?

Z.

Dear Mr. Guardian Monster,

Betsy wrote you a letter about the cancer. I tried to read it, but I don't understand any of the words. Betsy told me to tell you what I feel like because I don't know the doctor words for it. I have to stay in the hospital most of the time now, for medicine that makes my head really hurt and my heart skip rope in my chest. My bones really hurt, kinda like if dogs are chewing on them. I drew a picture of hellhounds biting on my legs, but it made my little sister cry and my mummy's voice got really high and tight when she called me disgusting. Mummy threw it out but Betsy saved it and I gave it to her to send to you. Do you like it? That's you, the big man in the clouds with your thunderbolts so you can save me.

Are you going to come and save me? Or is prison too far away to get here before I die?

xoxo,
Louise M. Lafayette

P.S. I am worried about you in prison. Do they at least have lollipops there? I love lollipops, especially the cherry kind.

Little Loulou,

Yeah, kid, I got the letter from Bets. You have Hodgkin's Lymphoma. I looked it up in the prison library. The bad news is, it's gonna suck to fight this and you're gonna get real tired doin' it. Good news? Those docs really know how to treat this shit. There are stages to cancer, kid, four of 'em and you are stage 2. This is really good, yeah? The odds of a kid beatin' this thing are high and the odds of you beatin' it? Even higher.

Really like the drawing, Lou. I got a few from my kids in my cell and now I got yours here, too. Makes the place a little brighter. And I don't got any lollipops, but gotta say, I don't have a hankerin' for 'em

AND STRAIGHT UP, KID? THOSE THINGS WILL ROT YOUR TEETH RIGHT OUT.

Z.

YEAH, BEFORE I FORGET AGAIN, CUT IT OUT WITH THE MR. GUARDIAN MONSTER, YEAH? JUST CALL ME ZEUS.

Dear Mr. Zeus,

My hair is falling out. Betsy told me it was going to happen and a bunch of other kids in the cancer ward don't have hair but I'm really sad. My hair was really pretty. Do you remember it? I think there was blood in it last time you saw me but mostly it's gold and thick and long. Nanny used to brush it for me before bed and it felt really nice. Nanny shaved the little bit I had left off so I'm bald. Now, my head is super cold. It doesn't matter really, I got to stay in the hospital right now and it's always warm in here. I'm fighting, Mr. Zeus, really I am, but I'm super duper tired and even though you told me I was too strong to cry, I cried last night.

I haven't seen my parents in three days and Nanny only brings Bea sometimes because she's too little to see me all sick. I'm really lonely and I know you are in prison but if you could get maybe a Christmas break or something, could you come visit me? It's really sad in the hospital but I think you could make me smile, maybe.

xoxo,
Little Loulou M. Lafayette

P.S. I'm happy you don't like lollipops so now I don't have to share. Betsy told me that in prison you don't get a lot of stuff. What do you miss most? Maybe I can send it to you!

LITTLE LOULOU,

LISTEN TO ME NOW. YOU DON'T NEED YOUR PARENTS. THEY AIN'T THERE, GOOD FECKIN' RIDDANCE, YEAH? THEY'RE TOO BUSY TO SIT WITH A GIRL LIKE YOU, SWEET AND KIND EVEN SICK AS A DOG? GOTTA SAY IT, LOU, THEY DON'T SOUND LIKE GOOD PARENTS. NOW, ON TOP OF EVERYTHIN' ELSE YOU GOT GOIN', THAT STRAIGHT UP SUCKS. GOOD NEWS IS, YOU GOT NANNY, BEA, AND BETSY OVER THERE IN YOUR CORNER. YOU NEED TO CRY, YOU GO TO ONE OF 'EM AND YOU TELL 'EM TO GET YOU A DAMN CHERRY LOLLIPOP OR YOU GET 'EM TO GIVE YOU A HUG. AND I MIGHT BE STUCK IN PRISON, LITTLE WARRIOR, BUT YOU STILL GOT ME, YOUR GUARDIAN MONSTER, KEEPIN' AN EYE ON YOU FROM HELL ON EARTH. YOU FEEL SAD, YOU WRITE ME ONE OF YOUR LETTERS OR MAKE ME A PRETTY PICTURE, YEAH?

DON'T MISS NOTHIN' SO MUCH AS I MISS MY KIDS. I TOLD YOU 'FORE, I GOT A SON WHO'S JUST TWO YEARS OLDER THAN YOU AND A DAUGHTER 'ROUND 'BOUT YOUR AGE. KING AND HARLEIGH ROSE. THEY'RE STAYIN' WITH THEIR MUM AND YOU KNOW HOW YOUR PARENTS SUCK? KING AND H.R.'S MUM SUCKS EVEN WORSE. SHE'S NOT A NICE LADY AND SHE'S A FECKIN' CRAP PARENT SO I GET WORRIED ABOUT 'EM. WORRIED ABOUT 'EM, WORRIED ABOUT YOU... A GUARDIAN MONSTER CAN ONLY DO SO MUCH FROM PRISON.

Stay strong, little warrior.

Z.

Betcha look pretty even without all that golden hair. You're too young to get this, maybe, but sometimes a person's got a soul so pretty it makes 'em glow prettier than anythin' else. You got that kid, trust me. About the cold head, I asked Betsy to get you one of those knit cap things from my garage. Wear it inside out, so the Hephaestus Auto logo doesn't show, yeah? Don't need your dad crawlin' up my butt about writin' you.

CHAPTER THREE

2009-2010

Zeus is 28. Louise is 9.

Dear Mr. Z,

Merry Christmas! I don't know if Santa comes to prison, so I got Betsy to send you a present. It's not really big or anything because I don't have a job yet. When I grow up and become a famous ballerina, I can buy you something even better. Betsy and I looked up what I was allowed to send you in jail and it's not really a lot... Do you like it? I spent my whole entire allowance on it and Betsy took me IN DISGUISE to the biker shop to get it. It was super fun. I wore the toque you gave me but not inside out, so people could see Hephaestus Auto on it. Betsy gave me sunglasses too! I looked just like a biker girl. One of the ladies in the shop even asked me if my daddy was a biker just like you! Don't worry, I didn't tell her that you are my guardian monster, but I did lie and tell her yes. Lying is a sin so I had to go to the hospital chapel and pray for forgiveness, but it was worth it.

Anyways, did you know it's my birthday in one week? The nurses are going to bring me a cake because I have to go in to get my medicine that day. I hope it's chocolate! I CAN'T WAIT to be 9 years old! I asked Mummy and Daddy for tickets to the Nutcracker ballet in Vancouver but they say I might be too sick to go. I hope not. I tried to tell them that I'm feeling better and I am. I think the chemo thing is working!

I don't want you to send me anything like last year. It was too big. I looked it up on the internet and when you work in prison you don't make really any money so I don't want you to waste it on me. Maybe you can buy King that dirt bike he wants! And then for my present you can send me a picture of him riding it. I think that would be really cool.

xoxo,

Little Loulou Lafayette

LOU,

DON'T CARE IF YOU'RE MAD. BETSY TOLD ME YOUR FECKIN' PARENTS DIDN'T GET YOU THOSE TICKETS, SO I DID. YOU ACCEPT THE PRESENT GRACIOUSLY, LIKE THE LITTLE LADY-IN-

TRAININ' THAT YOU ARE, AND YOU GET NANNY OR BETSY TO TAKE YOU TO THE BALLET, YEAH?

I DIDN'T GET PRESENTS FROM SANTA, BUT IN MY EXPERIENCE, LOU, SANTA DOESN'T HAVE MUCH TO DO WITH ADULTS SO ENJOY 'EM WHILE IT LASTS. DID GET A VISIT FROM MY KIDS THOUGH. THEIR MUM BROUGHT 'EM IN, DRESSED IN DIRTY CLOTHES WITH THEIR HAIR ALL TANGLED. FECKIN' KILLED ME TO SEE 'EM LIKE THAT. KILLED ME MORE TO HOLD MY LITTLE GIRL IN MY ARMS AND BREATHE IN HER SCENT. SHE SMELLS LIKE FLOWERS. DON'T KNOW HOW, GIVEN HER MUM PROBABLY WASHES HER IN CHEAP CRAP, BUT SHE STILL SMELLS LIKE A MEADOW. NOT GONNA LIE TO YOU, LOU—NOT THAT I EVER WOULD—BUT I FELT THAT SHIT IN MY CHEST. MISS THE WAY MY DAUGHTER SMELLS AND HOLDIN' HER IN MY ARMS.

YOU DON'T GET MUCH LOVE AND COMFORT IN THIS HELL ON EARTH, LOU. WOULDN'T WISH IT ON ANYONE. GRATEFUL FOR THE MAGAZINE SUBSCRIPTION. DON'T LIKE YOU SPENDIN' YOUR MONEY ON SOME OLD MAN IN PRISON, BUT GOTTA SAY I MISSED READIN' ABOUT BIKES.

Z.

CHAPTER FOUR

2010-2011

Zeus is 29. Louise is 10.

Dear Mr. Z,

The doctors told Nanny today that the medicine is working, and it looks like I am going into remission... it means that I won't be sick anymore.

I cried. I know you don't like it when I cry alone, but this time, it was good. I hugged my pillow and I cried so much my eyes were swollen nearly shut. But it felt really good. Can you believe it, Z? In a little while, I will be healthy again. I can go to the play-

ground and swing on the monkey bars with the other kids. I can have sleepovers! I don't really have any friends yet who would ask me, but now, I can make some! I can even take dance lessons again. Not right away or anything because I still get really tired and dizzy, but the doctor said I could start again in six months or something. How cool is that? Mummy cried when she came to visit, and she told me Daddy was really happy. My sickness kind of embarrasses him and he's running for mayor, you know, so now I can stand with him on stage.

My hair will grow back. I think it is probably vain to miss it so much, but I do. And when it grows back in, I am never, EVER going to cut it again. It's going to be long like Rapunzel's and no one will ever be able to tell that I was bald once.

It was a really happy day and I wish you could have been here, so I could tell you in person. Thank you for being my guardian monster and making me healthy again.

xoxo,
Little Loulou Lafayette

LOULOU,

FUCK, ARE YOU OLD ENOUGH NOW FOR ME TO CURSE WHEN I WRITE YOU? BECAUSE THIS IS CAUSE FOR SOME SERIOUS CURSIN' AND I MEAN THAT IN A SHOUT-AT-THE-TOP-OF-YOUR-LUNGS KINDA WAY LIKE FUCK YEAH! SO FUCKIN' STOKED, KID. I SHOUTED FOR JOY IN MY CELL, I KID YOU NOT. MY CELL-MATE, DIXON, ASKED ME IF I'D WON THE LOTTERY. FEELS LIKE IT, LOU, IT FEELS LIKE I WON THE LOTTERY KNOWIN' THAT

YOU'RE GONNA GET WELL AND SOON. I DIDN'T HAVE ANYTHIN' TO DO WITH GETTIN' YOU BETTER THOUGH. YOU DID THAT ALL ON YOUR OWN, LITTLE WARRIOR, AND I AM SO PROUD OF YOU. NEVER MET A STRONGER LADY AND YOU'RE ONLY TEN YEARS OLD. I CAN'T WAIT TO SEE WHAT KINDA WOMAN YOU GROW INTO NOW THAT YOU GOT THE CHANCE TO DO IT.

Z.

CHAPTER FIVE

2011-2012

Zeus 30. Louise is II.

LITTLE WARRIOR,

GONNA GET OUTTA HERE, KID. CAN'T FUCKIN' BELIEVE IT BUT I'M UP FOR PAROLE AFTER TWO AND A HALF YEARS. I GOT A GOOD LAWYER, BUT IT'S MY "GOOD BEHAVIOR" THAT'S DONE IT. FIRST TIME IN MY LIFE ANYONE EVER COMMENDED ME FOR "GOOD BEHAVIOR." I NEARLY BUST A GUT LAUGHIN' WHEN THEY TOLD ME. THINK THEY THOUGHT I WAS CRAZY.

MY GUESS IS, I GOT YOU AND MY KIDS TO THANK. SPENT SO MUCH TIME IN MY CELL WRITIN' TO THEM AND, MOSTLY, YOU, THAT I WAS TOO BUSY TO CAUSE TROUBLE. BEEN CAUSIN' IT ALL MY LIFE, SO YEAH, LOU, CAN'T FUCKIN' BELIEVE IT. IF I GET OUT AFTER TWO AND A HALF YEARS INSTEAD OF EIGHT? I CAN SEE MY FUCKIN' KIDS GROW UP. KING'S TWELVE YEARS OLD NOW, ALMOST A MAN. I CAN TEACH 'IM HOW TO BE BETTER THAN ME. KID'S SMART AS A WHIP, I'M TELLIN' YA. HE'S HEADED TO UNIVERSITY FOR SURE, FIRST PERSON IN THE FAMILY. H.R. IS TEN LIKE YOU AND SHE'S TOO SMART, TOO BULL-HEADED LIKE HER FATHER TO STAY WITH HER MUM ANY LONGER. SHE'S RUN AWAY TWICE AND THE STAFF SERGEANT AND HIS FAMILY ARE KEEPIN' HER AND KING FOR NOW WHILE MY SOON-TO-BE EX-WIFE GETS CLEAN AGAIN. YOU PROBABLY DON'T KNOW WHAT THAT MEANS 'CAUSE, CHRIST, I'M TALKIN' TO A KID 'BOUT MATTERS WAY BEYOND HER YEARS. YOU DON'T NEED TO WORRY ABOUT MY SHIT. YOU JUST WORRY ABOUT STAYIN' HEALTHY, YEAH?

SO, I GOTTA THANK YOU 'CAUSE THIS IS YOU. THIS IS YOU REMINDIN' ME ABOUT GOODNESS. I LOST SIGHT'A IT FOR A WHILE... BUT BEFORE YOU GET EXCITED, FUCK IF IT'S TOO LATE FOR ME TO REFORM OR SOME SHIT SO DON'T PREACH IT, YOU HEAR? I'M JUST...HAPPY. I'M HAPPY AND THAT'S A RARE THING IN THE LIFE OF A CONVICTED FELON, IN THE LIFE OF A MAN WHO FUCKED IT UP REAL EARLY FOR HIMSELF. SO THANKS, KID, FOR GIVIN' AN OLD MAN HOPE.

Z.

Dear Mr. Z,

I AM SO EXCITED! I AM GOING TO WRITE THIS WHOLE ENTIRE LETTER LIKE THIS BECAUSE I AM SO HAPPY I COULD SHOUT! YOU GET TO LEAVE HELL ON EARTH!? YOU GET TO SEE YOUR KIDS GROW UP? I AM SO STINKING HAPPY. WHEN WILL YOU COME AND VISIT?!

HURRAH HURRAY!
    Little Loulou

Dear Mr. Z,

HAPPY BIRTHDAY! I'm sorry I haven't ever sent you anything before but you didn't tell me when your birthday was so this year I asked Betsy and she told me so HA! I got you another biker magazine subscription, this one is called RIDE and I did lots of research so I think it is probably the best one. Do you like it? I know you don't have much to do in there but exercise and work on the farm. I can't believe you are 30! That's super old. Do you have grey hairs and stuff already? I wish I remembered better what you look like. I tried to look you up on the internet but there aren't any pictures of you. How is that possible? I looked myself up too and there are a few articles with pictures of me because Daddy's mayor now. Happily, there are none of me bald. My hair reaches my shoulders now, just barely but still, I can do a hair flick and everything.

When is your meeting with the hell warden people to find out when you can go home? You didn't answer me last time but when can you come and visit me?

xoxo,

Little Loulou

LITTLE GIRL LOU,

MEETIN' WAS YESTERDAY. LOU, I'M GETTIN' OUT. I LEAVE AT THE END OF THE MONTH. GOTTA TELL YOU, IT FEELS FUCKIN' GREAT TO KNOW I'LL GET TO SEE MAIN STREET AGAIN, CLAP MY BROTHERS ON THE BACK, AND FEEL MY BIKE BENEATH ME, ROARIN' DOWN THE HOT STRETCH OF ROAD LEADIN' FROM ENTRANCE TO WHISTLER LIKE A WINDIN' BIKER'S PARADISE. CAN'T WAIT TO *LIVE* AGAIN.

WISH I COULD VISIT YOU, LOU, I DO. THAT SAID, I WON'T. YOU DON'T GET THIS YET, BUT ME WRITIN' LETTERS TO A LITTLE GIRL IS SEVEN DEGREES OF FUCKED UP. ME AND ETHICS AIN'T EVER BEEN THAT CLOSE AND DON'T EVEN GET ME STARTED ON MORALS, BUT STILL, A MAN HAS GOTTA DRAW A LINE SOMEWHERE AND FOR ME, THAT'S MOVIN' THIS STRANGE PEN PAL GIG WE GOT GOIN' INTO THE REAL WORLD. I DEBATED NOT EVEN WRITIN' YOU ANYMORE AND, IF YOU PUSH ME ON THIS, I WON'T. BE HAPPY WITH THIS 'CAUSE IT'S ALL YOU'RE GONNA GET. AND BEFORE YOU GO WHININ' ON ME, THAT'S THE TRUTH OF THE WAY LIFE WORKS, LOU. KNOW YOU GOT A HARD KNOCK WITH THE CANCER, BUT YOUR PARENTS SPOIL YOU SOMETHIN' ROTTEN AND YOU NEED TO KNOW REAL LIFE IS FULL'A PAIN, DISAPPOINTMENT, AND DARK DEEDS. I'M HERE TO HELP YOU

THROUGH THE CRUD, BUT ONLY AS A VOICE WRITTEN IN INK ON PAPER, YEAH?

Z.

LOU,

BEEN HOME A WEEK NOW AND I DON'T KNOW WHAT THE FUCK I'M DOIN' TALKIN' TO A KID 'BOUT SOMETHIN' LIKE THIS, BUT THERE IT IS. SOMEHOW, YOU'RE THE ONLY WITNESS I WANT TO THIS. 'CAUSE THE THING IS, I SHOULD BE HAPPY TO BE HOME WITH MY KIDS, MY BROTHERS, WORKIN' IN THE GARAGE ON BIKES I LOVED ALL MY LIFE. YOU KNOW WHAT I FEEL, KID?
WEIRD.
FUCKED UP AS ALL GET OUT.
I CAN'T SLEEP 'CAUSE MY MATTRESS IS TOO SOFT. YEAH, TOO SOFT AFTER THE CRAP MATTRESS I RESTED MY WEIGHT ON FOR TWO AND A HALF YEARS. SO, I'M SLEEPIN' ON THE FLOOR. HARLEIGH ROSE CAME IN YESTERDAY MORNIN' LOOKIN' TO CUDDLE AND I NEARLY BIT HER HEAD OFF. JUST TOUCHED HER OLD MAN ON THE SHOULDER, INNOCENT LIKE ANY TEN YEAR OLD KID, AND I NEARLY CLOCKED HER HEAD CLEAN OFF HER SLIP OF A BODY. YOU DON'T TOUCH IN HELL. YOU DON'T SMILE, AND IF YOU LAUGH IT'S A HARD LAUGH THAT'S MEANT AS A THREAT. MY DAUGHTER DOESN'T GET THIS. I DON'T WANT HER TO *HAVE* TO GET THIS. WHICH MEANS I GOT TO MAN THE FUCK UP AND GET OVER THIS SHIT. BUT FUCK IF IT ISN'T HARD.
I KNOW I'M SWEARIN' TOO MUCH, I KNOW I SHOULDN'T TALK TO A TEN YEAR OLD GIRL WITH HER OWN PROBLEMS (YOU

STILL HAVIN' PROBLEMS AT THAT PRISSY BALLET SCHOOL?), BUT I FIGURE, I'VE GOTTA TALK 'BOUT IT TO SOMEONE AND IT SURE AS HELL AIN'T GONNA BE A SHRINK. YOU COOL WITH THAT, LITTLE LOU, BEIN' MY LITTLE WARRIOR AGAIN SO I CAN REST SOME OF THIS WEIGHT ON YOU FOR A SPELL AND CATCH MY BREATH?

Z.

Dear Mr. Z,

I think I need to teach you two lessons because even though you're an adult and I'm just a kid, I'm pretty sure I know these two things better than you do.

One thing, you don't apologize to friends for needing them. I don't know this because I have a lot of friends, you know that with the cancer and missing school and stuff I kinda lost all my friends. I know this because in all the really good books and movies, friends do everything and anything for each other. Obviously, you would do anything for me seeing as how before we were even friends, you saved my life by taking a bullet for me, and I'm trying not to be mad that you don't know I would do the same for you. You want to curse? You want to talk to me about your kids? Or the hell you went through in prison because of me? It's my duty as the girl you saved, my pleasure as your bff (best friend forever) and my honour as a girl who respects you more than she even respects her parents and whole family, to listen to whatever in the world you want to say to me.

The second thing is harder to teach but I've been thinking about it a lot since I got out of the hospital. We all have scars. Some of them, like the one you and me share, you can see with your eyes. Some of them, you ink, like you do, on your skin so that they tell the story like a picture book. Like a badge of honour that you overcame something really bad. Then there are others, like the scar that stays in your heart when you're left alone in a hospital room for a week without anyone visiting you, or when you sleep on a metal bed in a concrete prison filled with bad men or weak men who only touch each other to sin in one way or another. I think it's harder to talk about those scars and it's harder to get over them because they wrap around you like poison ivy, making it hard to breathe and pump blood through your heart in the normal way. At least, that is how it is with me. I feel my heart skip when I talk to my friends now at school and they talk about boys they like and what they want to be when they grow up, and I know that sometimes, a lot of the time, kids don't even get to grow up. They die.

I think bad things happen to everyone, not just bad people. My grandfather is the pastor, you know? And he says all the time that religion will absolve us of our sins and lead us to heaven if only we follow all God's rules. I don't think you are the kind of man to follow rules, even if they are the Almighty's, but I do know that you definitely deserve to be happy so I think there must be special exceptions for men who are good but whose lives went bad. I think sometimes God sends us bad stuff, like cancer and prison and crappy ex-wives and too-busy daddies to see how we hold up. If we are strong and we endure, we are rewarded.

I don't know if that makes you feel better, to know that I kinda know what you are going through, that our scars make us different and they make us hurt all the time and feel a little lonely.

Only, we are lucky because we are bffs so we have each other. So, I guess what I'm trying to say is, I got you, Mr. Z.

xoxo,
   Loulou

P.S. Harleigh Rose won't care if you don't want to snuggle or you flinch when she touches you. You'll get used to it again and I bet you she's just happy to have you back. I know I am.

CHAPTER SIX

2012-2013

Zeus is 32. Louise is 13.

Zeus,

Tell me another story, a good one where the hero is kind of the villain and the happily ever after isn't easy coming. I want to hear about adventures and bravery and living life outside of the lines. I read On the Road like you recommended and I loved it. The Zen of Art and Motorcycle Maintenance was good too and I really loved

Fear and Loathing in Las Vegas. Our housekeeper found my copy under the bed and turned it over to my mother who immediately threw it into the fireplace and informed me that I would be going to church camp for the summer again. I hate church camp. Remember last summer when those girls told me I was impure because I was wearing coloured lip chap? I know you said that they were dumb, but it still really bothered me, and I know they'll be there again this year. They go to my school and I bet you when I go to EBA for high school, they'll be there too. They call themselves "the angels." How self-righteous can they get?

My life is so boring. I can't seem to stop thinking about it. It feels like I'm a Barbie, dressed by someone else's hand in sensible shoes and sweater sets (did you know I have fourteen different strands of pearls, one for every occasion? Did you even know there was more than one occasion to wear pearls!?). Living the life someone else wants me to live. I'm good at it. I got honours with distinction again this year, which was cool but honestly, kind of easy. Apart from the angels, who are mean and don't like me because I don't pretend they're cool, I have some friends. Not good ones, not like you. I dance five times a week, I do my homework, I obey my parents, volunteer at the Autism Centre, and I go to church on Sunday and whenever else I need absolution (a lot, I admit, and it's getting worse). I'm a normal thirteen-year-old girl. A woman officially. And I still feel like such a dumb, dull girl.

So, tell me something exciting. I know you are probably driving through the California hills on your bike, drinking beer in some bar or flirting with some really pretty girl because who wouldn't want to flirt with you?

xoxo,
  Loulou

Loulou,

Sure, kid, I'll tell ya a story.

Once upon a fuckin' time, there was a princess named Lou with a shit ton of golden hair and a smile that lit a person's heart up. She was sweet and kind, but curious. The Queen and King kept her in a big tower away from the rest of the world and only let safe, boring folk through to see her. The princess grew fuckin' tired of that shit, as anyone would but 'specially a girl as curious, as wild at heart as Lou. So, she made a plan. Instead of runnin' away, she staged a quiet rebellion in her soul. She made friends with the dull boys and did her duties, so her parents would be happy with her, but inside, she worked away at becomin' the kind of woman she wanted to be when she got old enough to do things her way. She listened to rock n' roll, read copies of banned books by the light of her fish tank late at night, and doodled in the margins of Gideon's Bible. She was a good kid, a good girl, and when the time came that she turned eighteen, she was ready to take off into the sunset, no man, no rules, just a rucksack filled with booze and jerky, a head full'a crazy dreams and a heart brave enough to do 'em.

Z.

P.S. You aren't dumb and next time you say somethin' like that, Lou, I'll stop writin' ya.

Zeus,

You always threaten to stop writing me... Is it because you don't want to anymore? I get it. Betsy doesn't deliver my letters for me anymore. I drop them myself on the way to ballet every Sunday. But she asked me if we still wrote to each other when I saw her a little bit ago and when I said yes, she looked unhappy and told me I was probably bothering you. Am I? You're my best friend in the whole world but I get that you have kids and a life and a job because you're an adult and I'm just a girl with like zero real problems. So if you want to stop writing me... I'll deal with it.

Loulou

NOT SO LITTLE WARRIOR,

DON'T BE LIKE THAT, LOU. I GET THAT YOU'RE TURNIN' INTO A WOMAN SO THIS PASSIVE AGGRESSIVE, EMOTIONAL SHIT IS GONNA COME UP, BUT I'M TELLIN' YOU RIGHT NOW, THAT KINDA INSECURITY IS FUCKIN' POISON AND IT'LL EAT AWAY AT YOU IF YOU LET IT UNTIL YOU BECOME A BITTER, HOLLOW SHELL OF THE COOL KID YOU ONCE WERE. YOU'RE THE SHIT, LOU. WE'VE BEEN WRITIN' FOR NEAR ON FIVE YEARS NOW (FUCK) SO YOU SHOULD KNOW BY NOW THAT I DON'T DO ANYTHIN' I DON'T WANT TO.

I WANT TO WRITE YOU. IT'S FUCKED UP, BUT YEAH, WE'RE

FRIENDS. AS LONG AS IT STAYS LIKE THAT, WE KEEP THIS THING TO PAPER AND PEN, I'M NOT GOIN' ANYWHERE.

NOW, TELL ME MORE ABOUT THESE "ANGEL" BITCHES SO WE CAN GAME PLAN HOW YOU'RE GONNA WIN 'EM OVER.

Z.

CHAPTER SEVEN

2013-2014

Zeus is 33. Louise is 14.

Z,

Okay, so can I ask you something kind of weird? I would ask someone else only I don't really have anyone else... Dad wouldn't know what to say, Mum is never around, you know they got rid of Nanny last year and Bea is too young to get it. The angels don't know anything so I can't go there. Which leaves you.

Okay, I'm just going to go for it here.

Over the summer, I, well, I "became a woman" or whatever.

Late bloomer and all that. So now my body has erm, changed, and all the boys at school are suddenly talking to me! It's super weird and I don't know what to say to them. They tease me and tug on my hair or call me fat and stuff like that. It's mean but I can see the way they stare at my, like, private areas so I know they like me, I mean I think they do. I don't like any of them, though. They're all stupid little boys and I just want them to leave me alone. What do you think I should do?

Loulou

LOU,

JESUS CHRIST, LOU, THERE HAS TO BE SOMEONE FUCKIN' BETTER THAN ME TO ASK 'BOUT THIS SHIT. I'M A MAN. YOU OBVIOUSLY DON'T GET THIS YET, BUT MEN TALK 'BOUT THREE THINGS: BOOZE, SEX, AND SPORTS. FOR ME, THAT WOULD BE WHISKEY, SEX, AND BIKES. EACH MAN'S GOT DIFFERENT PREFERENCES, BUT WE ALL STICK MOSTLY TO THAT STRICT RULE.

REMEMBER THAT, LOU, BOOZE, SEX, AND SPORTS.

THAT SAID, I GET THAT YOU GOT NO ONE ELSE TO GO TO, WHICH SUCKS. SO, KID, I'LL TALK TO YOU 'BOUT THIS BUT ONLY THIS ONCE SO RELISH IT AND **NEVER** ASK ME AGAIN.

LISTEN, IT'S SIMPLE, BECAUSE MEN ARE SIMPLE. A GUY LIKES A CHICK, HE NEEDS TO GET HER ATTENTION. THERE ARE A COUPLA WAYS TO DO THIS. THE DICKS, THEY DO IT BY BEIN' A DICK TO THE GIRL, INSULTIN' HER HAIR OR HER MAKEUP OR SOMETHIN' TOTALLY MADE UP JUST TO START A CONVERSATION.

BEST THING TO DO IS IGNORE 'EM. THE BETTER ONES, THEY'LL TRY AN' BE YOUR PAL, BUDDY UP TO YOU ABOUT SOMETHIN' THEY THINK YOU MIGHT LIKE EVEN THOUGH THEY DEFINITELY FUCKIN' DON'T. THESE GUYS ARE HARMLESS, LOU, JUST FRIEND ZONE 'EM FOR LONG ENOUGH AND THEY'LL GIVE UP.

THEN THERE ARE THE BEST KINDA MEN, YEAH? THE ONES THAT MAN-UP AND CLAIM A WOMAN THE WAY A WOMAN WANTS AND NEEDS TO BE CLAIMED. HE SEES SOMETHIN' HE LIKES, HE GOES UP, LAYS IT OUT, AND ASKS HER OUT. HE DOES WHAT HE NEEDS TO DO TO GET TO KNOW HER, LISTENIN', SPENDIN' THE MONEY, AND, BETTER, THE TIME TO KNOW HER MIND SO HE CAN ROCK HER WORLD. SOMETHIN' FUCKS WITH HER, THAT MAN IS GONNA THROW DOWN TO MAKE IT RIGHT AGAIN. SHE WANTS SOMETHIN' HE CAN'T IMMEDIATELY GET HER? THAT GUY'S GONNA WORK HIS FUCKIN' ASS OFF TO GET IT FOR HER JUST FOR A CHANCE TO GET SOME MORE OF HER SWEETNESS. THAT'S THE KINDA MAN YOU'RE GONNA GET YOURSELF ONE DAY, LOU. NOT NOW, YOU'RE JUST A KID, SO BE PATIENT. IGNORE THE DICKS THAT WILL BE IGNORED AND THROAT PUNCH THE IDIOTS THAT WON'T. MAKE FRIENDS WITH THE PUSSIES WHO LET YOU DO THAT TO THEM. AND WAIT.

Z.

Zeus,

I think I know what kinda guy you're talking about...
Also, I wanted to throat punch one of the dicks that wouldn't

take no for an answer, but good girl Louise Lafayette wouldn't do that, so I spit in his Coke when he wasn't looking at lunch and watched him drink it after. It was nearly as satisfying.

xoxo,
    Loulou

CHAPTER EIGHT

2015-2016

Zeus is 35. Louise is 16.

Zeus,

It's my sixteenth birthday today. Mum threw me a massive Sweet Sixteen party with like four people I actually like and one hundred people I actively can't stand. They were all hoards of plastic Ken and Barbie dolls littered around our backyard like a kid's playroom. Only, I didn't have fun with them because I refuse to play with them. I stood in the middle of all the pastels and polo necks listening to my parent's friends talk about politics and vacation homes and I was more than the usual bored. I felt like I couldn't breathe and honest to God, I think I was having a panic attack. Suddenly, I couldn't stand my own life anymore. I wanted to rip off my double strands of pearls, tear the Tiffany charm bracelet from my wrist and run away. Do you know whom I wanted to run away to, Z?

You.

All I could think about was racing to you, finding you already straddling your great metallic dragon, the rev of the engine like a warrior cry as we took off into the night. Not sunset. There are no sunsets for men like you and women like I am at the heart of me. Only inky night that clutches at you as you tear past, moving through the darkness like we own it, like we are only free inside the shadow vortex of it.

I'm being nonsensical. I snuck a few extra glasses of champagne and my head feels like it's filled with helium. What I'm trying to say is that I want to run to you. It doesn't have to be away with you. You've got kids, really great ones from the looks of things, so I get that we probably have to stay here. I get that it'll be hard because you're a mechanic and I'm the Princess of Entrance, because you're nineteen years older than my sixteen. But I know it'll be okay just as long as I can get to you. I'll leave whenever you want me to. Just say the word. And Z, say it soon.

I love you,
Loulou

Louise,

Can't write you anymore. Don't ask me why or try to change my mind about it. It's not cool, a grown ass man writin' to a teenage girl and it's my fuckin' fault that you got confused and you think you're in love or some shit. You don't love me, little girl. Fuck you don't even really know me. Happy to have been here for you

THROUGH THE CANCER, THROUGH YOUR GROWIN' INTO A SERI-
OUSLY COOL YOUNG WOMAN. IT WAS MY FUCKIN' HONOUR TO BE
YOUR GUARDIAN MONSTER. BUT TRUTH IS, YOU DON'T NEED ME
ANYMORE. YOU'RE GOOD, HEALTHY AND GROWN. SO, I'M
GONNA DUCK OUT HERE, TELL YOU TO KEEP LIVIN' TRUE AND
FREE. FORGET YOUR PARENTS AND THEIR BULLSHIT, FORGET
WHAT ANYONE ELSE EXPECTS FROM YOU. LIFE'S TOO SHORT
AND YOU KNOW IT, LITTLE WARRIOR, SO LIVE WHILE THE GOIN'
IS GOOD.

Z.

CHAPTER NINE

Loulou

May 2017

NO MATTER how devout you are, Sunday service is never fun.

Trust me, I'd been the pastor's grandchild and the mayor's daughter for long enough to know what I was talking about. I'd tried counting backward from one million, naming every important figure in the Bible in order of the gravity of their sins, conjugating French and Latin verbs until my eyes crossed. Anything, however tedious, was better than listening to my grandpa read yet another passage from the Bible.

I had tried for years to be pious, good and strong in the face of all the evils Christians believed to walk the earth and tempt the weak. I had tried and I had succeeded so well, I was a kind of paragon of virtue in Entrance, BC, an example that mothers used to teach their little girls how to grow up right, the ideal wife for young men who stayed true to the path of righteousness. Louise Lafayette was a pillar of the community just as her mother and father were, just as her grandparents had been.

All that goodness, all that *trying* so hard and how did God repay me?

With cancer. Again.

I'd lived through an entire two-year period in my childhood with it running hot and corrosive through my blood and yet, now that it was back, I still wasn't used to the taint of it, how it blackened my vision both literally sometimes and metaphorically. It was hard to believe in the things I was supposed to believe in when I felt so miserable, so beyond the help of prayer.

They'd just diagnosed me as stage two and the possibility of chemotherapy loomed on the horizon.

I'd lose my hair again.

It was such a vain thing to be concerned about but even though my parents were Sunday churchgoers, they were human enough to practice pride and superficiality. Heck, they were the King and Queen of Entrance; they *lived* for those things. Mum had been more devastated than I when they said I'd lose the thick mass of pale blond hair I'd had since birth, hair that I'd inherited from her. She'd cried and clutched big handfuls of it in her fists, wiping her tears in the strands. I would have been grossed out if I weren't devastated myself and trying so hard to hide it.

It was the end of my grade eleven year of high school, less than twelve months from graduation and all that entailed, including prom. And I was going to be bald for all of it.

Mum said they'd get me a really good wig but everyone would know it wasn't my hair and that was somehow worse than rocking a naked scalp.

My friends were nice people so they wouldn't make fun. They would just ignore it, as we all ignored the ugly things in life, and move on.

I was so tired of hiding the ugliness. It lived inside of me now. It was impossible to ignore its presence in everyday life.

Worst of all, I couldn't tell Zeus about it.

I'd gotten through my first bout of cancer *because* of him and now that I was sick again, I couldn't imagine doing it without him. Each letter I'd received written in his surprisingly cool graphic script had been a balm to my ragged soul. A little girl needed a champion, someone to believe in and someone to believe in her. He'd been right in saying that I'd grown up but he'd been wrong to assume that I no longer needed him. I'd learned that women needed a champion maybe even more than little girls did. Men forget to treat women with tender affection and platonic encouragement. Lust was no worthy substitute for pure care.

I wanted to send him a letter anyway because a part of me knew that he would come back if only he knew I was sick again. It was that exact reason that I left well enough alone. Did I really want a pity pen pal?

My mother reached over to quell my fidgeting hands. We were in the first right pew, front and center for everyone to look at. She didn't want me to look bored or inelegant. So, I stopped twisting my fingers even though my body ached all over and it felt good to distract myself by tracing each digit. I smoothed my sweaty palms over the demure length of my pastel pink skirt and tucked my modestly heeled feet under the bench.

Mum patted my thigh.

Good girl, it meant.

I gritted my teeth.

Thankfully, the service wrapped up soon enough. Unhappily, the next half an hour would be dedicated to mingling, my least favourite part of the entire ordeal.

"Benjamin," Tim Buckley boomed out in his loud, sport's announcer voice as he ambled up to my father and did that shake all men did, the one with a hard clap on the back. "How is our mayor doing this fine Sunday morning? It was an excellent service, as per usual."

"Thanks Tim, I'll be sure to pass that along to Dad. Life is good, can't complain about a thing," my father said.

It wasn't surprising that he didn't complain about my illness. My parents may have informed everyone about what they liked to call "my condition" but they felt it was tacky to talk about it, to draw attention to the poor little sick girl.

My younger sister, Beatrice, gently bumped her shoulder into me before her hand found mine and held it fast. We were used to the song and dance of Sunday service but neither of us liked it. The pageantry that was our lives had fused us together from an early age and even though Bea was three years younger and at an age when girls are pretty screwed up by hormones, boys and insecurity, we were still thick as thieves. The only time we argued was about who had it worse, her or me. Bea liked to argue that our parents didn't care what she did. She was right, at least to a certain extent. As long as she performed well in school and kept her nose out of trouble, Mum and Dad were pretty oblivious to her as a human being.

I argued that being their super-star was harder. There wasn't a moment of my day they didn't want to plan, a nuance of my person that they didn't want a hand in forming. Mum liked me because I was pretty, just like she felt she was. Dad liked me because I was brainy in a bookish kind of way but also charming, just like he felt he was. Their interest in me was relatively recent, as of puberty when my good looks descended and my intellect was noticed. They liked me because I was a useful tool to them.

Poor Bea had pretty bones but she hadn't grown into them yet and she was smart but not in a showy way. She worked hard and was driven to succeed, which in my mind was even better than being naturally gifted. Plus, she was sweet as sugar pie and funny as all get out.

She was the only one who cared for me when I woke up from nightmares about death or when I was too run-down to get out of bed in the morning. Even then, she didn't like to talk about why that was but she was there and that was good enough for me.

"I heard tell that your girl got into UBC, U of T and McGill. You must be proud of her," Tim continued, his attention now on me.

His gaze was appreciative but in a way that wasn't strictly about praising the intelligence of his good friend's daughter. He liked my curves even though they were dressed down in the conservative shift and sweater set my mother made me wear.

"I never doubted her. She's her father's daughter," my dad crowed, tugging me closer so that he could beam down at me, pretty as a picture.

I wanted to let Tim know that it was all for show, that at home neither he nor my mother had time for us, but I knew Tim wouldn't really care so I kept my mouth shut.

My bones ached. I was tired of standing for two hours singing dumb hymns that didn't mean anything because I didn't think I believed in God anymore and I just wanted to go home.

"Of course, of course. Now, do you have a minute to come talk to James and me about the strip mall proposal?" Tim asked.

"All the time in the world for you, buddy," he replied with a super charming smile.

I rolled my eyes at Bea who giggled behind her hand.

"Dad, you have to drive Bea to her dance lesson, remember?" I reminded him with a smile so that he wouldn't see how frustrated I was with him for forgetting.

Normally, I would have just taken her myself but I was going to a youth cancer support group after service and, as much as I wanted to skip it, my oncologist had insisted to my parents that I attend. Something about how two bouts of cancer in ten years could lead to depression or something. I didn't know about depression but I was sure as hell angry, and growing angrier by the day.

Dad frowned but extended his hand to Bea, flicking his fingers for her to follow behind him.

"You good?" Tim asked, having already started to move away.

"I've got to take Beatrice to ballet but she can be a bit late," he said before following Tim to the other side of the church, already talking about his ideas for the project, Bea trailing behind dutifully like his shadow.

Benjamin Lafayette had been mayor of Entrance since I was eleven years old and he hadn't lost his love of it. I was actually proud of him for the work he did for Entrance. I just wished he worked half as hard at being a good dad.

"Louise, darling, you look so well today," Mamie Ross crowed as she swept up to my mother and me.

She pinched my chin to give me two smacking kisses on each cheek. I knew she left red lipstick on my skin but before I could wipe it off myself, she licked her thumb and rubbed it against the marks with a little giggle.

The woman wasn't a day under fifty-five. She should not have been *giggling*.

A year ago, having such a spiteful thought would have made me sick to the pit of my stomach. Now, I was always sick to my stomach so I didn't have as hard a time with the evil thinking.

"She does, doesn't she?" Mum demurred, smoothing a hand down my hair. "A little too brown though, maybe."

There was no maybe about it. She had almost blown a gasket when I'd come in from sun tanning the other day. *Peasant brown*, she'd called me. I had inherited her platinum hair but I had my dad's golden skin. She didn't mind when his tanned, which it did because he loved to golf and he loved to fish. She minded with me because I was supposed to be a little lady.

What my skin tone had to do with that, I'd never know except that her family had come from England and parts of British Columbia were still behind the Tweed Curtain.

"No, she looks lovely. And so thin! Have you been dieting?" Mamie continued.

Everyone in Entrance knew I had cancer. When my parents found out, they had put out an announcement in both the *Entrance Herald* and the parish newsletter. Still, no one out and out talked about it.

Which I found, increasingly, frustrating as hell.

What were they going to say when I lost my hair?

Oh darling, what a fashion-forward statement you're making!

Such bullshit.

I smiled widely at Mamie. "No diet, just trying to stay healthy."

She nodded sagely. "Wise girl. I yo-yo dieted for years and now my skin doesn't fit quite right."

"She's sick, Mother. She isn't on a fucking diet," Reece Ross sneered at her as he stepped up to our little grouping.

He was wearing a suit, as was proper for Sunday service, but the tie was loose around his neck and the top three buttons were undone. He was one of the handsomest boys at Entrance High and in most of my classes. We didn't talk much though, mostly because he was cool in a burgeoning bad boy way and I was a good girl.

So, I was surprised that he'd come to defend me.

Especially against his own mother.

I'd wanted to do that countless times with my own mother but never found the gumption. It made me look at Reece Ross, who was known around town as a hotshot basketball player and all-round *player*, with new respect.

Mamie's mouth opened and closed uselessly.

My mother glared at Reece, disgusted by his lack of decorum.

"That said, you do look pretty great for a sick girl," Reece added, his gaze roving languidly over my modest dress, the curves beneath it.

I'd been blessed when puberty hit with an abundance of breast and ass and a small waist that, with my blond hair, made me look almost like a Barbie. It was ironic and cruel given the family I was born into. I was a Lafayette and as such, I was to be defined by certain qualities such as piousness, generosity and grace. Not sexuality, wickedness and beauty.

Anger burned clean through the murkiness in my blood, purging me clean for one glorious second before I remembered myself and became boring again.

"Thank you," I said, idiotically.

My mother smiled, as did Mamie.

Reece glowered at me.

The older women bent close, cutting us out of their heart to heart. Reece took the opportunity to step closer to me, his cologne strong in my nose.

"You dying?" he whispered harshly.

Anger again, a brief flare. "You care?"

"Do you?" he bit back. "I watch you live your pretty life, Louise, and it looks fucking dull. Worse than death, some might say. If you're truly dying, don't you think it's time you lived a little?"

"Let me guess, you're volunteering to show me how?"

His grin was a slim slice across his face. "Interested?"

"Why are *you* suddenly so into me? I don't think we've

spoken ten words to each other and I've known you all my life."

Reece stepped back slightly, crossing his arms and affecting that teenage boy stance that spoke of artificial bravado and casualness. "I was hoping you'd be more interesting now. With the cancer and all."

"Are you trying to be a massive asshole or does it come naturally to you?" I snapped.

My hand flew to my mouth to cover my gasp. It wasn't that I never swore. I just never did it in public or even anywhere outside my head. I'd never said an ill word to anyone and yet at the slightest provocation, I was being absolutely vile.

"I'm sorry," I whispered.

"Don't be." He lunged forward into my space again but not so close that the busybodies in the congregation would titter about it. "Doesn't it feel good to be mean?"

"It shouldn't matter if it *feels* good or not. Meanness is not something to aspire to," I preached.

He rolled his eyes. "You're so boring, I'm surprised you don't put yourself to sleep with talk like that." Suddenly, my hands were in his. "Look, let me help you here. You're a seventeen-year-old girl with absolutely no life experience and you could die soon. Doesn't that scare the pants off you?"

"You wish," I muttered darkly before I could censor myself.

His eyes caught fire with humor and I realized just how pretty he was. "There, doesn't that feel good? Saying what you really think."

I swallowed because it did.

Triumphantly, he grinned into my face. "Listen, you can think about it, yeah? I'm not asking you to do a line a coke or anything. I'm just urging you to *live* a little while you got the chance."

"Why do you care?" I asked again, this time softly because what he said was under my skin.

"I care because I've got half the crap you've got to deal with and I hate it." He indicated his mother, who was still gabbing away with my own. My parents were King and Queen of Entrance society and Mamie Ross was firmly on the fringe despite years of trying to be otherwise. I couldn't count the number of times I'd seen Reece dragged to the same boring events I was forced to attend.

"I'll think about it," I whispered, afraid to even have the words in the air.

The rebellion that was churning hot and slow under my skin had always been just a feeling, a rumbling heat that growled sometimes but never erupted into words or actions. I felt the release of my promise to Reece, felt the crack in the shell of my hardened exterior. It was both ominous and entirely beautiful.

I hadn't felt so free since Zeus had stopped writing to me.

So, when my mother returned to my side and excused us by saying that we had an important meeting to get to instead of just saying that she had to take me to the Youth Cancer Support Group in Vancouver, I decided to dip my toe in independence.

"I'll drive myself," I said, firmly.

Mum hesitated as we crossed the parking lot, surprised by the iron in my voice. She'd molded me to be her ideal child and her ideal child was supposed to be a pushover.

"You're so busy with all your charity work and there's the dinner with the Anholt's tonight so you have to make sure Chef isn't serving anything with dairy because of Mrs. Anholt's lactose intolerance... You have so much on your plate and I can easily drive myself down to Vancouver."

I waited, holding my breath, for my mother's response.

She took her time thinking about it and, by the time she answered, I was probably purple in the face. "Fine, but be home by dinner."

"Will do," I said behind a curtain of hair so that she wouldn't see my enormous smile.

It was such a little thing, driving myself an hour both ways to Vancouver, but it felt like a massive triumph because my mother dictated almost every aspect of my life and I spent most of the time with her when I wasn't in school.

"Use the slow lane and watch out for those idiot motor-cyclists who think that road rules do not apply to them," Mum said as she ducked into her sleek black BMW.

"Of course," I said.

I watched her pull out of the parking lot before making my way over to the silver Mazda hatchback I'd named Optimus Prime. It wasn't anything to write home about, but it was a zippy little machine and it was my very own. I absolutely adored it.

I was pulling open the door when I felt him behind me. I knew it was Reece before he said, "So, where are we going now that you got rid of mommy dearest?"

"The Youth Cancer Support Group in Vancouver," I deadpanned, turning my head just slightly so that I could watch his expression fall out of the corner of my eye.

Strangely, he didn't look disappointed. "Cool, let's hit it."

I watched him round my car and open the passenger door. "You're actually going to go with me to group?"

He crossed his forearms over the roof of the car and leaned toward me. "If that's where you want to go."

I pursed my lips. I hated the support group. It was utterly depressing, especially given that of the nine kids in it, four were terminal and three had fought the good fight more than once to get to remission only to slide back into its clutches years later. Everyone there tried hard to be open and optimistic but the second came hard and struck a discordant note. They got something from the morbid camaraderie the group provided for them but I didn't.

I was tired of pretending to be happy and group was just another stage for me to act out my false contentment.

"Not really," I admitted. "Did you have something else in mind?"

"Yeah, friend of mine is having a kegger out in the boonies. You down for a party?"

I'd never been to a party before. My girlfriends hung out with a group of guys sometimes but we never partied. We hung out at Mary's house mostly because her parents had an awesome home theatre bigger than most actual theatres, or at Joe's because his family had an Olympic sized pool with a three-tiered diving board. None of us drank because we were all athletes and scholars. Well, I'd been an athlete, a dancer, before the cancer decimated my energy.

"I don't have anything to wear," I said.

The shift and sweater set weren't exactly party clothes.

Reece cast a critical eye down my body and came to the same conclusion.

"Hudson has an older sister. She's smaller than you but you could probably squeeze into something of hers."

"Gee, thanks," I muttered.

He laughed. "I meant in the chest region, Lila is a lot smaller than you."

"Oh," I said, less offended because that was a fair assumption.

"Lila is cool. You'll like her."

"Will she like me?" I couldn't help but ask. Most of the kids at Entrance High thought I was a snob.

"They'll like you," he reassured me in a soft voice.

I wasn't sure why he was being so nice but I wasn't going to look a gift horse in the mouth. I was too much of a coward to do any of this by myself so I was grateful for his bad influence.

"Okay, let's do it," I decided with a firm head nod, proud of my decision and my conviction.

"Cool," Reece said before ducking into the car.

"Cool," I echoed softly, a little deflated at his lack of enthusiasm, and then followed him into Optimus.

"So," he began after we pulled out of the parking lot. "Let's go over the basics, yeah?"

"Okay?"

I saw him grin in my periphery.

"Have you ever done drugs?"

"No!"

"Not even blazed?"

"What?"

"Blazed."

"I don't know what that means," I admitted.

There was a short, stunned silence.

"You mean to tell me, you were born and raised in BC and you don't know what blazing means? What about taking a bong toke, getting high, greening out, doing dope, smoking grass, hot-boxing a car, rolling a joint?"

"Are you talking about marijuana?" I guessed.

I knew it was the leading albeit underground industry in British Columbia but that didn't mean I knew anything else about it. Most people in high school smoked marijuana but I wasn't most people and it kind of annoyed me that Reece was being condescending when he *knew* that. I was a paradigm of virtue. A paradigm of virtue did not know drug slang and they certainly did *not* do drugs.

"Yeah, Louise, I'm talking about Mary Jane," he said, again, like I was a moron.

I figured Mary Jane was another slang term.

"You can't even call yourself a British Columbian if you don't know a thing about BC bud. Our weed is the best in the world."

I shrugged.

"Fuck, you really are a good girl," he said, echoing my thoughts.

"Yes," I said, with a proud chin tilt.

Then I realized that being a good girl kind of sucked. I had friends, sure. A group of girls that called themselves the angels of Entrance High because they all came from established and, mostly, good Christian families, but more so because they were pretty, wealthy and they knew it. They weren't bullies to the rest of the kids but there was a lot of in-fighting about who was prettier, brighter and better liked. Ironically, the angels did not support one another's successes. Instead, they used guilt, manipulation and lies to hold each other back. I knew this because they had been my friends since birth just as our mothers had been. Old stock, I had come to learn, did not mean *good* stock.

I got good grades because I was, thank God, born smart and even if I didn't try hard, which I did because I was a good girl, I would have done well.

I volunteered at the Autism Centre. It started out as an obligation because my mother made me pick a charity organization to patronize when I hit twelve years old, but now, I loved it, and I wished that I had more time to dedicate to both it and other charitable organizations. I loved the kids at the center even though some of them were really hard to love because they didn't have the cognitive ability to discern social cues. One such kid, an adorable ginger-haired boy named Sammy, was one of my best friends. I still remembered the day that he informed me of our best-friends-for-life status. He'd written me a letter and asked me to sign it, officially making us bffs. I'd burst into tears.

So the volunteering was great, it made being a good girl worthwhile.

But the part where my parents showed me off like a prized pony and pretended that my illness didn't exist because it didn't fit in with their ideal life was beginning to consume me. I was fed up and repressed in a way that made me sick of spirit as well as of body.

I was seventeen years old. I was basically an adult; a fully formed human being. And I had no idea who I was outside of my parents expectations, outside of the mirror Entrance society held in front of me, more a painting of their own making than a true representation of myself.

"I don't even know who I am. How cliché is that?" I whispered.

"Pretty fucking cliché," Reece agreed easily.

We were silent as I chewed over my suitably teenage brooding thoughts and Reece stared out the window thinking about whatever Reece thought about. "You know what else is cliché? Rebelling against your parents," he finally said, leaning over the console so that he spoke right into my ear.

I shivered but my thoughts had led me down the same path. "Yeah."

He grinned at me. "It's going to be fun, Louise. You'll like normal teenage life and all the bad decisions you get to make when you don't give a fuck who you'll disappoint."

I frowned because that didn't sound like fun. It wasn't so much that I didn't want to disappoint my parents. In truth, I was angry with them for a variety of reasons and all of them had to do with their response—or lack of one—to my cancer.

I didn't want to let myself down by making stupid decisions that could harm me or someone else.

Reece put a warm hand over mine on the gearshift, his voice gentle when he said, "I'll watch out for you. I want you to have fun, get into just enough trouble to taste life, not end up dead in a gutter somewhere."

"Okay," I agreed, as if I wasn't terrified.

"Okay," he repeated.

CHAPTER TEN

Loulou

THE BASS PULSED LIKE A MUSICAL HEART BEAT BENEATH MY bare feet as I stomped them to the rhythm of the Kygo song that blasted through the massive speakers set up throughout the main level of the house. There was a red Solo cup in my hand filled with warm beer Reece had tapped from a massive keg of Blue Buck in the corner and the contents sloshed over my fingers as I tossed my sweaty hair back and forth over my exposed shoulders. I'd already had a few cups of beer as well as two shots of vodka that Lila, Hudson and Reece had poured for me to start the evening off.

Reece was right, I liked Lila and she liked me.

She was three years older than us and back from UBC for summer break. I'd never met such a graceful, willowy woman but her classic beauty and the good humor in her huge hazel eyes enthralled me. She had me laughing before I could remember to be awkward and when she had offered me clothes, she'd only laughed a little bit at the absurd fit of the jean skirt and crop top I'd tried on. Lila was maybe five foot four and one hundred and ten pounds soaking wet. I was five foot nine and curvy.

After we'd both had a good laugh, we'd improvised. Now, I wore the fragile camisole that I'd been wearing under my shift and a stretchy black skirt that on Lila went to just below her knees but on me came up to mid-thigh. I wasn't wearing shoes because my sensible, low heels were *not* party shoes. Lila had done my makeup, taking the time to teach me how so that I could do it in the future.

I didn't know when I'd have the opportunity to wear red lipstick ever again but it looked pretty cool with all the blond hair I had, mussed with a bit of styling goop that smelled like coconuts. When I'd come downstairs to join Reece and his friend Hudson in the kitchen both of their mouths had fallen open like the hinges broke.

When the rest of Entrance Bay Acad—and it really seemed like the entire school minus my squad of preppy kids was there—showed up, they had similar reactions to my presence. Shock, awe and finally, laughter. Apparently, it was amusing to see Little Miss Goody Two-Shoes dressed like a teenage tramp, drinking warm beer and grinding up against the masses. I wasn't insulted because sometimes I was so saccharine that it made even *my* teeth ache and because it *was* pretty funny and became funnier as the night grew long and I grew drunk.

The sun had set a long time ago but the air was still warm so a bunch of us were hanging in Hudson and Lila's backyard. Reece, true to his word, hadn't left my side all night and he made sure we always had booze. He was super handsome and actually pretty fun, always telling jokes and sharing stories so as the night wore on and he grew closer, a hand on my shoulder then an arm around my waist with his fingers settling intimately over my hip, I didn't protest.

For the first time *ever*, I was having fun.

He brushed my hair over one shoulder and leaned into my neck, his breath hot on my exposed skin as he whispered, "Want to go inside, find a little quiet?"

I wasn't really surprised by his question. I wasn't totally naive.

Part of me didn't want to go with him. I liked Reece but in the easy way of friends and partners-in-crime. I didn't think I wanted his tongue in my mouth, let alone his hand down my pants. But I told myself I was being snobby and a little unreasonable. I'd never had a tongue in my mouth or a hand down my pants, so how could I know that I wouldn't like his?

The answer was, I couldn't.

I'd loved one person in my life thus far and I'd only ever seen him twice. What was I going to do? Cling to the idea of my childhood prison pen pal for the rest of my life? Pine after someone who didn't want me and, I was fairly sure, wouldn't be good for me even if he did?

No. Absolutely not.

So, reaching my drunken conclusion, I answered him by grabbing his hand and tugging him inside.

I saw Lila watching with a concerned frown and even Hudson looked a little wary, but I smiled sloppily at them in reassurance as Reece took the lead, ushering me inside and up the stairs to an empty bedroom.

As soon as the door was closed, he was on me.

The tongue that I'd been curious about was in my mouth and it tasted like yeast and hops. It was warm and slick, ickier than I'd expected as it thrust between my lips and ran over my teeth.

His hands though, I liked. One pressed between my shoulders so that I was tight against him and the other trailed down my back so that he cupped my butt. It felt good to have his large, hot hands on me. Even better to feel his response to my body in the groan that worked its way into my mouth from his. I could definitely get used to a man's hands on me.

Slut, the conservative Louise cried.

The new me, an entirely new person without a name or family, without a care in the entire world but for what pleased her in that very moment, grinned at the name calling and kissed Reece back.

He had me pressed to the bed, his long body on mine and his hands under my shirt, palming and squeezing both of my breasts with unabashed fervor when the nausea hit me smack in the middle of my gut.

"Oh, no," I mumbled against Reece's lips.

He hesitated, pulling away slightly to ask, "You okay, sweetheart?"

I was scrambling away from him before he had even

finished speaking but I only made it to the edge of the bed before I was throwing up.

"Shit," I heard him curse over the sounds of my ceaseless vomiting.

I was mortified but so sick that my entire body ached with it. Belatedly, I realized that drinking was a terrible idea. Even though I'd just been diagnosed and hadn't started any treatment yet, my body was worn down and I'd never been intoxicated before.

On the heels of my embarrassment, self-loathing came snapping.

"*Idiot*," I managed to breathe between heaves.

"Okay, wait right here. I'm going to get Lila," Reece said.

I groaned and he must have taken it as confirmation because he ducked out the door.

A minute or two later, I was puked out.

I lay there panting for what felt like ages but must have been only a few minutes because Reece didn't return. My stomach had settled but I was still drunk as a skunk and probably just as stinky so I decided to head back outside to get some fresh air. My legs were surprisingly steady as they carried me down the crowded stairwell, past my peers who smiled and called to me with caution, maybe worried that I was a tattle-tale or that I was just a good girl playing bad. I ignored them, pushing through the front door and gulping in deep lungfuls of clean air.

There was nothing like the air on the coast of British Columbia. I'd been on a lot of family vacations across the globe and there was nothing as sweet as the air I breathed in after getting off the plane when I was back home.

I closed my eyes, leaning against the wall beside the door

so I could figure myself out. There was still a heavy tread to my thoughts like they waded through thigh high swamp water but the urge to be sick had retreated.

I was almost asleep against the side of the house when the low rumble of approaching motorcycles roused me.

In Entrance, that thunderous growl was not uncommon. The Fallen MC had been a staple of the town almost since the MC was founded in 1960. I'd grown up seeing the leather-clad bikers swarm the streets in rigid formation on the backs of great metal beasts, their hair long, their beards wild and their skin covered in permanent art. I'd always watched them with a strange kind of envy because I'd never seen anything as free as those men seemed to be, riding off as a brotherhood into the sunset.

After the shooting, I'd watched for them wherever I went, desperate to catch sight of Zeus, even when I knew he was in prison but especially after I knew he got out. I didn't know if he was a part of the infamous gang because he had never answered my questions about his involvement that day at First Light Church and my memory was too hazy to recall if he'd been wearing the cut of The Fallen.

I deeply suspected he was a part of the rebel group and it thrilled me each time I heard the rumble of a bike, thinking that I might finally, after nearly ten years, see him again.

The thunder grew so close that I struggled to sit up from the wall and open my leaden eyes wider. Seconds later, three yellow-lighted bikes swung around the corner and slowly rolled down the street.

My eyes were riveted on the scene and I suddenly *hated* myself for getting drunk for the first time in my life because, though my traitorous eyes could have been deceiving me, I was certain that the powerful figure at the head of the trio was my guardian monster.

I watched, my heavy eyelids peeled back wide but I would have taped them wider if I could have. I didn't want to miss a second.

I shot to my feet to say something or, maybe, to run to him but the effort was too much for my alcohol-muddled brain and I promptly passed out.

"What the fuck?" Zeus was growling somewhere very close to me.

I blinked as I came to, but my vision refused to clear so I lay still and focused on not throwing up again instead.

"She was letting loose, man. It's not a big deal. Everyone gets like this before they understand their limits," Reece responded.

Even from within the fog of my inebriation, I knew that was *not* a good thing to say to Zeus.

I was proven right when the wall I was lying against grew impossibly harder and I realized, as arms tightened brutally around me, that he was holding me against him.

"You brought her here, yeah? To party and get in her pants?" Zeus asked, deceptively casual.

There was a long pause.

Zeus took one step forward.

"Yes, yes, okay? So what?" Reece asked nervously.

"So, you got a girl with you, a girl you want a piece of and you let her get fuckin' wasted like this? There are two types of men who do that shit. One, the pigs that need to get a woman drunk to stick their dicks in 'em willing or not. Two, the jackasses like you who don't give a shit about 'em till your dick gets hard and you can use 'em to get off on or in. Which one are you?"

Wow. I blinked again and finally my vision cleared. I stared at the steep edge of Zeus's bearded jaw and decided it was time for me to step in.

"Zeus, he didn't mean any harm."

He stiffened even more and cut his burning gaze down to me for one horrible moment. "I'll deal with you later."

Um, what?

"What?" I asked, confounded by his fury.

This was the first time I'd seen him since I was *seven years old* and this was how he was going to talk to me?

Then again, it was the first time I'd seen him in a decade and this was how I was going to see him, drunk, dumb and seriously disgusting.

The inebriated side of my mind chose to point out that at least I was in his arms which was nice.

More than nice.

So my drunk mind won out and I curled closer into his marble slab of a chest, my fingers pushing past the edge of his leather vest so I could rest my palm over his heart.

I could feel the breath stutter for a moment in his chest before he recovered and it made me smile.

"I'm not either of those guys. I did her a favour, man. You obviously don't get this but Louise is fucking repressed and she needed to let go. I helped her do that. Though why the fuck *you* of all people care is beyond me," Reece said.

He had bigger balls than I'd originally credited him with or he had a death wish.

"In fact," Reece went on, proving that he must indeed have a death wish, "*I* should be defending her from *you*."

A low, menacing growl thundered through Zeus's chest. I peeled open my sticky eyelids to see Reece step back in fear at the look on my biker man's face.

"Listen here, you motherfucker. You obviously know who I am, you obviously got no respect for anythin', but if Lou thinks you're worth her time then you better prove fuckin' worthy of it or the entire weight of The Fallen will fall heavy on you, you hear me? I personally will cut off your dick and shove it up your ass if you treat her like anything less than fuckin' gold. Under-fuckin'-stood?"

Reece blinked at Zeus then looked at me and back to him. I watched his Adam's apple work as he swallowed painfully and said, "Yeah, Mr. Garro. Understood."

Zeus nodded curtly then turned on his heel and stormed out of the house. I noticed vaguely that there were no more teenage partygoers. Instead, leather-clad bikers appeared through the open doorway to the kitchen laughing and drinking leftover booze.

"You kicked everyone out?" I asked weakly, safe but curious in his arms.

"Shut the fuck up," he ordered without looking down at me as we stepped through the front door and made it to his huge motorcycle.

Maneuvering me in his arms so that I was wrapped around his front like a koala bear, he reached for the helmet strapped to the back seat of the bike and plunked it on my head, clipping it closed with one hand. He stared at me with dark, angry eyes for a second before he swung us *both* over the bike and let go of me to put his hands on the bars.

"Hold on tight and don't fuckin' throw up on my bike," he demanded.

I swallowed and closed my eyes against the misery of my pounding head, twisting stomach and wounded pride. I closed my eyes, held on tight and hoped with every molecule that I would wake up and this would have all been a terrible nightmare. Miserably, I noticed that he smelled like leather, tobacco and some kind of tree, cedar or pine. It was better than any high drink or drugs could give me. His big, hard body was warm against mine as the cold night wind rippled over us as he pulled into the street and I snuggled close to the scent and the warmth.

"I missed you so much," I murmured, half-asleep and fully drunk.

"Fuckin' pissed at you for pullin' this shit, Lou," he told me over the loud rumble of his bike and the rushing wind.

"I know," I agreed sleepily. "I'm pissed too. I don't know if I'll remember this in the morning and thinking about forgetting the way you smell makes me want to cry."

"No tears," he ordered.

"But I'm not alone this time," I reminded him. "I've finally got my guardian monster back."

Zeus was silent but the level of fury vibrating through his body stilled and I fell asleep listening to the steady thrum of his heart thinking that nothing and no where had ever felt so close to heaven as *this*.

When I woke up it was in my deeply shadowed room and Zeus was somehow there, dropping me gently into my bed.

"How did we get in here?"

He hesitated pulling the covers over me then shook his head like he couldn't believe me. "Tell your dad you need better locks."

Oh.

"How did you know you'd be able to get inside?"

"Lou, shut up. I'm still fuckin' pissed at you and the less you talk the better. I got some things to say and then I'm leavin'."

"Okay," I agreed easily because now that he'd found me, gotten over whatever made him think we couldn't be together, I knew I wouldn't lose him again. "Sit down beside me."

Zeus looked down at me, a muscle clenching in his jaw. "No. I'm tellin' you what I got to say then I'm leavin' and Louise, I am not coming back. I'm pissed because I found you tonight drunk outta your fuckin' mind with a dumbass kid who woulda fucked you without thinkin' a fuckin' thing about anythin' but gettin' off. You can barely speak, walk or keep your eyes open. You think I wrote to you through the cancer and all that fucked up shit you had to go through as a kid just to see you piss your life away like this? I stayed away so you would stay good. I'm warnin' you now, you don't smarten the fuck up, not only will that buy you never seein' me again but I'll get in touch with your cunt father and tell him exactly what you're doin' and he'll send you to a fuckin' nunnery. You get me?"

Somewhere deep in the shroud of my drunkenness, my heart was breaking.

"I don't want to be Louise Lafayette anymore," I admitted.

For the first time that night, Zeus softened. I couldn't see him in the darkness of my curtained room but I could feel his gentling in the air and it made the pain in my chest loosen.

"You can be whoever you want to, Lou. I'm not tellin' you

to be the girl Benjamin fuckin' Lafayette wants you to be. I'm tellin' you to be who *you* want to be, not anyone else and I'm tellin' you to do it smart, yeah? Right now, you don't know who you are, what you want or where you're goin', your head is stuck so far up your ass."

"You don't have a right to talk to me like this," I whispered brokenly.

"I have every fuckin' right. As the man who saved your life once, don't make me save it again," Zeus ordered then turned on his heel and left.

He left and even though I woke up the next morning with a headache that clanged worse than broken church bells between my temples and a memory filled with holes, I knew Zeus had reentered my life only to tell me he was leaving it for good.

CHAPTER ELEVEN

Loulou

FOUR MONTHS LATER.

THE BRICK WAS hot against my mostly bare back. In fact, it burned, and the texture was rubbing my sweaty skin raw but I didn't move. I'd spent a long time perfecting The Lean and I finally had it down. One foot, encased in kickass super tall espadrilles that I kept hidden beneath my floorboards, was wedged up against the wall while the other was straight and long, showcasing the long length of my yoga toned leg beneath the beyond short shorts I wore. My arms were crossed loose enough to be look casual but tight enough to press my boobs together, to ride the hem of my white crop top up even higher on my tummy. My chin was tipped down, pale hair perfectly mussed, unlit joint hanging between my lips.

In short, I was *rockin'* The Lean and I was absolutely not going to fuck it up by wiggling like a moron.

The sun was practically set but it could get hot in Entrance and it had been a record breaking October. I had the deep brown tan to prove it, tiny tan lines and only around my hips, over my crotch and cut through the cheeks of my ass because I sunned in a thong every chance I could get to slip off to the little knoll in the forest behind my house. I only owned a few and I had to keep them hidden under my floorboards but the effort was worth it to be brown all over.

If Mum or Dad ever caught me, they would've killed me but I'd stopped worrying about that a long time ago. They were always telling me not to waste my brain, that I was too smart not to use it. So, I did, just in ways they didn't like.

To be fair to me though, I always did my homework, got straight As, sat in the front pew of church every freaking Sunday at what felt like the butt crack of dawn, volunteered at the Autism Centre every weekend and never, *ever*, did anything to disrespect the Lafayette name.

At least, not when I was Louise Lafayette.

As Loulou Fox, I did everything my family stood against.

I gambled, partied, smoked, lied, cheated and generally disrespected all authority, every government given rule.

I was a seventeen-year-old teenage dirt bag and I fucking loved it.

Which was why I was doing The Lean against The Wet Lotus, Entrance's one and only strip club.

It was a sleazy place with poor lighting, sticky everything

and a female owner who was beyond bitter and disillusioned and hated the club even though it was the only one in town and made her a crap ton of money.

She didn't know who I was or, more specifically, who my father was, or she wouldn't have let me anywhere near her place.

Loulou Fox, though, she loved.

I was underage but even if she knew it, and Debra Bandera was a wily one, I had the generous curves and the fake ID to pull off nineteen.

Besides, Debra liked me. She liked me because when I'd taken to hanging out after dropping Ruby off and picking her up again at the end of the night, I'd started to help out around the bar and who doesn't like free labor? Four months later and I was Debra's unofficial assistant.

I did a bunch of the ordering, everything from nipple tassels to cocktail napkins. I sewed the girl's minuscule costumes, learned to mix drinks, flirt with men without promising them anything more, mop and sweep the floors, wax and shine the poles and take care of the twelve very high-maintenance dancers. I wasn't there every night but I was there three times a week on the nights I pretended to go to the support group and it had become, in a way, more of a home than my actual home was.

No one knew Loulou Fox had cancer because none of the bikers, scoundrels, dancers, bartenders or regulars that hung out at the Lotus read the local newspaper or the parish newsletter. I'd be surprised if most of them even knew either publication existed. They probably knew of Louise Lafayette, the Goody Two-Shoes daughter of Benjamin and Phillipa Lafayette. It would just never cross their minds to associate the Loulou they knew—fun loving, brazen and ballsy—with the staid, boring girl they had heard about in passing.

I laughed as I leaned, as I always did when I thought about Louise vs. Loulou, good vs. bad, my very own naughty and nice combination split down the middle into two very separate people.

I much preferred Loulou.

And three nights a week, I could be her without impunity.

"I'll never get used to seein' you like that," the woman who was largely responsible for my new two-sided nature said as she pushed open the emergency door and stepped into the alley beside me.

Ruby Jewel was her honest-to-God given name. Her mother had been a prostitute that found a decent John who married her and provided for her and their two kids. They weren't a poor family. Ruby wasn't abused as a kid, she didn't need the money and she was pretty well adjusted as far as twenty-one-year-old girls went. She just loved to dance, she loved expensive shoes and she loved The Lotus.

We'd actually met at the one and only Youth Cancer Support Group I'd gone to in Vancouver. Ruby had been diagnosed as a kid with brain cancer. She'd battled it for four years before finally going into remission. She'd succumbed to the disease again when she was seventeen, this time in her bile ducts. After a year of intense treatment and three surgeries, she'd beaten that too. Ruby Jewel was a fighter. I'd known it the second I had seen her sitting in the depressingly empty classroom on a plastic chair waiting for group to begin. She was wearing a tiny dress held together with silver safety pins and her hair was out to *there*. Somehow, even rocking all that, she didn't look like a whore. She just looked super cool, someone who had grown to love themselves and was comfortable not only in their own skin but in their own personality, flaws and all.

I'd sat beside her and left two hours later with a new best friend.

"Is it the joint?" I asked mildly, as she pushed her dark red bangs back from her sweaty forehead and waved a hand to cool herself.

She was wearing blue, red and white spandex short shorts and nipple coverings shaped like miniature American flags. It was one of my favourite outfits she wore.

"Nah, it's the complete ease you got goin' on out here. I've seen you, from afar obviously, livin' the classy life. You go to a church every Sunday and to a school where you wear uniforms for Christ's sake. And yet here you are, Louise Lafayette leaning against the wall of a fucking strip club as if you were born an' raised here."

She shook her head but it was with awe and warmth that she turned to me to say, "You're incredible. Weird as shit, but also incredible."

"Back at you, babe," I said.

We smiled at each other before hers broke off and her eyes darkened.

"How're ya feeling?"

"Why?" I snapped.

I didn't like to talk about the cancer, about Louise and her life when I was at the bar. Ruby knew that and, normally, she respected it.

She bit her scarlet painted lip and shifted on her heels.

"Just that something weird is going on tonight and I don't know if you should be here or not."

I straightened instantly, my foot jarring against the pavement as I stood up. "What do you mean?"

She shrugged. "Dunno really. Debra told us girls that tonight had to be the best show we put on in our lives."

A little shiver scuttled down my back. I knew Debra was frustrated with The Lotus. It was a lot of work and she was tired, not just of the club but of hard living. Her third husband had left her five months ago for a newer model and she hadn't recovered.

I'd had a feeling for a while that she wanted to sell but the thought of her doing so slayed me. I'd found a little oasis of crazy calamity in my perfectly ordered life. It was what got me through the hours spent hooked up to poison that was supposed to cure, it was what pulled me through the teeth aching monotony of my day-to-day existence.

"Shit," I swore.

It was a bit excessive but I'd found out that I liked cursing. There was some kind of release attached to the words that always made me feel better.

It didn't then, not with the thought of losing The Lotus weighing on my mind.

"The new owner might not want to change things up," Ruby offered. "I mean, they'll definitely keep on the dancers and probably the serving staff too."

"What use will they have for me though? I'm an underage, unpaid hang around."

"Yeah, but you're super cute so let's hope that the buyer is a man with good taste," Ruby said with a smirk.

I snorted but her attempt at easing me fell short. There was anxiety like arsenic in my blood.

"Cool it, Lou, everything will be golden," Ruby said.

I chuckled darkly and dropped my joint to the ground to crush it beneath my high heel. "Nothing in my life is golden, Rue."

"Your bush is," she quipped which startled a laugh out of me. "If you had any that is."

I rolled my eyes at her. "Come on, let's go see what's going on."

We linked arms as we headed inside, laughing about something Molly, a sweet but dumb dancer, had done the night before. I was mid-laugh when I noticed Debra heading into her office behind a few shadowy shapes. She caught my eye and looked uneasy. I raised an eyebrow at her in question but she only bit her lip and shook her head slightly, like she was sorry.

A shiver of trepidation shot up my spine.

"Deb," I called out to her.

"Behave tonight," was her response in a voice that brooked no argument.

Ruby and I shared a look after she'd closed the door.

"Shit," we both cursed at the same time, then broke down into giggles.

HE'D BEEN WATCHING me all night.

I'd felt his eyes for hours but not in the way I was used to the men in a strip club looking at a woman. That was the feeble falling to sin and temptation, hoping to prey on the assumed weaker sex. Those eyes left hot greasy marks against my flesh, disgusting but easily washed off, easily ignored.

These eyes were not. They tracked me across the room, embedded under my skin like some clever device, not losing track of me even when I left and entered again, even amid the glittering mass of mostly naked women and excitable men, between the high backed semiprivate booths and the tall, mirrored bar.

I hadn't looked his way, positioned with his back against the wall to one side of the main stage, his position open to the entirety of the club. It had taken more determination than I wanted to admit, I was curious about a man like him, a man who watched someone the way a computer might, or a camera, without bias or emotion. Only stone-cold calculation.

I wanted to meet him because I wanted to learn that.

I wanted to never meet him because it was dangerous that he watched *me* like that.

I had secrets, big ones, though none so scary as to threaten my life.

Something about the way those eyes watched me though, warned me that he could become that threat to my life and more that he *wanted* to.

The hair on the back of my neck had been on end all night and a little voice at the back of my head told me one peek wouldn't hurt.

The rest of me knew better.

So, I avoided the watchman and continued my Wednesday night as if he didn't exist. I helped Ruby tuck her curves into a tiny sequined costume, sewed the buttons onto half a dozen more just like it, served drinks because Margie had called in sick and mopped up the puke in the bathroom after the bachelor party went awry thanks to too many tequila shooters.

I was mindful of the women, dancers and customers alike, who gravitated toward him as the night carried on. They were beautiful women who had no qualms about displaying their wares and their interest but the man seemed to have no qualms about rebuffing them, sometimes brutally if their sour mouths and thunderous brows were anything to go by.

Still, he watched me.

It was quarter to two in the morning and things were winding down at The Lotus. The bachelor party had long since departed, the couples looking to heat up their love life had found their ignition and left back to their beds and it was only the devout that remained. It was my favourite time of night at the club because the men who lingered were regular enough to have made friends with the crew, including me.

"Been watching you all night, girl," Harlow told me as I handed him a frosty new pint.

I wiped my hands on the dishtowel tucked into the back of my shorts and shrugged as if I didn't care, as if I hadn't been aware of that gaze the entire night. As if it and the man behind it weren't driving me crazy.

"Nothing new," I said, because it wasn't.

I was pretty and men seemed to have a sixth sense that I was young, too young. It made them unusually hard for me.

"You noticed 'im too."

I shot Harlow Barton a look over my shoulder as I wiped down the counter. He had once been a large man, fit and virile due to his years in the navy, and though age had softened his figure, not much slipped by the old coot's sharp eyes.

"No shame in admiring a pretty face," Tinsley quipped as she skipped up to the bar, her doctor-given breasts bouncing becomingly in her brief white crop top. "I've been staring at him all night. He's been holding court to dangerous looking men all night and half of them weren't bad-looking, either."

"You stare at all the pretty men," Reno interjected, leaning back in his chair to gesture to himself. "That's why I always catch you looking at me."

Tinsley rolled her pretty brown eyes. "This guy isn't just pretty, he's, like, magnetic or something. The only woman in here who hasn't hit on him yet is Loulou and you know how she is."

"Yeah, stuck up," Reno muttered, but the sides of his slim mouth crooked up so I would know he was joking.

I shrugged. "I've got high standards."

"You've got that Reece Ross," Tinsley said, her face taking on a dreamy quality as I handed her the drinks for her last table. "Anyone with the good luck of landing that kid wouldn't look elsewhere."

I didn't fully agree with her but I couldn't argue that Reece was an awesome guy. Ever since the night he'd corrupted me, his words not mine, we'd been pretty much inseparable. We partied, both with drugs at friends' houses and with tea at church luncheons. He occupied both of my worlds and took pride in the fact that he'd introduced me to the dark side of Entrance. He liked Louise *and* Loulou but I had the feeling he thought I was having a gag, that Loulou was this fun alter-ego pastime I had going so that I could forget about the problems that faced Louise.

He was right and he was wrong.

He was right because Loulou had cancer but it didn't define her so, it wasn't a problem for her.

He was wrong because in every way that mattered, Loulou was the woman I wanted to be. She was the dark heart of me brought to life, unbound from the scripture and familial guilt of my youth. It was the section of my soul that found violence a necessary tool of retribution. That felt passion like a thunderclap and hatred like a burning thing in my gut that *needed* to be acted upon. Loulou was base, instinct and brimstone. She had so many flaws so beautifully accepted, that they became honed weapons and gleaming treasures.

She was unashamed and *free*.

If anything was a phase, it was Louise. And she was fading fast to give way for Lou.

Zeus's Lou.

The girl who had recognized Zeus Garro as a kindred soul from across the church parking lot and run toward him as bullets flew all around.

I couldn't have him. I knew that and felt it like the echo of the bullet wound in my chest.

But I could be the woman he'd created, the one he gave me the confidence to be.

So I liked Reece. I liked kissing him because kissing was fun, and I liked talking to him because he had things to say unlike most of the friends I'd had all my life. But I didn't love him, and I never would.

"Look at her gone all gaga over the boy," Reno cackled as he slammed down his warm mug of beer. "He's a lucky feller, I'm sayin' it right now."

"Damn but if I was ten years younger," Harlow said with a sigh.

Tinsley giggled. "More like forty."

Reno laughed too but I reached over to pat Harlow's hand and give him a little wink. "Ten's more like it, Harlow baby. I like my men older."

The old man's creased face creased even more with warmth. "You're a good girl, Loulou. Too good for the likes of Zeus Garro anyways."

I froze.

"What?" I whispered, my lips barely moving because for some reason, I was afraid to move.

"Zeus Garro, Prez of The Fallen MC and a meaner motherfucker there never was," Harlow explained.

"I know who he is. Why did you bring him up?"

He frowned, his eyes skittering over to Reno and Tinsley who both watched me with concerned confusion.

"Babe," Tinsley was the one to say, stepping backward to open up my line of sight to the man who had been sitting in the booth all night watching me. "Zeus Garro's the man who just bought The Lotus from Debra."

My eyes burned with the need to look over, tears building from the tension of holding back the impulse.

"Tinsley, don't fuck with me," I whispered and somehow there were tears in my throat too.

"Honey, I'm not. *Look*," she urged gently, no doubt wondering if I was a crazy person.

I didn't care.

I didn't care about anything in the world in that moment except for the fact that Zeus Garro was in my space.

Did he know I was there?

Yes, of course he did. He'd been watching me all night.

What the *fuck* was he doing here?

A muscle below my left eye ticked.

I had to look.

My heart beat thrummed like thunder in my ears and sharp thrills of anxiety and excitement zipped across my skin like fingers of lightning as I swiveled my head to look over at the booth, to take in the man I'd been in love with for what seemed like forever.

And then I saw him.

Gorgeous, more gorgeous somehow than ever before. His enormous frame took up the entire back of the red velvet booth and his mess of curling brown hair caught in the light like it was dipped in gold. He looked powerful and dark. A god in his den of iniquity.

And his eyes were on me. Even across the room as I was, I could see the glint of silver, feel the intensity of his intent.

His eyes were on me, but his arms were around Jade, locked tight around her topless body as she ground her latex-covered sex against his leg and licked a long line up his neck to his bearded chin.

Then, as he'd done when I was a little girl, he winked at me, and turned his head just enough to take Jade's seeking lips with his own. And all the while, his eyes still hooked mine.

My heart seized and not for the first time in my life, I felt like I was dying.

CHAPTER TWELVE

Zeus

I LIKED MY GIRLS A LOTTA WAYS.

I liked thin, plump, thick with muscles, or soft with curves.

Liked blonde, brunette, or red, anything in-between but a little more partial to light, the mostly fake kinda blonde women found in a bottle. They reminded me of the biker babe posters I'd first jerked off to as a kid. Still any woman with some gumption no matter her looks or stylin' would do.

As I said, I liked my girls a lotta ways and I liked takin' her a lot more ways than that.

They only thing I did not like was young ones.

Seen enough old bikers stick their wick in fresh honey to

know it didn't lead to good things. Plus, I had a teenage daughter who didn't need to catch wind of me fuckin' a girl closer to her age than mine.

Then came Louise Lafayette.

The mayor's daughter.

Same age as my youngest fuckin' kid.

And the fuck of it was, I'd never wanted anyone more than I wanted her.

Which explained why I was sittin' in The Lotus, a piece of shit titty bar on the outskirts of Entrance that most of my brothers and I couldn't be bothered to go to because the dancers were decent but the décor had more stains than even bikers were comfortable with and that was sayin' something.

I was there 'cause of the girl I'd known most of her life who had somehow turned into a woman, and a fuckin' fine one at that. I'd watched her all night, wonderin' at first if she knew it was me sitting at the back booth 'cause she was makin' an art of avoiding my eyes and the last time I'd seen her, I'd brow-beaten her pretty bad. Wanted to get my point across, get her set on the straight an' narrow, only looking back I'd been too harsh. Despite my reputation, I wasn't a harsh guy, at least not with my family and definitely not my kids, yet I'd been fuckin' brutal to Lou that night. I'd sat on that for a few weeks, wonderin' why and when I'd come up to the answer, I wished to God I hadn't tried to figure it out. The answer was simple as fuck. I'd been angry and surprised that the little girl I'd been writing to for years—too many years—was *not* a kid anymore.

Even drunk as fuck and rank as shit, Louise Lafayette took my fuckin' breath away.

It mighta been all that pale hair that mussed up in sexy disarray all around that heart-shaped face. I wanted to drive my hands into it, fist it tight and bring that phenomenal bee-stung mouth to mine. Wonderin' what she tasted like had been drivin' me crazy for months. In my dirtiest fantasies, she tasted like cherry lollipops, the kind she'd liked as a kid.

I was sick. Sick with lust for a girl nineteen years younger than me and morally sick because of it.

So, if I'd been too hard on her it was to take my mind off the way her out-fuckin'-rageous curves felt against my body when I'd hauled her into my arms. It'd been 'cause of the fury I felt at some dumbass preppy fuck touching her while she was outta her mind with drink. It'd been 'cause I'd forced myself to stay away so she could live a good life, the kind of life a girl with a soul as beautiful as hers should live. And I'd seen her throwin' it away.

Problem was, as harsh as I'd been, Lou didn't seem to give a fuck.

I'd started watchin' her again. Not creepy, you get me, but just a casual eye. Have one of my brothers do a drive by her house, get my son, King, to keep watch of her at school where she seemed to excel—no surprise, she'd always been a smart girl—and keep an ear turned towards my H.R.'s chatter on the off chance I caught a hint of Lou's name.

So, I'd learned Lou led a double life. My kids reported Louise Lafayette was a good girl who did her homework and hung with those religious "angel" bitches I'd once told her to charm. My boys told me different. They told me about Loulou Fox who wore next to nothin' and worked at the shitty titty bar off Highway 99.

The temptation was too fuckin' great. It seemed that the

sweet kid in the frilly white church dress with the bows in her hair had grown into a rebel, a woman not content unless she was livin' hard and livin' free.

I couldn't say I was surprised. I couldn't say I didn't have a hand in nurturin' that in her but now I could see it'd always been there, just waitin' to take over.

With or without me, Loulou Lafayette was going over to the dark side.

And I'd decided I'd be the welcoming committee.

So there I was sittin' in a booth in The Lotus, makin' out with one of the dancers so when Lou finally got her head outta her ass and realized I was there, she'd know I wasn't there for romance or fuckin' flowers.

I was there to teach her right and proper how to live the kind life she was barrelin' toward without gettin' herself pimped up, drugged down or washed out. She was givin' in to the devil on her shoulder and I was bound and fuckin' determined to be the voice of Satan.

There would be no hearts, not even any fucking.

Louise was a seventeen-year-old daughter of the bastard who'd been makin' my life a livin' hell for years.

She was the definition of off-fuckin'-limits even for a man like me who didn't go in for rules.

As solid as I was on the point, it still rocked me like a sucker punch to the gut when she finally turned those massive blue eyes to mine, our gaze connecting like two mechanical parts meant to work in sync.

Fuck me, she was a wet dream come to life.

Then the hurt came.

It washed over her features like acid, contorting her

features until she was as close to ugly as she could ever become.

I felt that pain in my chest. Had to fight the instinct to punch myself in the face 'cause that's what I woulda done to any other motherfucker that put that look on her face.

Instead, I hammered that final nail in the coffin of her childish dreams with a ruthless bang.

I winked at her.

Just like I had when she'd come to visit me that first time in the hospital.

I fuckin' winked at her and her acid washed face crumpled into ash, skin pale, features lax.

Fuck me but I ruined her with that wink.

Remorse burned through me and I nearly gagged into the bitch whose mouth I was eatin' at.

"You okay, baby?" she purred into my ear.

I didn't take my eyes off Lou even as she jerked outta her misery and turned away from me to talk to the old-timers sitting at her bar. She said somethin' real quick then hustled out of sight.

"Done with you, sugar. Go wax a pole or somethin'," I told the dancer, gently but firmly shoving 'er off my lap.

She blinked at me but she was a dancer, she knew how it was, and she strolled off without givin' me lip.

I was grateful. It was hard to tell if I wanted to rage at someone, beat 'em senseless to get rid of all the guilt under my skin or burst into fuckin' tears like a twelve-year-old chick.

"Z," my brother Bat called out as he rounded the booth. "Let's roll out, brother. Nova's got a party goin' with those biker models back at the compound."

I nodded at my now-warm glass of bourbon and tipped it back. The burn settled me some so I could look up at Bat without lookin' like a pussy.

"Wow, what the hell's up with you?" Bat asked.

Damn the perceptive bastard.

"Nothin'," I said as I made to get up from the booth.

"Nothin' my pasty white ass," Bat snorted as he sat down, blocking my exit. "Tell me what's got you lookin' so fucked. Last time, it was Farrah O.D.ing again."

I rolled my eyes. "Don't fuckin' mention that bitch's name. Haven't seen her in three years an' another fifty wouldn't be long enough."

"Z, brother, you know I won't push if you gotta keep it down but there are some serious ghosts in your eyes and fuck knows, I gotta sense what that looks like."

My mouth twisted in a grimaced smirk because if anyone knew pain, it was Bat. He'd served in the military for fifteen years before being honourably discharged after the rest of his battalion was killed in action durin' an air raid in Iraq. He'd been my best friend before he'd been my brother and I knew better than to keep shit from him 'cause he was a fuckin' hound dog at sniffin' it out. I'd kept 'im outta Lou-surveillance duties for exactly that fuckin' reason.

Still, he knew enough of the story to get me when I said, "Lou's here."

"The fuck?"

"You heard me."

"Please tell me that isn't why we bought this shithole?"

I glared at him. He may have been my brother, but no one questioned me, especially about the betterment of *my* fuckin' club. "King had a point about diversifying our investments. We got the garages, the trucking company, the tat shop, Eugene's bar and now a titty bar. They're cash cows and it'll keep the boys happy, they got a place closer than Vancouver to go to get some quality pieces."

"The only thing of quality here is your little church mouse," Bat argued.

"We bring in Maja and she'll get 'em sorted," I said, referring to my VP Buck's old lady. She'd worked at a titty bar over in Calgary for years before hookin' up with Buck and she was a class act, just what this place needed.

That and about thirty gallons of bleach.

"It may be a good investment, I get you wouldn't do bad by the club, Z, but this is about way more than that. This is about the fuckin' girl."

"Watch your fuckin' tone, brother," I growled, my fingers flexing around my empty rock glass.

I needed to work out this sick fuckin' feeling. A bag at the gym, a warm pussy in my bed and a couple hours of physical therapy with both ought to do it.

"You want someone to bow and scrape to the almighty Zeus Garro, go to one of the fuckin' prospects or get some pussy 'cause I've been tellin' it to you straight for twenty-five years and I'm gonna keep right on doin' it 'til you drive us both into an early grave."

He stared at me dead in the fuckin' eye, serious as shit.

I threw my head back and laughed because he was the only man still walkin' on this earth that would throw back at me like that.

"Fine, you fuck. It's about the girl too," I conceded.

Just then, the girl in question came striding back into the bar, walking amidst the now empty tables picking up used glassware and empty bottles. My throat ran dry at the sight of those curvy long legs in those tiny little black shorts, the thick wedge of deep brown skin between the low rise of the hem and the edge of her thin, white crop top. Couldn't tell if she was wearing a bra but it was clear she'd gone outside to recuperate from her shock 'cause her hard little nipples were clear from across the room where I sat watching her.

I licked my lips at the thought of those sweet tips between my teeth.

She'd like it rough, I thought. My Lou was a spitfire and I knew she'd give as good as she got in the sack.

Fuck.

What the fuck was wrong with me?

I'd practically raised this girl from the time she was seven years old. I could tell myself 'til I was blue in the face that I hadn't actually *seen* her grow, that she'd been a little girl one moment and a grown woman—a damn fine woman—the next, but it was still seriously fucked up.

It was even more seriously fucked because I didn't care. I wanted her. I wanted her worse than I'd ever wanted anythin' in my life, even my first Harley that I'd saved for startin' when I was eight years old and first saw a bike in one of my uncle's car magazines. I didn't care that she was a little girl. If I was being honest, it was hot as fuck that she was so young, so fresh, like a blank wall in front of a graffiti artist, I wanted to stripe her in paint, draw her up in anarchy.

I wanted to be the one to fuck her that first time, her blood on my cock and her cries in my mouth as I claimed her.

The only problem as I saw it was this.

I'd keep her.

Knew myself well enough to know the truth. I was a monster, sure as shit. Violence was second-nature to me. Greed was an instinct I didn't care to curb. Lawlessness was my code and brotherhood was my anthem.

I didn't believe in rules 'cept the ones I decided to make for others.

And for the last twenty years of my life, my religion had been two-fold. The Fallen and my kids.

At one point, I'd lumped Lou into "my kids".

I was realizin' I needed to un-lump her quick or I'd be a seriously sick bastard.

But where did that leave her?

I tugged at my beard as I watched her hips sway between the tables, as she laughed at a guy who tossed her an empty bottle, as I thought about how good it would feel to throttle that guy with my bare hands and feel his life leave 'im under my fingers.

"You're so fucked," Bat said, shakin' his head. "The only thing keepin' you away from her was knowin' us brothers had an eye on her, now it's not enough. You've seen her, watched her too long. You're a predator if ever I fuckin' saw one, Z, you ain't the kinda man to sit back and deny himself his kill."

I was about to agree with him. To say "fuck it", storm up to Lou, haul 'er over my shoulder and take her to the nearest wall so I could pin her like a pretty little butterfly and have my ruthless way with her.

"Fuck, Zeus," Blackjack called gruffly, swinging through the doors with Nova, Lab-Rat and Priest at his back. "Fuck man, the warehouse on Jackson is on fucking fire."

The warehouse on Jackson. One of the thirteen warehouses we used to stockpile our shipments of prime grade marijuana.

"Fuck," I cursed at the same time as Bat.

But I wasn't just cursin' about the potential loss of near thirty Gs of weed.

I was cursin' because Blackjack had just reminded me of the biggest reason to stay away from Lou.

She'd been through enough in her short life already. She didn't need a man-slaughtering, drug-pushing outlaw dragging her into the depths of depravity. She was better off in the shallow end, playing at wicked and lookin' like a treat doin' it.

I'd stay away, mostly. There was no way I was leavin' her to her own devices, not when she was operating on the fringes of my world, but I'd guard her like I'd always done.

No contact.

Strictly as a watchman.

No emotion.

Only calculation.

No sex.

Not one fuckin' kiss.

No even thinkin' about it.

Even as I swore it to myself, I caught sight of her bendin' over a stool to pick up something from the floor and noted the perfect ripe peach shape of that ass, thought about my cock wedged between each cheek, weeping against her skin as I came all over it and marked her as mine.

And I knew I was fucked.

CHAPTER THIRTEEN

Loulou

HE WAS IGNORING ME.

The Fallen MC had officially owned The Lotus for three weeks and the brothers were around constantly. They'd been stripping out the old, stained upholstery, the cracked linoleum floors and lopsided stage to replace it with all new, all wicked cool stuff. The booths were now black velvet with glossy blood-red tables, the bar was made up of faceted sections of mirrored glass so that it sparkled under the lights and reflected distorted visions of the girls dancing on the new massive and greatly improved main stage as well as the three smaller stages amid the floor seats. We had top-shelf liquor behind the bar, three new dancers that were so sexy even I drooled over them, and a manager named Maja who was tough as nails but also wicked cool.

This was all good—great, really—because I wanted The Lotus to succeed and when we'd reopened after two weeks of renovations, there was already a ton of business. It was the good kind—horny men with cash in their wallets and loneliness in their eyes, and bachelor and bachelorette parties from the right side of the tracks as well as the wrong.

And Maja, she liked me.

I'd been nervous even though I'd tried to hide it behind my usual sassy contempt when she'd approached a few of the serving staff while I'd been behind the bar. She'd taken a good hard look at me with hard, wise eyes for so long, I'd started to sweat.

Then she'd said, "Cute earrings, where'd you get 'em? I've been lookin' for feathers like that for an absolute age and no luck. You tell me your secret and I'll give you a Friday night bar shift."

So, I'd told her where I got the earrings and we'd gone together on Friday afternoon before my shift to get her a pair. She was cool but maternal. It was a weird combination but it worked for me because my mother was neither.

Loulou's life was kicking ass but for one thing.

Zeus was finally everywhere and he was nowhere.

He was in the club nearly every night, holding court in the same booth as the first night he'd appeared like some kind of underworld god doing dealings with mortals. Bikers, businessmen in smart suits with slicked hair, and random civilians came to speak with him and it was clear in every interaction that Zeus was the one in control.

He sat in the deep shadows, the red and blue neon lights

cutting his brutally constructed face into even harsher lines. His sheer size seemed magnified by the darkness, by his riotous brown-and-gold hair and the thick lines of black ink turning his dark skin into fallen angel wings. There was casualness to his posture as he sat straight-backed and spread out, yet his huge hands were always nonchalantly on display like a man who placed a gun on the table to make a point. They were his weapons, huge God-given weapons of sheer violence and force that anyone who looked at them knew it.

He was breathtaking in every sense. Terrifying beyond comprehension and so gorgeous, it was a physical blow to the senses.

People watched him nearly as much as they watched the dancers.

I know I did.

I fell helplessly into his orbit, a small, insignificant planet sucked up into his gravitational pull. Through the night, I watched him and not once, not *one* time, did I catch him watching me.

At first, I was so hurt it felt like a second cancer, this one a sticky, fibrous mass melding my lungs shut so my breath came through thin and wheezy. I circled through The Lotus three nights a week without the usual joy and freedom I'd felt each time I walked through those doors before.

I felt spurned worse than a lover because Zeus had never been that. He'd been in some sense *more* than that. He'd been my guardian monster, the saviour who had first taken a bullet for me and then saved me from living through my first round of cancer alone.

He'd been, quite simply, my everything.

And now, it seemed, I was nothing to him.

Now, it was a Saturday night, the busiest night at the club we'd had since Debra sold it off and moved to fucking Jamaica.

When word got out that The Fallen were spending time at The Lotus, the seats filled to the brim each night from open to close. Most of them were criminals just like before but a higher caliber, the kind that made their lackeys take the fall and kept themselves from jail by greasing endless hands.

It was great for making tips, especially for a girl like me who didn't mind tossing an effective hair flick or bat of my eyelashes in the right direction to earn just another couple dollars added to the total of each bill.

These new criminals weren't as grabby and offensively disgusting as the old clientele but they were something worse. *Entitled.* A few girls had learned this the hard way but acquiesced easily, both because it was their job to but also because they were paid well for their time and attentions.

I wasn't a dancer so I had no obligation to sit on anyone's lap. Some of the wait staff were more generous with their bodies, but I was seventeen years old at the end of the day and I had a boyfriend.

So no laps for me.

Of course, these entitled men didn't know that and, more, they didn't care. Even though at least a small group of The Fallen had been there every night since we'd reopened, it was obvious that a few of them had been assigned to look after the girls and they were put to good use at least once or twice a night.

"Two-hundred dollar tip and all I had to do was let the

guy kiss my feet," Ruby told me as she swung up to my spot at the bar in her glittery red sequined bra and hot pants. "I told him to come back and see me regular. I mean, that was the easiest money I ever made."

I laughed with her even though one eye was still on Zeus. He was sitting with a guy who had been in once before to see him, a man I recognized because he'd been a regular here back when it was seriously sketchy. Quentin Kade was a drug dealer from Whistler who sold drugs to the ski bums, Australian snowbirds and wealthy vacationers there. The dancers liked him for the tips but they tried to avoid going to one of the semiprivate curtained booths with him because he liked to get rough and often left bruises along with his generous tips.

What was Zeus doing with a man like him?

"You are so not listening to me," Ruby accused me.

"I'm so not," I agreed easily, sliding an iced water across to her. "What do you know about The Fallen?"

"Loulou…" she cautioned. "I told you, don't get involved in that shit. In fact, I specifically remember telling you to get outta here before they realized who you were and did you take my advice?"

"No, so what makes you think I'm going to take it now?" I asked with a wry grin.

She snorted, lifting her heavy fluorescent red hair from her pale neck so she could fan the sweat off her chest. "Fine but I get to say I told you so when you get fucked over by one of them, deal?"

My heart clenched but I agreed.

"The Fallen are the shadow puppeteers of the entire North American west coast. About ten years ago they had some problems in their ranks that started a shoot out in a fucking church of all places." She snorted into her water, too preoccupied to notice my flinch. "They've had some problems with bad drugs lately. Not sure if it's the MC or not cooking them up, but the high and mighty mayor hates them something fierce and he tried to get the town to turn against them last year at a town meeting. Now *that* was funny."

I remembered it. Not the meeting because Bea and I hadn't been allowed to attend, but I remembered the fury my father felt at the drug-related crime, at the fact that the same motorcycle club involved in the First Church Shooting were still ruling strong and true in *his* town. My dad had worked for years to gain his office and he was absolutely not going to let "thugs" out-influence him.

"Yeah, yeah, I know that stuff. Tell me about the men," I told my friend.

Her eyes shadowed and she leaned forward in the universal girl friend gesture that signaled "real talk." "Who's got you asking?"

I shrugged one shoulder and plucked a glass from the drying rack to polish. "I'm curious."

"Curiosity killed the cat, Loulou."

"Yeah, well, this cat has cancer, so she's not really concerned at playing it safe," I retorted. "Are you going to tell me anything or what?"

Ruby's slick red mouth pursed with hurt and I realized I was taking out my irritation on her.

"I'm sorry, babe. Bad day." I reached over to take one of her thin hands in my own. Needle marks scarred the backs just as they'd scarred mine.

"I didn't mean to sound like my mother." She laughed. "I

get more than anyone that you gotta do what you gotta do with the time we are given on this earth. You feel you have to do something, even if I think it's a bad idea, I'm gonna support you and more, I'm gonna urge you to go for it."

I hated talking about the cancer while I was Loulou but a tidal wave of sorrow and fear swallowed me whole as I looked into my friend's empathetic eyes. She didn't know much about my life outside the club, other than the fact that I had cancer, but she knew what it was like to wonder how long you'd live, to wonder if you were strong enough to survive.

She knew what it was like to be dying.

I blinked past the hot well of tears. "Don't make me ruin my makeup," I whispered hoarsely.

She ran her thumb over mine and squeezed. "I'll just say this, okay? You can love an outlaw and he can even love you back, but that doesn't make him any less an outlaw. You get me?"

"I got you," I told her, jumping up over the counter slightly to press a kiss to her cheek. "Now, get back there and get dressed for your next number or Maja will be at you."

Ruby shuddered in mock horror as she slid off her stool and strut away, drawing a dozen eyes to her ass as she did.

I laughed softly at the familiar spectacle before turning my eyes back to Zeus. Quentin was still talking as one of the bikers led him away, his face twisted with impatient passion, but Zeus seemed unmoved, one arm dangling over the booth clutching a nearly empty glass of Canadian whiskey.

I knew he drank Forty Creek Double Reserve because Felicity, one of the bartenders, had bragged to me about it the other day. How he only ever asked for her to bring him his drink. How he made sure to tip her big and how, the other day, he'd told her she had a damn fine smile.

A damn fine fucking smile.

Hearing it made me want to take a knife to her smile and turn her into a female version of the Joker. How would Zeus find her smile then?

I shook my head free of the jealousy and decided to take action. I'd given him three weeks of faux distance, but I wasn't going down without a fight. Not now, not when Ruby had just reminded me that I might not have much time left.

And what time I did have left, I wanted to spend with him.

In fact, if I was being honest with myself, I would have traded the next fifty years for one good one spent with him.

I reached on my tiptoes for the top-shelf liquor and poured him a glass, neat.

"That for Garro?" Felicity asked me, sliding up to the bar with an empty tray. "His brother Nova is joining him with a Johnny Walker Blue. I was just coming to refresh them."

"I got it covered," I told her, quickly pouring out a measure of the whiskey and then sliding both drinks onto my tray.

My red-headed co-worker laughed at me condescend-ingly. "Honey, trust me, you wouldn't know how to handle a man like that."

I smiled at her with all my teeth as I walked around the bar and slid past her. "Let's just see, shall we?"

He clocked me before he looked over at me. I could tell by the way his great big body tensed subtly, a rolling of immense muscles that brought to mind a predator about to strike. My belly quivered at the thought.

"Gentlemen," I said in a practiced purr.

I say practiced because I had. I was a good student and a competitive dancer. There was no way I was going to rebel and not do it properly, so I'd watched about fifty classic outlaw movies, read a ton of books, and watched Scarlett Johansson's interviews on YouTube until I had the throaty roll of my vocal cords down pat.

Even as focused as I was on Zeus, I couldn't help but stare at his Fallen brother. He was without any doubt the prettiest man I had ever seen in my life. As I slid his drink across the lacquered table, I took note of the wicked way his pink lips curled up at the corners, of the roguish hank of wavy hair that fell across his forehead. When my gaze reached his, I blinked, half-blinded by the beauty of his thick-lashed brown eyes.

"A refill for you, handsome," I said breathily. Not because I meant to but because I was still recovering.

He beamed at me and it truly didn't seem possible that a man so pretty could exist in real life. "Thanks, gorgeous."

I recovered my wits when I felt the change in atmosphere emanating from the man to my right. The feel of his fury against my skin excited me.

I kept hold of Zeus's glass because despite his obvious displeasure, he still wasn't looking at me.

"Canadian whiskey," I murmured, dangling his refill from my fingers, swirling it around under my nose. "Something my grandpa might drink."

I was watching carefully so I saw the heat waves of irritation roll off him.

Nova laughed. "The girl's got a point."

I laughed with him, leaning one hand on the table so

that my cleavage was closer to them both, but it was Nova who took an appreciative look.

The air solidified so suddenly, I felt paralyzed in the concrete mass of it.

Zeus looked up at me slowly, the shadows sliding from his face in a loving caress. His eyes glinted like the edge of a well-honed blade, silver and filled with deadly intent as he spoke in a sinuous rumble that was deceptively soft. "Take a sip of it, little girl. Let's see how well you swallow the fire down that delicate throat, how you like the burn of it in your belly. I think I might like the sight'a ya with tears in your eyes as you try to take what I give you."

My belly heated for a different reason as I felt those eyes like a hand at my throat, squeezing just right.

I squeezed my thighs together and noticed the way his eyes darted down to watch me before he could help himself. His clenched jaw and fisted hands gave me the confidence to laugh lightly and tip the glass at him before bringing it to my lips.

Watching him, I traced my tongue over the rim of the rock glass. His slashing brows drew down over his eyes, shadowing them but not enough to conceal the gleaming hunger there.

Confidence warmed my insides. I parted my lips, opened my throat and let the burning liquid race down my gullet. It was probably one of the most seductive moments of my life, a powerful man caught up in my snare...

And I utterly ruined it by planting a hand on my belly as I bent over to cough furiously as the liquor tore a strip off my throat and seared my gut. Through my hacking, I heard Nova's bright laughter and Zeus's lazy, dark chuckle.

When I recovered, my eyes were filled with tears and my skin was redder than spilled blood. I was more mortified than I'd ever been in my life and floundering with how to handle it with any sort of class when Zeus's soft words penetrated my haze.

"Teary-eyed n' pink-cheeked with the effort to take it all for me. Appreciate the effort, kid."

I blinked at him because he'd managed to both soothe my ragged pride and gently tell me off at the same time.

"I'll get you another," I rasped.

His eyes were heavy on me as he nodded. "You do that."

I turned on my heel before I could embarrass myself further, both angry and thrilled with the incident. Zeus had flirted with me. Sure, he'd been a prick about it. But the intent was there, the hunger in his eyes had little to do with missing dinner and everything to do with eating me for dessert.

I was distracted as I made the rounds of my section so I didn't react quickly enough when Quentin Kade pulled me into his lap.

"Saw you flirtin' with Garro. How come I never see you waitin' on me with that pretty smile, huh? I promise I'd treat you sweeter than him."

"Hands off the merchandise, Mr. Kade," I told him with a winsome smile because I was used to grabby hands and arrogant criminals.

Quentin wasn't an unattractive man, slim all over in a way that looked like he'd been compressed between two walls as he grew, he was still mildly handsome if you looked at him in profile. He wore expensive, designer clothes and he smelled rich, musky and artificial. It was obvious that he believed his wealth and reputation would get him whatever he wanted, even human flesh.

His narrow face creased up in laughter. "'Course, there's always a price for sweet merch like you. Tell me and I'll pay it, see if we can't put this ass to some use, eh? Just 'cause you can't get Garro doesn't mean you have to go without."

He and his posse of men laughed like he was a stand-up comedian.

My smile grew strained. "No price. It's like the Mastercard commercial says, some things are priceless."

"HA! Got a sweet behind, girl, wouldn't say it's priceless," he snorted.

"No," I agreed because it was a fantastic ass but I wasn't *that* arrogant. "But my self-worth is, and while I don't judge anyone for doing it, I don't sell myself for sex."

The good humor fell through the false bottom of his charm and his mouth grew hard. "You think you're too good for me, or something?"

Fuck. I hated the ones who made it about their own inadequacies. Couldn't a girl just reject a man based on her lack of desire to be wooed or taken?

"I don't." I smiled again. "Like I said, I just don't go in for that kind of thing. Now, if you'll excuse me, I've got rounds to make."

"Yeah, showing off that ass to see who's gonna be the highest bidder," he sneered, shoving his face into my neck so he could lick a slimy trail up to my ear where he whispered, "Trust me, it's gonna be me who takes you home tonight."

I planted my hand on his shoulder and shoved, all politeness forgotten in my haste to get away from him but his hands had curled into my hips like heavy anchors so I couldn't move.

"Kade."

The one word echoed through the room like thunder.

It was a warning that the lightning wouldn't be far behind.

Zeus, the God of Thunder, was finally paying attention.

"Back off, Garro. Get yourself another girl for the night," Quentin laughingly called over his shoulder.

But his bluff wasn't good enough. I could see the fear spark behind his eyes and the thin crown of sweat that bloomed high on his forehead.

"Let the kid go, Kade," Zeus said again, his voice a low rumbling force that had Quentin's hands flexing anxiously on my skin.

I took advantage of his fright to scramble off his lap and put a huge partition of space between us. It took me a minute to realize that I'd subconsciously come to a stand still beside Zeus.

"A woman tells you to let her go, do it," Zeus growled, taking a step ahead and to the front of me, shielding me from Quentin's sight.

I didn't know or care if he was conscious of the protective gesture, it sent hope fluttering to life in my heart.

"This is a fuckin' titty bar, Garro. Can you blame a man for trying? Or is that particular girl you got an issue with me taking?"

"Yeah, I fuckin' well can because this titty bar is property of The Fallen and if you don't know this by now, Kade, listen close, yeah? You fuck with the The Fallen, you court death. Simple as that."

Even though I was slightly behind him, I could see the cruel cut of his smile across his face, as if the idea of Quentin defying him, of courting that death, turned him on.

A dark shiver rasped like a calloused finger down my spine.

"Now, if a girl wants your attention, go for it. I hear you try to corner another one of my girls, you're banned for life. And, Kade, I don't just mean from this bar."

I chewed on my lip because I got it. Quentin Kade was one of the biggest drug dealers in the province. The Fallen was one of the biggest producers and distributors of weed in the *country*. If Kade got cut off, he'd be crippled.

"Yeah, got you," he said, face twisted with wounded pride and bitter anger. "Just like I got that you don't give a fuck about getting my business anymore."

"Just spent way too much of my fuckin' time tryin' to get that through your head so gotta say, glad you've finally got the message."

Something feral and nasty slithered across Quentin's narrow face, something that looked a lot like *evil*.

Zeus crossed his enormous arms over his chest and tipped his chin up. "I'd say it's time for you and your boys to move on for the night."

"Yeah, I'm fuckin' beat," Quentin agreed with a grin that was more of a grimace.

As soon as they left, I took a step toward Zeus, eager to thank him, wanting to touch him.

He took a huge step away from me before I could gain any ground and spun to face me. "I'm lettin' you stay on because at least here I can keep an eye on your crazy ass, you get me? This is what you get when you flirt with dangerous men, little girl. You're too fuckin' young to know what you're dealin' with here and honest to Christ, I wish you'd go back to your pretty, ordered little world and stay the fuck outta mine."

"Zeus," I breathed with what little air was left in my compressed lungs.

"Got two kids already, Louise, you think I got time for a third?" he asked with a cruel raise of one scarred eyebrow.

I opened my mouth to say something but there was no air left in me, only hot blood that coursed through my veins like flames. It was impossible to believe that my saviour could so suddenly have turned into a demon.

"Believe it," he whispered darkly, and I wasn't sure if I'd spoken aloud or if he'd read the disillusion fragmenting the dreams at the backs of my eyes.

I watched in mute horror as he turned and walked away from me.

CHAPTER FOURTEEN

Loulou

BY THE END OF SIXTH PERIOD THE NEXT DAY, MY HURT HAD calcified into something else, harder and offensive. I was spitting mad and righteous with it. If Zeus Garro thought he could just flick me away like a fucking bug, he was sorely mistaken. I wasn't a little girl anymore and I'd made it my mandate since my diagnosis that absolutely *no* one could tell me what to do.

Not even my guardian monster.

Especially when he was being a fucking *prick*.

"You got fire in your eyes," Reece noticed, leaning away from his position at my side so that he could push my hair behind my ear and peer at me. "What's up?"

I chewed at my lower lip as shame swirled in my belly.

Reece and I had never talked about whether or not we were "dating". It wasn't so simple as that these days when there was a spectrum of togetherness that ranged from one-night stands, hook-ups, friends with benefits and "seeing each other" to the more serious stuff. I figured Reece and I were the latter of those options but seeing as how we had never rubber stamped it, I tried not to feel too guilty that I'd spent the past few weeks consumed with thoughts of another man.

"Just thinking about how excited I am for the Winter Hoops tournament next week," I told him with a huge fake smile.

He frowned slightly because he had a good bullshit meter but talk of basketball always distracted him enough for me to get away with it. "Yeah, scouts are coming from U of T, Western and UBC."

"That's so great," I said genuinely.

Reece was an amazing player and honest-to-God, the kind of boy I knew I should want. He was handsome and smart, moneyed and going somewhere bright but with that bit of an edge that made him interesting. He liked to party on Saturday nights and golf hung-over but functioning on Sundays with his father.

He was the kind of cool a normal teenage girl could hanker after safely.

Too bad I was the kind of teenage girl who dreamed of men who could murder with their bare hands, who swore like it was essential to the English language and believed in brotherhood more than the law.

Eh, everyone had their crosses to bear and I figured that was mine.

"Louise," he called again, squeezing my bare thigh under the hem of my kilt.

"Distracted, sorry," I murmured.

Instantly, his handsome face softened with empathy. "How're you feeling?"

I bit my lip so hard it drew blood because his question shouldn't have annoyed me but it did. I didn't need or want the constant reminders, which was why I kept Loulou cancer-free. People didn't want me to be honest about my response. Did they want to hear that it was hard to get out of bed in the morning because my body felt *wrong*, broken then mended in a way that meant I looked fine but couldn't breathe right or pirouette in dance class anymore because my world didn't stop spinning when I did?

The symptoms weren't that bad at the moment. The one round of chemo I'd had during the summer had slowed the progress of the cancer but not stopped it, not reversed it. I was due for another, more intense, round in December and I knew it would be worse then. The shortness of breath, the itchy skin and constant weariness would be magnified by endless nausea and bone-deep aches.

So, for now, I was okay physically. I was fighting, feeling optimistic about it because that was the only way you could feel if you had a hope in hell of surviving.

But I was living on an island. It was the second kick in the gut of cancer, the way it isolated you from your loved ones, made you feel like no one could understand you and that no one *wanted* to, really, because you'd turned into some kind of hope-devouring monster, infected with nightmares and frighteningly contagious.

There was no one who could understand that.

No one, I'd thought, except for my own guardian monster.

The bell signaling the end of sixth period rang out, shattering my depressing reverie. Reece immediately threw his arm around my shoulders and ducked close to me, his eyes on mine as he whispered, "I'm here, Louise. You may not see that and damn, you might not even want it, sometimes I can't tell. But if you do want me, I'm here."

I nodded mutely, guilty and stricken by how on target he was. He searched my eyes for a long moment more before he nodded then moved away to join the crowd of students funneling out the door.

"Louise," Mr. Warren called out to me as I swung my messenger bag over my shoulder and made to follow after Reece. "Stay a minute."

I nodded then waited for the last few students to leave so I could close the door behind them. Mr. Warren didn't like to speak with the door open.

"What can I help you with, Mr. Warren?" I asked in my practiced, saccharine voice.

My biology teacher wasn't my favourite teacher; that spot had been taken by Miss Irons, my former IB English and History teacher who had since quit amid a flurry of gossip about her banging a student. I didn't believe the rumors and anyone who knew Miss Irons wouldn't have either. She was the soul of discretion, a mild-mannered woman with a smile that made you feel like an angel was grinning down on you. She was the only person I'd told last year when I'd first been diagnosed and I missed our infrequent tea dates in her bookish classroom.

So, no, Mr. Warren wasn't my favourite teacher.

But I was his favourite student.

He was beaming his beautiful smile at me as he came around his desk to lean against the front and hook his thumbs in the pockets of his bright blue dress pants. He was a pretty guy, the kind of immaculately groomed man that offended my sensibility because wasn't a man supposed to be, well, manly?

"How's my favourite student doing?" he asked.

I perched my butt on the end of a desk in the first row across from him and shrugged. "Good, excited for Winter Hoops."

I wasn't excited.

Being a cheerleader was something the women in the Lafayette family had been since Entrance Bay Academy was *founded* so I didn't really have a choice in the matter.

School colours and pom-poms were so *not* my gig.

"Of course, the highlight of the fall semester." He nodded. "Well, I won't keep you long. I just wanted to ask if you'd be interested in being my teacher's assistant this year. I know it's a few weeks into term, but I like to take my time with these decisions and make sure I find the right pupil for the job."

I blinked into his car salesman smile but the well-trained part of my brain was already saying, "Of course. Thank you for considering me."

I didn't have time to be his teacher's assistant. I was training in the dance studio four times a week while my body could still stand to do such rigorous activity, I spent at least a few hours each week with my Autism mentee, Sammy, and I was in the full International Baccalaureate program at school, which was the equivalent of taking university-level courses.

And that was just as Louise.

As Loulou, I had an equally packed schedule and now the Zeus problem to figure out and spend additional hours each week stewing over.

But Mr. Warren was my dad's best friend.

And what Benjamin Lafayette wanted, he got.

So I didn't bother to refuse him because it was obvious that the two of them had already talked about it, decided on it and this was just a formality.

"Great." He grinned and stepped forward to grasp me in a quick hug. "I'm so glad to have such a capable young woman on my team. I'll need you every Wednesday after school for two hours. You can work in here with me."

"Cool."

His smile softened slightly and made me realize that he stood a little too close after giving me that awkward hug. I flinched slightly when his hand came up to tuck a piece of hair behind my ear.

"Glad to see you aren't losing your hair," he murmured.

"Me too," I said, somewhat harshly because I didn't like having him in my space.

"Looking forward to spending time with you, Louise. It was nice to see you so much this past summer," he said, referencing the countless times I'd been forced to attend church functions, charity picnics and political events with my parents. "You've grown into a very beautiful and intelligent young woman."

A timid knock on the door had him stepping away from me before I could react—negatively—to his over familiarity.

"Sorry, I can come back," Lily Foster, a girl from the grade below me with pretty yellow hair, said from the door.

"No, Lily, you know I always have time for you." Mr. Warren smiled that same smile at her, warm and fake as artificial light. "Louise was just leaving."

Hot and cold flashes erupted across my skin as I shouldered my bag once more and brushed past an eager looking Lily on my way out the door and I couldn't tell if it was a common side effect of the lymphoma or because Mr. Warren had seriously creeped me out.

CHAPTER FIFTEEN

Loulou

I WASN'T PAYING ATTENTION.

Later, I wouldn't blame myself because I was still reeling from the complete loss of my childhood idol, the broken heart I nursed at realizing my first love was nothing but a dream.

Still, I was taking the trash out to a poorly lit back alley behind a titty bar. It was straight up dumb-blonde of me not to take note of my surroundings.

I paid for it when something heavy slammed me into the brick wall. The trash bag fell to the ground beside me as I tried to bring my hands up to push away but someone strong captured them in one hand and brought them around to the small of my back.

"Stupid bitch," Quentin Kade hissed into my ear. "Think you're too fuckin' good for me to fuck, huh?"

I tried to buck him off but there was no torque.

"Fuck yeah," I bit out, enraged by my helplessness, so angry with myself for being oblivious in a dark fucking alley.

He chuckled in my ear. "Don't worry, bitch, I'm not going to stick my dick into a bitter cunt. I have a better idea. We're going to play a little game, okay? Zeus fuckin' Garro thinks he can intimidate me? He's not the only game in town anymore and it's about time he knew it."

He spun me around, kicked my legs apart and pressed something cold and hard to my left temple.

A gun.

Fear spilled over my head like an ice bucket and for a moment, I was afraid I was going to pee myself.

Instead, I worked the minimal saliva left in my mouth into a pool and spat it at him. "You think I'm the right thing to send a message to the Prez of The Fallen? I'm just some girl that works in his titty bar."

Quentin's grin glinted dimly in the grimy light cast from the red stripper sign over the side door. "You know, you're probably fuckin' right? But I don't really give a shit. He'll know it's a message when I kill one of his filthy new dancers and if I don't kill you, I want you to give it to him for me. Tell him that the Nightstalkers are back and they aren't fucking around this time."

I watched as he stepped back, the gun in front of my face now, leveled just between my eyes so that they crossed as I stared down the small barrel. He kept chuckling as one of his lackeys handed him a shot glass.

"Hope you like vodka," he said as he placed the shot on top of my head. "Now stand real still or this game will be over a lot quicker than either of us want it to be."

I frantically thought about who might come out into the alley to see us, who might save me. There was no one left inside but Michael, a sweet middle-aged man with Autism that I'd convinced Debra to hire a few months ago.

Everyone else was gone and I didn't think Michael would recognize the sound of a gunshot and come running.

I closed my eyes. Maybe dying from a bullet in the head would be a better way to go—quick and done—than from the cancer, slow and creeping.

Silver lining, right?

I opened my eyes again and glared at him as he took position two yards away from me in the narrow alley. I decided if I was going to die, I was going to do it with sass.

"Betcha twenty bucks, you miss," I goaded him, like a reckless fool.

He laughed as he brought the gun up in his right hand, used the left to steady it, squinted one eye and... *POP*!

The bullet exploded up and over my head to the left, shards of metal and brick raining down on my face. A tiny sliver caught my left cheek but I didn't flinch because I didn't know what he'd do if I spilled the shot myself.

He laughed uproariously and it was clear he was higher than a fucking kite.

I was going to die at the hands of a coked-up drug dealer just because I wouldn't grind on his lap. Sometimes, I seriously questioned my morals. As in, were they necessary?

"Told ya," I sneered at him.

"Bitch," he chuckled, waving the gun erratically back and forth. "You talk like that when *I* got the gun? You're whacked."

I managed a small shrug without dropping the shot, keeping an eye on his loose gun hand. If I could disarm him enough, I figured that I could make a run for it and duck back into the bar before he could get a clean shot off.

"I'm just saying," I continued, as if I was having a casual conversation instead of a deadly one. Panic was a knife's point at my throat but I forced myself to take a deep breath and forge on. Zeus had once told me that being high made you feel like a king, invincible in an ironic way because being high made you anything but. "I don't think you can hit it clean off. Ask your buddies, I bet they agree with me."

Bringing his friends into it was the right move.

He turned to them with exaggerated horror, flapping the gun around as he demanded that they vouch for him.

It was my moment and I took it without conscious thought.

I pushed off the wall, leapt over the mounds of garbage and sprinted the four steps to the huge metal door, yanking it open just as a shot *pop*ped against the brick beside me. I slammed the door shut, my heart thudding in my throat, then bolted it shut with a finality that made me want to cry.

Seconds later, I heard them cursing as they tried to get in.

I didn't wait around even though I knew the door would hold. We still had a front entrance and I couldn't afford to be stuck there all night. It was already two in the morning and I had school the next day.

I turned and ran through the darkened halls. They were so familiar that it was easy to grab my rucksack from the back room and dash back into the main bar toward the front.

When two huge hands grabbed at me, I screamed and swung around to thwack my bag against the intruder.

"Stop." A tall, broad shadow of a man ordered as his strong hands held me still by the shoulders.

"Get off me," I ordered, struggling under the hold.

He didn't budge.

"Brother of The Fallen," he explained in a low voice that seemed rough with disuse.

Immediately, I settled, peering harder through the dark to see the glint of the small white patch on the front of his leather cut that claimed he was a member of the MC.

"Thank God," I said in bone-deep relief, sagging against him.

He stiffened in intense discomfort, so I sprung away from him instantly. I wasn't normally an overtly affectionate person, but I'd been weak with relief that I wasn't alone with a group of four stoned, misogynistic assholes just outside.

"Sorry," I muttered. "There's a group of guys outside that literally just tried to shoot a shot glass off my head."

The Fallen brother blinked huge brown eyes at me then turned away, squatted slightly and jerked his chin at me from over his shoulder. "Up."

I stared at him a little slack jawed because if I didn't know better, it seemed like he wanted to give me a piggyback ride.

"Up," he repeated.

A guy that clearly didn't like to be touched was going to give me a piggyback ride out of the bar?

"Um, I don't think that's necessary," I tried.

He sighed impatiently then lifted his hands to show me the small black gun in one palm and the glint of a sharp blade in the other. "Up."

I swallowed my fear and climbed onto his back. He stiffened as soon as I touched him, so deeply *not* okay with my body against his that I immediately wanted to get off him.

"Hold on," he ordered.

I barely had time to blink before he was running, *running*, through the bar as if I was light as a shadow. I could feel the immense power in his body as he thrust us through the front door at an incredible speed and immediately fired off two shots to the left of us where my abusers would be emerging from the side alley if they were indeed following me.

There were shouts and another shot rang out somewhere behind us.

Yep, they were following us.

What the absolute *fuck*!?

I clung to the stranger beneath me and ducked my head into his neck as he ducked behind a van and halted in front of a motorcycle. Without any degree of gentleness and all haste, he *threw* me off his back and onto the tiny backseat of the bike before he swung a leg over it and gunned the engine.

"Hold. On," he gritted between his teeth as he peeled out into the streets, the bike at such a horizontal angle to the pavement that my hair brushed across it before we righted and shot forward into the night.

The shouts faded behind us when we took the first

corner. A few minutes later, the eloquent biker pulled over to the side of the road to make a call.

"Got 'er on my bike," he said into the phone.

I tried to listen to the other end of the conversation but couldn't hear anything because I'd released him from my tight hold as soon as we pulled over. I was used to an aversion to touch because a lot of kids I worked with at the Autism Centre were touch sensitive. I didn't want to cause my hero any further discomfort than absolutely necessary.

"Yeah. Yeah. Back at Lotus. Yeah. Yeah," he responded. "I'll bring 'er."

Bring her?

Bring her where?

He hung up the phone and immediately started the bike again so I didn't have time to question as he swung back onto the street into the dark. I'd lived in Entrance my whole life so I knew immediately where he was taking us when he veered away from the ritzy coastal neighborhoods and into the east side of town.

We were going to The Fallen Compound.

I'd only seen it from outside the huge chain-link fence encircling the industrial lot. I'd been sixteen, just after Zeus had ended our correspondence and I wanted to catch a glimpse of him. I'd waited for three hours across the street in a small strip complex before one of the brothers, a nondescript until you looked at him kind of man with white skin and copper hair, had noticed me. He'd approached me and told me gently to get lost.

I'd obeyed.

And I'd never gone back because I was still living scared and obedient back then.

Now, I watched with my heart in my throat as the metal gates to Hephaestus Auto and Mechanics groaned open and we swung up a slight incline on to the lot.

Zeus's inner sanctuary.

He was waiting for us at the door to a long, low brick building slightly behind the main garage complex and as soon as my silent companion killed the engine, Zeus was coming at us.

Before I could speak, he plucked me from the back of the bike and plastered me to his side with a heavy arm belted around my hips. Then he promptly ignored me.

"Mute, brother, you did good tonight," he told the silent man who'd helped me.

Under the huge industrial lights of the complex, I could make him out better and was surprised to find he couldn't have been much older than me. Mute, appropriately named, was over six feet tall but stocky, so wide with muscle with a face so craggy under his severely buzzed hair that he looked almost like a cartoon drawing of a thug. Then I noticed the way his fingers thrummed against his left thigh in a staccato rhythm, the way his face was blank and absent as he nodded at his Prez.

He was busy with a ritual.

I frowned as I recognized the trait from Sammy, my best bud at the Autism centre who had similar rituals, having to stomp his feet five times whenever he put on his shoes, eat his dessert first thing in the morning before he'd ever have anything savory... I frowned at my hero and wondered if a biker could be autistic.

"Sent Bat, Priest and Axe-Man," Zeus was growling, his fury a cloak I pulled tight around myself because I found it, strangely, comforting. "They'll pick 'em up and bring 'em back. Get me when it's done."

Mute nodded then turned to walk into the clubhouse but stopped just as abruptly and walked over to me in the circle of Zeus's arm. He stared hard into my face with an inscrutable expression before he reached out to tug a little too hard on a lock of my pale hair.

"Stay safe," he ordered with a solemnity I felt in my chest.

I nodded slowly, a gesture he echoed before he turned to go into the brick building.

"Got shit to do so let's get this over with, yeah?" Zeus finally said, though not to my face because he was already walking us inside.

"I need to go home or like, call the police," I said, so discombobulated by the turn of events that I didn't know which way was up or down.

As always in those moments of panic and pain, all I knew was Zeus. So, even though I knew I had to return to Louise's life in less than six hours, I leaned into Zeus as he propelled me forward and enjoyed his proximity. I took the opportunity to learn his scent, something I'd wondered at for years.

Dark forest; pine and cedar, fresh air bitten with the slight tang of tobacco. I dragged the heady mixture into my lungs, closed my eyes and committed it to memory.

"No police," Zeus growled as he propelled me through the dark interior and then lifted me up as if I weighed nothing to plunk me on a tall stool beside a bar. "Wait here."

He didn't wait for me to respond but stalked off down the hall.

I took the time to take a deep breath and instead of

focusing on the craziness of having a gun in my face (somehow *not* for the first time in my life but the second), I studied The Fallen MC clubhouse.

It was a fairly enormous open room wrapped in dark wood paneling but coloured by the plethora of neon bar signs on the walls that signaled things like "Live Free, Die Hard But Only If You Can't Kill 'Em First." There was also a collection of prison photos lighted by an overhead lamp leading down the hallway Zeus had disappeared into. I noticed his immediately, dead center, his scowl fierce, tongue out, rock on symbol constructed by his fingers just beside the plaque he carried so that at first, the emblem of rebellion wasn't noticeable.

There were two pool tables covered in black felt at the far end of the rectangular room, a jukebox between them that even now was playing hard rock (Zeppelin), and a couple of high tables with stools. A huge antique Harley was mounted on one wall, a massive TV on the other fronted by a couple long, low black leather couches. The recreational space and the bar area that I sat in was partially divided by a black chain-link wall that made the entire place wicked cool and would have been my favourite feature but for the fact that the massive square bar I sat at was absolutely covered in graffiti, the biggest of which was a huge image of The Fallen logo, a skull with fiery, tattered wings, and their motto: Live Free, Die Hard.

"Wow," I breathed.

"Fuckin' somethin' else, isn't it?" A tall, skinny guy covered in tattoos appeared beside me, sliding onto a stool with a wide smile.

He wasn't a bad-looking guy despite being vaguely terrifying but there was something about his smile that rubbed me the wrong way, like he expected my panties to melt off at the sight of it.

I crossed my legs, suddenly extremely conscious of the tiny length of my work shorts.

"Yeah, it's a cool place. Cleaner than I thought for a group of bikers," I admitted.

He laughed. "Got bitches who keep the place clean."

I tried not to wince at the terminology or the thought of one of those women with Zeus. "Figures, only women would know how to keep a place this clean."

Another chuckle. "Should see it after one of our shindigs. Fuckin' *mess*."

I wrinkled my nose at the thought, which made him grin even wider at me.

"You're a real treat, you know that?" he asked me, leaning forward to put his forearms on his thighs, which brought him much closer to me, his face on level with my breasts in my deep-cut crop top.

I leaned back slightly but winked at him to soften the rebuke. "I've been told."

"Get a taste, figure it'll be just as sweet," he continued, eyes sparkling.

It was my turn to laugh, covering my mouth with my hand as I did it loudly. "You're kidding me with this, right?"

His grin was unrepentant when he straightened with a shrug. "Can't blame a man for tryin' now, can ya?"

"She might not, but I fuckin' well can. Back off, Skell. Lou's too smart to fall in for your cheesy fuckin' lines," Zeus grumbled as he prowled back into the room, a skinny ginger kid barely older than myself and a man with an eye patch following behind him.

The guy named Skell held his hands up in surrender. "Girl looks like a fuckin' Barbie doll, Prez. Gotta say, I'd put up with a beatin' if it meant I could have just one minute with my face up her skirt."

I didn't know whether to be strangely flattered or seriously offended but Zeus took matters into his own hands by hooking a foot in Skell's stool and tugging so that the biker went tumbling to the ground.

The other men burst into laughter and even Skell chuckled good-naturedly as he rubbed the back of his head and rolled to his feet.

"If you weren't six foot fuckin' five an' harder 'an a concrete wall, I'd fight ya for that."

Even I laughed when Skell jumped around on his toes, his hands up in faux fighting posture.

"Breathe on ya right and you'd fall over, brother," Zeus said, his lips tilted to the left in a small grin. With his arms crossed over his wide chest, one booted foot over the other and lean hips against the side of the bar, he was the picture of badass biker guy.

I had no doubt he could blow on someone just right and bowl them over.

I also didn't doubt that he could blow on me and I'd go down, but probably for different reasons.

"Right, brothers, this here is Loulou," Zeus introduced with a chin nod. "She'll be around seein' as she won't leave me the fuck alone."

I beamed angelically up into his scowling face as he continued, "Lou, got Cyclops, Skeleton and Curtains, other wise known as Cyc, Skell and Curtains."

"Why Curtains?" I asked warily, because the other two biker nicknames made sense but I couldn't picture the skinny, stoned-looking ginger biker sewing curtains.

His pale skin went as red as his hair when the others burst out laughing but he continued to pass out the cold beers he'd grabbed from the bar fridge.

Zeus clapped him on the back, rocking his slight frame with the movement. "Think you'd be used to answerin' that by now, Prospect."

"It's, uh, cause the curtains match the drapes," the poor kid told me.

I blinked at him before I dissolved into laughter. "That is too funny!"

When I stopped laughing long enough to see him frowning at me, I laughed even harder. "You should feel grateful no one thought to call you 'Fire Crotch.' At least Curtains is kind of subtle."

"Fire Crotch," Skell snorted beer through is nose and all over the bar. Immediately, Curtains grabbed a rag to wipe it up. "Damn, we missed out, boys."

"Do I get a nickname?" I asked, leaning forward to bat my eyelashes at Skell who stopped laughing and blinked dumbly at me.

"Uh, you want one, I can think of a few things to call you, sugar," he finally responded on a wide grin.

"Don't you fuckers have better things to be doin' like, oh, I don't know, findin' those scumbags that scared Lou so fuckin' bad?" Zeus asked, deceptively calm.

Immediately, the men snapped to attention like soldiers,

only Curtains tossing me a wave as they moved in formation out the doors of the clubhouse.

I turned back to Zeus, watched him as he collected an unopened bottle of Knob Creek Canadian whiskey and pried the cork out with his teeth. It was astonishingly sexy, watching him manhandle the bottle like that. I wanted his teeth on my body, his big hands plumping my flesh before those strong white teeth bit into it.

He caught sight of my expression and scowled at my flush.

"I'm gonna make you a deal, Lou," Zeus started, his voice and face stern like a parent lecturing a child. I didn't care because he hadn't called me Lou once since I'd seen him again and the sound of those syllables in his mouth were better than a song.

"Okay," I agreed, apparently too eager, because his face darkened with disapproval.

I squirmed in my chair because he was impossibly sexy in stern Dad mode. I resolved to be naughty more often.

"There are rules. You know I didn't want this life for ya, but you seem hell-bent on it so I figure the only way to get you through is to show you myself."

"Show me what?" I breathed.

"Show you how to live on the wild side. You wanna drink, party and rebel? I'm the safe place to learn that shit."

"Definitely," I agreed again, this time carefully trying to hide my enthusiasm.

It didn't work.

His scowl deepened. "Before you get too fuckin' excited, there'll be rules."

I echoed his frown. "I thought bikers don't follow rules?"

"So young and naïve, little girl." He leaned forward, his messy tumble of hair framing his rugged face. "See, without rules, a person is aimless. You gotta believe in somethin', adhere to some kinda code or your soul can wander down some dark fuckin' paths. We got rules; brotherhood, bikes and bitches you treat like fuckin' queens because they give you the kinda sweet a rough man can't find anywhere else. And you know who enforces those rules, Lou? Me."

"You aren't the boss of me," I told him because I couldn't help myself. Something dark and eager inside my soul called out to him, wanted to test his edges like a sharp blade point against my thumb. I wanted to see how far I could push him, if it was farther than anyone else ever had and what he would do when I finally went too far.

Something told me, it would be just as dirty and dark as I'd always imagined.

"I'm the boss of this world. All those monsters you picture under your bed, in the dark corners of hospitals and night black forests? They're fuckin' real, Lou. And I own 'em. So, yeah, you want this world, you better believe I'm the fuckin' boss of ya."

"Fine," I pouted just to watch his hot eyes fall like a kiss on my lips. "What are your rules, then?"

"No touchin'," he responded immediately as he dragged his eyes away from my mouth. "As in, you don't get to touch me."

"What?" I cried, thrusting my arms in the air so that he had to duck away from my flying hand. "That's so unfair."

"Tough shit, kid. I don't need you touchin' me, cuddlin' or some shit when you get scared and, trust me, little girl, you'll get scared livin' this life. Can't coddle you every time somethin' goes sideways."

I crossed my arms under my breasts and glowered at him. "I'm not seven years old anymore, Zeus. And don't tell me you haven't noticed, because *you have*."

His beautiful mouth twisted into a sneer as he landed a heavy palm on the table and leaned close. "Yeah, I fuckin' noticed 'cause I'm a man with goddamn eyes and any man —monk, eunuch or married—is gonna get off on the sight'a those tits, that ass, and a waist that spans one fuckin' hand and not think about touchin' ya. Difference is, I don't wanna touch you. I don't even wanna fuckin' think about it."

"Because you're tempted?" I whispered, my hope like a dove struggling to take flight in my chest.

"Nah, 'cause I'm a man. The kinda man that needs a woman to satisfy him. Little girls, however stacked, don't do it for me and, Lou? They never will so kill that hope in your eyes. I quit talkin' to ya before because of these little girls dreams and I'll do it again, you don't obey my rules."

Ouch.

I tried not to let the colossal amount of hurt radiating through my chest crack through my eyes and let the tears spill through but it was a monumental effort that left me strangely breathless.

"Got it," I murmured.

The heartbreak of his words was that he spoke the truth. The man sitting across from me was all man, from the top of his wild mass of gold dipped brown waves to the tips of his heavy motorcycle boots and the ends of his deeply calloused fingers. He smoked, drank, marauded and fucked like he was on Death Row, like every single moment counted more than the next.

Who was I to claim a man like that?

I closed my eyes as I took a deep breath to settle the ruckus of insecurity that surged through my mind.

I was Louise Lafayette and that obedient, sad excuse for a woman didn't deserve a man like Zeus Garro.

But, I thought with sudden verve, Loulou Fox could give him a run for his money.

So, I opened my eyes and knew they burned on his skin as I said, "Fine, no touching. But you never said you couldn't touch me, and I'm telling you now, Z, I'm going to do everything in my power to make these tits, this ass and this tiny waist as tempting to you as possible."

He stared at me for a long minute, inscrutable and arbitrating like the God of Olympus on his throne casting judgment on a mortal. And then, to my utter surprise and delight, he threw back his great mane of hair exposing his corded brown throat in the process, and laughed.

The sound was just as rich and warm as I remembered from my childhood and I let it wash over me as I stared at his throat and thought I'd never known how sexy an Adam's apple could be.

"Finished?" I asked snottily when he finally wiped the tears from his eyes with the back of a hand.

"Don't figure I'll ever finish bein' surprised havin' you back in my life," he said through his grin. "Can't believe little Loulou just threw down with me."

"You bet your ass, I did," I said with a defiant chin tilt. "I'm not a kid anymore, Zeus Garro. And with or without you, this is who I am and I'm in this world to stay."

"Then it'll fuckin' well be with me," he growled, his smile so quickly replaced with a scowl that I lost balance and leaned toward him. "Hear this, little girl, you got what you wanted, yer guardian monster is back but this time, he's teachin' ya how to keep the monsters at bay yourself so when the time comes that you no longer need me, you'll be good."

I rolled my lips under my teeth and held out my hand to secure his promise with a shake. His eyes sparked with humor as his huge, rough hand engulfed my own and then his lips stretched into an arrogant grin when the warm contact made me shiver but I didn't say anything.

I was too busy thinking, *Game on, Zeus.*

CHAPTER SIXTEEN

Zeus

TO SAY MY LIFE WAS A FUCKING MESS WOULD HAVE BEEN AN understatement of epic fucking proportions.

I was elbow deep in blood, debt and drugs, none of them my own and all of them fucking poison. Just 'cause they weren't mine personally didn't mean they weren't my problem.

The Fallen MC had a problem, it meant I had a problem. And right now, we had a big fuckin' problem.

The Nightstalkers were back.

Cut off the head of the beast and three more grow back, right?

'Cause it seemed that no matter, I'd sliced up the bastard

in charge less than a year ago, the fuckin' MC was back and still lookin' to take over *my* operation.

I'd bled, sweat and fuckin' killed for The Fallen, for the success of each of my brothers and there was no way in heaven or hell I'd hand over shit to those fuckers.

There were a coupla problems with that though.

I stood starin' at one; the ashen remains of one of the biggest warehouses we had just outside Vancouver tucked away on a supply route off Highway 99. It wasn't a grow-op, thank Christ, but we had nearly three million dollars worth'a grade A weed in that fuckin' warehouse.

Now, it was grade A trash.

And that wasn't even the worst of it.

'Cause I stood there holdin' a eight by ten glossy photograph of my daughter, Harleigh Rose, that'd been staked to the ground just outta range of the fire. I hadn't noticed it when we'd put out the fire the night 'fore last and we'd had to let the scene cool before we came back to assess the damage but I'd seen it right quick when we'd pulled up that morning.

In it, she was laughin' as only a beautiful, confident teenage girl could do, lips pulled back over teeth, chin tipped back and hair streamin' behind her. It was a fuckin' great photo, one my son's woman had taken durin' the summer. I had a copy of it on my desk at the garage, framed in kickass chrome and gifted to me by Cress for Christmas.

I treasured that fuckin' thing.

And now I was holdin' a copy with H.R.'s eyes punched out by bullet holes, her neck slashed open by a jagged knife.

A warnin'.

A warnin' that those fuckin' scumbags were back and

they were gonna play dirty, play for wives, children and families.

A warnin'.

It had been ten years since we'd had to deal with shit like this. Ten years that my brothers had lived an outlaw life of recklessness, boozin', smokin', ridin' out into the night like midnight raiders but without the real violence a life like that could bring. I'd made sure of it when I'd killed Crux, ex-Prez of The Fallen MC, a decade ago. The same night he'd shot a bullet through Lou and me.

"Prez," Lab-Rat called to me, scuttling like his namesake through the mess of burnt wood. "They took it 'fore they lit it."

I blinked slowly at him, careful not to crunch the photo of H.R. in my clenching fist. "Say again."

"They took the supply 'fore they lit the buildin'. There's no weed left here," Lab-Rat explained.

Fuck me.

"You're fuckin' with me," I growled.

"He's not," Curtains said, appearing with his laptop open balanced on one arm, clickin' through things on his screen like a maniac. "Got surveillance from Evergreen Gas Station. A sixteen-wheeler with blacked out plates stopped for fuckin' gas yesterday at five pm."

I reached out to drag the prospect closer by the hood of his sweater so I could see the screen. "Show me."

"The fuckers," I muttered as I watched the truck pull up for fuckin' gas like it was nothin' and two tall, familiar motherfuckers crawled outta the cab.

One went into the store.

Lysander fuckin' Garrison pumped the gas and did it starin' right into the fuckin' security camera.

I roared, the fury hot and fuckin' alive in my chest as it burned out over my tongue. I spun away from my brothers and stomped into the debris, picked up a charred plank and snapped it over my knee.

"Fuck," I shouted again. Another plank crumbled between my hands. Pretended it was Lysander Garrison's fuckin' neck givin' way to my grip. Or that fuckface defector Ace Munford's skinny spine snappin' like a fuckin' twig over my knee.

"You 'bout done?" Bat called over, standing at the top of the incline with his hands in the pockets of his army fatigues as if it was a normal fuckin' Thursday.

I rolled my shoulders back, cracked my neck and grinned menacingly at the prospect just to see 'im flinch 'cause I was in that kinda mood.

"Yeah, I'm fuckin' done. Get the brothers to fuckin' Chapel and call in some of the Nomads if they're around. I'm not havin' another war on my fuckin' hands without reinforcements."

Bat nodded as I climbed up to him, his eyes cold and calculating, battle mode. "They're gonna go after families."

"No shit," I said, swiping down to pick up the mutilated picture of my girl.

"You gonna call King?"

"Fuck." I ran a hand over my tangled mess of hair and across my beard. "Gotta. He'll fuckin' hate it, but they gotta be careful even down at the university. The fucks won't stop at nothin' to get what we have."

"They didn't learn their lessons last time," Bat noted.

"No shit," I growled. "But last time we were on the fuckin' defensive. This time, we'll take this war to them."

"You ready for that, brother? Got a lotta other things on your mind lately," the fuck chose to remind me.

I glared at him but he did have a point.

I was a thirty-six-year-old man with two kids, both born before I'd been old enough to grow a full fucking beard. One of them was off at college livin' a mostly clean life that I fuckin' loved for him and his woman. Missed him like hell-fire in my chest but knew it was good for him.

Got another kid, Harleigh Rose, grew up like an angel and only now had discovered how to be a serious pain in my ass. She was too gorgeous for her own good and she'd discovered it young, given how she'd grown up around a group of men that were all men and made sure she knew that 'cause she was such a beaut, they'd beat on any man that mistreated her. My girl found she liked the attention, both from my protective brothers and from other darker men. She was dating a two-bit drug dealer called *Cricket* of all fuckin' things and she was "in love with him." Keepin' track of her was a bitch and now with this new threat, there was no way I wouldn't shackle her to her fuckin' bedroom so I'd know she'd be safe. She'd fuckin' hate it, cause a drama because she was too much her mother's kid sometimes. Not that I gave a fuck, so long as she was safe.

Then there was Lou.

What the fuck was I gonna do about Lou?

I was a man who kept his fuckin' word and I'd promised to teach her about the outlaw life.

It wasn't the place for a girl like her, with a soul too wise for such a young thing, with eyes the colour of pure, unblemished skies and hair like pale gold. She may have had the body of a sinner but she had the looks of an angel and the heart to match.

Too good for the likes of me and this life.

But she was in it now, I told myself because I wanted to believe it, she was in it and if there was trouble brewin', she'd be at my side for all of it.

No one could keep her safe like me.

"Garro."

Just what I fuckin' needed.

Cops.

I turned around, crossed my arms over my chest and tipped my chin at the young officer Danner and his partner, Riley Gibson, as they stepped outta their squad car.

To say "fuck the police" was The Fallen's mandate would have been an understatement. Cy actually had the words tattooed on his back over The Fallen symbol.

I hated the fuckin' pigs.

"Long time no see, Garro," Danner said, strollin' toward me as if he didn't have a care in the world.

"Not long enough," I told him as I felt my brothers take my back. "What can I do you for, pretty boy?"

I grinned at his frown. The kid was always tryin' to prove himself. He was somethin' like sixth generation British Columbian cop and his daddy was staff sergeant. He'd been tryin' to use the MC for years to make his mark but fuck if I was gonna let 'im.

"Seems the question is, what can I do for you?" he asked, recovering quick enough to indicate the wreckage. "Wasn't aware you had property up here but seems like you've had something of an accident."

I snorted. "Yeah? What makes ya think that?"

His partner, more impulsive than Danner, stepped forward. "Stop screwing around, Garro. We've got forensics coming up behind us. Before they get here, why don't you tell us what the story is?"

"Can't say for sure, boys." I shrugged and rubbed at my bearded chin like I was confounded by the situation. "Just bought an empty building up here, thinkin' about demolishin' it and making myself a pretty ranch like home on the land. Not surprised it went up in flames, givin' how old it was and how dry the weather's been."

The cops stared out at the scrubby, remote wilderness and looked back at me skeptically.

I fought the urge to laugh and won. Instead, I shrugged. "Like bein' alone."

"Cut the bullshit, Garro. It's obvious there was foul play at work here," Gibson snapped.

I pressed a palm to my heart. "Now, why the fuck would anyone want to do somethin' like that to little ole' me?"

Gibson looked ready to beat me but Danner just smiled slightly and shook his head. More cop cars pulled up and my favourite cop of all time emerged into the sunlight.

"Hutchinson," Danner greeted the other man with a grimace as he approached.

The other cop, *a Fallen* cop, grinned at him and clapped him on the back. He was an older man with serious seniority in Entrance police ranks and he'd been livin' in my back pocket for a good nine years. Older, yeah, but the old codger sure as fuck loved the weed we gave him to soothe his arthritis.

"I'll take it from here boys. Let's let the experienced men

get to the bottom of this, hmm?" Hutchinson told the rookies, already roundin' em to shake hands with me and Bat. "Spot a trouble here, Garro?"

"Not much. The old thing crapped out on us. I'll file an insurance claim and all that shit but I gotta be gettin' home to my kid. You cool to catch up with me later if you find anythin' in your investigation?"

Hutchinson nodded like the good ole boy he was. "Sure thing, Garro."

I grinned at Danner and Gibson as I passed them on the way to my bike but I noticed the way Danner's eyes caught on the photo of H.R. peekin' outta my back jeans pocket, the flash of apprehension in those sharp eyes, and I knew he wouldn't drop it for shit.

CHAPTER SEVENTEEN

Zeus

SHE WAS BENDIN' LOW, HER TIGHT JEANS STRAININ' AGAINST her round ass, and every man in the fuckin' room was lookin' over at that pretty sight, droolin' like a fool.

I knew 'cause dammit if I wasn't one of 'em.

A kid with hair the colour of a fire engine sat between her spread legs, laughing up at her as she swung her long gold hair back and forth over them like a curtain. He grabbed a fistful of it and yanked so hard it musta hurt but her laugh only rang out louder, musical in a way I'd never heard music played before. She dropped to her ass, legs splayed around him like a bracket as she brought him into the fold of her body and smothered his face in kisses.

Felt my chest tighten like a bottle top closed too tight, the pressure buildin' behind my ribs until I thought I might have a fuckin' stroke.

Never seen anythin' more beautiful than that teenage girl playin' with a little kid like he was her own.

Before I could control it, the heathen inside me reared to the surface and thought about it. About claimin' her for my own and plantin' my seed inside that sweet body, watchin' it grow even rounder 'cause a me. Thought about a sweet kid who looked just like my little warrior who I would call my own fuckin' kin.

I clenched my fists against the impulse to throw her over my shoulder and spear her on my cock right there against the wall in front of everyone, so they would know she was mine. The only thing that held me back was knowin' that even if no one else was aware of it, Loulou Lafayette was mine and she had been since she was seven years old whether it was fucked or not.

"Angel," Mute grunted from beside and behind me, his eyes riveted to her like she was Mary Magdalene descended from heaven.

"Fuck me if you're wrong," I muttered.

Even though I'd spoke quiet, Lou perked up suddenly, her spine slammin' straight and her head spinnin' with unerring accuracy in my direction. I waited with pleasure as she took her time lookin' me over, from the worn boots at my feet to the ball cap I wore backward over my unruly hair. Watched her lick that lush mouth and loved that she was too young to hide how much she wanted me.

"Zeus," she breathed before clearing her throat and

unconsciously dragging her kid closer to her chest like a shield. "What're you doing here?"

As soon as we'd finished at Chapel, I'd set out to find her. Mute told me she spent every Thursday afternoon at the Autism Centre on the outskirts of downtown Entrance. He knew because he'd been tailin' her for me since she'd cropped back up in my life at that fuckin' party all those months ago. At first, it'd been a rotation of brothers who shouldered the duty but it was Mute who took a shinin' to her and so it was him who I sent after her most often. He was a strange kid, my son's best friend and like my own son after all these years. His bastard dad had ousted him from the house when he was just a kid because of his "fucked up" tendencies and he'd lived at the clubhouse or my place ever since. There wasn't a soul I would trust more with Lou than him so he was with me, so I could introduce 'im properly as her new bodyguard.

"Time to live and learn, little girl," I told her with a wide grin, enjoying the looks of the receptionist and a few of the caretakers as they milled about the large space.

"Really?" she asked, excited like the girl she was.

My dick twitched at that enthusiasm, how it might be better applied to other things.

"Yeah," I said roughly. "If you're done here?"

Snappin' back to reality, she looked down at her fire-haired charge and ducked down to rub noses with him.

"What time is it, Sammy?" she asked him softly.

"You can't leave for nine minutes," he declared in a loud voice.

"Hmm," she stroked his springy hair back and peered up

at me through her long fuckin' lashes. "Do you want to meet my friend, Zeus? He likes to build things just like you."

The kid, Sammy, stared up at her in awe then turned to me with his little mouth open in a perfect O. Fuck, I'd forgotten how cute kids could be.

"You like to build things?" he demanded.

I moved closer, noting the complex building blocks carefully ordered all around them and crouched low just in front of 'em. "Yeah, kid. I build bikes and cars."

"No," he breathed, his eyes so wide thought they'd fall straight outta his head.

I beamed at him. "Better believe it. My brother Mute does too." I looked over my shoulder at Mute who lingered awkwardly by the door still. "Come 'ere, brother."

He stalked forward, his mouth set in a firm line and I knew it was because Lou was spendin' time with another kid. It was one of his things, he either liked ya or he didn't and if he did, he wasn't a big fan of sharin'.

Loulou seemed to notice 'cause she patted the ground to the other side of her and said, "Nice to see you again, Hero. I half expected you to be wearing a cape after your heroics of the other day."

Then, for the first time since King had gone off to university and left his best friend behind, I saw Mute's lips twitch then turn into a full-blown grin.

He reached out to tug on her hair as he lowered himself to the carpet. "Sammy, Mute."

Sammy stared at 'im for a minute before saying, "Loulou's my best friend so if you wanna play with us that's okay but she signed a contract and everything so it's kinda up to me to share her. If you can build something really, really cool, I'll let you play with us some-times too."

The two kids, more alike than I woulda thought, stared at each other for a long minute before Mute nodded and reached for the Lego blocks.

I waited a tick as they both started to play before I reached out to knock Lou gently on the edge of her chin with my knuckles. "How ya doin', kid?"

Her face was soft from watching her charge and her hero playing together and it socked a wicked punch to my gut that took my goddamn breath away when she smiled at me and tried to lean her face into my retreatin' hand. I hesitated then spread my rough fingers against the silk of her cheek for a sec before pulling away.

"Good now," she told me.

Fuck me, had I ever stood a chance against her?

"Wanna take you to Smoke's Range," I told her, tryin' to focus on the reason I was there in the first place.

Tryin' to remember my own damn rule.

No touchin'.

Fuck but that was provin' harder than expected to follow.

"BBQ?" she asked, her brows twisted up in an adorable frown.

Christ, a grown man thinkin' a frown was 'adorable.' What was I becomin'?

"No." I grinned. "Gun range."

"You're going to teach me to shoot a gun!?" she cried out too loudly.

Sammy immediately ducked into himself and covered his ears with a whimper. Lou cringed and took a moment to stroke his back and head, leanin' close to pepper kisses

173

against the back of his neck until he poked outta his shell, forgetting his discomfort in favour of Lou's kisses.

Couldn't blame the little guy.

"Sorry, one of Sammy's aversions is to loud noises," she explained then giggled softly. "Unless he's making them himself. I've always, always wanted to learn to shoot a gun. Dammit, I'm not wearing the right clothes for it though!"

I took in her jeans and turtleneck. Normally that much clothin' on a woman did nothin' for me but I'd never seen a woman fill out a shirt the way Lou did. 'Sides, the thought of pullin' out the knife I kept in my left boot and cuttin' it off her was a fantasy now firmly rooted in my brain.

"Look fine," I grunted.

She giggled again. "Okay, well in that case, hell yeah, I want to go to Smoke's Range with you."

I bit back my smile and nodded. "Good, now give me some a those blocks so I can show these two why I'm the boss, yeah?"

Her answering smile grabbed holda my heart and squeezed.

"ZEUS, ZEUS!" Lou called even though I was right fuckin' there, one foot over her shoulder watchin' her as I had been for the past ninety minutes. "Did you see that?"

Smoke and I chuckled but I was the one to say, "You're a fuckin' natural, Lou."

She glanced over her shoulder, her pretty face obscured by ugly fuckin' protective eyewear and ear mufflers and she was still the prettiest thing I'd ever seen, gun pressed to her tricep, finger on the trigger and massive grin on her face.

"I am, aren't I?" she said.

Smoke laughed rough and wet the way only a man who'd smoked a pack a day his whole life could laugh. He was a hard man, an MC brother who couldn't ride much anymore but who taught all the brothers how to handle a weapon when they prospected The Fallen. He was like a dad to me, only better 'cause my dad had been an abusive alcoholic fucktard who'd cheated on my mum and took all her hard-earned money whenever he felt like it.

He liked Lou and, given the way he kept raising those wire brush eyebrows at me, he liked her for me.

I tried to ignore the old bastard, but problem was, I liked her for me too.

"Sniper rifles are way cooler than handguns," Lou was saying to him as she took off the mufflers. "I want one of these."

"Not near as practical, girlie. I'll get you set up with a Sig Sauer P238."

"Don't I need to apply for a gun permit or something?" she asked.

Smoke and I blinked at her.

She bit her lip and laughed self-consciously. "Yeah, no, never mind. Sorry."

"No need to 'poligize, Lou," I crouched down beside her. "You want a permit, we'll getcha one, yeah?"

"Yeah, okay," she breathed, starin' into my face as if it was the first and last sight she'd seen or ever wanted to see.

She made a man who'd felt like a monster his entire life, feel like a fuckin' angel.

"This is serious though, Lou, so I want you to drop the rifle and practice with the handgun again, yeah?"

She nodded immediately. "What's going on?"

I sighed as she pushed her eyewear into her hair, flipped the safety on the gun and got up to follow me over to the handgun section of the range.

"Shit's goin' down with another MC," I decided to tell her. "Not the kinda thing I talk about with outsiders, Lou, so don't get used to it but you gotta know that things might get rough for a while and I need you to be careful, yeah? Mute's got your back and you need to let him. Fuck, even introduce him to your parents if you need to so he can get access to your house."

She laughed. "My parents are barely home. If Mute needs to hang out with me and Bea while we do our homework, that's cool. They won't be around to question why there's a biker in their house."

"Hate that for you," I told her, not for the first time.

"I've got you back now and something tells me you've got family to spare," she said with a soft grin, moving her body into mine as I came to a stop before a target.

The feel of her soft breasts against my chest was excruciatin'.

"No touchin'," I barked.

She had the fuckin' gall to smile at me and turn on her Converse heel like the cheerleader she was to grab the pistol.

"Like this?" she asked over her shoulder, squaring her arms and leveling the weapon.

Her small pink tongue stuck between her teeth as she concentrated. It was the same pink I imagined her pussy would be when I spread it open with my fingers and dived in with my tongue.

I'd noticed a red lollipop stickin' outta her front jeans pocket and couldn't wait to watch her suck on it. Wished I could know if she'd taste like cherries all over.

"Zeus?"

I adjusted my half-chub in my pants and stepped closer to maneuver her shoulder, readjust her hips between my palms. The contrast between her little waist and my mitts was such a turn-on that I took an extra beat to stare down at myself touchin' her. She took the opportunity to arch her back, stickin' her ass up like a present wrapped in denim.

"Behave," I ordered.

"Yes, Daddy," she answered, humor rich in her voice.

I reached out to smack her ass, *hard*. She squealed, her free hand coming to rub over the hurt as she frowned at me.

"Um, ouch!"

"Don't fuckin' tempt me, Lou," I warned her. "Now, you hit the inner ring of the target twice and I'll let you ride on the back of my bike insteada Mute's, yeah?"

Those blue eyes lit up like I'd given her fuckin' diamonds. Without another word, she angled away from me, donned her protective gear, steadied herself and popped off six rounds.

When I dragged my eyes from the sexy as fuck sight of 'er, I noticed she'd hit three within the inner ring.

She shrugged at me as she ripped off her mufflers and goggles. "I've always been an overachiever."

I threw my head back and laughed, snaggin' an arm around her hips and draggin' her to my side as I'd wanted to do all day. She wasn't a short thing but anyone was little compared to me and she fit into my side just fuckin' right.

It was gettin' harder to believe this girl, this teenage daughter of my arch-nemesis and renowned good girl, wasn't fuckin' made for me.

I grinned down into her face and loved the way she blinked up at me as if I was the sun. "You earned yourself a ride on my bike."

She shivered against me, leanin' all her weight, all those soft curves into the wall of my body in a gesture of trust that eviscerated me. "I've been dreaming of it since I was seven years old."

I squeezed her hip, dipped my head 'cause I needed to be closer to the pure blue of those fantastic eyes. "Been on it before, little Lou."

"Don't remind me." She rolled her eyes then grinned wryly up at me. "I'm choosing to believe this is the first time. Although if I remember correctly, I liked the way you held me Koala style, front to front."

A low hum of approval worked itself up my throat before I could stop it 'cause the memory of holdin' her so close, her warm crotch up against my own as I pressed her chest to mine... it'd been a feature fantasy one too many nights of jerkin' off.

"Let's try it traditional this time," I said.

She rolled her eyes. "Such a boring old man."

I swallowed thickly as she trailed her hand down my arm and casually wrapped her little fingers through my own so she could tug me forward.

"Bye Smoke, thanks for letting me use the sniper rifle!" she called, waving madly at the man.

He lifted a hand and his chuckle followed me as I let Lou lead me over the grass to my waiting Harley. It was a FXR model I'd outfitted and customized myself over the years so that it suited me to a fuckin tee. She was a beaut and anytime I left 'er outside a truck stop on a run with the club, I'd find bike enthusiasts crowdin' around takin' pictures of the silver-and-black beast. Soon as they saw me, they were quick to back off but I didn't mind because a thing of beauty deserved to be 'precciated.

I shot a look at Lou and watched her eyes reverently caress the bike like it was a loved one.

Her hand was shaky as she placed it on the bitch seat and stroked the soft leather. "My knight in leather on his beast of metal," she whispered, looking over her shoulder at me. "That's what I thought when I first saw you. What kind of knight was that?"

"One part of a different kinda brotherhood."

"Yeah," she agreed. "Modern-day warriors."

"Don't romanticize it, little girl," I warned her. "You know what they say about those scary folk tales, there's a kernel a truth to 'em."

She slanted me a look that was wiser than her years and reminded me of the precocious girl she'd been, writin' to a man in prison and advisin' him like she'd been born to do it.

"Don't insult me. We met amid a hail of gunfire and the

first time we touched, a bullet connected us chest to chest. Don't pretend I don't know all that you are."

"You know shit about it," I insisted, leanin' forward to loom over her.

She blinked placidly up at me, unaffected the way most grown fuckin' men were by my sheer size. She placed a hand above my heart where the scar we shared marked my own chest. "I know enough and when you're ready to share more, I won't run away scared because you're the person I've always run to when I am."

"No touchin'," I rasped, hatin' that my heart beat harder against her palm like it wanted closer to 'er.

Surprisingly, she backed off with her hands in the air and a wicked smile on her full mouth. "Sorry, Daddy. I'll be a good girl."

I ran a hand down my face, scrubbing at the wariness behind my eyes as I listened to her laugh at my reaction.

Fuck me, I was too old for this shit.

And fuck me if it didn't make me feel young again and freer than I'd ever been before.

I swung my leg over the bike, tossed her the helmet, and braced myself as she carefully perched on the seat behind me.

"Gonna have to hold on, Lou," I reminded her sarcastically.

"Oh, I'm allowed to touch you, then?" she asked innocently.

I revved the engine and grinned at her resultin' squeal as her arms shot around my chest and wrapped tight, bringing her hot body against the back of my cut. Then, 'cause I knew it'd make her laugh and the sound'a that laugh was quick becomin' my Achilles heel, I gunned outta the parking lot, fishtailin' slightly so for a brief second, it felt like we were flying.

I was right, she laughed and she did it loud, pressed against my back and right into my ear.

CHAPTER EIGHTEEN

Loulou

I HAD A PLAN.

It had been a long week of spending time with Zeus again and it was, by far, the best week of my life. I'd spent an evening at Eugene's Bar with a bunch of the brothers and met more of them, including two guys I didn't like much, Blackjack and the creepy, silent copper haired man named Priest who I recognized as the man who'd told me to stop watching The Fallen Compound years ago. They both gave me the creeps because they always watched Zeus or me with inscrutable expressions on their faces, so it was impossible to tell what they were thinking.

I didn't linger on it though, because I loved everyone else and was beyond thrilled to see Lila again, she'd embraced me as if I was a long-lost sister. The bar was epic, the same style as the clubhouse and when I'd asked Z about it, he'd explained that the massive man who owned the bar was also an artist specializing in graffiti art and neon signage.

I'd done tequila shots with Lab-Rat, a huge blond Viking named Axe-Man and Bat, who was no-nonsense but had taken a shine to me. A brother named Boner had taught me how to play pool like a pro even though when I'd challenged Zeus to a match, he'd wiped the floor with me and done it laughing.

Mute was my constant shadow and one I found I loved. I liked his largeness, his quietness, and the way he lumbered in a manner that was somehow graceful. I never would have told him to his face, but he reminded me somewhat of Frankenstein's monster, a creature made for violence with a surprising kindness of spirit. It was fairly obvious to me that he was on the autistic spectrum though at the low end, and I was happy that he was forced to come with me three times a week to the Autism Centre. He and Sammy were quickly becoming best friends and Sammy had asked me just yesterday to help him draw up another best friendship contract for his new biker bff to sign.

I was spending less time as Louise. Dance classes were still a priority, but everything else I ducked out of as much as I could. Reece was patient with me, the cheerleading squad as well, and my teachers offered to give me extensions on my work even though I stayed up late to finish it each night. I was taking advantage of their pity while I could because December was drawing nearer with each cold day and with it would come more chemo and the end of my stamina.

So, I'd decided to take action while I could.

I waited until the club was empty in the wee hours of Saturday night.

It didn't take long.

As soon as the performers were done, everyone cleaned up quick and left to parties or bed, or the special kinda parties that take place in a bed. No one wanted to hang around an empty stripclub.

But I knew Zeus would be there, sitting in his black velvet booth finishing the end of a cigarette, maybe talking to one of his brothers.

That there would be other people to witness my scene didn't concern me.

I was too preoccupied with the thought of Zeus, of his burning eyes on me, scoring every inch of my skin in invisible ink that branded me as his.

The music kicked up because my girl Ruby promised to turn it on before she high tailed it out of there.

It was my moment to make a very serious point.

I wasn't a little girl anymore.

I was a woman, one with dark thoughts and deviant desires. There was no changing the tapestry of my psyche now. Whether it had been the violence of the shooting, the rigidity of Lafayette family rules or something intrinsic to my DNA, I craved the darkness.

Even more, I craved the god who ruled from it.

I knew he'd been hyper aware of me all week. His resolve was eroding and he needed only one final push. I couldn't touch him but I was serious about making him want to touch me.

The swell of AC/DC's "Sink the Pink" spilled through the huge room hot and slick as whiskey from a barrel. I waited for my cue, took a deep breath to calm my spastic heart and then strutted out onto the lacquered black stage in my wicked cool, clear plastic platform high heels.

I couldn't see the audience because of the pale blue, pink and white spotlights shining down on the stage, but I was grateful for it. I may have been a classically trained ballerina but I was a virgin about to do a strip-tease for the Lord of the Damned and I didn't need any distractions.

Besides, I could feel his eyes on me like dark tunnels channeling through the light.

I closed my eyes as I hit center stage, took a deep breath to find that cavern of peace music always unlocked in my psyche and then, I moved.

My body dropped to the stage as the beat did, knees bent but closed, before I swung upright with my spine arched so the long length of my hair swished against the top of my ass.

Again.

This time legs opened, hand dipped into the shadowed crevice cast by the harsh lights between each thigh. Just a tease, a flutter of my fingers disappearing before I shot up again. The beat controlled me, shoved me to the ground with my knees turned out farther, my little frilly skirt flipped up enough to show the frilly white thong barely covering my sex beneath it.

On the next drop, I thrust my knees apart with my hands, trailing my fingers up from the insides of my knees to the edge of those girly panties. I imagined Zeus's eyes mapping the path of my fingers, noting each valley and hill of my topography so that later he could explore it himself.

The pulse of the music was inside me now, at the center of my groin and the tips of my breasts. I stood again then spun away, my skirt rippling up to show a glimpse of my ass before I bent over with my legs straight and hands on the floor. The hem of my skirt tickled the bottom edge of my ass cheeks as I swayed my hips side to side and then sinuously took one leg off the ground and then the other. Standing on my hands for a moment, skirt flipped up, breasts precariously close to spilling out of my bra, I took a deep, steadying breath before bringing my legs down again on the other side. Right beside the pole.

I may not have been a stripper, but I'd been around long enough to pick up some tricks of the trade amid giggles and tequila shots with the girls after a slow night. So I knew how to plant my hands against the bottom of the pole, turn vertical to the ground and swing upside down again, this time off the ground, the pole and my body one long, unbroken line.

Sweat beaded on my brow as, achingly slowly, I let my legs fall apart into a horizontal split. With a quick, careful flick of my wrist, my skirt fluttered to the ground and I hung from the pole like a blasphemous Christmas ornament, rampant with corrupted symbolism, the virgin laying prostrate on an altar of sin in wicked offering.

With my heart pounding in my ears, I wrapped my legs around the pole tight enough to support my weight and flipped my torso up. It was an extremely uncomfortable position but I'd watched Ruby do it for months and knew how effective it could be when a woman thrust her chest forward and with an insignificant flick of her fingers, sent her bra parting down the middle.

I could feel the hot light and even hotter eyes of the men in my audience sear the tender skin of my breasts. The large, red sequined pasties I wore concealed my nipples but caught the light in a way that made my breasts look even more voluptuous, Pictionary definitions of sin.

My mind had stopped being the mind of a girl long ago, maybe when I woke up that morning in the hospital with a bullet hole in my bones and cancer in my blood. But my body had been a woman's body for a few years now too, generously rounded curves all finished in a creamy satin that shone like fresh-water pearls in the pink light.

Abruptly, the music stopped and an indecipherable shout heralded the return of the main lights. I slid from the pole on muscle memory, eyes blinking against the sudden change from harsh spotlight to warm overhead glow.

"Fuckin' out," Zeus roared like a thunderclap from where he sat in his booth.

He didn't have to repeat himself.

Mute held the side door open as Nova and Bat slid out of his booth, the former with a quick but uncharacteristically uneasy smile sent my way while Curtains, Boner and Priest appeared from the control room and hustled past the stage without casting even a flicker of a glance my way.

"Good fuckin' luck, girl," Boner muttered before he was out of earshot.

I crossed my arms over my mostly bare breasts and watched everyone depart.

"Get down here," Zeus ordered.

"Fuck you," I shot back, infuriated by his anger. "You can boss around your bikers but not me."

He prowled forward quick and lethal as a great black panther as he came for me. I was distracted enough that I didn't take the time to back away like I should have. When he hit the end of the stage and lashed out with one huge paw to snap me around the hip and tip me over the stage, free-falling onto his shoulder, I screamed.

He spanked me with one hand as the other kept me secured in the fireman's carry. "Quiet."

I slammed my fists against the iron wall of his back. "Let me down, you oaf!"

"Need to stay?" Mute asked in his stilted, rough voice.

"Yes!" I cried out at the same time Zeus growled, "No. Leave and lock the door behind you."

A violent shudder tore across my skin at that threat.

"Be outside just in case," Mute said after a few seconds, a slight warning in his voice.

It warmed me to know he was concerned about me just as it frightened me that he had reason to be concerned.

Zeus might have nodded but we were moving again toward his booth and when he deposited me roughly across the slick red surface, we were alone. I tried to get up but he was there, looming over me like the devil. His full mouth was twisted into a braided pink rope as he stared down at me, his silver eyes eclipsed by the deep shadow of his furrowed brows.

I jumped as his hand came slamming to the table beside my head. He leaned into it, his muscles bulging as he leaned down low, so low I could taste his whiskey-flavored breath in my panting mouth.

"Is this what you wanted, little girl? You wanted to see what would happen to a room fulla men when you took your clothes off? Wanted to see 'em pant and lust after ya?"

I whimpered because his big, hot body was nearly pressed to mine and the small sliver of space he kept between us was just as exciting as full-body contact. Without meaning to, I arched into that space, my nipples scraping along the thin fabric of his tee over the hard muscle beneath.

He planted a hand on my lower belly to still me, his rough fingers splaying slowly across the entire naked span of my hips.

"You know what I saw up there? Not your tits or your ass, not the way you worked that pole like you were born to dance. Nah, not me, little girl, because I ain't just some man to you. Saw the scar just here." His fingers abraded my skin as he arrowed his hand up, between my breasts so it could rest just above one tit, over my rioting heart, on top of my puckered gunshot scar.

"Saw all this hair," he said in that dark, delicious growl that vibrated through his hand and against my skin as he moved it up my neck to tug menacingly at my locks. "Remembered the way you worried 'bout losin' it all, how fuckin' thrilled you were to have it back. See you stayed true and haven't cut it since. Like the length, like the colour, but like the weight of it more 'cause I know what it means to ya."

I didn't understand what he was doing. His position was threatening, and he was clearly angry with me, but his hand on me was sexual, driving me wild as his fingers rhythmically released and tugged on my hair, as his thumb swiped up and down across my jugular.

And he was reminding me of our history as if it mattered to him, as if he ached with memories just as much as I did. Which couldn't be true, or he wouldn't have ignored me for the past three weeks.

"What are you doing?" I whispered, staring up at him with wide, unblinking eyes.

He dipped even closer so that his lips whispered across my own and his thick-lashed crazy-beautiful eyes were the only things I saw. "Seducin' ya properly."

"What?"

I gasped as his teeth nipped into my lower lip and rasped over it. "You heard me."

"I..." I swallowed. "You're fucking me."

His chuckle was hot against the bare skin of my neck as he tilted my head with the hand in my hair and bit sharply at the junction of my throat and shoulder. He smiled against my skin as I trembled.

"No, but I fuckin' well plan on it. You wanted me to touch you, Lou, you wanted to tempt the fuckin' beast? Well, here he is. Now, tell me has anyone been inside this young, fresh pussy, Lou?" he asked me in a way that suggested the answer had better well be *no*. "Anyone stretched you so much it burned but ya loved it anyway?"

I was panting loudly already but when one of his big, hot hands clamped over my panty-covered sex and he ground the heel of his palm against my clit, I struggled for breath.

"Answer me."

I felt his command down to my bones because he had helped form me. His words in ink on paper were my Bible, his attention my place of meditation and his hands on my skin? The same hands I'd dreamt of every day for a decade. That I'd prayed for with more fervency than any virtues I'd been told to worship at church. They were my ultimate blessing.

My mind rolled like a loose marble in my sexed-up head but I still found the nerve to say, "Why don't you find out for yourself?"

A snarl rolled up from his gut, through his barrel chest and into the air between us. I stared into his eyes as they stormed, whipped up like a sky at siege with itself.

"Remember you asked for this, little girl," Zeus ordered, his face savage with desire and all I could see as he leaned over me. "You begged me to touch your pretty young pussy and now I'm not going to stop until your cum is drippin' from my fingers like honey."

His strong fingers tightened around my neck as I strained against him. Pinned against the table top like a butterfly, splayed open by the width of his hips between my legs and held down by the hand at my throat and the other pressed deeply into the sensitive place above my pubic bone. I was utterly helpless, held captive by a man with warning labels sewn into the very lining of his soul.

And I wanted him so badly, I shook with it.

"I dare you to try," I taunted, poking the bear just to see what it would do.

A wicked grin cut across his face. "You say my name when you come."

I opened my mouth to refute his arrogance but the sharp sound of fabric rending and the slight pain around my hips distracted me.

He'd torn off my underwear.

My fingers curled around his rocky biceps instinctually, just in time for me to brace against the first touch of his blunt, thick fingertips to my shamefully wet sex.

He hummed his approval low in his throat. "So wet. You like the thought of me finger-fuckin' you on this table, in the middle a this club? Betcha wish there was someone to watch, to see how goddamn magnificent you'll be when you break apart at the seams."

I groaned as he slid his entire hand over my sex, up and down so that my wetness spread everywhere, all over his fingers, from one side of my groin to the other and all the way over my asshole. It should have been embarrassing to have him play with my arousal like that but I loved the sloppy sounds my pussy made under his touch, the way he trailed his index finger deeper to play over my entrance and his thumb lagged behind to brush hard at my clit.

He hadn't even penetrated me yet and I was shaking.

"Wanna feel this pussy leakin' all over my dick while you work it," he rasped in such a low rumble it was nearly indecipherable. "Wanna see your face as you struggle to take alla me in this tight cunt. Tell me, Lou, when I first break through, will you cry pretty tears for me?"

"Fuck," I cursed as one finger swirled at my entrance, deeper and deeper with each pass until he was at the thin barrier. Panting but unable to give in without one last barb, I said, "You don't like it when I cry."

"New rule. You're allowed to cry when I claim you as mine."

"Zeus." I squirmed under his firm hold as another finger joined the first and thrust shallowly in and out of my sloppy pussy. "Please, take me."

His chuckle wafted across my mouth as he bit into my bottom lip again. "No fuckin' way the first time I'm takin' my girl is on a table in the middle of this fuckin' club. 'Sides, you gotta earn my cock, little girl."

"And how do I do that?" I whined as his calloused thumb

rubbed tight, firm circles into my clit, working my orgasm to the surface like a cork from a bottle.

I was going to burst open, rational thought evaporated and blood carbonated with pleasure as my cum spilled forth against those sinfully thick fingers playing between my thighs.

"Show me how fuckin' gorgeous you are when you come all over my hand," he said.

And just like that, I broke apart. The orgasm crashed through me like a great wave, pulling everything that I was into its wake until I shattered and spilled between the junction of my thighs, against the great boulder of the hand against my sex.

I had orgasmed before, both with Reece and by myself at home in the dark hours of the night with only girlish thoughts of Zeus to lead me there.

This was so much better than that.

I lay spent and boneless against the table, twitching slightly in the aftermath, pussy pulsing against his hand as he shifted to cup his big palm over my sex.

I jerked when he gave it two quick, gentle pats and said, "Good girl."

Fuck me but that was hot.

Using the little energy I had left, I went into a crunch so I could watch him as he brought a wet thumb to his mouth and smeared my cum against his lower lip before sucking it into his mouth.

"Fuckin' delicious," he groaned.

"Please let me touch you now."

His heavy-lidded eyes studied me splayed out on the table for him for a long minute before he reached down and carted me into his arms. Immediately, I wrapped myself tight around him even though I could feel my sex drench his tee where I pressed against him. I shoved my face into his neck, breathing deeply of his forest-and-tobacco scent, and I struggled not to cry.

One hand supported my ass while the other dove into my hair, twined it around his fingers and held me close.

After everything, the vulnerability of dancing for him, the overpowering sensation of breaking open against him, it was this hug that sank my heart to him forever.

There was no going back now.

I'd made a deal with the devil, tasted his brand of sin in hell and as the fables always said, once you indulged in the food of the underworld, you were stuck in its depths forever.

"Stuck with me," I croaked, trying to be brave and strong and unmoved but completely unable to because how often does a girl live a dream come true?

He turned his lips into my hair and kissed me. "It's you who's stuck with me, little warrior. Not lettin' you go now. Not fuckin' ever."

"Good."

His chuckle vibrated through my body. "Not as easy as all that, jailbait."

I pulled back from him enough to say, "The age of consent in the province is sixteen years old unless you're an authority figure. You can't go to jail because of me. Not again."

His face softened into something so beautiful it made my breath catch and my heart stop beating. It reminded me that I hadn't told him about the cancer coming back, about how I had chemo coming up. It reminded me that I didn't *want* to because I was finally a woman to him, whole and sexy and filled with promise.

I wasn't going to be the destroyer of my dreams.

"Wasn't your fault, Lou, and even if it was, gotta say, I'd do it again. If I have to kill every single fuckin' man on this goddamn planet to be with you, Lou, you better believe that I fuckin' will and I'll do it with a fuckin' smile."

I wish I'd known back then that his words would be tested again and again over the next few months and that, in the end, death would stalk me anyway.

CHAPTER NINETEEN

Zeus

SHOULDA KNOWN IT WAS COMIN'.

She'd been too good, too Louise Lafayette in a smokin' hot bod wearin' Loulou Fox's tight, barely-there clothes. She'd been too content to straddle our sketchy line between devil and devotee. The girl was followin' my rules, even the no touchin', and doin' it with a smile.

Shoulda known and shoulda braced for it but, fuck me, I was surprised.

Honest to Christ, never expected the girl to give me a damn strip-tease on the stage of The Lotus like she'd been takin' her clothes off for a livin' for years.

The second the lights went out and the spotlights cranked on, shoulda told my brothers to get *the fuck out*.

197

But then that fuckin' song came on. "Sink the Pink" by my favourite fuckin' band AC/DC. She'd done it on fuckin' purpose, knew from our letters that I loved the band, listened to the lyrics and knew they'd mean somethin' to me.

And they did.

So insteada kickin' my brothers out or puttin' an end to the whole fuckin' thing like I shoulda, I was frozen when Lou went struttin' out on the glossy black stage, wearin' pink and blue light, a little girly skirt that barely covered her ass and a tiny bra with cherries on it.

How the fuck she'd known about the cherries was beyond me. It couldn'ta just been a good guess that she'd dress like a little girl. Had to have known my dick was a fuckin' steel pole in my pants the second I saw 'er, so fuckin' young and so fuckin' ripe for the pluckin'.

She had to have known that I was fucked in the head 'cause the sight'a her like that was the sexiest thing I'd ever seen.

Then she moved.

It was clear she'd learned some moves from her stripper sisters, but it was also clear as fuckin' day that my Lou was a ballerina 'cause the way she flowed from one move to another didn't just make my dick hard, it made my heart stop. She was so goddamn sexy and so goddamn pure it was like watchin' two different girls up on the stage.

I wanted both. The princess and the sinner.

My mouth was drier than a morning-after hangover when she flipped upside down against that pole and dropped those long gold legs into the splits.

No man could withstand the sight'a that.

Any man says different, he's fuckin' *lying*.

But it was over for me the second she reared up like some beauty on the bow of a ship and undid her bra. Her big round tits fell into the candy-coloured light like fuckin' gumdrops.

"Out," I tried to yell but my voice was gone probably 'cause my breath was gone.

The brothers at my booth, Nova and Bat, ripped their eyes away from Lou, blinkin' like they'd looked too long at the sun

My fuckin' sun.

"Out," I growled.

Never seen Bat scared but he noticed the seriousness of my threat immediately and started to push Nova out the other side.

Nova—the fuck—tried to reason with me.

"She's just a kid, Z, take it easy on her."

Fury tightened like a fuckin' collar round my throat as I turned my glare on him and watched him flinch, just slightly but it was enough fear to appease the beast in me. The beast that wanted to rip out his fuckin' eyes for seein' Lou anywhere near to fuckin' naked.

"She look like a kid to you?"

Even in the dark, Nova paled and swallowed roughly.

"Fuckin' out!" I roared.

Thank fuck my brothers knew me enough to know when I meant fuckin' business. Within seconds, Curtains had the music and spotlights off and the club lights on, and the rest of my lingering brethren were makin' quick for the door.

They didn't dare look up at Lou as she slid from the pole and crossed her arms under those fan-fuckin'-tastic tits.

"Gonna have your hands full with this one," Bat had

muttered to me, clapping a hand to my shoulder as he moved past me. "Good fuckin' luck, brother."

I didn't need luck.

All I had was the force of my fury carrying me forward as I took her over my shoulder. The force of possession makin' me splay her out on my table and finger fuck her 'til she creamed all over my hands. And then only the force of my fuckin' need for her when I dragged her into my arms and told her she was mine.

I'd cleaned her wet pussy with her broken panties before shovin' them in my pocket 'cause I was sentimental that way. Then I'd sent her to get dressed and called Mute who'd been waitin' outside the entire time like he'd said to give her a ride home.

I wanted to be the one to give her a ride home.

No, fuck that, I didn't want her to go home.

Now that I had her, I wanted her at my side under my fuckin' roof.

I wasn't a patient man and I couldn't see that changin' now after thirty-six years of it, but I had more pressin' concerns so I shoved thoughts of claimin' Lou as my old lady and what that all would mean to her and me and my kids, and I slid into my role as Prez. I'd been at the club only as an alibi just in case anyone wanted to put up a stink about the disappearance of a fuckin asshole dealer. You never knew with the Entrance cops just how invested they could get in takin' The Fallen down, so I liked to cover my bases.

Now though, and especially after what I'd just had with Lou, it was time for some fuckin' vengeance.

"You good?" Blackjack asked when I showed up at Angelwood Farm just outside of Entrance.

It was a hundred acres of fertile land I'd bought and gifted to my old prison cellmate Dixon when he'd got out three years ago. He'd liked the farmin' we'd done as prison labor and I needed a safe place to bury bodies so it worked. I gave 'im the land, he bought a shit-ton of pigs, and we were in the body-disappearing business.

"Good," I repeated as I fell into step with him.

Blackjack grinned. "Heard Foxy's givin' ya a run for yer money."

"Foxy?" I asked even though I knew he was talkin' about Lou. It was only a matter a time before they give 'er a nickname but didn't mean I had to like it.

He shrugged. "It was either that or Barbie but she threatened to cut off Boner's dick when he suggested it and you know how fonda that thing he is."

I smiled at the thought of my girl sassin' Boner, who was lean as hell but carried about nine concealed weapons on his person even in peace times.

It wasn't peace times though, which brought me to the reason I was even at Angelwood and not in bed discoverin' my Foxy girl.

"Callin' King home this weekend. Cress too. Gotta have a family dinner to talk about this shit and get it sorted. King won't want a bodyguard but I'm thinkin' of sending a brother down there to keep an eye," I told Blackjack.

He wasn't a lieutenant but I'd known B.J. almost as long as I'd known Bat and that was sayin' somethin'. He'd lived across the street from my uncle and his dad had been a member of The Fallen too, so we'd hung out at family BBQs and charity fundraisers. He was a decent guy, not so pretty 'cause of a car accident as a kid, but loyal to a fuckin' tee.

He'd taken my side in the revolt ten years ago when I'd exposed what a bastard my uncle was and taken the presidency from 'im. A bunch of old-timers had left, includin' Blackjack's dad, but my brother had stayed.

He proved how well he knew my family by sayin', "Queenie's gonna freak, she figures out yer sleepin' with Foxy."

"Not sleepin' with her yet, brother, and don't plan on doin' any sleepin' when I got her in my bed for a good long fuckin' time."

He laughed even as he shook his head at me. "Luckiest fuckin' man I ever knew."

My grin turned into a grimace. "Try tellin' me that again when Queenie and H.R. rip into me about Lou."

His laugh was even louder. "Fuck but I'd like to see that."

"Makes one of us," I muttered.

"Yer serious about the girl, then? I mean, can't blame ya, I got young pussy like that lustin' after me," he whistled, "Well, I'd near to sell my soul for a shot'a that."

I grunted as we came to a stop at the doors to the storm shelter round the side of the farmhouse. "Give ya a pass on that one, B.J., but next time you call my woman 'young fuckin' pussy' I'm gonna have to tear a strip off you."

His pale eyebrows shot into his pale hair but he laughed as he held up his hands. "You got it, Prez. This one means somethin', good to know."

I nodded at him, done with the conversation because talkin' about Lou had reminded me of the rage eatin' away in my gut at what that fucker dealer had done to her. I'da been pissed he played those fucked-up tricks on any one of the girls at The Lotus but that it was Lou made me feel like skinnin' the man with a dull blade. I let the anger dope me up like a shot of heroin as B.J. held open the doors to the storm shelter. The air hit me like it always did in the deep cellar, earthy and decomposing. I rolled my shoulders and cracked my knuckles as I descended into The Fallen owned corner of hell where we kept the worse kind of sinners.

Traitors.

"Quentin!" I called out happily as I rounded the corner into the big concrete room and saw the drug dealer danglin' by his shackled hands from a metal hook in the ceiling.

Priest had already gone at 'im. The right side of his torso was purple with bruises, red with blood and lumpy in a way a man's ribcage should never be.

He'd left Kade's face for me.

I nodded at my brother in gratitude as he cleaned his bloody hands over at the sink against the wall. The blood was the same colour as his hair and it always seemed kinda poetic to me that the club enforcer had hair like that.

"Did the rat bastard give us anythin'?"

"Nah, boss, he was feelin' real tight-lipped. Was about to take out the pliers when Axe-Man told me you were on your way."

I nodded as I pulled my tee up over my head from the back of my neck. No reason to get blood on anythin'.

"Oh Kade, you think you're gonna get outta this alive? Let me tell you," I said conversationally as Priest handed me my favourite brass knuckles and I fitted them to my fingers. "You're gonna tell me everythin' you know about those motherfucking Nightstalker bitches and you're gonna do it screamin', then garblin'. Why's that, you ask? 'Cause I'm gonna cave your motherfuckin' face in for playin' fucked up games with my girl."

"Your girl?" the rat bastard finally sniveled, fear sparking so fuckin' pretty in his eyes. "She told me she was nothin' to you!"

I grinned, flexed and released my fist as I drew closer to 'im and then reared it back as I said, "She's every fuckin' thing to me."

My bronze fist hit him straight across the left cheek. I felt it crumble under my force. Heard the brutalized scream of the man a second later and knew, a second after that, when my fist reared back to connect again, I'd hear the pathetic excuse for a fuckin' man break and start fuckin' talkin'.

"They're comin' for you," he said through his tears. "And this time, they've got help."

CHAPTER TWENTY

Loulou

THE NEXT NIGHT AT THE LOTUS WAS CRAZY BUSY. IT SEEMED every single brother of The Fallen and every single one of their friends was in the club, laughing, drinking and reveling in the beauty of the dancers. I was so busy behind the bar and backstage helping the dancers that I didn't have a single moment to make my way over to Zeus's booth. I'd had a brief flare of creativity and a good giggle that morning when I'd gone into the big department store halfway to Vancouver and got a little plaque made specially for the booth. *God of Thunder*, it read in red letters on a black lacquered background. I'd had Harlow help me drill it into the end edge of the table that morning so that when Zeus arrived, it would be there glowing under the red-tinged lights for him.

I'd been too busy to see his reaction when he showed up just after eleven and I was dying for a chance to hear what he thought. It was a stupid gift really, the kind a little girl might give her dad. But in some ways, I knew I would always be that little girl Zeus had saved in the parking lot of First Light Church and he would always be that guardian monster. There was something beautiful about the fact that our relationship had changed and evolved as we aged but that purity would always remain.

I caught glances of him whenever I could though, unable to keep my eyes from straying his way.

I couldn't stop watching his hands, his enormous, strong-enough-to-kill-a-man hands. They rested on the blood-red table, one loosely wrapped around his sweating glass of whiskey on the rocks and the other relaxed palm down on the lacquered wood. I found myself sweating just like that glass, imagining the way those fingers could destroy me, how they would tear apart my body at the seams with rough, sure strokes and unceasing pressure. I was certain to my bones that those hands had killed a man, maybe many but definitely all who had dared to fuck with him. And I now knew from personal experience that those hands could be yielded with the same amount of passion and ruthless intensity on and deep inside a woman's body.

I wanted those weapons of mass destruction on my skin, wrapped around my wrists like shackles, parting the folds of my soaking wet cunt like a hot knife through butter. I wanted the stretch and burn of each thick digit inside me and then I wanted him to wrap the other big paw around my throat like a threat, like a benediction and claim me as his while I came all over his palm.

I had the time now to go over because the club had just closed and only a handful of The Fallen remained, most of whom I recognized. The low murmur of voices from the back was dissolving into quiet as the girls left for their beds and most of the other servers had already gone home. Only our janitor Michael and my manager, Maja, remained.

But Maja had her eye on me as she had done all night, so I didn't want to scamper over to Zeus like some eager beaver when I didn't even really know where we stood on things.

Sure, he'd said I was stuck with him, but what did that mean?

I'd never felt so young in my life as I did when I tried to answer that question.

I was wiping the bar down and cleaning the runoff from the beer taps when Maja scooted onto a stool and said, "Pour me a big vodka, will ya?"

I pulled the Grey Goose off the top shelf and slopped three shots into a rocks glass for her.

"No ice, already dissolved it," I explained as I pushed it across the slick bar and into her waiting hand.

"Leave the bottle," she told me when I went to put it back. "And grab a glass. I have a feelin' a girl talk is in order and I only do that shit when booze is—heavily—involved."

I bit off my grin as I grabbed a glass, poured myself a thimble full and hefted my ass onto the counter on my side of the bar.

"What's up?" I asked.

She was a middle-aged woman who looked her age because of her hard living but still wore it well. I'd never seen her without big hair, smoky eyes and seriously tight, flared jeans on. She was a biker babe and she rocked it *hard*. I didn't know much about her history other than that she was married to Buck, the VP of The Fallen, and I only knew that because my friend Lila liked to come have a drink at the bar sometimes and she was a font of biker knowledge.

She looked at me then like she had some serious shit to say, serious shit that I wasn't going to like.

Without meaning to, my eyes darted over to Zeus at his booth where he sat talking to Buck, Bat and Nova.

Maja laughed her loud, smoker's laugh. "*That's* what's up, baby girl. You eyin' the beast like you don't care he bites."

A blush worked its way into my cheeks before I could stop it, but I shrugged casually, desperate to pull it off. "He's hot. A girl's allowed to look."

"Oh, she sure is and it'd be a crime not to appreciate a great, big beast like that. So pretty you could just walk up and stroke him, hmm?"

The woman was playing with me, smiling over the rim of her glass like a tigress playing with a cub.

I bared my teeth at her in something meaner than a smile. "A beast is just like any other animal... touch them just right, even they purr."

This time, Maja threw her head back as she cackled and slapped the table with her free hand. "Yes! Damn, I knew I liked you, girlie."

My grin softened. "Thanks, Maja."

"That said, I still gotta tell ya to go carefully with this one. It's my responsibility as an older woman to stick my nose in where it ain't wanted and give advice, so bear with me a tick, yeah? I wouldn't be sayin' nothin' if it weren't for the fact that Zeus Garro hasn't even blinked twice at a woman since he got shot of his bitch ex-wife and now he won't stop fuckin' starin' at ya like you're his last meal on Death Row."

"Oh," I said because *wow*, it felt good to hear someone say Z wanted me and that it wasn't just all dreamt up in my head.

"*Oh* is right. You ready to take on the beast, girl? He's fuckuva lot'a man for a grown woman, let alone a young one and he comes with a wealth of fuckin' baggage. You ready to be a mom to two kids your age and a whole host of brothers in the club? 'Cause any woman of Zeus Garro's is gonna have to pick up that mantle. Don't get stuck in if you don't intend to stick."

"You're really laying it out, huh?" I asked her to buy myself some time.

I took a sip of the vodka and hated it. Tequila was so much better.

She nodded, drained her glass and poured another. "Only way to do it. It's part of the life, girlie. You live balls to the wall, say what you think and do what you feel. Know you got a life somewhere outside of here and I seriously doubt it's a life like that. Remind me too much of my girl, Queenie. I can smell the blue in your blood."

"My blood's not got anything to do with this."

"Like fuck it doesn't. You want to take on not just a biker but *the* biker, you better be willin' and eager to drown that blue out with green and black, the colours of The Fallen, 'cause that's what you'll be."

I crossed my arms under my breasts and blinked at her,

done talking about my relationship with Z with a virtual stranger. "Who says I even want to take him on?"

"Girlie, there's only one man I know with hands that large," she said with sparkling eyes as she gestured to my bare midriff under my cropped top. "Next time you want to keep somethin' a secret, maybe hide the evidence, yeah?"

I looked down to see the faint bruises Zeus had left on my hips last night and glared at her. "One of the brothers blabbed about the dance, didn't they?"

She laughed like a wicked witch again. "You betcha. Brothers are worse than a group of old biddies but don't tell 'em I said that. Nothing stays secret in the club for long, not once you're accepted into the fold."

I rolled my lips under my teeth and voiced one of my worries. "Bet that's easier said than done."

"Darlin' the Vice President's wife just sat down to have a drink and a chat with you. Think that process has already begun." Maja downed the rest of her drink with a wink then slid off the stool and sauntered into the back.

There was a commotion at the doors and I turned my eyes from Maja's great ass to watch as Cy and Boner escorted a well-dressed man into the club.

I recognized him immediately as one of the men with Quentin Kade the night he'd shot at me. My heart leapt into my throat as my eyes swiveled to Zeus. He was watching me too and the moment I looked over, he tipped his chin at me. I didn't know what that meant exactly but I stayed behind the bar, relaxing slightly when Mute appeared from out of nowhere and sat at the bar beside me.

"Garro," the newcomer said, grinning uneasily as he sat down in the guest seat at Zeus's booth. "How's it goin', man?"

"Good, Hiccough, how's the trade?" Zeus asked casually, adjusting one of the silver rings he wore on his big hands.

The man named Hiccough looked down at those hands and swallowed so roughly, I could see it from all the way over at the bar.

"Good, can't complain. Got rid of the last'a that fucked up shit the Nightstalkers sold me last year, just like I told ya I would."

"Yeah, 'bout that. Haven't seen you around in a while. If business is so fuckin' good, where you gettin' your shit from?" Zeus finally looked up from his hands, slowly exposing his face to the reddish light in a practiced way that was still cool as fuck and so scary it gave me tingles.

"Oh, uh, man, you know I actually decided a while back to maybe diversify and try to support the small guys, ya know?" Hiccough laughed nervously, and it sounded exactly like his name.

"You happen to go to the same 'small guys' as Quentin Kade?" Z asked as he adjusted enough to pull a wicked curved blade from somewhere on his person. It glinted in the light as he laid it on the table, gleaming red like a physical foreshadowing.

I gulped at the same time as Hiccough did.

"Well, man, I mean it's a small community really so there, uh, may have been some overlap. You know how these things work," the stupid man tried to backtrack but even I could see he was falling backward and right into their trap.

Zeus was playing with him.

"'Course." He nodded sagely. "Get that, Hiccough, you gotta think 'bout your business. What's loyalty if you don't have any cash to back it up, right?"

"Right." Hiccough jumped on his chance to agree with Zeus. "Knew you'd understand."

Zeus nodded slowly as if he was distracted then called, "Lou, bring me another whiskey. Hiccough, you want somethin'?"

He nodded like a bobblehead. "Beer would be great."

Zeus tipped his chin at me and when I hesitated, Mute nodded from beside me. I didn't want to get close to the guy but I quickly poured the drinks and made my way over to them. Hiccough was facing away so he didn't see me until I was beside him, planting his drink on the table. He looked up to smile at me or maybe thank me but then caught sight of my face, the faint scratch the falling brick from the bullet had made across my cheek, and froze.

Before he could do anything else, Bat and Buck were hemming him in and Cy was tugging me out of the closing circle. Zeus's mighty hand went slamming down on top of Hiccough's and he tugged it forcibly in his grip while he began to talk, and as he began to talk, he took that wicked knife in his other hand and worked it slowly into the back of the other man's hand.

"You think you can go behind my back and make a deal with the fuckin' Nightstalkers and I won't know about it? Think you can come into my house, the business of my brothers and scare one of our fuckin' girls, Hiccough? I don't fuckin' think so."

Hiccough whimpered and tried to pull back his hand as Zeus opened a flap of skin, held it to the blade with his thumb and slowly began to pull it back over the length of his hand like he was skinning an apple.

"Now, my boys are going to take you to the fun farm to

ask you a few questions about the motherfuckin' Night-stalkers and if you answer correctly, you'll be free to go back to your pathetic fuckin' life. If you don't, I have 'bout twenty pigs who haven't eaten dinner yet." Zeus's grin was wide and manic as he ripped the last bit of skin and let go of Hiccough's hand with a flourish that had blood spraying across the table.

Hiccough was howling and whimpering now, and I was struck dumb with shock at what I'd witnessed. Zeus wiped his bloody blade on either side of Hiccough's cheek to clean it.

I'd always known Zeus was a monster, but this made it an irrefutable *fact*.

I didn't have time to process it because the brothers around me were moving, two of them carting a sobbing Hiccough between them out the back while Nova pulled out a fucking *handkerchief* and cleaned the blood off the table with it before putting it back in his jeans pocket.

"Meet you there," Zeus told his brothers then turned to look at me.

I turned on my heel and fled behind the bar. It wasn't that I was scared of him—though I *was*—it was that I needed the space to think about what I'd seen and how it made me feel.

Mostly, I wondered if it was wrong that I felt vengeance burn like the satisfying heat of whiskey down my throat and in my gut; that I loved the look of that fucker's fear because it so accurately mimicked my own when his friend had leveled a gun at my face.

I was thinking these thoughts as the club emptied out, leaving Zeus and I alone.

A predator and his prey in one big cage.

"Lou, look at me."

His voice settled over me like a cloud of marijuana smoke, sweet and heady enough to make me forget myself.

I looked at him.

He stood at the entrance to the bar, blocking my exit. I watched as he prowled toward me and I instinctively backed up until my ass hit the opposite end. His grin shone in the shadows cast by his wild mass of hair.

"You scared, little girl?"

He leaned into me, looming so close that I could feel tingles erupt over my skin just from the proximity and the threat of his touch.

"No." I swallowed thickly.

"Do you know why I wanted you to see that shit?"

I dragged a deep breath into my lungs, caught the forest and smoke scent of him and forgot to breathe again. "To scare me."

"To *show* you. This is me. This is the monster you're so desperate to make your own. There's no goin' into this with eyes closed shut, Lou. I'm the kinda man, someone wrongs you, I cause him the equivalent in pain. I'm a man of loyalty and vengeance, violence and sex. Won't make apologies for it and won't have you romanticizin' it. I'm an outlaw and this is an outlaw's life. You sure you still want that?"

I hesitated, caught in the silver web of his gaze.

He wrapped his huge hand around my delicate neck and squeezed. "You want me, little girl? You want the man who'll always right your wrongs with blood and teach you all'a the dark ways of life, includin' how to take a cock and make it come? Who'll tell you what to do to please him and expect you to obey?"

My eyes flashed rebelliously but I knew he felt me swallow hard against his grip.

I was terrified of him like this, a man turned volcanic with rage.

There was no getting around the sheer masculine power of his enormous frame or, beyond that, the cold intelligence that lurked at the depths of his blade-grey eyes. It didn't help that I'd just seen him peel a strip of skin off the back of a man's hand with his Swiss Army knife as if he was casually peeling a carrot.

Yes, I was terrified of Zeus Garro, and rightly so.

The little girl who'd been drawn to his dark spirit now understood as a woman the violent realities of it.

But that fear pooled between my thighs like a hot tide that ebbed and throbbed with the tempo of his temper.

I was a woman now and that seed of intrigue had blossomed into something darker, edgier; a desire that was watered with danger and fertilized by fear.

And he was dangerous with fury now. Angry with the men who'd wronged him, angry with the Nightstalkers for fucking with him and his kin, angriest with me for being seventeen years old, off-limits and constantly in his face.

"You get me," he murmured darkly, reading my thought through my hammering pulse under his thumb. "You want to get up on this counter and offer your sweet, wet cunt to me. Open up those golden thighs nice and wide under that little skirt so I can see exactly what it is you're offerin' me. I'll teach you to touch that pretty pussy for me until you're so wet I can smell it, then you'll come exactly when I tell you to, and we'll see if you're good enough to be mine."

"Yes," I hissed, tipping my head back in his grip like a beta wolf submitting to her Alpha.

With one hand at my throat and the other at my ass, he hefted me on the counter and grinned that wicked grin. "Open wide."

I stretched my thighs open as far as the counter would let me and swallowed thickly again as he flipped up my skirt to expose the seam of my slit, overstuffed with a swollen clit and plump, glistening lips.

"Spread yourself open for me," he ordered as he took a step back, crossed his thick arms over his thick chest and leaned a hip against the counter to watch me with half-lidded but fervent eyes.

I used two fingers to hold myself open for him, feeling the heat of his eyes on the wet pink skin like a physical touch.

"Two fingers on your clit, gentle circles so it stands up nice and high for me."

"Oh God."

"You feel you've gotta pray to get through this 'fore I give you the okay to come, you do that, little girl," he drawled. "Now dip one of those little fingers into that tight cunt but careful not to break the seal. My cock'll do that soon enough."

Holy fuck, he was fire and I was wax, melting under his attentions. My wetness trickled under my ass and onto the counter.

"Harder on your clit, another finger in your pussy," he told me a minute later.

My eyes closed as I tossed my head back. It was too much, his voice coiled around me like wicked bondage, my fingers attached to puppet strings he maneuvered over my sticky flesh.

"Eyes on me," he barked.

I opened them with effort but was rewarded by the sight of him palming the huge bulge in his black jeans. My mouth opened and my tongue darted into the air as if I could taste him.

His lids fell even lower, his voice a deep rumble as he said, "You come for me really pretty, Lou, I'll reward you with my cock next time we play."

"What if I want it now?" I dared to ask.

I watched his eyes flare open then sink back down. "You want me, you do what I tell you to do, little girl."

A full body shudder ripped through me.

He stalked closer and leaned down to stare at my pussy like I was some interesting painting on display in a gallery. I watched him watch my fingers churn through my juicy pussy and knew I was close to coming.

So did Zeus.

"You can come whenever," he muttered then blew a cool gust of air over my clit, leaned forward and gave it a short, wide lick with the flat of his tongue.

The sight of his head and broad shoulders between my thighs turned me from solid to liquid. He watched my cum splash out against my fingers, watched me jerk against the counter and whimper. Then, when I was finally done, he used a single finger to follow a trail of wet up my inner thigh and then licked it off his skin.

"Good girl," he praised with dark eyes.

I narrowed my droopy eyes at him and closed my legs over his hand. "You sound surprised.

"Can't surprise a man like me, little girl. I've seen it all."

"Yeah?" I taunted, too vulnerable and hating his coldness. "Because you're an old man?"

"No, 'cause I've seen more in one year of my life than most people ever see in the entirety of theirs. I've seen grown men weep, loved ones kill loved ones over money and greed, little girls get shot because they were in the wrong place at the wrong time and other kids hungry in the fuckin' dirt 'cause their parents are too weak ass to provide for 'em."

"Seems like all you've seen is bad," I ventured softly, my anger cooled by the travesty of his words.

His gaze collided with me like a hand at my neck, squeezing and lifting until I felt unbalanced, unable to breathe.

"Saw you in the parking lot of First Light with velvet fuckin' bows in your hair lookin' at me like I was your saviour. Saw you drunk as fuck outside Nova's girl Lila's house lookin' like somethin' I dreamed up even stinkin' like you did. Saw you again in this club in hardly anythin' at all charmin' near everyone around you with that halo of good you wear in your golden hair... Little girl, I told you, I've seen it all. But until you, didn't know if any of it was worth it."

He closed the sliver of space between us then spread his whole hand across my chest, over the spot where the scar we shared rested beneath my shirt. "Need to make sure you were cool with it, the monster in real life. Now I do, you need to know. I was serious about not lettin' ya go. And by that, I mean fuckin' ever."

I snaked my arms around his back and pressed him to

me, relief and love so bright a thing in my chest, it burned.

"The first seventeen years of my life, I fasted. I kept my body clean and my spirit pure. Now, I want to feast like a glutton, spread lust on my breakfast toast, shoot violence and sip greed. And I want you to teach me, sinner man, because you're the only man for the job," I told him.

His workingman's hands abraded the sensitive skin of my neck as he worked them up my throat to cup my face in his wide palms. My breath caught in my throat as I wondered if this would finally be the time he'd kiss me. If this would be the kiss I'd been waiting for in one way or another since I was seven years old.

His thumb ran the length of my jaw then up to pull down my full lower lip. My tongue came out to taste the salt of my sex on his thumb and his eyes flashed like neon lights. I gasped as he dipped down to glide his tongue over the inside of my pouting lip then groaned low in his chest like a beast after his first taste of blood, and sealed his mouth to mine.

He tasted like whiskey and smoke, hot and sinful on my tongue and I knew if wickedness had a taste, it would be him. I moaned as he tilted my head and plunged deeper, his tongue like hot silk in my mouth and his beard rough against my cheeks. I sank my fingers in his soft, tangled mane and clung to him mindlessly because no amount of little girl dreaming or hoping could have prepared me for the earth-tilting reality of Zeus's mouth on mine.

When he pulled back, he smoothed that thumb over my kiss-bruised lips, his eyes reverent and dark with the kind of desires a virgin couldn't understand. I shivered as he bent his knees so we were on eye level and said, "Welcome to the dark side, then, little Lou."

CHAPTER TWENTY-ONE

Loulou

THE WATERFORD CHINA WAS OUT.

I walked into my four-story mansion on the corner of Mulberry Rd. and Pinewood St. and noticed the set-up immediately through the open door across the marble-floored foyer. The room was littered with fractured gold shards of light from the low hanging, six-tiered chandelier over the formal dining room table and the soft swell of Beethoven played over the surround sound system.

Fuck.

I was tired to my bones after a sleepless night dreaming about the ways Zeus had touched me and the impossibilities that faced us now that we were going to be together. This was followed by a rough morning with Sammy, who had thrown a fit because his exhausted mother had forgotten to buy enough of his favourite sticky toffee pudding, so he'd had ice cream for breakfast instead. It seems like a small difference, but to a child with Autism, routine could mean everything and even though I'd tried to right his morning, poor Sammy was completely thrown off by the change and even Mute's presence hadn't brought him peace of mind. When I'd left, I was surprised but touched that Mute had offered to stay with Sammy and his single mum, Margie, who'd practically cried at the offer of help even though it was from a biker.

To top it all off, even though I'd texted him, Zeus hadn't been in touch all day.

So, I was too tired for what I knew the Waterford China meant.

Company. The kind that my parents wanted to impress.

"Louise, thank God you're home. Really I know I encouraged you to volunteer, but it seems like you spend every spare moment at the centre," Phillipa said as she breezed into the room on a cloud of Nina Ricci perfume and kissed the air at the side of my cheek. "You have fifteen minutes to get ready before the Venturas get here. Wear the dress I had Yasmin put out on your bed and the pink pearls, not the cream or the white."

"Mum, I'm really tired," I said softly, swaying slightly on my feet because honest to God, I was fading fast.

She pursed her lips at me. "Louise, you can't play the sick card only when it suits you. Besides, chemo doesn't start again for another week so I know you can't be feeling that badly."

You know *shit*, I screamed inside my head.

Instead, I nodded. "Okay, I'm just going to lay down for ten minutes and then I'll get ready."

"Fine," my mother said with a dismissive way of her hand. "I need you on your game tonight though. These people are *very* important. Javier Ventura is one of the richest men in Mexico and he's decided that Entrance of all places could be a marvelous place to open a Canadian branch of his business."

"Great," I muttered, dragging my feet to the grand staircase so I could find some brief solace in my room.

"Oh, and Louise? Make sure Beatrice looks presentable, will you? I do wish she'd grow out of this awkward stage."

I waved a hand over my shoulder as I walked away but otherwise ignored my mother's criticism of my sister. I wasn't surprised when I opened the door to my pink-and-white room to find said sister, sprawled on my bed reading one of my *Cosmo* magazines.

Immediately, she said, "Do you wanna take a quiz to see what kind of man you'll end up with?"

I snorted as I dropped my bag to the ground, kicked my loafers off and face-planted to the frilly bed beside her. "No."

"Yeah, I got Skater Boy. I mean, do skater boys even exist anymore? Aren't they like *so* early 2000s?"

I could feel her swing around on the bed so she was sitting facing me and then I hummed as her hand stroked over my hair.

"How's my favourite sister?" she asked softly.

"Better now," I said, like I always did.

I turned my cheek into the bed so I could look at her and smiled tiredly. "Ready for another dog and pony show?"

"Yep. I'll be the dog, you be the pony," she said with a wide, brace-filled grin.

I closed my eyes as I smiled. "How was your day?"

"Good. I got a 99% on my biology test today. Mr. Warren told me that one day I may even surpass you in brains and beauty," she said with a girlish giggle.

Immediately, I frowned and leaned up on my elbows. "Bea, baby, you *already* surpass me in both. I hope you don't need Mr. Warren to tell you that, and I hope you don't take what he says too seriously."

Bea blushed slightly and wrapped a long strand of my hair around her finger. We had the exact same shade of pale hair but other than that, we didn't look much alike except for our stature, five foot nine. She'd yet to fill out like I had, and something told me she would be long and lean instead of curved like me, but I knew she longed to be exactly like me even when I told her she could be better.

I fit our hands together, feeling the ridges in our skin line up and locked tight as I braided our fingers tight.

"Love you, Bea," I said before pressing our joined hands to my heart.

She grinned, wide and happy, so carefree it took my breath away. "Love you more."

The sharp vibration of my phone buzzing in the front pocket of my jeans broke our moment. I flipped over and had it in my hand, screen unlocked before Bea could blink.

Guardian Monster: Pick you up 'round the block at 9pm tonight. Tell your parents you gotta sleepover or somethin'.

My heart filled with helium and threatened to float into my throat. I hugged the phone to my chest and tried not to squeal like a little girl with delight.

"What's going on?" Bea asked, lunging for my phone when I just shook my head at her.

"Buzz off," I told her, laughing as I held her forehead back with the palm of one hand. "It's private."

"Oh come on, Loulou, tell me! I'm your best friend. Who else are you going to tell? Is it Reece?"

Fuck.

Reece.

God, I had barely talked to him all week and even though we weren't officially exclusive, I had pretty much physically and emotionally cheated on him.

Damn, I really needed to talk to him.

"I'm going out tonight and I need you to cover for me in case Mum or Dad decide to care for a change. I won't be back until tomorrow night."

"Ooooh," Bea crooned while waggling her eyebrows. "Are you finally going to go *all the way* with Reece?"

I bit my lip, grateful beyond all belief that Reece had never pressured me to have sex with him. We'd done hand and mouth stuff—*a lot*—but we'd both hesitated about the final deal and until now, I hadn't realized just how much I'd wanted to wait for the impossibility of giving it to Zeus.

Now that impossibility was on the verge of becoming a reality.

"Maybe." I grinned at my little sister and pounced forward to pepper her face with kisses, loving the sound of her giggle in my ears and loving for the first time in my life, the possible future that was unrolling like a red carpet at my feet. "I've gotta take a shower and get ready."

"Make sure you shave your legs. Nothing worse than a missed patch of stubble," she called after me through my laughter as I bounded off the bed, rejuvenated by the plans for the night. "Even you can't pull off Sasquatch legs."

I flipped her the bird over my shoulder as I shut the bathroom door on her giggles.

"LOUISE, DARLING, THERE YOU ARE," my mother cooed as I swept into the formal dining room, twenty minutes later than expected. "You'll have to excuse our daughter, Javier. She is just *so* busy these days with her extracurriculars. You know, she's a talented ballerina, an IB student, a cheerleader, a member of the school board—"

"Please, Mother, I'm sure Mr. Ventura doesn't want a laundry list of my accomplishments. They must be nothing compared to his," I interrupted with a sweet, subdued smile cast at my mother and another, more appropriately awed one aimed at the tall, immaculately groomed Mexican man beside her.

He clasped the ends of my fingers as I held my hand out for a handshake and brought them to a surprisingly full mouth. "Modest and beautiful. You have a rare breed here, Phillipa."

"Thank you," I said softly but I'd already taken the measure of this man in the expensive, custom-made suit and

Italian loafers, with the slick hair and the gold ring on his pinky.

He was candy coated, poverty enrobed in class. It was obvious in his manner, in the shrewd almost feral look that made his brown eyes murkier than most; swamp water that held hidden depths, most of them filled with monsters.

I knew monsters, I'd had one as a guardian growing up, so I knew what to look for.

And Javier Ventura was one of them.

"She is lovely, isn't she?" my mother agreed after taking a sip of her dry vodka martini with a lime twist.

I'd been making her that cocktail since I was a young girl. Whenever my father cut her off and the serving staff had to refuse to serve her, she used to send me into the alcohol closet for the copper cocktail shaker, a plump green fruit and a martini glass she made me chill in the fridge first.

It was one of the reasons Debra had been willing to keep me on at The Lotus. I made a *mean* martini.

"Smart as a whip too," my dad said, rounding the table where he had stood with Mr. Warren, Headmaster Adams from Entrance Bay Academy, Harold Danner, the staff sergeant, and his handsome officer son, Lionel, all of whom were frequent guests in our house. "You should see her IQ scores, Javier. She gets it from me, of course."

His laughter was meant to play his comment off as a joke, but I knew better and as I watched Javier smile thinly, I knew he realized it too.

"I'm sure," he demurred before his eyes came back to me. "You must meet my wife, Irina. She'll love you."

As if on cue, a glamorous dark-haired, pale-skinned woman floated into the room, probably from the restroom.

She wore a white dress that hugged her curves indecently and so many diamonds she looked like walking star shine.

Cue the trophy wife.

"Ah, you must be the Louise we hear so much about," Irina purred as she glided forward to take my hands in hers. Her red lips blossomed into a beautiful smile. "Just lovely. You know, I mentor many young girls just like yourself. You must come to my studio some day and pose for me."

"My wife is a skilled photographer and director back in Mexico," Javier explained.

I pursed my lips but didn't say anything even though their Mr. & Mrs. Smith perfectness was giving me the creeps.

"Let's sit down for dinner," my mother suggested and began to usher people to their assigned chairs.

I took my place in the middle of the table on the left, between Mr. Warren on one side and Javier on the other. Immediately, they both leaned toward me, moths to the flame of my youth and beauty, to the glimpse of my breasts nestled in the draped folds of my satin pale pink chemise.

"Louise," they both said at the same time and then chuckled.

"Please, guests first," Mr. Warren said with an elegant wave of his hand. "I can speak to Louise any time."

Javier's lips thinned but he nodded his acceptance then waited until it was Mr. Warren's turn to frown and turn away to speak with my mother on his other side. Only then did Javier lean even closer to me to say, "You look absolutely lovely in that dress, Louise."

"Thank you," I said neutrally, curious to see where he would take the conversation.

In my experience, it was either to issue a backroom invitation to test my virtue against their lascivious intentions or to offer me up as a possible candidate for their son or grandson.

In this case, I thought it might be something else.

"I can see why your parents are so proud of you," he continued as our cook, Mrs. Henry, served him an individual portion of her famous French onion soup.

"They raised me right," I preached.

I was almost surprised I remembered how. It'd been awhile since I'd had to do any ass kissing but I guessed after years of it, it was muscle memory.

"I'm sure," he agreed but there was vein of dark humor in his voice that I wanted to excavate.

So, I said, "What is your business with my father?"

He laughed softly. "Assertive. I like a woman who knows what she wants."

I sent a skeptical glance at Irina that had him laughing again, this time louder so that my parents both sent me approving glances from each end of the table. This was, after all, what I was there for; lubricating the guests with my looks, youth and charm so that my parents could swoop in and take from them whatever they needed: political merit, money, social connections or extramarital affairs.

"Irina would surprise you, I think. She is very *involved* in my businesses and quite successful with her own."

"Mmm."

"As for my business with your father, I hope to open a Canadian branch of my import/export company. In order to do this, I need his political support getting the right tax exemptions and his moral support, as I won't open a business in a town where outlaws run rampant."

I startled slightly, hesitating with a spoonful of gooey onion goodness suspended and dripping halfway to my mouth. Carefully, I settled it back down and turned my eyes to his bright, intelligent gaze.

"What do you mean by that?"

"I mean you have a cancer..." His dark eyes caught the light of the chandelier and reflected like obsidian, inhuman and deadly sharp when pointed, as they were at that moment, at *me*. "In this town, I mean. The Fallen MC, as I understand it, have run roughshod over this city for years. I plan to rectify that."

"And how might you do that?" Lionel asked from across the table.

I wasn't surprised he was listening. We weren't friends exactly because he was a good nine years older than me, but we'd been around each other all our lives and I knew him well enough to know that he listened to everything and missed very, very little.

Javier smiled at his wineglass as he stroked the faceted stem of it. "When there is an infestation, you must not kill one rat at a time, you understand? You must take them all and to do that there is an order to things. First, you take away their food, their basic means of survival. If there is no food, the rats will panic. Then, you set the traps. Those eliminate the stupid rats, the young and the old, the women and the children, maybe. All that remains are the male rats and they are hungry, growing mad. Finally, you smoke them out and as they spill out their little rat holes you shoot them one by one until the last rat remains, the strongest rat of the bunch but the one who had to watch all the other rats die before him. And then you put a bullet in his brain too."

There was a long stagnant silence full of disgust like a still pond filled with breeding mosquitoes.

"I've heard rat poison works too," Lionel suggested drolly.

I hid my surprised laughter behind a cough I covered with my napkin, but our eyes caught and danced at each other from across the table. His were green, greener than wet grass and ripe Granny Smith apples.

"Of course," Javier said with a one-shouldered shrug as he dabbed daintily at his mouth with his napkin after finishing his soup. "Less poetic of course, but if we're talking about rats then I suppose that would work."

"But we aren't talking about rats," I stated softly.

His eyes glittered again as he shot me a sly smile. "No, Louise, I don't believe we are."

A shiver rattled the backs of my teeth as it worked down my spine. I looked over at Lionel with wide eyes, letting my fear seep into them slightly. He had no reason to know that I was afraid because those "rats" Javier spoke so eloquently about included people I cared for, a person I loved more than anything else. He probably thought I was just some scared, naïve pampered little girl frightened by a man talking about rat killing at the dinner table. Still, his eyes were sympathetic as he inclined his head at me then shook it slightly.

He wouldn't let it happen, I knew, seeing that. Lionel Danner wanted The Fallen MC put away just as much as the rest of the police force, maybe even more as long as he could claim the glory over it, but he was a *good* man, one of those throw-back policemen you saw in old Westerns. He had a moral code and everything, which meant he wouldn't let

The Fallen be smoked out and shot like rats, not if he could help it.

It didn't bring me much comfort though, because I very much doubted he *could*.

I looked back to Javier and found him watching me with those crow's eyes, black as bad omens. "You'll see, *zorra*, within the year The Fallen will be wiped clean from Entrance."

CHAPTER TWENTY-TWO

Zeus

I WAITED A BLOCK AWAY LIKE A FUCKIN' TEENAGE CHUMP sneakin' out with his teenage girl after curfew. The fuck of it was, I sure as hell wasn't a teenager anymore—the grey comin' in slow at my temples and the crow's feet 'side my eyes proved that—but my girl *was* a teenager. It was a reality I had to face 'cause I knew, if I was serious about 'er, which given my plans for the evenin', I *was*, it'd be a fact I'd have to face with brutal regularity.

I tried not to sit there in the cold dark of the mid-November night and think about all the ways this thing with Lou could go wrong but there was somethin' about being drenched in shadows that made a man contemplative and there sure as fuck was somethin' about knowin' you were about to take a woman's cherry that made ya careful.

So, I was thinkin' about H.R.'s reaction when she found out I was seein' a woman her age, about King's face when he realized I was fuckin' a girl two years younger 'an him, and my brothers rowdy cheers each time there was evidence that I'd taken her to my bed. Grown up not givin' a shit what people thought but I'd also spent most of my grown life bein' a father to two kids I'd give my life for a hundred times over so the idea of them not likin' the woman I chose sat so wrong in my chest it felt like a cancerous lump.

I thought about it, hated it and moved on from it 'cause I didn't have the willpower to start my Harley and drive away like I shoulda and I sure as fuck wouldn't have it tomorrow when I woke up beside Lou, her gold hair spread over my pillow like a fuckin' halo, her virgin's blood gone dry on my cock.

This was happenin'. Me and Lou. If I was bein' honest, it had been happenin' since I saw that pretty girl with her velvet bows and Mary Janes running at me from across a parking lot rainin' bullets like I was Jesus come to save 'er. I knew in some freakish place deep inside the gut a me that Lou was made for me.

She was it.

My ex-wife had been a mistake, every other woman a blip and Louise Lafayette, the forbidden girl, the *worst* option, was the only one for me.

So, I leaned against the side of my bike smokin' my one cigarette a day as I waited for her, tryin' not to get too worried or too fuckin' turned on about my plans for the evenin' when finally I spotted the glow of her moonlight coloured hair in the moonlit night.

She ran at me.

Hair flying, arms pumping, smile spread clean across her prettier-than-all-else face, Loulou ran at me like she'd done when she was seven and she would, I knew, until she could run no more.

And, like I'd done when she was seven and like I would, I knew, until I could stand straight no more, I caught her in my arms and hefted her tight against me.

She buried her head in that place she liked under my right ear, her nose pressed to my throat, her lips to my pulse point and her forehead in my hair.

And fuck, it felt like home to have her there.

"Zeus," she said, and I got the feeling she said it just to say it, just 'cause she knew she could and knew now that she had a claim to that name. To me.

And just 'cause I knew I could, I titled her head back by that lush white-blond mane and claimed that pouty mouth as my own. As soon as my tongue swept through her lips, she groaned softly into my mouth and opened for me. I angled her head to get deep, explorin' that hot mouth like it was my job and I had all the time in the world to do it right.

It settled me deep that I *did*. Nothin' would stand in the way of me and this girl; not her fuckface father or her age or even my own kids.

She was mine.

"Mine," I tore away from her, leaving her lips open, moist and swollen.

Couldn't help myself and licked at the sweet red bottom lip while she breathed, "Yes, always."

Before I took things too far and fucked 'er on my bike—keepin' in mind to save that for another day—I walked her over and dropped her carefully onto the bitch seat. As soon as I settled my bulk over the bike, she was plastered against my back with her clever little fuckin' hands divin' down to my lower stomach, rubbin' at the hard abs she found and the ever-hard cock stretchin' at the front of my jeans.

"You want me to crash this bike?" I rumbled, prying her hand from me.

She giggled in my ear but happily slid her hands up my tee and black hoodie so that they rested palm down on the skin of my lower chest. It'd be cold, my belly exposed to the winter winds rippin' past the bike, but I couldn't'a given less of a fuck.

"Ready," she told me huskily and I felt it in my dick.

I shook my head at her, which gifted me another laugh, and then I shot us forward into the dark. She whooped loudly as soon as we merged onto the Sea to Sky Highway, liftin' her hands in the air until they were blocks of ice before slidin' them up under my clothes again. She felt my growl of complaint against her fingers and laughed louder than the wind in my ears.

It was an hour drive across the rollercoaster ups, downs and curves of the mountainside highway. A lot for a girl's first serious time on a bike and she didn't have a leather jacket, just a little pink denim one that made her look all'a fourteen years old. But she didn't complain and somehow I could feel 'er enthusiasm radiating against my back. A coupla times, she swirled her fingers over the ridges of the bullet wound in my chest and it felt like a direct line to my heart. A coupla more times than that, she trailed cool fingers down my abdominals, skiing 'em like moguls and it felt like a direct line to my hard-as-steel cock.

So, when we finally reached the wood cabin I'd built into

the treed mountainside, I was off the bike in less than a second and had Loulou squealing in my arms the next.

She laughed but wrapped her arms and legs tight around me, Koala-style as she'd called it, and played her fingers in the ends of my hair as I carried her to the house, unlocked the door and kicked it shut.

"What has you so impatient?" she asked me, humor and confidence ringing in her voice.

I pressed her against the wall beside the door, the house dark and stale all around us and growled, "Ten years waitin' for you to grow up so I could do this." Then I slammed my mouth to hers.

In about a nanosecond her lips parted on a soft moan of surrender and her tongue came out to tangle with mine. Her fingers in my hair slid up to the back of my neck and fisted, anchoring me to her tight as if her straining thighs weren't keepin' me close enough. I fuckin' loved that she gave back just as good as she got, biting at my lip until I hissed just this side of pain. Somehow, she managed to shuck off her jacket and reveal the dainty little tank she wore underneath, her nipples pebbled from the cold ride.

I had to taste her, been thinkin' about the taste of her for years and it was *this* fuckin' close to drivin' me crazy. So I hoisted her higher against the wall with one arm wrapped around her back and up under her ass then gripped the fragile left strap of that tank in my teeth and snapped it in two. Her gasp ruffled my hair as my lips followed the path of the fallen tank. Loved the taste of her smooth tanned skin, salty and sweet under my tongue as I pressed hot, open mouthed kisses to her chest, to the deep crease between her plump tits. I rubbed my bearded jaw there, felt her shiver at the abrasive contact and then pulled back to stare at the sweet tips of her exposed tits, red and furled like fuckin' raspberries.

My mouth watered.

I nipped one between my teeth to make it harder, then did the other.

"Zeus," Lou panted, writhing against the wall where I'd pinned her.

The sound'a my name in her mouth, comin' off her lips like a prayer sounded both blasphemous and right. She was done prayin' at the alter of another man's church, now she worshipped at my feet and made me feel like my namesake, God of fuckin' Olympus.

Thunder gathered in my chest and rolled up my throat as I hefted her higher and sank to my knees, ready to bless her with my tongue and taste her holy fuckin' waters.

She gasped as I dropped to the floor, unbuckled her jeans with my teeth and then shucked them off but she sassed me when I ripped off her little panties with a rough yank by sayin', "You better buy me more of those or I won't have any left for you to rip off."

I wrapped my arms over her hips and between her golden thighs so I could pet the smooth skin either side of her wet slit.

"The less the better between me and my new favourite meal," I told her as I spread my fingers on either side of her swollen clit and pulled back so I could lash it roughly with my tongue.

She screamed.

I shut her up with my mouth pressed tight over her pretty, weeping pussy. The second my tongue parted her folds and her sweet cherry taste exploded in my mouth, I knew I'd hit heaven, kneelin' there with my mouth on the sweetest pussy any man had ever dreamt of tastin'. I yanked her tighter to my mouth and feasted.

Two noisy, thrashing minutes then she was coming and she was doin' it loud, long and glorious, pulsin' against my tongue and callin' out my name.

"Fuck, God, no, Jesus," she chanted but her hands were in my hair and usin' it like reins to keep my tongue workin' her even as she came down.

"Don't interrupt a man when he's eatin', little girl."

"Again," she begged, practically sobbing.

"Thought you were a good girl, little Lou, so where are your manners?" I asked, circlin' my thumb 'round her entrance.

My cock was so hard it ached like a motherfucker but I needed this, needed to see this girl I'd wanted since before it was legal beg for me and say my name while doin' it. So, she knew for sure whom she was inviting into her body and her bed.

"Zeus, *please*."

I tilted her hips so I could drag my tongue over her cream from pretty pink asshole to swollen clit. She rattled like a cage around me, so fuckin' close already.

"Fuck, I need you. Please, I want to come on your cock. Please, please," she sang, yankin' at my hair to move me away from her cunt.

Fuck but that sounded like a good idea, feeling that snug virgin cunt come all round my cock. I tried to focus, tried to remember why I shouldn't take a seventeen-year-old virgin on the floor of the kitchen in a cold, dark house she didn't know.

Tried and fuckin' failed.

I dropped her down so we were face-to-face again then swapped out my teasin' thumb at her cunt with two fingers and thrust just inside 'er. Her hips jerked up against me, trying to fuck down on my hand at the same time lookin' down to watch me unbuckle my belt one-handed.

"Yes," she hissed and her eyes sparked. "Show me."

"You've dreamed 'bout this cock, haven't you?" I asked her, still fuckin' her with my fingers bumpin' up against the virginity I was about to obliterate. I unbuttoned and shoved my jeans down my ass just enough to show her the rock-hard length of me pressed to my thigh behind my boxers.

"Oh God," she breathed, her eyes gone so heavy it was a wonder she could fuckin' see me. "So big."

"You want it, take it out."

Her eager hands sprang out to fumble with my boxers and even though they were clumsy, I bit on my tongue to keep from comin' when they slid under the fabric and exposed my cock. It was hot as fuck to see her eyes wide and full'a fear and fuckin' excitement as she tried to wrap her hand around the base of my cock and failed.

"Hands around my neck, Lou," I rasped out, replacin' her hand with my own so I could rub the tip of my dick against her hot velvet pussy.

She moaned and wiggled her hips closer but I held her still with my hand at her hip. I pressed my forehead to hers and my cock against her tight hole.

"This is it," I warned her. "I'm it for you after this."

"You've always been it for me," she gutted me by saying.

Then, because I was no saint and I'd held out long enough, I slammed my mouth on hers and swallowed her harsh moan as I thrust up into her drippin' cunt.

My mind splintered. It was the only way to explain how the monster in me broke free of his chains and gripped Lou harder than I shoulda, tight at the hips, hard in the hair, drivin' her wet, raw cunt up and down over my cock until my thighs were a mess of her juices and sweat dripped down my back. It was the only way to explain the way pleasure popped the lid off my head and left me thoughtless of the fact I was kissin' her 'til she nearly couldn't breathe, bitin' her neck until it blossomed with flowery hickeys all over.

It was the only way to describe how I fucked her so hard, I marked her in every heathen way as *fuckin' mine*.

And she loved it.

My seventeen-year-old ex-virgin moaned and groaned, scratched up my back like a feral fuckin' cat and begged me when she had enough breath to do it, to fuck her harder. It had to hurt her, the way my big cock stretched her and made her bleed, but she loved it so fierce she even loved the pain.

We were sweaty, gruntin' animals on the floor of the kitchen. So far past fuckin', we were just rutting, greedy beasts.

Her fingers slipped in the sweat on my shoulders then dove into the damp hair at my temples to hold my eyes steady.

"Watch me," she managed to pant. "Please, watch me as you make me come."

My hand in her hair trailed down her back so I could grab two handfuls of her plump ass and buck up into her like a fuckin' pile driver.

"You come for me, you do it sayin' my name. You do it knowin' you've got me inside you and you do it knowin' all that I am."

Her cunt was ripplin' and spasming already, drawing me impossibly deeper into that tight, burnin' sheath. My balls drew up and I knew I was gonna come too, deep inside her like I'd only done in my darkest fuckin' fantasies.

"You be a good girl and come for me right fuckin' now," I said then ducked down to take the junction of her left shoulder and neck in my mouth, holdin' her still with my teeth.

"Fuck, Zeus," she screamed on a dyin' breath, her body already gone, already shakin' on me, squeezin' around me.

She chanted my name the whole way through, her cum warm and wet on my dick as I churned in and out of her then finished with a fuckin' roar. Each jet of cum I shot tight up against her womb jerked my whole body against her, draggin' everything outta me until we both fell exhausted against each other.

With the last of my energy, I dropped back to the cold ground and lowered her on top of me. She settled like a cat in the sun, fallin' to sleep quicker than I could blink at her and notice the smile that kept at her face even in slumber. A smile that said she was the cat who'd finally eaten the canary.

I knew how she felt 'cause my heart was beatin' too fast and too hard, not stoppin' or slowin' like it shoulda after the hardest orgasm of my fuckin' life. But I couldn't sleep, couldn't even really relax, not with the way my blood was pumpin' and my mind was whirrin'.

Her hair was fuckin' everywhere, warm silk on my chest,

arms and abs but I loved the feel'a it, the smell of burnt sugar and warm cherries all around me. Couldn't stop touchin' her even though she was asleep sprawled over my body like a heavy blanket. Loved the feel of her on me, her curves against my edges. Loved the weight of her on my chest against my heart.

Loved fuckin' everything about this girl.

If I'd had any doubt before, it was fuckin' clear to me now that Lou was mine.

Didn't give a single fuck that there were a million and one fuckin' things that made her forbidden to me.

That her father would try to toss me back into prison for it.

That my enemies would try to maim, torture and kill her for it.

That my own kids might throw a shit fit 'cause of it.

I was keepin' her.

"No one should be that tense after sex that incredible," Lou muttered.

I chuckled. Smoothed a hand down her hair and twisted it all up in one of my hands so I could tug it back and force her eyes to mine. They unveiled like heavy curtains, the kinds in old movie theatres my uncle had taken me to as a kid. Glamorous. That was the old Hollywood word for what Lou was, all woman, all sass, all fuckin' gumption all the time with a sweet center just for her man.

Just for me.

She gave that to me now, that sweetness rough men like me craved.

"Want to make you happy enough to relax," she whispered up at me.

Damn that sweetness and the ache it sent straight to the heart of me.

"Can't relax when there's still fuckers out there who'd keep you from me," I told her honest.

Her eyes flared. "You want to keep me?"

I rolled my eyes at her and slapped at her sweet behind so she squirmed. "You think I tell every bitch I fuck that I'm 'it' for them? Fuck, takes a helluva a guy to step inside my shoes after I've been there but I don't warn women off of it."

Lou planted her boney little elbows in my chest so she could prop her face in her hands and glare down at me. "Sorry, I think I lost your point when you implied you've slept with and ruined dozens of women."

"Little girl, I've fucked and ruined hundreds of 'em."

Her beautiful face collapsed into shock and then she surprised me by laughing loudly, leanin' down to do it right in my face. When she recovered, she fell against me to give me a full body hug and say into my chest, "Good thing for me, then, that you want to keep me and not them."

I grinned into her hair and hugged her back, almost wrapping her up twice over in my arms. "Good thing."

"I woulda made you keep me, you know?" she told me, tippin' her head back so she could look up at me.

I propped my hand behind my head and snorted, "Figured as much. I like to fool myself into thinkin' I make my own decisions so I had to sort it out quick, I wanted to keep ya."

She giggled and closed her eyes, sighing until she was melted against me.

"So happy," she muttered. "Never been happier and doubt I ever could be."

I thought about all the things she had left to look forward to in life—graduation, marriage, travels, kids—and I thought about all the things I was lookin' forward to givin' her—celebration parties, my ring, vacations, baby Garros—and I knew she was wrong.

"Gotta lot more of life to live, kid."

This time she sighed, it was a sad thing. "I like to live a day at a time, Z."

Kicked me in the face to hear her say that but I got it. You don't live through cancer to take life for granted and I was fuckin' proud of her for decidin' no matter what to live it to the fullest.

"I can do that," I told her even though I was already thinkin' and plannin'.

I mighta been a biker but I'd been a planner, a smarter guy than anyone ever gave me credit for 'cause of my bike, my tats, my size and my cut. I'd always known what I wanted and got it, even if I got some surprises along the way.

And I wanted Lou. So, I knew I'd get her and tie her to me in all the ways normal society and biker society would allow.

But despite what she said, I knew we had all the time in the world, so I wasn't in any fuckin' rush. I could enjoy lyin' on the floor of my cabin holdin' my girl and do it knowin' I'd have a lifetime with her.

CHAPTER TWENTY-THREE

Loulou

I WAS TOO HOT.

It confused me in my state of half slumber. I was never too warm. The cancer sometimes gave me hot flashes but mostly, I was always cold. It almost scared me the most—the coldness—because it made me think I was already halfway dead, stiff and frozen but clinging to life.

So, the heat pressed heavy and close around me confused me enough that I opened my eyes.

I saw tattoos.

A long quilted expanse of heavily muscled back covered edge to edge in beautifully detailed body art. In the center was The Fallen emblem, the large demon skull with *The Fallen MC* arched above it and *Entrance, B.C.* bracketing it below.

Then the wings.

They started at the edges of the skull but flowed over his shoulder blades and around his tree trunk thick arms. I touched a finger to the perfectly rendered feathers like I had when I was a little girl, filled with the same awe that I had a real-life angel under my hands.

His skin was smooth under the black ink but riddled with small and large scars, the ragged scar from where the bullet we'd shared had passed clean through him and into me, a longer, thin white scar that crossed diagonally from right hip to mid-back that looked like the swipe from a blade and the dozens of little scars breaking up the skin of his knuckles from too many fist fights.

It was a warrior's body and it was tucked all around me protectively, guarding me even in his sleep with his great big back like a chest plate over my torso, his right leg thrown over my lower body and right arm curled around my hips to tuck me even closer.

No wonder I was hot. The man was a fucking furnace.

I loved it.

In fact, I loved every single thing about the past ten hours with Zeus. From seeing him leaning up against his big black bike with a curl of smoke drifting into the air around his handsome, rugged face, to the way he'd taken me in the kitchen as if he'd *die* if he didn't have his hands on me in the very next second. Even the pain, I'd loved. Loved knowing that I was suffering through it to accept him because I knew the best things were always hard to come by and I loved working for it, for him and his monster cock. Finally, I loved the intensity of his need and the totality of his care. He treated me roughly, bending my bendable body just to see how it could form new positions for him to fuck and do it hard, but outside of the sexual, he treated me like gold. Not glass, not like something fragile and overly precious, something to be looked after out of necessity. No, something made of gold; priceless, worthy, but difficult to destroy. He wanted to defile me and defend me in equal terms, a dirty knight in his leather armor.

I'd never experienced anything transcending. My grandfather had always told me that being cured from cancer when I was a little girl was a miracle, that God had heard everyone's prayers and that I had been saved by the grace of heaven.

I'd never felt that, especially not after being diagnosed a second time.

But I did feel the grace of God last night, a different kind of god, one made of thunder and motor oil and wicked deeds, held together by leather and ink.

It was that kind of god I had transferred my religion to the night before.

I'd always believed that Christianity wasn't for everyone, that faith was a special and intimate kind of thing that had to occur to you naturally, and express itself through you organically.

Now I knew what deity I'd pray to and die trying to please.

Zeus Garro.

I felt settled in a way that I'd never experienced before, like the last piece of me had aligned and I was finally whole with myself.

I felt calm and sure, so wise I could burst with it.

I knew the feeling would pass because I was seventeen and I may have been through some things but I was no Yoda, but that feeling of completeness would remain as long as I could be with Zeus.

"No thinkin'," Zeus growled in such a low, barely decipherable meter that I laughed.

He pried an eyelid open to reveal his silver-as-star-shine eye. "Was fuckin' serious."

"I know." I pressed a kiss to his beard and then rubbed my fingers in it just because I could. "But I promise, they're happy thoughts."

He grumbled, dragging me further under his body so that my legs were forced open so his hips could slide through. I wrapped my limbs around him and held him to me.

"Fuckin' better be, I gave you all my best moves last night."

I laughed. "You liar, I know you were gentle with me."

He smiled against my neck as he buried his face in my hair and kissed my pulse. "Gotta break you in slow. Don't want any long-term damage 'cause I plan to have you regular from now on."

"Oh yeah?" I asked on a gasp as he adjusted his hips and the crown of his hard cock slid against my entrance.

I hadn't cleaned up after the last time we fucked last night because I was asleep before my orgasm had even fully faded, so a combination of our cum lubricated his way as Zeus notched his head at my cunt and slid home on a smooth, strong glide.

"Yeah," he rasped as he worked himself slow and lazy in and out of me. "Startin' right fuckin' now."

"Okay," I breathed, clinging to him and wiggling because

my sex ached, but in a way that only the stretch of him inside me could soothe.

He turned my head to take my mouth, plundering it deep and thorough. I loved his tongue in my mouth, how it mimicked his cock in my cunt. When he pulled away from me, I whimpered.

He grinned as he kneeled between my legs, leaned back on his heels so his wet dick was displayed like a trophy in his hand.

"Such a good fuckin' girl takin' all'a this in that tight little cunt," he praised me.

My mouth went dry at the sight of him before me like that.

He was a big man in all other respects, so I should have known he'd be a big man *there*, but the sight of him naked and erect, so thick and so long with a flared head the size of a plum and just as purple made my mouth water and my heart kick with pride knowing I'd had him inside me. I watched him wrap one of his massive hands around the base of his cock and squeeze before pulling forward to the tip in a smooth, tight motion that brought a pearl of liquid to the crown.

My tongue flicked out against my lower lip as I imagined the taste of that pearl. Would it taste just as briny and smooth as one plucked straight from the sea?

I was desperate to roll it over my tongue, to define the taste of him with my lips.

"You want it, come get it," he dared me, eyes bright under his dark scowl.

I loved that he looked terrifying in his arousal, the devil

that would kill you soon as fuck you. It gave an edge to the sex that made me feel wetter, dirtier, even more alive.

I swung around lithely so that I was on my hands and knees facing him.

"Head down, ass up. Wanna see that sweet peach as you suck me off."

God.

No one had ever spoken to me like that. It was almost degrading but instead, so fucking hot because I knew this man admired me, cared for me, would kill anyone who disrespected me. His demands, his crude mouth made arousal pool between my legs and leak down my thighs.

His sharp smile told me he knew his effect on me.

"Do it, little girl."

I groaned, loving the dirtiness. Loving our age difference only like this, between the two of us in bed where he was the big, bad experienced man and I was his eager little girl, so willing to please.

So, please him I fucking well would.

I dipped my head to lick that pearly drop of precum from his tip and moaned at the sensational taste of him.

"Better than a cherry lollipop," I told him, looking up at him with my mouth hovering over his dick.

His hands lashed out to tangle in my hair. "Let's see if you can fit it all in your mouth like you can one'a those suckers."

I knew how to give head. It wasn't a skill I was going to tell Zeus how or when or with whom I'd acquired it, but it was definitely one I was going to use on him.

First, I used my tongue on him. Just the wet length of it on the tip of him, dipping into the well of his precum, swirling over the defined head and lashing across the sensitive underside. His strong thighs quivered slightly when I opened wide and sunk my mouth down over as much of him as I could fit in my mouth.

I couldn't take all of him. Nowhere close and I knew it would take practice but for now, I used one hand to jack the base of him and the other to tug lightly at his balls.

When he tipped his head back and groaned long and low, I thanked God for *Cosmo* magazine.

My mouth watered at the taste of him and I loved the sounds I made over his cock as I tried to fit more and more of him in my mouth, down my throat. I was so into it, I knew if I reached down into the puddle between my legs, I'd come just from tapping my clit.

Before I could do so, Zeus had me tumbling backward, sprawled unladylike on the bed. He was on me in a second, his rough hands gripping my ankles and raising them into the air before spreading them wide into a deep split.

"So fuckin' flexible," he groaned as he held me lewdly open for him.

We watched together as he sank his dick deep inside me then slowly took it all the way out again before repeating it over and over. It was slow, deep and so fucking hot my legs shook in his grasp.

"Watch me fuck your cunt," he demanded, his hair a crazy gorgeous mess around his frowning face, his muscled chest gleaming with sweat.

I tried to strain against him, get him to fuck me harder but he held me still and instead of moving faster, he ended each stroke on a grinding motion that rubbed his rough pubic hair against my sensitive clit.

"That's it, little girl. Come for Daddy," he growled.

Immediately, I was gone. The bottom fell out of my mind and I went free-falling into hot, sparkling oblivion. Vaguely, I was aware that I was sobbing with pleasure and Zeus had closed my legs together to create a tighter vice around his now-pounding cock.

I came to slightly just in time to see him come.

His bronze skin shone in the morning light, highlighting the contorted plane of his forehead, contrasting the deep red of his mouth as it opened to let loose a low roar of completion as he shot off warm and deep inside my still grasping cunt.

He dropped to his forearms on either side of me, his face achingly handsome as he smiled lazily at me. He dropped a kiss to my breastbone then ran his fingers lightly across my forehead and into my hair as he stared down at me.

"Mornin', little warrior."

My heart stopped, tried to restart and failed. I took a deep painful breath before it kicked back into gear.

"Morning, monster," I said, smiling back at him.

"Pickin' you up tonight again. Don't care what time it's gotta be, want you in my bed tonight."

Warmth flooded me. "Yeah, okay. Will we come here again?"

He rubbed at his mouth like I'd noticed he did when he was worried about something. "Yeah, gotta get you introduced proper to my other girl before I take you home to her."

"Oh, God. I totally forgot about Harleigh Rose," I told him, my eyes bugging out of my head. "*God*, how the hell are you going to tell her you're banging a girl her age?"

He scowled. "First off, I'm not bangin' you. I'm fuckin' you regular and I plan to do it for a long fuckin' time to come. I also plan to take you out for sustenance between fucks and teach you to party like I said I would 'fore we fucked 'cause I'm a man of my word. I know it's gonna be fuckin' complicated but I was serious last night, Lou. You're my woman now. Maybe you don't understand that."

"Maybe I don't," I agreed, too afraid to hope or guess at what being an MC biker's woman could mean.

"You'll be my old lady. You'll stand by my side at club parties, at functions. You'll sleep in my bed as much as possible until I can get it so you do that every damn night. You'll meet my kids and suffer through that drama with me 'cause they're my life and so're you. You'll take my cock whenever I want to give it to you and you'll take my words whenever I need to give 'em to you. And when I'm an asshole, 'cause I'm a man and I got that in me to give, you'll give me a piece of your mind and then forgive me."

"So we're, like, dating?" God, I sounded like a kid but I didn't know enough biker speak to translate what he was saying into English I could digest. And this was too important to misunderstand.

His full lips twitched and he bit on the bottom one to keep himself from laughing. "Sure, kid, we're datin'."

"Don't be an asshole, Z. This is important!"

"Not bein' an asshole, Loulou, just enjoyin' the fuck outta you, outta this. Figure I'll be laughin' and smilin' a whole helluva lot more from now on."

"Wow," I whispered as I hit the wall of his sincerity and had the indignation knocked right out of me. "Sometimes you're so sweet, I forget you're a monster."

His grin turned dangerous. "Don't got time to remind you just now how dangerous I am, and you're probably sore as shit, but think I can work somethin' out for tonight."

"I'm your girlfriend," I told him, awed and unable to move on from it just yet.

This was my childhood dream come true after all, so I cut myself some slack.

"Old lady," he corrected.

I wrinkled my nose. "I think between the two of us, you're the old one, Z."

He laughed loudly. "Fuck if that ain't true. It's what we call the women we got that we don't plan to share or drop, ever. It's good, yeah?"

"Okay," I agreed. "I've got a lot to learn about biker culture."

"We'll get started on your lessons tonight. Wanna tell my kids sooner rather than later 'bout you so let's get you up to speed quick."

"Scared shitless about that," I admitted.

"That makes two of us," he said but he was grinning and doing it so wide, the beauty of it took my breath away. "Now, gotta get you to school, gotta get myself to the Compound and gotta do it quick 'cause we slept late. You need me to forge a note or somethin' so you don't get in trouble at school?"

I laughed. "No, thanks, *Dad*. I won't get in trouble."

I wouldn't because Headmaster Adams was a dear family friend but also because the faculty was used to my lateness and absences. They all knew I had cancer.

My lover though, did not.

"Watch that mouth, little girl, or I'll put it to better use, yeah?" He glowered at me but his grey eyes were bright with warmth.

I rolled my eyes at him. "Whatever."

"Whatever, she says," he muttered, shaking his head. "You a teenage girl or the woman who's all woman I took to my bed last night twice and again this mornin'?"

"Both, and you love it, you dirty old man," I said as I leaned up to nip him on the chin. "Now get off me so I can have a shower and get ready for school."

He rolled off me but stayed in bed, propped up against the headboard with his bulging arms behind his head, the sheet pooled in his lap. I stopped for a minute to stare at the beauty of him like that, covered in my blood, sweat and cum and never more gorgeous.

"Thought you were in a rush."

"The day I can't take a minute to appreciate something of beauty is the day I don't want to be alive," I told him primly before turning on my heel and skipping into the bathroom.

His laughter followed me.

CHAPTER TWENTY-FOUR

Loulou

THE AIR SMELLED LIKE SWEAT AND POPCORN, SWEET AND SALTY on my tongue as I set my voice to the chant rising over the crowd.

Griffins, Griffins, Griffins!

It was the Winter Hoops tournament; the biggest sporting event at EBA and one of the biggest in the entire province so everyone and I mean everyone was there, even my absentee parents who held court in their own private section of the stands, and my so-called boyfriend, who was the star of the show.

I shook my pom-poms along with the rest of the squad when Reece knifed into the air to intercept the opposing team's pass and sprinted down the court, the orange ball a blur of movement under his palm. When he reared up to slam-dunk in a version of athletic poetry that took my breath away with only three seconds left on the clock before half-time, the crowd erupted into ear-splitting wails and cheers of *Reece, Reece, Reece!*

We sports fans weren't a creative bunch, but we had enthusiasm.

Reece clapped hands and backs with his teammates then turned toward the stands and I knew he was coming for me.

My palms sweat against my pompoms.

It had been a week since I'd lost my cherry to the Prez of The Fallen MC.

A week of spending each night with him in his bed in a cabin he built with his own bare hands. When he'd told me that, I'd made him take off his shirt in the cold late November air and chop wood for me. I'd goaded him into it by saying I didn't believe he'd do such a menial task himself, but really, what girl didn't want to see her man sweaty and bare-chested chopping wood?

The cabin was more than that though. It was a chapter in the life of Zeus that I'd never known about, one that my little girl self wouldn't have understood no matter how precocious I'd been.

It seemed my man had shit parents. Not shit like Benjamin and Phillipa with their neglect and superficiality. Shit parents like a dad who drank himself silly, couldn't hold down a job and stole money from his mother who, on her bad days, beat her own son because she was so far past the end of her rope.

The fact that someone had beat on little boy Z made my gut churn like a violent sea and if he hadn't assured me that they were already dead, I would have used my newly acquired gun skills to hunt them down and use them for target practice.

His uncle Crux had takin' him in as much as a terminal bachelor VP of an outlaw motorcycle club could take a kid in. Crux, it turns out, was Eugene's dad, which explained the similarity in size and gruff handsomeness between Zeus and the bar owner. When Zeus was old enough to move out of his parents' house, Crux had given him the supplies and told a teenage Zeus Garro that the only way to make something out of yourself was to do it with your own bare hands.

So, Zeus had built himself a house and then he'd prospected The Fallen MC just like his uncle.

No one but Eugene and Zeus knew about the little cabin, so even though it was rustic in the extreme, three rooms with a bathroom that was seriously lacking in amenities, I loved spending my nights there.

But between spending late nights and early mornings with Zeus at the cabin, my last week of ballet classes before I'd have to stop for chemo, hanging out with Sammy and Mute, and studying for end of term finals, I hadn't had time to see Reece.

Which meant that I'd been an ex-virgin for a week and my boyfriend still didn't know it.

"Fucking epic, right?" he asked me with a wide, boyish grin as he scooped me into his arms and pressed a self-congratulatory kiss on my lips.

"Epic," I breathed, because through my guilt I also felt something dangerous hit my radar.

Surreptitiously, I looked around the crowded gym over my shoulder as shivers chased themselves across my skin.

"Babe, be ready for a wild after-party when I bring this

home for the team," Reece panted in my ear before squeezing my hip and taking off after his team into the change rooms for a team chat.

I watched him go but that feeling of wrongness remained and before Cassidy, my cheer captain, could rally us for the halftime show, I ducked away into the crowds of people going to the washroom and concession.

I scanned the bleachers, trying to discern a face amid the sea of green and yellow colours supporting EBA and the red and white on Entrance Public High School's side but nothing jumped out at me.

What I did notice was Mr. Warren.

He was partially concealed by the side of the stands, but I recognized him because he was the only man I knew who wore bow ties. I moved closer, rounding the corner of the benches just enough to see him talking to Talia McCutcheon, his teacher's assistant from last year who went to the local college now, and Lily Foster, the girl in the year below me that had shown up just as I was leaving his classroom last week.

Curiosity burned through me even as the saying *curiosity killed the cat* reverberated in my head.

Still, I stalked closer.

It was too loud in the echo filled gymnasium to hear what the three of them were saying but both girls were curved on either side of Mr. Warren like brackets, listening quietly and so attentive.

I didn't have the first clue what they could all be talking about.

Mr. Warren reached out to take Talia's hands in his, pulling her close so that her body obscured my view. After a few seconds, she moved away with a deep blush on her pretty face and quickly fiddled with her purse before ducking her head and taking off into the crowd.

Lily lingered, looking pale and terrifyingly excited. Mr. Warren took his time with her, drawing her closer and closer until he was curled around her but not touching. She had her lime green backpack close to her chest like she didn't want him to get closer and I was *this close* to interfering when she took off into the crowd.

Mr. Warren stood there for a minute, little smile of satisfaction on his face, his hands in his pockets and his weight on his heels. He looked like a man about to declare checkmate on his opponent and it sent a ripple of alarm down my spine.

I wondered if that was the man who had me seeing warning flares everywhere I turned.

Then I felt a hand on my arm and knew before the rough, wide fingers had even closed around me that the real danger had arrived.

Without turning me to face him, Zeus led me with a hand at my back and the other on my arm deep into the shadows Mr. Warren had just absented. Instead of stopping there though, he pushed me deeper, into the small gap between the metal siding of the bleachers and the wall of the gym. We entered the dark space and the noises of the court immediately receded.

Zeus had me flipped around and pressed against a pole before my eyes could adjust to the dark.

"You still seein' that motherfucker?" he asked me in a voice that was lower than a rumble and so controlled, I knew I was in trouble.

"Erm, technically, I don't know if we were ever dating in the first place," I tried to explain. "The logistics of modern dating are kind of complicated."

"You fuckin' with me, little girl? You playin' with a grown man for sport to learn a few things 'fore you go back to limp-ass teenage dick?"

"Zeus," I called to him through the fury and pressed a hand against his AC/DC tee-covered chest, right where I knew his scar would be. "I didn't break up with him because every spare moment this week I've spent with *you* and when I wasn't with you, I was so busy getting everything done so that I *could* be with you that I did not have time to see him. Chill, Z."

His body turned to stone beneath my hand. "You think a man sees his woman kissin' another man, he needs to chill? I'll remember that next time I got bitches hittin' on me at the clubhouse, yeah?"

"Okay, that's fair," I admitted, because the idea of any of those women touching Zeus made me manic with violence.

"You're damn right it is. Come to see my girls cheer and instead, I see H.R. wearin' her uniform but suckin' face with her trash boyfriend behind the gym. Then I come in 'ere thinking, at least my good girl will cheer me up, wearin' that pretty little outfit, and doin' the splits in a way that'll remind me how I had 'er doin' them naked around my cock just this mornin', and instead I see her suckin' face with another trash boyfriend. You see the fuckin' theme here?"

"I see it, definitely," I agreed solemnly but then pressed up on my tiptoes to take his chin between my teeth in a gentle nip. "I'm sorry."

He stared hard at me for a minute and then nodded.

"Right. Turn around, bend over and hold on to your fuckin' ankles."

I blinked at him because even though my body was already growing wet, my brain took longer to understand. "Excuse me?"

He leaned into me with a soft sneer and said, "Bend over and hold on to your fuckin' ankles. I'm gonna fuck you in this cheerleader getup like I planned to do later tonight, only I'm gonna do it here so when you go back out and break up with that kid, you'll have my cum inside you."

A shiver ripped through my body so hard it unbalanced. God, he was almost too hot to handle.

Good thing I was always up for a challenge.

I glared at him even as I spun away and reached down easily to grab my ankles over my frilly edge white socks. Immediately, his hand was on my ass, kneading it under his callused fingers, palming the whole cheek as easily as a basketball. I was wearing full-bottom cheerleading panties, too thick to rip off easily, so instead he shucked them off me and the fabric disappeared into his pocket. Then he flipped my skirt up and ran his thumbs down the seam of my ass, spreading me open so he could see all the way from my asshole to the slippery slit of my sex.

He cupped the entirety of me in his big palm. "This is mine now. My cunt to eat, fuck and play with. Mine to take whenever I want."

"Yes," I hissed as two of his fingers slid inside me and hooked against my walls, curling and rubbing slow but hard in a way that had my legs shaking.

"This is for me, little girl. I'm fuckin' you as a reminder and I don't want you gettin' off on it. You hear me?"

Oh God, I barely could through the roar of blood in my ears. I could vaguely make out the dance music as my fellow cheerleaders flexed their bodies for the halftime show. I loved the contrast, loved knowing that I was flexing my body, holding it open in a private halftime show for only one man.

A sharp *crack* rent the air a second before pain radiated through my ass.

"Lou," he growled. "No comin', you understand?"

His fingers played in the shallows of my wet pussy, dipping one inside then two and three, but never deep like I wanted. I was squirming from foot to foot, my face hot from shame and arousal.

"Yes," I croaked because I knew he wouldn't fuck me until I agreed and I needed him inside.

I listened to the soft clack of his belt unfastening and the metallic gasp of his zipper. As soon as his hands returned to my hips, I was thrusting back against him.

"So eager for my cock," he growled before slamming balls-deep inside me.

I cried out, my shout merging with the cheers of the crowd as the teams returned to the court to warm up for the second half. My pussy convulsed around him, struggling and failing to accommodate his girth without pain. I loved the harsh bite of hurt, the way the head of his cock knocked against my cervix. He dragged himself slowly out of my tight pussy, even tighter because I was folded in half, and then gripped my hips hard as he slammed back into me.

A whimper escaped me as I struggled to hold on to my ankles, as I struggled not to come.

"Let me hear you, Lou. Maybe someone above us will notice you moanin' and beggin' for me to fuck you. Maybe they'll get excited and come down here to try and find the source of those sexy-as-fuck moans. Maybe they'll catch you bent double, takin' my cock in your sweet teen pussy."

"Fuck," I cursed as his next thrust jolted me forward.

"My good girl is so fuckin' dirty. Gettin' off on the idea of being found out," Zeus continued to taunt me with his rough voice, the sound of it like an extra pair of hands stroking all over my burning flesh.

I groaned loudly for him as he drilled me harder and harder, the loud slap of our skin and the heavy sound of my breath the only clear sounds in the muffled, dark space under the bleachers.

I jolted like I'd been electrocuted when one of Zeus's thumbs slid into the crease of my ass and swirled my wetness around the pleated entrance of my asshole. Pleasure spiraled tight in my lower belly, drawing all my muscles up like a powerful magnet so that I felt my center of gravity in my cunt, my body drawn tight all around it

"Zeus, I, please, *fuck*," I muttered.

"Wanna come?" he grunted, his thumb pushing hard at my asshole so it popped just inside and burned. "Does my dirty cheerleader wanna come all over my cock?"

"Fuck, yes, you fuckin bastard," I cursed him through gritted teeth, then let go of my ankles, placed my hands flat on the floor and spread my legs even wider so he could fuck me harder and I could—finally—fuck back.

His chuckle was a deep, dark thing, wicked and prideful. "I let you come, Lou, you go out there and don't leave this gym without finishin' things with that fuck."

"Yes, yes, okay. Just please," I whimpered as the thumb in my ass rotated and he lowered his stance slightly so he could fuck up into me at an angle that had his cock raking against that sensitive spot inside me. "Please, you fuck, let me come."

He laughed again, carted me up so I was only balanced on the floor by the tips of my toes and the arm now banded around my waist, and he said, "Come, then, Lou."

I did, exploding at the joints and seams of my body so that I felt pleasure even from the roots of my hair to the tips of my toes. I came so long I could feel my body unraveling like a ball of yarn, loosening from that tension of preclimax to the loosening of ecstasy. My breathy gasps and curses disappeared under the crushing sound of the supporters in the stands coming to their feet and cheering as the buzzer sounded for the second half of the game to begin.

Zeus finished silently, the kick of his cock in my cunt and the tightening of his hands on my hips the only indication of his release.

I preferred it when he roared.

He stroked his thumbs up the inside crease of my ass then palmed each cheek and gave them a rough squeeze. "Love this ass."

"I've noticed." I tried to stand up and felt the blood rush painfully to my head.

Zeus caught me in his arms before I could lose my balance and fall over but it took me a second to reorient myself against his chest before I could look up at him with a smile.

He was frowning. "You okay?"

"Well, my man just thoroughly fucked me to make a point so I'd say I'm fan-fucking-tastic," I said with an enormous grin.

He stared at me for a moment before he was satisfied

then hauled me up tight against his barrel chest and said, "Come 'ere."

"I'm here," I told him the obvious, but I pressed my curves even tighter against his hard planes and put a hand in his hair, the other on the steep ledge of his bearded jaw.

"Yeah, but haven't kissed my girl yet today. Want you to wear my kiss on your lips so even though I can't have you by my side like I want, every time I look over at ya in your sweet cheerleader skirt shakin' those pom-poms, I'll know it was me who put the red on your mouth."

I swallowed the lump in my throat. "So kiss me, then."

He did.

His mouth closed over mine like the gateway to hell, flooding me with flames and smoke, incinerating my insides until everything but my heart crumbled to ash and all I had left was a pulse that beat just for him.

When he was done—and he took his time—my legs were boneless and the inside of my mouth felt seared with the taste and feel of him.

He dropped me down to the ground so my breasts slid against his hard chest and made me shiver. Then with a face more tender than I'd ever seen and strangely handsome on such stern, rugged features, he dipped down to run a ringed finger over my swollen mouth.

"Prettiest mouth I ever saw but even prettier marked from my kiss."

I clutched at his forearms and blinked up at him, dazzled by the reality that the six-foot-five god of a man was just as dazzled by *me*.

I startled out of my dreaminess when one of his hands

glided up my inner thigh and dabbled in the wet mess between my thighs, smearing his cum across my entire sex.

"My cheerleader filled with cum and swollen from my kisses," Zeus rumbled with male satisfaction.

I hit his chest. "You are such a caveman."

His hand came out from under my skirt and he brought his wet thumb to his mouth to suck off our juices. "Not a caveman, little girl. A biker, and lucky for you too, 'cause another kind of man wouldn'ta just fucked a teenage girl at her high school basketball game and made 'er fuckin' day."

I rolled my eyes as I tagged my panties from his pocket and stepped into them. "Oh, yeah, lucky me. Every little girl grows up dreaming about their very own biker, not Prince Charming or a CEO."

"You did."

I landed against the wall of his chest with a thump as he pulled me off-balance and glared up at him to find the creases I loved beside his smiling eyes. I ran a finger lightly over the tanned fan of wrinkles and said softly, "I did."

"Now go out there do your pom-pom thing then break up with the douchebag. I'll pick you up tonight from ballet at seven, yeah?"

"Bossy." I shook my head at him, but my heart wasn't in it. "But fine."

He nodded, tucked himself back in his pants and buckled up then grabbed my hand to lead me back out the slim divide under the bleachers and into the light.

I blinked rapidly a few times to adjust to the bright yellow light of the gym so it took me a minute to notice Mute standing sentry just to the side of the bleachers, his thick arms crossed over his thick chest and his face as inscrutable as those soldiers outside Buckingham Palace.

I blushed fiercely and kicked Zeus's foot as I hissed, "Z, you couldn't have warned me that fucking Mute was, like, aware of what we were doing down there?"

He looked over his shoulder at me and laughed. "Think Mute knows about what happens between a girl looks like you and a man acts like me, Lou."

I turned to Mute to say, "Sorry, Mute."

His flat mouth twitched slightly as he shot me a sidelong look. "'S cool."

Zeus pinched my ass to draw my attention to him and said, "Later, little girl. Remember why I let you come. Make sure you do it 'fore you leave here today."

Mute cleared his throat to hide his laughter.

I glared at Z, flipped him the bird and slipped back into a line of people walking into the stands so I could rejoin my cheerleading squad. When one of the girls asked me where I'd gone, I'd told them I was feeling dizzy and needed a moment (which after that orgasm Zeus gave me, *I did*) and when one of my old angel friends told me she *loved* the shade of my new lipstick, I told her it was called Monster Red.

CHAPTER TWENTY-FIVE

Zeus

"So, who's the girl?"

I was sittin' in the stands pretendin' to watch my daughter sulk in her cheerleadin' uniform on the other side of the court, her pom-poms held in her hands like they were deadweights. She was so unimpressed with bein' at the game but she needed extracurricular credits to graduate and it'd been too late to sign up for anything else so cheerleadin' it was. She'd been *pissed*. She was a smart kid, but she wasn't like her brother, King. She didn't go in for books and the normal high school experience. Nah, my girl was too much like her fuckin' mother. She liked to drink beer with men who were too old for her, make bad decisions like it was a class she was acin' at school and disobey me at every turn.

Loved the kid, loved her more than my next fuckin' breath, but she was a Grade-A pain in my fuckin' ass.

Still, I was there to support 'er because that's what Garros and The Fallen did. We went to the important things and the unimportant things because at the end of the day, the only thing you had supportin' ya was your family and I wanted H.R. to know we had her back even when she didn't like what she was doin'.

My boy, King, and his woman, Cressida, were with me too. I'd called King back home for Thanksgiving a few weeks before to brief him on the fuckin' Nightstalkers but now both of 'em were on break studyin' for university exams and they were doin' it from Entrance. It was cool as shit that my son was the first Garro to go to university and I was proud as fuck about it but it was good to have him home. He occupied a weird space between prospectin' the club and bein' raised by it to be the next Prez, and things didn't feel wholly right to me when he wasn't a part of things.

And things were goin' down.

So, King and Cress were back even though they'd left Entrance in a cloud of scandal, they were both back at their old stompin' grounds supporting Harleigh Rose.

Loved 'em for it.

See, Cress had been my kid's English and History teacher last year and they'd fallen into it together. It was complicated, as any story involvin' a smart, mouthy woman was gonna be, but they'd ended it good and in love. Even now, King had her scarred hands in his, rubbin' at the marks in her palms absently like he still wished he coulda changed the fact she got 'em in the first place.

So did I.

The Nightstalkers had gone after family before and it'd resulted in Cress bein' nailed to a chair with spikes through her hands. I'd killed the motherfucker in charge of the Nightstalkers that night, stabbed him clean through the back of his fuckin' skull. But like I'd said before, you cut off one head and three more grow back.

I was just glad as fuck that Cress was with us today, sittin' between me and her man in ripped jeans and her signature bookish tee under a leather jacket as though she'd been born an' raised as a biker babe.

"Zeus?" she asked, bringin' me back to the moment. "I asked you a question."

"You know Dad doesn't date, Cress babe," King said on a laugh, slingin' an arm over her and pullin' her even closer so she was half in his lap.

People around us watched, drawn to the leather and the confidence, the prettiness of our Cress and the fierceness of the men beside her.

People always watched and what they coveted but didn't have the fuckin' guts to take for themselves, they hated.

So, the three of us, we were good, used to the looks and not carin'.

"Man's got a point," I said, tippin' my chin at my boy. "Don't date."

Cress peered at me suspiciously. "You disappeared for fifteen minutes at halftime and I know it didn't take you *that* much time to threaten H.R.'s dumbass boyfriend, Cricket, to get the freak out of here."

King rolled his eyes. "Babe, seriously, you *need* to start cursin' like an adult."

She stuck her tongue out at him and then faced me

again. "Please tell me you aren't taking a walk on the Norman Rockwell side and banging a housewife?"

I laughed and hard 'cause that shit was so funny, I couldn't even wrap my mind around it. When I was done, I rubbed my smile outta my beard and tried to take her question seriously. "Nah, teach, I'm not bangin' a housewife."

She relaxed. "Good, because seriously, I know these Entrance mums and I've heard them talk about 'taming the bull' and having a round with you. Women like that don't know the first thing about handling a man like you, Zeus Garro, and you should know better than to get involved with them."

I looked at King. "Did the woman just give me a lecture even though I didn't do what she fuckin' thought I did?"

"It was a preemptive strike," she explained like the prim and proper little teacher she'd been. "And I'm not a teacher anymore, so don't call me 'teach'."

"She did," King confirmed, ignorin' her. "She does that."

"Don't know how you put up with it," I told 'im, purposely ignorin' the irritation makin' Cress bristle. I liked buggin' the fuck outta her, she was cute like a little yappy dog when she was mad. "Knew I raised a strong man, didn't know I'd raised a saint."

King laughed, throwin' his head back just like his sister and I did when we laughed. He was blond like his mum, skinnier than me but fillin' out now he was nearly twenty, and other than the colour of my eyes, he didn't look a thing like me. But fuck he was so much my son it slapped me in the face sometimes. Like me but, thank fuck, better.

"Oh shut up, both of you," Cress snapped but there was no real heat in it. "Zeus you're trying to distract me from the topic at hand and I will not be deterred. Something's different about you."

Fuck if that wasn't true. I was sittin' there in my cut, my normal scowl on my face to intimidate the dads and brothers in the stands and turn on the repressed mothers and curious little girls, and I was doin' it leanin' forward with my forearms on my knees so that the rows of people behind me could clearly see the cut I wore, The Fallen symbol on the back. I wasn't smilin', doin' a fuckin' jig or singin' some pop song about it bein' a beautiful fuckin' day.

Yet somehow even I knew I looked different. There was something wrong with the air around me, like a near invisible shroud of misery had been lifted and people could see me clearer. Hell, even I could see me clearer.

I was fuckin' *happy*, and after years of gettin' by on rations of happy moments stolen from seein' my kids grow good and strong, memories my brothers gave me ridin' behind me in formation down the hot roads of the province and the brief flares of pleasure to be had from fuckin' random pussy, this kinda happiness *rocked* me.

Yeah, I was different and Cress was too smart not to see it.

There was no reason to lie to her. She'd meet Lou sooner rather than later 'cause I planned to bring my girl over for Sunday dinner to "meet the family".

But I was a selfish man and I wanted just one more night with my teenage woman as my dirty secret.

"Mute, brother." King stood up with a loud cry to greet his best friend with a backslappin' hug. Mute didn't like to be touched but he was used to King, loved 'im more than anyone else in the fuckin' world, and he embraced him back like they'd been parted for years insteada weeks.

When they broke apart, they were both smilin'.

"You been here this whole time? Why aren't you sittin' with us?" King asked, wavin' a hand at the man sittin' beside him to make room for Mute.

The man blinked at my son, looked to me and the entire size of me, then forcefully shoved into the person on his other side to make room. I grinned at him manically and watched him swallow.

Laughin' under my breath, I caught the end of Mute sayin', "Got a job to do."

Fuck.

I stiffened before I could tell myself to stay cool. Cress was a fuckin' hawk when it came to sniffin' out secrets and I had a feelin' mine was about to be blown to fuckin' bits.

King was frownin'. "A job? At a fuckin' high school basketball game?" He laughed, lookin' at me as he did it to confirm that Mute was bein' ridiculous.

Mute was never ridiculous and, un-fuckin'-fortunately, he never lied.

"Gotta keep an eye on Foxy," he said, lookin' over at his charge as she did a fuckin' backflip on the opposite side of the gym.

"Foxy?" King and Cress both said at the same time.

It woulda been funny if I was in the mood to find the situation funny.

I closed my eyes and pressed my palms to 'em 'cause I knew what was comin'.

"Louise Lafayette," Mute explained, pointing at her. "The one with gold hair and gold skin and blue eyes like Barbie."

God, the kid never talked and now he was fuckin' Shakespeare.

I opened my eyes and peered between my fingers to see Cress lookin' at me like a fuckin' pedophile and King's mouth wide open enough to swallow a Quarter Pounder without chewin'.

I sighed, dropped my hands and shot Mute a look. "You do that on purpose or is this one of those things you can't help doin'?"

Mute blinked at me.

No fuckin' help there, then.

"Zeus, please do not tell me you're sleeping with Louise Lafayette," Cressida breathed. "She's a *kid*!"

"Cress babe," King muttered, sittin' down beside her in a —useless—effort to control his woman. "Think 'fore you speak."

"She a kid like King was a kid when you two started fuckin'?" I asked blandly, adjustin' one of the skull rings on my finger where it'd gone crooked from finger-fuckin' Lou twenty minutes before.

I brought my fingers to my nose and caught the salted caramel scent of her. Tried to focus on that insteada bein' annoyed with Cress.

"That was—" Cress opened and closed her mouth. "That was different and you *know* it!"

"You know shit about it bein' different," I told 'er. "Careful here, Cress."

"Queenie," King said, firm. "Let Dad explain."

She rolled her lips under for a second, tryin' to reign in her sass.

No surprise, she failed.

"No, seriously, what the hell, Zeus? Louise is the seventeen-year-old daughter of the mayor! A man, I don't have to remind you, who just last year held a freaking town meeting in an attempt to run The Fallen MC and, more specifically *you*, out of this town."

"Memory works fine," I told her between my teeth.

Didn't want to scare her, didn't want to 'cause even more of a scene than we were already makin'. Lou needed to finish high school 'fore we went public in her mainstream society. We didn't need my son's woman outing us in the middle of a fuckin' high school basketball game.

"I'm trying really hard not to say something I can't take back, but Zeus, help me understand how this isn't wrong?" she begged me, her eyes wild with caged accusations.

She'd been raised by parents so stuck in the mud, they were permanently rooted in it and their stifled, judgmental ways. I knew it, I'd witnessed it and defended her from it then watched her grow away from bein' that herself, so told myself to calm down even as the anger rolled through me like thunder lookin' for a place to land.

I leaned toward her, closer than was necessary but I needed the threat to be real for her and I didn't want to use my hands.

"Listen here, *teach*. I met you, you were a repressed sad little woman livin' a life you hated and the only thing you wanted, the only thing that could take you outta that, was my boy. Why do you think I gave you the go-ahead to fuck your student, to stand beside my son? 'Cause I'm a rebel and I didn't give a fuck either way. How 'bout *fuck* no? How 'bout I knew what it was like to want someone younger, to want someone so fuckin' forbidden it made you dark and corrupt even to think'a having 'em? I know love when I see it and you think I got that from bein' with my fuckin' ex-wife? No fuckin' way. I know that shit 'cause I helped raise a little girl with the soul of a fuckin' angel and when she turned into a woman and *still* somehow had that fuckin' soul after everythin' she'd been through and I got the chance to hold that kinda woman in my arms, you think I was nuts enough not to take it?"

Cress blinked at me.

King did too, his face slack and younger lookin' than I'd seen it in a long time.

Mute looked satisfied, his arms crossed over his chest and a hint of a fuckin' smile round his mouth.

Yeah, the bastard had done it on fuckin' purpose.

"Sometimes, Cress, you're even younger than my son," I told her with a disappointed frown.

She gasped slightly and leaned back into King who banded an arm around her hips and dragged her the rest of the way into his lap.

"The letters," King said. "Remember you writin' 'em, even when you got home you'd still write 'em every week. H.R. thought you were workin' or some shit but I knew it was somethin' else. You'd always get angry after writin' 'em, frustrated."

"Always been a smart kid," I told him, leaning forward to punch him lightly on the chin.

"You're in love with Louise Lafayette," Cress said soft and fulla wonder. "Zeus Garro is in love and it's with my heartbreaking and beautiful favourite ex-student, Louise Lafayette."

"Second favourite," King amended.

"She prefers Loulou," I told 'em. "And I'm bringin' her over for Sunday dinner so you two better be fuckin' gems 'cause I still got Harleigh Rose to think 'bout."

The three of us looked over to where my daughter was leanin' against the wall to the exit door of the gym, smokin' a cigarette when she shoulda been cheering. A teacher hurried over and told her to put it out. She did, in the guy's coffee.

"You're fucked," King said.

"Don't I know it," I agreed.

CHAPTER TWENTY-SIX

Loulou

THE GAME WAS OVER AND SO, UNFORTUNATELY AND fortunately, was my relationship with Reece. He'd taken one look at me after the game, at my swollen mouth and remorseful eyes and known.

"Wish I could say you'll regret dumping me, but I have the feeling you won't," he'd said and then because he was one of the best guys I'd ever known, he'd hugged me. "It was a hope and a dream that I could tame a wild one like you."

"You were the one who taught me to be wild." I'd laughed wetly, because for some reason I wanted to cry. It felt like the end of something, like I was shedding the last vestige of Louise. At least, the last part of her life that I actually liked.

Reece's beautiful face screwed up as he tugged on my

ribbon-tied ponytail. "It was always in there, babe. Just needed a little coaxing."

"I'm so sorry," I whispered past the lump in my throat.

He nodded. "Not more than me. Listen, you need anything, I'm here and I won't even ask for a kiss as payment, okay?"

God, he was amazing.

I wondered briefly if he'd ever stood a chance with me, even if Zeus hadn't sucked me into his life and planted me there for good. I looked over at the crowd of people leaving the gym and immediately caught the back of Zeus's dark hair, head and shoulders above the people around him. There was a break in the flood and I caught sight of the wicked skull and flaming wings across his leather jacket and knew without a flicker of a doubt, that I'd never been meant for anything or anyone else.

Reece had read the resolve in my face, squeezed my hand and shook his head ruefully before walking off to join his celebrating teammates.

I'd felt like shit but also strangely relieved. It was one thing crossed off the laundry list of obstacles threatening to take down my man and me.

Speaking of obstacles, my parents took the time to find me after the game and walk me to the car. Phillipa had her arm around my waist, her head bent close as she giggled about the gossip she'd learned that day. It wasn't that she wanted to share it with me particularly, it was that it made her look younger, our blond heads together like sisters instead of mother and daughter. People looked over as we passed and praised my mother for being just that, a mother and a good one at that.

The irony made my teeth ache.

Benjamin had Bea under his arm but they both looked uncomfortable, especially when a local reporter stopped to take a picture of them and ask them some questions. Dad didn't know how to bring Bea into the conversation because he didn't *know* her at all, and Bea didn't know what to do because she rarely had the opportunity to shine alone.

It was vaguely depressing, but I was still riding my orgasm high as we stopped at the curb of the parking lot and stood talking with random family friends like the school was our home and we were thanking people for coming to visit.

In a way, we were.

EBA was my parents', grandparents' and great-grandparents' high school. It was the seat of youth in Entrance and so now, Bea and I went there and with us as a viable connection, my family could rule there too.

It wasn't that I didn't understand the appeal of that power, of having men come up to my father in search of endorsements and political favours, of my mother raising and lowering women in her society with the twitch of an eyelid or the flip of a hand.

It was heady stuff, that kind of power.

But as I understood it, being Queen and King of Entrance was hollow. Mayors were elected out of office, society queens grew elderly, old families moved out of town and new ones moved in.

No, I wanted power but the real kind, the kind that was deeply rooted in fear and reverence, power and genuine cleverness that kept you at the top of the greedy pile of bodies that had tried and failed around you.

Zeus's kind of power.

The kind built on blood, sweat, threats and tears in credence of a lifestyle based on freedom of expression, brotherhood and defiance of the man just because he was the fucking man.

That was real power worthy of sacrificing your kids, their health and dreams for.

I was willing to play the power game, but only if I was doing it by Zeus's side and playing it his way.

I was distracted by my rebellious thoughts when I heard the piercing scream.

One second, I was in the parking lot of EBA about to get into my car and the next second I was on the ground, my face crushed to the rough pavement and my hands and knees scraped up from the fall.

"You slut!" a girl shrieked from where she dug her knees into my back. "You disgusting filthy slut."

Um, okay, *what*?

I tried to wiggle out of her hold but she was strong.

"Who the fuck are you?" I asked even though I had a horrible sinking suspicion.

How many girls would blindside someone with a side tackle in a parking lot and call them a slut for everyone to hear?

A biker's girl, that's who.

"Harleigh?" I asked, straining to turn my head in order to look at her.

It was at least half an hour after the game had finished but these sorts of things were a social occasion in Entrance as much as anything else and people still lingered, mingling. People, including my parents who were frozen in horror at the scandalous sight before them.

"It's Harleigh *Rose*, bitch," she said as she pushed my head back into the ground. "And if you think you can fuck my dad and get him in trouble with the cops or something, you are so fucking wrong."

"Harleigh Rose," I tried again as the asphalt rubbed my cheek raw. "Let me up and let's talk about this somewhere private."

"Fuck private. You want the world to know you're fuckin' my dad so you and your dumbass family can attack The Fallen. Why the fuck else would you disappear under the *fuckin' stands* for everyone to see?" she hissed in my ear, thankfully low enough for only me to hear.

I was officially tired of this. Despite the cancer, I was still strong. A lifetime of ballet dancing gives you the kind of mean strength that's hidden in long, lean muscles. I used it to buck up to my hands and knees then toss Harleigh Rose off me.

Immediately she got back to her feet, her thick blond-streaked brown hair a crazy mess around her sneering face.

"I don't want to fight you, be reasonable here," I told her, holding my hands up in the universal gesture of pacifism.

She spat at me. "Touch him again and I'll do more than fight you. You probably think you're too good for the likes of us but it's the opposite way around."

I shook my head at her and spoke in a low voice because people were converging on us and I knew there were only bad endings in store for Harleigh Rose.

"You don't know what you're talking about and if you'd just give me a second to explain or find Z—" I tried.

And failed, because the next second she was slapping me across the face, one of her rings cutting me across the cheek.

"Don't you dare say his fucking name when you're trying to con him!"

I staggered back, blinking rapidly so I missed the chaos as men erupted out of the gym doors and flooded the scene. I bent over to plant my hands on my knees and blink the tears out of my eyes when two hands lifted me up and spun me around midair so that I was deposited on a broad, hard back.

Mute.

He stood strong with his booted feet spread apart, glaring forward at the scene but keeping me at a distance from it. Officer Lionel Danner, my parents, and Zeus argued with each other while King Kyle Garro held back his struggling sister.

"Mute, put me down, I need to get in there," I told him, trying to wriggle out of his hold.

His hands were iron shackles around the backs of my thighs. "Stay."

I stopped struggling because it was fruitless, my cheek hurt like a motherfucker and I didn't want to miss anything else.

"Your daughter is a menace, Garro," my dad was claiming, his finger pointed like an ineffective weapon at Zeus. "This is what happens when you raise girls in a *gang*."

"Girls get worked up over boys all the time, Mayor. Not sure this is anythin' to write home about," Zeus drawled.

"Danner, aren't you going to arrest this girl?" my dad demanded, turning to Lionel when he failed to rile up Zeus. "She *assaulted* my daughter."

Lionel's usually stern face looked years younger when he fought a smile as he did then. "Mayor, I understand you're angry, but really, I think this was a harmless bit of teenage drama."

"Detention then, at least!" my mother tried, her hands shaking as she pressed one to her heart and one to Bea's shoulder to bring her even closer to her side. "Your daughter needs to understand there are consequences to attacking someone. Maybe in your... home or wherever it is people like you live...you encourage behavior like this but in the *real* world, it's completely unseemly."

I thought it was funny that my parents were so staunchly defending me when they didn't even know I'd been saved and piggybacked by one of the very bikers they hated so much.

I rested my cheek against Mute's shoulder, my chin in his neck. He stiffened for a second then rested his head lightly against mine. My heart melted even in the midst of this chaos.

"H.R., you gonna do somethin' like this ever again or have you learned your lesson?" Zeus called to his daughter, his voice mild like he was bored with the conversation and was only placating my parents.

They noticed and both their jaws went tight with anger.

"I'm on my period," Harleigh Rose admitted with a defeated scowl.

Zeus nodded like that explained everything. "Look there, my girl's on the rag. 'Course she's feeling emotional. I think we all can understand that, can't we, Officer?"

I laughed into Mute's neck.

Officer Lionel looked about ready to laugh himself, but he schooled his face admirably and frowned at Harleigh Rose. "I've picked you up more times than I care to count for minor offenses. Let's not level up to a bodily assault charge, okay?"

To my surprise, H.R. blushed and ducked her head so that a soft curtain of hair partially hid her expression. "Yeah," she muttered petulantly. "Whatever."

"Looks like this thing is all cleared up, then. I'll just be takin' my daughter home and we'll let you folks get on your merry fuckin' way," Zeus said magnanimously, already moving his family to the other side of the parking lot. "Okay, Mute, let Louise go."

I giggled again as I slid from Mute's back and made my way back over to my parents who stared at me in horror.

"Louise," my mother breathed. "Are you... *friends* with one of those men?"

I smiled at her, pulled a highly entertained Bea into my arms and started walking toward the car. "Yes, Mum. Mute's been one of my best friends for ages now."

"Ages?" Phillipa echoed as she followed us to the car, casting a fearful glance over her shoulder at Zeus and King, standing so fierce and proud on the other side of the lot beside their huge motorcycles.

I understood her fear. They were like gargoyles, horrifying at first sight in their ferocity but utterly beautiful up-close, intricate with detail and gruesome because their role as guardians called for them to be so.

I was glad my mother feared them. She had cause to.

Men like that only protected the innocent and the loyal, and my mother was no such thing.

"Yep," I confirmed as I pushed Bea into the car and then opened the door of the Lexus SUV for my mother. "He's been over to the house nearly every day for the past few weeks."

"Oh," she said as I closed the door on her after she'd gotten in.

"Dad," I called to Benjamin who was arguing with poor Officer Danner again. "Come on!"

They ignored me and as I walked closer, I caught sight of the utter disgust on Lionel's face as my father spoke.

"You better get on board with things here, son," my dad was threatening, his habitually immaculate hair gone slightly astray in the ruckus. It was a small thing but it reminded me of my father's fallibility. "Your father is always vouching for you but I'm beginning to doubt your investment in this."

"I'm invested, Ben, and I don't have to answer to you," Lionel said.

"I'm the mayor," my dad said as if that explained just how wrong Lionel was.

"And Javier is the one with the money and the connections. My dad is the one with the intel, Jack and Ace are the ones with the inside track and Mitch is the one with the dealers. That makes us equal."

"Fuck," my dad swore viciously, so unlike him I stayed frozen between two cars, only a meter away from them. He ran a hand through his mussed hair and looked, for a moment, utterly lost. "I don't know how it got to be this way, Danner, I really don't."

Lionel squinted at him. "As a cop you learn pretty quick what motivates people and you know what it is 85% of the time, Ben? Greed. Plain and simple."

"I have money," my dad muttered.

"Vengeance and pride work a close second," Danner retorted. "Garro hurt your daughter, undermines your respect and makes more money than you do each year in around about a month with the operation he's got going. Trust me, Ben, you're chin-deep in shit and it stinks of greed."

With that parting shot, Officer Danner inclined his head and prowled over to his personal vehicle, an old Mustang convertible.

My dad stood there for a second, looking so lost that I almost didn't recognize him. All I knew was that my dad was doing more than his usual bit to incarcerate The Fallen, and in his quest, he might end up precariously close to incarceration himself.

CHAPTER TWENTY-SEVEN

Zeus

I was fuckin' livid.

Don't know where the fuck H.R. got off on bein' a bitch to a woman she didn't even know. What did it matter that Lou was her age in number if not in fuckin' maturity?

The woman made me happier than Harleys, Canadian whiskey and any kinda high.

But my kid didn't want to hear it.

The second we'd got home, I'd called her out on her shit. Fights in the Garro house were usually loud bursts of shoutin' and screamin' followed by hours of brooding silence. We all had tempers but H.R.'s was worst of all.

She called me disgustin', cryin' as she did it as if I'd broken her little girl heart by fallin' in love with a woman. She'd never had a hope of her mum and me gettin' back together and when that childhood pain had drained away, she'd grown up likin' her dad's full attention.

She wasn't gonna get as much of it now and my spoiled brat didn't like it.

"You'll be nice to her on pain of bein' turned out on the street," I'd growled at her when she'd called Lou a slut for the last fuckin' time.

I'd sent Cress on ahead before gettin' involved with the confrontation at the school and when I'd come home, she'd been ready. She had her jacket on, purse across her shoulder and keys in hand. She knew it'd come to H.R. stormin' out, so when she did, tears streamin' at my dishonest threat, Cress followed her with a gentle smile my way.

She'd do what she could with my girl.

The cat was outta the bag now and it was fuckin' scratchin' and wailin' like a wild thing but I had hope H.R. was mature enough to see that Lou made her old man happy.

I wrenched a kitchen chair out from the table and dropped myself in it with a loud fuckin' sigh.

King did the same.

"Why do I feel like my son is 'bout to give his old man a lecture?" I griped, running my hands through my hair to relieve some of the stress runnin' through my body.

He shrugged. "Spend a fuckuva lota time with Cress, it's not a bad guess."

I sighed, slid the pack of cigarettes from my back pocket and laughed despite my fuckin' fury when I saw that Lou'd drawn a disgusted or dyin' face on each cancer stick. I looked up grinn' as I put the pack back in my pocket. "Have at it, then."

"'S not really a lecture, Dad. Just me tellin' ya that I get it. I get what it's like to see the face of an angel and covet it so hard, you'll do anythin' to posses it. And I know what it's like at the end'a that road when you got her beside you and you wake up to that face of beauty every fuckin' day like you're livin' a dream."

King paused for a sec, searchin' my face before he continued. "Yeah, I get that you're on that road now and I get you know it's a fuckin' rough ride, but you gotta do what you gotta do to secure that kinda happiness for yourself. Don't regret a minute of the pain that was securin' my woman to my side and know you won't either. H.R.'s a little girl still but she'll come 'round."

I stared off over his shoulder, rubbin' my fingers through my beard as I thought over my son's wisdom and blessin'. He'd always been a smart kid and I liked to think I'd given him that. He'd stopped bein' a son to raise a long fuckin' time ago and now he was more like one of my brothers, one of The Fallen.

"When you comin' home to prospect?" I asked, because as far as I was concerned, the other conversation was wrapped up tight.

King laughed and slapped his messy hair into a knot at the back of his head. "Why'd I know that was comin'?"

"As I said, smart boy."

"You serious though, Dad? 'Cause Cress and I are havin' a fuckin' blast down in Vancouver but you need us, we'll be back faster than you can say 'The Fallen.' Hope you get that."

"Got it. But nah, it was just the wishful thinkin' of an old man. Shits goin' down with the Nightstalkers and I'm not sure who to trust, to tell you the fuckin' truth of it."

King frowned. "You think you got a rat?"

My phone buzzed in my pocket. I held up a finger for King and answered, "Yeah."

"Prez, there's another fire," Nova said over the sound of revving engines in the background.

"*Fuck*, where this time?"

"The grow-op near Squamish. We got Officer Hutchinson over there now, he'll deal with keepin' the illegal nature of the warehouse on the down low, but there's more."

"Say it," I growled.

"They hit the tattoo parlor and the truckin' company too. There's graffiti everywhere and they took all the money from the till at Street Ink Tat Parlor, but there wasn't anythin' to take from Edge Trucking. This was to make a fuckin' point."

"Motherfuckers," I spat. "How the fuck they'd know about Edge Trucks, huh? Buck's owned that company since before he was even a fuckin' member and it's under his old fuckin' name. Explain that to me, would ya?"

"Can't," Nova said grimly. "Got that kid Curtains on it. I'm headin' to Street Ink, Bat's over in Squamish and Buck's at the trucking company."

"I'll meet Bat," I said.

"Uh, I'd meet me, Prez, the staff sergeant's at Street Ink and he's claimin' the business was 'unsafe' and in violation of about a dozen fuckin' codes."

"Fuck," I roared. "Who the fuck told them about this shit? I swear to motherfuckin' God that heads will fuckin' roll for this shit."

I hung up, jammed the phone in my pocket and stormed over to the door.

"Later," I called over my shoulder to King,

He was up and movin' though. "I'm comin'."

"You're not a member of this club, kid."

His eyes flashed grey as a lightning strike just like mine. "Fuck that. We both know I was born a member and I'll die a member. Just 'cause I ain't prospectin' doesn't mean this isn't my goddamn family that's been fucked with."

I clapped him on the back and brought 'im close to press our foreheads together and squeeze the back of his neck. "How'd an old fuck like me end up with such a kickass kid?"

He grinned and clapped me on the back. "Pure luck."

IT WAS LATE, OR FUCKIN' early dependin' on how you looked at it. It'd been a long fuckin' night of puttin' out fires, literally and metaphorically. Our friendly neighborhood cop, Hutchinson, had dealt with the fire at the grow-op but we'd lost the entire fuckin' thing. It was a huge loss even for the scale of an operation like ours and to say I was pissed woulda been the understatement of the fuckin' year.

There were three more of those glossy eight-by-ten photographs, one at each scene and each mutilated violently. King's stuck in the empty till at Street Ink, Cress's plastered on the gates to the Edge Trucking lot and Lou's on the mailbox at the grow-op.

More warnings.

Only they weren't warnings anymore. They were threats and I wasn't havin' fuckin' anymore of that shit.

The problem was, I didn't know where the fuck these fuckin' Nightstalkers were. They weren't actin' like bikers. I didn't see 'em drivin' down the streets of Entrance in their colours or hear tell of them in any biker bars on the Sea to Sky. They were just these invisible enemies playin' a game I didn't want any fuckin' part of.

They were bein' smarter than last time, which meant that they had someone else helpin' 'em. Someone smarter, and I intended to find out who that fuckin' well was.

None of the brothers would be sleepin' for a long fuckin' time, includin' me, but I was tired as shit, mad as hellfire and I wanted—fuckin' needed—my girl.

Which was why I'd parked my bike down the road from her house and was calmly breakin' into the backdoor of the Lafayette mansion. They had a weak ass alarm that I disarmed easily with a little help from The Fallen's resident computer hacker, Curtains, and then crossed softly in my boots through the house and up the epic fuckin' staircase.

Wasn't a man who liked opulence, gold plated this or eighteenth century that, but even I could recognize that the place was worth a fuckin' mint. It was fucked to me that my Lou grew up in a place like it, like a fuckin' museum. There were no pictures of the kids on the walls, only old guys with huntin' rifles, and there was no life in the house. No clothes on the stairs or keys and shit on tables. Just rich furniture and a smell like clean money.

I knew which bedroom was Lou's from the letters. She'd always talked about the huge willow tree outside her bay window, about the fact that her nanny had let her paint her door pale pink in defiance of her parents and then promptly been fuckin' fired for it.

So I knew when I pushed open that pink door that Lou would be asleep in her bed but I wasn't prepared for what the sight'a her curled up in a fuckin' frilly white-and-pink bed would do to my cock.

I felt like the fuckin' monster under the bed come to play with the little girl bedded down in it.

My cock hardened with each step as I crossed the room and sat on the edge of the bed to take off my boots.

She didn't stir.

It was the first night she hadn't spent in my bed in a week and there was no way after a night like the one I'd just had that I was okay goin' to bed without her warmth beside me.

When I'd shucked the boots, I shrugged off my leather jacket, unbuckled my jeans and tugged off my shirt before leanin' down into the bed to get a closer look at the girl who'd stolen this monster's cold heart.

Her eyelids were pale purple and there were faint bruises at the tops of her cheeks. I frowned as I brushed a thumb over the silky bruises and wondered if I wasn't lettin' her get enough sleep. Those lids pulled slowly open when I slid my workingman's hand 'cross her cheek and down her neck.

She stared at me without fear, her pure blue eyes filled with wonder instead.

"Zeus," she breathed like I was a fuckin' dream come true. "You're here."

I kissed her warm, sleep-soft mouth. Without hesitation,

she kissed me back, sliding her small wet tongue against mine in an innocent way that had me groanin'.

When I pulled back to look into her face, she was frownin'.

"Bad day for my guardian monster," she whispered, her hand comin' up to stroke my cheek and into my hair.

Fuck but her sweetness did me in.

"Roughest in a while, all good now I got my girl with me," I told her honestly.

"What happened?"

"Not tellin' you much, Lou. Not ever and that's for your own good, yeah? But there's stuff goin' down with another gang, Nightstalkers, and shit's gonna get violent and real before it gets gone. Need you to know and need you to be fuckin' careful, yeah? Don't leave Mute's fuckin' side when you're not with me."

"You're more than angry. I think you might even be scared," she noticed like the sharp shooter she was.

I rubbed a weary hand over my tired eyes. "They went after King's woman last year. Seems they're gearin' up to go after family again."

"But why?" she asked, and I forgot that she was so fuckin' innocent in all of this.

"Got a business that keeps me cash rich and morally poor, Lou. Lotsa people want a piece of that, good ones and bad. This club wants what The Fallen has and they've decided the best way to take it is by cripplin' us with death and debt."

"Fuck."

"Burned down coupla our operations but it's the threats, I'm not down with. Can't have my kids gettin' hurt," I leaned down to suck her bottom lip into my mouth. "Can't have my girl gettin' hurt, either."

She bit the lip I'd sucked, not realizin' how it made my dick twitch. "I think my dad's involved in it somehow. I heard him talking to Lionel after my cat-fight with H.R. earlier and it seemed like he was in trouble."

I went solid. "Tell me exactly what happened."

She did, her eyes faraway as she told me the names involved in the scheme.

"Don't know who the fuck Mitch, Jack and Javier are, but Ace fuckin' Munford is the motherfuckin' rat who's the reason things went down the way they did at First Light Church the day of the shootin'," I told her. "He's Blackjack's deadbeat dad."

I didn't realize I was vibrating 'til Lou's warm hands slid up my arms and squeezed. "Text someone else to take over for the rest of the night and get in here with me. The bad guys and conspiracy theories will still be there in the morning. I want to feel my man beside me."

My heart burned 'cause the old thing wasn't used to feelin' so much. Her easy acceptance of my violent life and me was a gift I'd never get tired of receivin'.

"Lose the pants," she added when I got up to get in.

I chuckled softly but did as my girl wanted and lost 'em. Her eyes tracked over my chest and abs, down my legs and back up to the hard-on pressin' hard against my boxers.

"I'm in your little girl's room, you think that's not a fuckin' turn on?" I asked her as I slid into the bed and hauled her against my body.

She settled warm and womanly against me and laughed.

301

"You think I wasn't wet the second I saw you in here like some dark demon come to use me?"

I snarled quietly and rolled her to her back, pressing my cock into the hot apex of her sweet thighs.

"You got any of those lollipops around?" I asked as I ran my hands over her silky skin under her sleep shirt and pulled it up over her head.

The second her gorgeous tits were exposed, I took one of the peaks in my mouth and bit down hard.

Her thighs squeezed my body as she thrashed. "Fuck, yes. Why?"

"Get one out," I ordered, plumpin' her other tit in my hand.

Loved the contrast of my dark, calloused hands against all her creamy flesh, her deep curves so fuckin' ripe I wanted to bite into each and every one of them, feel her cherry tang on my tongue. I could barely fit one of her perfect tits in my big hand but I could fit the other from little finger to thumb across the entire span of her little waist.

In the dark, sneaking into her house like I had, I felt like a filthy fuckin' intruder 'bout to take the virgin girl in her bed.

I felt the strain in her body as she reached for somethin' on the bedside table. Reverently because she was better than any fantasy I'd ever had, I traced the long lines of strong muscle dancin' had given her, rubbin' my thumbs through the divots on either side of her belly and down to her shapely thighs and sweet plump calves. She was beautifully constructed and the mechanic in me got off on seein' how her body worked, how it moved. Loved bendin' her just to see how flexible she could be, touchin' her just to see how high her engine would rev.

The crinkle of a wrapper had my eyes jerkin' away from her body and up to her face. Her lids were low as she placed the head of a round red lollipop in her mouth and swirled it over her tongue.

Fuck, she was gonna put me in an early grave.

I reared up took her mouth, the cherry flavored candy still between her lips. We sucked it together, our tongues racin' over the sweet sugar then over each other. She rolled her hips against my groin and moaned.

My girl liked the games we played in bed.

As if she wasn't fuckin' perfect enough already.

I pulled back and took the sucker with me, tucked into one side of my mouth as I braced on one arm over her and looked down the long hourglass shape of her below me.

"Hold still," I ordered. "And be quiet. Don't want Mum and Dad hearin' their little girl cryin' out now, do we?"

Her skin erupted in goosebumps.

I grinned around the candy then pulled it from my mouth and drew a lazy circle with the wet red tip over her wet red nipple. Her breath was shaky, her eyes glued to my hand as I moved over one tit and then the other.

When I was done, I studied her pretty strainin' tips, the way they heaved and jiggled with her heavy breaths. Then I dipped down to take one of those candy-coated treats in my mouth and hummed.

"Fuck," she rasped, her hands flyin' to my hair to hold on tight.

I sucked hard at her flesh then raked it with my teeth, pulling it away from her body and lettin' it go with a wet pop.

"Fuckin' delicious," I told her as I flicked the damp nipple with my fingers.

Her hips were wriggling against my thigh, her wet sex slidin' up and down, searchin' for more friction than my leg could give her. I grinned wickedly at the sight of her wanton and depraved, golden like a fuckin' angel but fallen to this bed so I could have my fuckin' way with her.

I attacked the other nipple with my tongue and teeth, listenin' to her mewl and feelin' her scratch my shoulders like a fuckin' cat.

I brought the cherry lollipop to my mouth, got it wet again then trailed it between her breasts and swirled it over her belly button. She stiffened then writhed when she figured out where I was goin' with it.

I let her tit go with a harsh bite that had her shakin' then lowered my shoulders between her thighs, tossin' her legs over my shoulders so I had complete access to her bare golden cunt.

She watched me roll the candy in my mouth, pantin' hard, her eyes all black with arousal.

"Always wondered if you tasted like cherries down here," I told her in a voice so low and rough I barely recognized it. Dippin' the tip of the sucker in her honey, I said, "Now, I know for sure you do."

I locked a forearm over her canting hips to still her while I traced the folds of her glistenin' pussy with the red candy, turnin' her cunt into a red flower I wanted to bury my face in.

So I did.

I replaced the sucker with my tongue and went to town lickin' up every single scrap of sugar laid down in those juicy folds. I was noisy and messy as I ate her, her wetness in my beard and nose, my tongue up her grasping cunt and my fingers glidin' in a tease on either side of her clit.

"Zeus, please," she cried out. "Finish me off, please."

"Such a pretty cunt," I praised her. "Even pretty smeared with my cum."

"*Jesus*," she cursed, her legs shakin' violently on my shoulders.

"*Zeus*," I corrected her before bitin' into the tender junction of her groin and thigh. "There's no God but this devil in your bed."

"Ohmigawd," she cried out as I twisted three fingers deep inside her.

It was too much too soon but just that side of pain and it triggered an orgasm so massive, her entire body thrummed with it, like a live wire in my hands and against my mouth. I kept my lips sealed to her floodin' sex as she thrashed through it and licked up every single delicious drop of cum before I was done with her.

Her eyes were closed as she recovered but she opened her mouth obediently when I pressed the cum slicked head of the lollipop at her lips. She hummed as she sucked it, her eyes openin' so she could see how much she turned me the fuck on.

My cock bobbed in the air, so heavy it felt like a fuckin' steel pipe attached to my groin.

"I want another one," she panted.

It took me a second to figure out what my foxy girl wanted. I wrapped my hand around the base of my dick and worked it tight toward the head. "You want a taste of this?"

She licked her lips and nodded. "Please."

I moved up, straddlin' her chest so that my ruddy dick was pressed between the still slick valley of her breasts. Her eyes were round as I told her, "Press 'em together for me and I'll give you something else to suck."

We both moaned when she wrapped an arm around her breasts and tightened the pressure around my cock. I spit down on the flesh to lube it and got another moan for my efforts from my dirty girl.

"Gonna fuck these pretty cherry-tipped tits and cum on your cherry-red lips," I growled.

"Such a fucking poet," she sassed because only she would sass me while I titty fucked 'er.

"You complainin'?" I asked, thrusting deep so the crown of my cock hit her chin.

She ducked her chin in so on the next thrust I hit her open mouth. "Not at all," she purred, then swallowed the head of me.

I tipped my head back and groaned.

"Magnificent like a fucking god," she breathed as she looked up at me, a strand of drool connecting her mouth and the cock wedged between her breasts.

"A goddess," I told her back then leaned forward to press a hand to the wall and warned her, "Gonna fuck you hard and cum all over these tits."

She hummed her approval and opened her mouth wide, showin' me how ready she was to receive each thrust.

Fuck yeah, but I had a dirty girl.

I went to town, fuckin' her soft, slick globes until my balls tingled and the base of my spine went hot. Loved fuckin' her like this in her pretty princess bed in her pretty fuckin' mansion owned by a man who hated my fuckin' guts.

The thought tipped me over the edge and I started comin' with a low snarl. I fisted my dick in my hand and directed my hot seed all over my girl's tits and open mouth, her pink tongue stickin' out to catch as much as she could.

I squeezed out the last dribble of cum onto her skin then looked down at my handy work, breathin' hard. She was covered in me and smilin' like I'd bought her a real damn pearl necklace. Then as I watched, her tongue between her teeth, she smeared my cum into her skin until her tits glowed white from me and red from the lollipop in the bright moonlight comin' in through the curtains.

"Fuuuuck," I groaned as my spent dick twitched at the sight. "Musta been a saint in another life to deserve this."

She giggled as I ducked down to kiss her forehead then swung outta bed. "You were a saint, I don't think you'd fuck a teenage girl under her father's roof."

"And you wouldn't like me half as much then either, would ya?" I teased her as I went into the little bathroom off her room and wet a cloth to wipe her down with.

When I came back she was still smilin', her eyes half-closed and a hand playin' idly with her left nipple.

I raised a brow at her when I sat down and started to clean her. "Not enough for ya?"

"Don't worry, I get that you're old and I have more stamina than you," she tried to taunt me but she was laughin' like a loon before she could even finish gettin' the words out.

I bit her nipple sharply and leaned down menacingly into her face. "Watch what you say, little girl or I'll keep you up all night provin' just how much gas I got left in the tank."

"Easy, stud," she said through her laughter. "You've got

bad guys to catch and maim and I've got Sammy, studying and The Lotus tomorrow. We need our rest. Honestly, not that I'm complaining, but you should have gone home to bed, Z. You look beat."

I scowled at her as she pulled back the covers for me to get into bed. The second I did she was plastered to my side, her left arm and leg thrown over me and her head on my chest. Her fingers played in my short chest hair and up over the ridge of my bullet scar.

"Could probably sleep without you," I admitted. "Just don't want to."

She sighed happily into my shoulder. "You gonna sneak out before my parents wake up in the morning?"

"Nah, thought I'd join the Lafayettes for fuckin' porridge at breakfast."

She laughed. "Porridge? Ew."

I shrugged. "Figured that's what borin' folks ate for breakfast."

"Dad does like porridge in the winter..." She laughed softly as she traced the dips and valleys over my torso. "What does a big badass biker man eat for breakfast?"

"Virgins," I deadpanned.

Her startled laugh was like fuckin' church bells.

It didn't make sense but that's what my time with Lou always reminded me of, a religious experience. I felt cowed and unworthy of her goodness, moved to the point of reverence and devoted to the point of worship. I wanted her to be my religion, the reason the sun rose and fell each day. The reason for my entire fuckin' existence.

"No seriously, I made you breakfast yesterday at the

cabin but all you had was cereal. If I get the chance to cook for you again, I want to know what you like."

My girl, so fuckin' sweet. "Meat and potatoes kinda guy, Lou. No surprise there, I hope."

"Nope. Any vices? Like me and my cherry lollipops?"

I groaned. "Damn don't remind me of those fuckin' things ever again 'less you want me to fuck you soon as you do."

"Perv," she said, pinchin' my nipple.

"You bet your ass," I agreed easily which got me another one of those fuckin' beautiful giggles. "My vices are longer than my virtues. Like Canadian whiskey, Lucky Strikes cigarettes and pussy."

"Zeus, I can't make you any of those things!"

"Sure ya can. Pour me a whiskey, pass me a smoke and spread those sweet thighs for me whenever I get a hankerin' for somethin' sweet."

"Oh my God, you are useless. I'm going to sleep, shut up."

I grinned into the dark, playin' with the ends of her blond hair. It was so bright the locks shone even in the night shadows. When her breathin' was levelin' out into sleep, I pressed my lips into that hair and told her, "You wake up in my bed after a night of takin' my cock, it's me who'll make breakfast. You want lunch or dinner, I'm good with that 'cause breakfast is the only thing I got in me to make. It was a long eighteen years of microwave dinners for my kids and makin' fuckin' salads and shit so they got the right nutrients. Done with that now so I eat what I want and what I want is usually meat with a small side of veg. You wanna take over cookin' when I get you in my house permanent, like I said, I will not complain. But never breakfast. Want my girl warm, relaxed and ready for another round of cock in the mornings. You get me?"

I felt her smile against my chest before she pressed a kiss to it.

"Got you."

I lay in the dark for hours after my girl fell asleep curled up into me, strokin' her hair like rosary beads between my fingers. It settled me, bein' there with her, touchin' her. There was shit stormin' on the horizon and it was comin' straight for us but for the first time in a long fuckin' time, I felt at peace.

CHAPTER TWENTY-EIGHT

Loulou

IT WAS QUIET IN THE CHEMOTHERAPY ROOM OF THE HOSPITAL. It was the kind of silence that penetrated my nightmares. There was a texture to it, thick and slippery against my skin so that it refused to emit noise even when I felt my body should have made some. It lent a muffled quality to the sound of nurses bringing in new patients and administering their drugs, little Dixie cups full of poison pills and IVs full of a different kind of toxins. Patients often sat with friends or families while they waited for the drugs to obliterate their blood but even their conversations had a hushed property that made my ears tingle.

I sighed deeply and tipped my head back against the high headrest then flinched when the needle pulled painfully at the back of my hand. I had "unfavourable" stage two Hodgkin's Lymphoma, which basically meant that I didn't have a tumor they could nuke with radiation or cut with surgery. Instead, the cancer was an invasion of micro-ants in my system, spread above and below my diaphragm, which made it the "unfavourable" kind. I'd already had something called a Stanford V twelve-week round of chemo last spring but it hadn't done much so now the doctors were going for a short but dramatic combo; more drugs, higher toxicity but for a shorter amount of time. I'd have three cycles of treatment, once a week for three weeks with one week off so that my body could recover. The doctors had already warned me that the third cycle would be crueler than I'd ever experienced, that I had a high likelihood of losing my hair, vomiting excessively, diarrhea, infection and loss of respiratory function.

Something to look forward to.

I always wished someone would sit with me during the treatments. Bea would have if she didn't have school or extracurriculars, but my parents made sure she was always busy so she wouldn't be underfoot.

I knew Ruby would have, if I asked, but I felt she did enough by driving me to and from my appointments.

Zeus would have, but he still didn't know about the cancer and with each passing day it became harder and harder to explain to him why I hadn't.

Saying I wanted him to treat me like a normal woman—a whole person and not one half drowned by sickness—would *not* go down well with him. I knew that and still I put it off. We were having such an amazing time together despite everything going on with the Nightstalkers MC, with H.R. and my parents. I wanted to enjoy it while it lasted.

Which would probably be that night when I went over to

the Garro house for Sunday dinner. I couldn't believe that a biker family like that had such a banal tradition but Zeus told me that he'd started it after becoming Prez to encourage brotherhood and family. It wasn't always a full house but usually a handful of brothers and their women and family would roll up to the Garro house on the far rocky edge of Entrance Bay Beach for beer and food.

It sounded like the kind of family fun I'd always wanted but never had.

Only Harleigh Rose would be there and, apparently, she hadn't spoken to her father in the two days since our fight at EBA and most of that time, she'd been out with her boyfriend Cricket. So, even though I wanted to be excited about hanging with the brothers and seeing Zeus's house for the first time, I didn't have high hopes for the night.

This was exacerbated by the fact that I'd lied to Mute.

To say he'd become my best friend in the last few weeks seemed too trivial to define the way our friendship had developed. True to his orders, Mute was my constant shadow tracking all my daylight hours just one silent step behind me. Sometimes, I barely noticed he was there and didn't really know the extent of his watchfulness. He took me to school and picked me up like a dad would (though not my dad) but when I asked him, he told me he usually worked at Hephaestus Auto during those hours. Whatever the case, if it was school or ballet or an appointment, he was there the second I was finished, waiting outside on the curb beside his bike like he'd never moved.

We also hung out though. He ate breakfast with me in the mornings and surprisingly, he loved to cook, only healthy things packed with superfoods and nutrients, but each morning he made me a delicious smoothie and some nights we helped Mrs. Henry, my parents' chef, cook in the rarely used kitchen at the back of the house. We devoured cult classic films, played cards because I wanted to learn how to play poker and there was no one with a better poker face than Mute, and sometimes, I even read to him from a book. He liked books, he told me, but he couldn't read very well. He still didn't like to be touched unless I gave prior notice but he loved my hair and touching it, tugging it and wrapping it around his fingers seemed to center him in a way that playing with toy blocks soothed Sammy.

I found out a lot about Mute in the last couple of months and life before his presence in it seemed like a faint and lonely memory.

So, I felt like shit for lying to him. I'd told him I had cramps and would stay in my room until dinner at the Garros that night but instead, I'd slipped out the back door just in case he was watching and hitched a ride with Ruby, who'd been waiting a block away for me in her red convertible.

If he found out, he'd be pissed and even worse, so would Zeus.

"There's my darling girl," Betsy's voice sung out, the only thing to cut through that laminated silence.

I opened my eyes to smile at the middle-aged woman who'd nursed me as a child and passed my letters back and forth to Zeus until I was old enough to go to the post office myself.

She hooked a stool with her foot and slid it beside my chair then ducked down to look into my eyes and check the pulse at my throat.

"Always a nurse," I muttered as I rolled my eyes. "I thought you'd give me a kiss before you inspected me like a prize horse."

She clucked her tongue and then sank onto the stool. "You know I care about you, that's why I do it. I know this sucks, honey, but I think Dr. Radcliffe's course of treatment is the right one."

I nodded because we'd already talked about this. "I know."

She tucked a piece of hair behind my ear. "How are you, honey?

I bit my lip because I hadn't seen Betsy in a few months so she didn't know about Zeus.

Apparently, I didn't have to worry about telling her because her eyes widened like camera apertures zooming in on me. "You've seen him, haven't you?"

"You could say that."

"Oh God, he finally did it, didn't he?" she asked the heavens. "I don't know what's wrong with him."

"Absolutely nothing," I said fiercely. "You of all people shouldn't judge us."

"I don't, sweetheart. I'm just concerned. He's...an intense guy with an intense life."

"I know all about it," I told her with hard eyes.

She nodded slowly. "He told you about what happened with his uncle Crux?"

Fuck.

"Of course," I lied boldly.

Her face softened with empathy as she reached out to pat my thigh. "He didn't. You ask Zeus Garro what happened with his uncle ten years ago and then we'll still see if you have stars in your eyes over him."

I glared at her as she pulled out her knitting and went to town on a hideously ugly olive-green sweater. "This is for you," she beamed at me.

"Great," I muttered, looking away and hoping to hell that what she'd said about Zeus wouldn't destroy anything between us.

THE GARRO'S lived off the main beach drive down a packed dirt road behind a chain link fence, overgrown sea grass and about five signs that warned of Danger, No Trespassing and Cross At Your Own Risk.

It wasn't exactly a warm welcome but as Mute and I passed down the weaving road lined with parked cars, I looked around in awe at the surroundings. The ocean ran alongside the lane, the high tide line just a meter or two off the path. The blue water sparkled with fragments of shattered gold cast by the setting sun and the mountains cupping Entrance like a hand loomed up all around us, capped by snow and shrouded in perpetual mist.

I breathed the briny sea air into my lungs and then lost it all when we rounded a bend and caught sight of the house.

Zeus had built this one as well.

It was a pale wood clapboard house with thick slats around the windows and doors stained a darker wood. The roof had pale green tiles that blended in beautifully with the ocean at its side and the forest at its back. There was a wraparound porch with potted plants on it and a huge three-door garage built in the same style as the compact, two-story house.

I *fucking* loved it.

I was off the bike and running toward the painted forest green front door when it opened and Zeus stepped onto the porch, his feet bare beneath the frayed hem of his jeans and his torso snug in a criminally tight Henley the same colour as his pale grey eyes.

I launched myself up the stairs and into his arms.

He caught me easily with his hands splayed across my ass and planted a long, wet kiss on me before I could get a word out. When he was done with my mouth, I'd forgotten what I was going to say and blinked at him dazedly.

"How's my girl?"

I stared into his grey eyes, cracked and lined like an ancient boulder over time. They were beautiful eyes thick-lashed under heavy brows, given character by that radiating fan of wrinkles to either side of them. I decided right then that I'd be happy to spend the rest of my life looking into those eyes.

"I think you dazzled her," a well-known but surprising voice said from behind Zeus in the house. "King does it to me all the time, so I know."

I peered around Zeus's hair to confirm my suspicions and immediately jumped down to the ground as I yelled, "Miss Irons!"

She laughed as I used my entire body to move Zeus's bulk out of the doorframe and then pulled my ex-teacher into a full body hug.

"What are you doing here?" I asked as I stepped away.

It was only then that I noticed what she was wearing.

Miss Irons had been a young and pretty teacher that wore sweet little dresses and feminine suit combinations like a classy secretary. Now she stood before me in jeans with the knees ripped out and a purple tee shirt with a crown emblazoned on it that said *Queen*. Her long golden brown hair was wild all around her in a way that said she'd arrived on the back of a bike and enjoyed the hell out of it and, not only that, she hadn't bothered to fix her mane because she liked the windblown look of it.

Totally different woman.

I took a step back as I frowned at her.

She laughed lightly as she looked from me to Zeus, who stood leaning against the wall of his house with his arms and feet crossed, an unlit cigarette in his mouth. "I should have known it would be just as weird for her to see me as it would be for me to see her with you."

Zeus pushed his tongue against the cig in his mouth but didn't say anything and for another second, I got stuck on how goddamn sexy he looked standing there as the man of the house, cool and casual but potent with masculinity and harnessed power.

Miss Irons laughed again and hit Zeus in the shoulder

like they were friends. "Totally dazzled by you. Way to go, Zeus."

He raised an eyebrow at her. "As if it's that surprisin'."

I couldn't help myself when I rolled my eyes and said, "Yeah, you get dazzled first thing when you look at him but as soon as he opens his mouth, you come back to earth *real* quick."

"Oh my God, you two are freaking adorable," she breathed, her eyes sparkling with delight.

I felt like I was in the twilight zone.

"Queenie, you gotta start swearin'," Nova said, appearing behind her.

The golden light of the sunset hit him full in the face and highlighted the utter perfection of his bone structure. I bet if I took a ruler and measured it out, his features would be exactly symmetrical.

"Seems dazzled enough by pretty boy," Zeus grumbled.

Miss Irons or *Queenie* grinned and waved a dismissive hand through the air. "Oh come on now, you know any woman with eyes in her head is dazzled by Nova."

"This is true," Nova agreed with a wink and a rakish grin.

"Come 'ere, little warrior," Zeus ordered with a glare at his brother.

I went without thinking under his arm and leaned hard into his side before reaching up to pluck the cigarette from his lips and put it between my own. It was a strangely intimate thing to do and I knew Zeus understood that when his hand cupped my hip and pulled me closer.

"So, are you with him?" I asked, pointing a finger between Nova and my old teacher. "Because there were these bizarre rumors about you sleeping with a student when you left. I told anyone who would listen that it was utter horseshit—"

I stopped talking when a motorcycle came roaring into the wide driveway and King Kyle Garro swung off his bike. He turned to grab the bag of ice strapped to the back, and then his long legs ate up the space as he came up the stairs to the porch. I thought distractedly that it was easy to get dazzled by The Fallen men. If women knew how fucking handsome bikers could be, it would blow their minds.

I was thinking this when King's booted feet hit the landing, the ice hit it a second later and Miss Irons was hauled into his arms the second after that. He slid a hand to the back of her neck, banded the other over her hips and planted a hot, wet, super long kiss on my ex-teacher.

His ex-teacher.

"Um, okaaaaay," I said slowly.

They kissed on.

Nova smirked at me. "They do this a lot."

King pulled away from eating at her mouth but kept his face close to say, "How's my Queen doin'?"

She sighed dreamily, clutching his wrists as they cupped her face. "Better now you're back."

Zeus snorted. "Boy went to get fuckin' ice, woman. He didn't go off to war."

Miss Irons blushed fiercely but shot my man a sidelong look filled with sass. "Your women just ran from Mute's bike the second it stopped and jump into your waiting arms like you'd just returned from war?" she waited a beat for her point to sink in then grinned and placed a smacking kiss on King's smiling lips. "That's what I thought."

"So obviously, the rumors were true," I clarified drily.

Zeus's body rumbled against mine with a deep chuckle.

King's boyish smile was absurdly handsome with pride. "Better believe it. Worked fuckin' hard to snag her, let me tell ya."

She shoved him and then immediately followed him as he stepped back from the force of it and slotted herself into his side before looking at me. "Apparently, you've got yourself a Garro man so you can't tell me you don't get it."

"Oh, I get it," I said with a nod, tipping my head back so I could look up into Zeus's rugged face. "I almost feel badly that there are no Garros left for anyone else."

"There's one," Nova drawled as, on cue, a clunker of an old Toyota came barreling down the drive and fish tailed to a stop about five inches from the porch stairs. Even through the cacophony of the music thudding through the shit speakers, I could hear the couple inside yelling at each other. A second later, Harleigh Rose climbed out in tiny denim shorts over fishnet tights and combat boots, a tight black leather jacket zipped up to just below her cleavage and her masses of hair tossed all over her head. It was like an ad for the original bad girl, rock music playing in the background for special effect as she slammed the door and yelled, "Fucking fuck you!"

The car roared out of the drive and into the lane a moment later, kicking up dust that swirled around Harleigh Rose as she stood staring after it, flipping him the bird.

"Pity the poor bastard that gets saddled with H.R.," Nova muttered.

And Mute, my lovely friend who had been so quietly standing against the porch railing the entire time softly added, "Seconded."

The entire porch burst into laughter, which was shit timing because when H.R. turned on her boot and stomped up the stairs it looked like we were laughing at her. She scowled at everyone as she came to a stop in the middle of the porch, planted her hands on her hips and said, "Well if this isn't a motley fuckin' crew."

"Harleigh Rose," Zeus growled, tightening his hold on me. "This is Loulou. Think you two 'ave met but why don't we give the introducin' part a second go 'round, yeah?"

"Hey, Harleigh Rose," I said on a small smile, hyper aware of the healing cut her ring had left on my cheek and the fact that her dad had me pressed to his side from tip to toe.

Her jaw worked as she struggled not to say something mean. It wasn't necessary, her acidic eyes, an aquamarine blue that was so startling they seemed to glow, said it all for her. She hated my fucking guts.

She cut her eyes from me to her father and did something with her face that might have been a smile but seemed to me more like a painful grimace. "Welcome to our lovely home, Louise. Can I offer you a refreshing beverage?"

"A beer would be good," I suggested, careful because I wanted to show her I wasn't going to back down, but I didn't want another *throw* down.

"While you're at it, I'll take one too," King added casually but his eyes were sharp on his little sister.

"Me too, honey," Cressida put in.

It was only then that Harleigh Rose flinched like Cressida throwing down for me was the worst possible betrayal. Her head turned to look at her and even though I couldn't see H.R.'s face, I knew there was pain in it.

Clearly, she did not have the same problem with King's woman as she did with me.

"Beer, honey," Cressida said in a way that meant she expected Harleigh Rose to do as she was told and do it with a smile. "You need help carrying it out?"

"I'm capable of carrying some fuckin' beer," she muttered petulantly.

"You capable of rememberin' your fuckin' manners?" Zeus asked and immediately drew a glare from his kid. He shrugged. "Hey, you're proud of the way you're actin' like a fuckin' fourteen-year-old brat just cause I found a woman happens to be your age with twice your life experience, then go at 'er, sweetheart. Just thought I raised a girl bright, kind and true. Fuck me if I was mistaken."

His words hit her like a ton of bricks; the stubborn cruelty in her eyes shattered like mirrored glass and revealed the wounded heart of her.

I knew the words were coming before they came.

"She's a fuckin' Lafayette, Dad. You think the minute comes that she has to stand up for our family, she's going to sacrifice hers for ours? She lives in a house like a fuckin' castle up on Entrance Hill. You want young pussy, fine, who am I to stop you. Guess I just expected you to have better taste than that." She sneered as she waved her hand over me, her eyes like fingers ripping apart my big curled hair tied back with a black velvet ribbon, my pink lipstick and spike heeled black leather boots.

They seemed to tell me that I was too rich to be authentic, too young to be wise and too fuckin' privileged to be wild.

I stepped forward away from Zeus and smiled prettily at

her. "You can insult me until the cows come home, Harleigh Rose, I'm here to fuckin' stay and I don't care if it takes you two decades to be civil to me, *nothing*, not even you can take me away from Zeus."

Uncertainty made her blink like a lost little girl for a moment and it was a moment my man took advantage of.

Zeus stepped forward and tagged his daughter around the hips to haul her into his chest and wrap his massive arms around her in a great, big bear hug. He even growled for effect as he rocked her back and forth.

"You fuckin' suck sometimes H.R.," he said as he bent down in a pseudo squat so they were at eye level. "But I'd do fuckin' anythin' for ya."

"Yeah?" she asked hopefully, casting a sly look over her shoulder at me.

I laughed at her audacity, perilously close to liking her despite everything.

Zeus's grin was a bright wedge of joy in his dark, close-cropped beard. "Fuck yeah. Just a warnin' though, you ask me to stay away from my little warrior, she'd fight you and win. Even if she didn't, there's no way in heaven or hell my fallen angel would leave me in peace."

"You know it," I winked at him.

H.R. pouted but she did it in a cute way and she didn't gripe when Z slid one arm around her shoulder and reached out to grab mine with his other hand.

"Fuckin' starvin', let's get the feast fuckin' started."

CHAPTER TWENTY-NINE

Zeus

IT WAS DARK, LATE INTO THE NIGHT PAST LITTLE GIRL'S bedtimes but I had a surprise for Lou and I couldn't wait to see her put it to use for me. Her hand was in mine as I led her out of the house where some of the brothers lay crashed out in the livin' room and the two guest bedrooms, where King and Cress were makin' out like teenagers 'cause one of 'em was one, where my daughter was pretendin' to sleep in her bed 'til she could sneak off to Cricket.

We left that all behind for a moment or two of solitude in any man's paradise.

His garage.

We went through the side door and when I flipped the light switch, Lou gasped and declared, "Wicked."

It was.

Not only my cages—the huge GMC truck I used to haul dead bodies to Dixon's farm and wood for my fireplace to my hearth, and the black 1969 Boss 429 Mustang—but the entire space was admittedly pretty fuckin' wicked. Eugene had done up some of his neon light shit and I'd put up old street signs and license plates Bat, Blackjack and I stole as kids. I'd built the garage and the house with my own bare hands, so I took a fuckuva lot'a pride in it and I loved that Lou's dazzled expression said she did too.

Then she noticed her surprise, wrapped in a red bow in the corner of the concrete space with a workbench dragged in front of it just exactly for what I planned that night.

"Did you install a stripper pole in your garage?" Lou asked me, cocking out her hip as she turned at me with a sassy eyebrow raised. "Seriously, Z?"

I went over to the bottle of Crown Royal and glasses I kept in the small bar beside my wall of tools and poured myself a drink 'fore goin' over to sit on the bench in front of the pole.

"Want you to dance for me."

"I don't take orders, Zeus. I barely even take suggestions unless they happen to line up with what I already wanted to do. What makes you think I'm going to dance for you on fucking demand?"

"Dance for me, little girl," I ordered lazily, as if I had the right to command her. 'Cause I did and she fuckin' loved it. "If you impress me, I may let you make me come."

She glared at me. It took effort because she was sassy but she wanted what I was offerin' her and it showed all over her flushed face. Only my girl would look into the eyes of a monster like me and taunt, "Kiss my ass."

"You get to dancin' and you do it in a way that gets my dick hard, I may let you come too. You want it like that, I'll get you on your hands and knees and eat that sweet ass 'till you come on my tongue. But, Lou, warnin' ya, you want ass play, I'm down but that means I'll also be fuckin' ya there too."

She blinked at me then fisted her hands on those cocked hips and said, "What music have you got?"

Half an hour later, I was groanin' in my bed with my hands clamped over Lou's hips watchin' her glide up and down on my cock. "That's my good girl, ride me hard."

She blinked at me with heavy eyes over the deep, dark water blue of her eyes. It was a look that said she was lazy with pleasure, like a drunk gone tired after hours of reveling. Loved that look but loved it even more when I reached up to tweak hard at her cherry nipples and her eyes flared open with wicked surprise.

"Going to come," she warned me, bracing her hands on my chest to tilt her ass back and ride me even harder.

"Come on my cock, little girl," I ordered her, bringing my hands around to palm that peachy ass in my hands.

I traced a thumb down her crease until it was slicked with her pussy juices then brought it back up to her tightly furled asshole.

"You come for me and then I'll fuck your ass," I growled as I thrust up at her the same time I pushed my thumb into her tight backdoor.

She screamed. So loud and long it probably woke the entire Garro house, my daughter, my son and his woman and the brothers who'd passed out on the couches. I didn't give a fuck. In fact, I fuckin' loved that they'd know how much pleasure I gave my girl.

Couldn't help the arrogant pride that swelled in my chest and made me want to beat it like a fuckin' caveman. I was bringin' my girl pleasure like she'd never had, makin' her take everything I wanted to give her and makin' her do it while she cried out my name like I was the only man who'd ever existed.

As soon as her pussy stopped clenching around my cock like a fuckin' vice, I went out from under her and took my place behind her kneelin' body. With a hand between the fragile span of her shoulder blades, I pushed her face down and then canted her hips up.

"You remember what I said about eatin' this ass, Lou?"

A delicate shudder rippled her spine. I chased it with my hand movin' down her back the way you soothed a horse before mountin' it for the first time. Then 'cause I was addicted to the taste of her, I fell to my forearms and buried my face in that lush ass.

Her cum was sweet like salted fuckin' honey on my tongue as I cleaned her up with my mouth. I flicked at her rosebud with my tongue until it twitched then circled it with a thumb.

"You wanna give up this ass for me, little Lou?" I growled as my thumb popped through the tight ring of muscle and two of my other fingers slid deep into her swollen cunt and curled up against her sweet spot.

Her toes curled against the bed as she arched her back and panted loud.

I slapped my big palm down over one plump cheek just to see it spring back under my slap. She gasped so loud, I knew she wanted it again. I smacked the other one and rocked my thumb and fingers slowly in her holes.

"You want my cock in your ass, little girl?" I asked, lovin' her small size and plump curves. The way she was all woman and yet still a girl.

"Yes," she hissed and braced her hands against the wall so she could hump back at me. "Take it. I want you everywhere."

I reared up to slap my swollen purple cock between her cheeks, squeezin' 'em together against my dick.

"Prettiest fuckin' picture," I told her just to hear her moan.

My girl liked it when I talked dirty.

I leaned over to grab the lube I'd bought just for her outta the bedside table, ripped the cap off with my teeth and dumped the cherry-scented liquid all over my dick and that heart-shaped ass. I growled as I slid my cock up and down that warm, wet crease, coatin' me and coatin' her. The smell of cherries in my nose nearly made me want to come right there and then.

"Touch your clit while I try to work my dick in there."

Immediately, one hand disappeared between her steeply arched torso to do as she was fuckin' told.

"Good girl," I rumbled as I held her steady with one hand at the hip and pressed my cock to her smallest entrance.

She groaned and panted as she took me inside, wrigglin' her hips and clutchin' the blankets.

"Oh Zeus, oh fuck, *God*," she chanted until I was seated all the way inside her snug, hot as fuck channel.

I leaned back to look down at my trail of dark hair, the

root of the swollen cock inside her round, golden ass and thought I coulda died a happy fuckin' man just like that.

"Move, please," she begged me.

So I did.

I fucked long and slow into the tight grasp of her ass, workin' her 'til she was screamin' and whimperin' for more. She was comin' apart at the seams and I held the thread in my fuckin' teeth.

My balls were tight and heavy, so ready to spill my seed inside 'er, it was fuckin' ridiculous that I could even keep movin' like I was. But I wanted Lou to come with my cock in her ass and I wanted it bad.

So, I leaned over her, addin' two of my thick fingers to her cunt as she rubbed her clit and I fucked her ass.

"Come for me, Lou," I said, then I bit her hard in that place I liked at the base of her neck and felt her pulse throb on my tongue in tandem with her ass around my dick.

Fuckin' bliss.

I growled against her flesh as I spilled inside her.

With the last of my energy, I dropped to the bed and flipped her onto my belly. Her sweaty skin slipped on mine then fused us together.

She rested her cheek against my pec and played with my bullet scar.

"Did so good tonight, Lou," I praised her as I ran my fingers over her spine the way someone mighta played piano keys.

"Mmm, it was super fun," she slurred, so wrung out from her orgasm she didn't even open her eyes.

Pride rumbled through my chest, makin' her smile 'cause she knew why I loved her voice like that.

"Like the brothers so much. Not just Mute," she went on. "And the biker babes are hilarious. Never knew Cressida could be such a badass."

"She's gettin' there," I agreed.

"Harleigh Rose isn't so bad either," she mumbled.

"Nah, she's a good kid," I agreed.

And she was. She was goin' through a time but I figured it was normal for a teenage girl to rebel, however well she'd been raised. She partied too much and dated that fucktard Cricket, but she got good marks in school despite the lack'a studyin' and she loved her brother, her club and her dad like nothin' else.

And for that reason, she'd been good tonight. Not great 'cause it was weird as shit for her to see her dad who never brought women home—usually fucked 'em at the clubhouse—be all over a woman and that woman bein' the same age as herself.

I got it.

Lou got it.

It was cool.

H.R. was tryin' and she was tryin' by mostly leavin' Lou to her own devices but my little Loulou didn't seem to care. She'd thrown herself into befriendin' the biker babes, even Skell's woman, Winona, who was dull as death and Bat's bitch of a wife, Trixie.

By the end of the night, everyone loved Lou if they hadn't already before.

I was a happy fuckin' man.

That is until Lou shifted on my chest to ask, "What happened between you and your Uncle Crux?"

"The fuck that come from?"

Her eyes narrowed 'cause she knew I didn't want to fuckin' answer.

"Told ya I had an uncle who was President of this club 'fore me."

"Yeah... why'd he step down?"

I rubbed a hand over my beard and up into my hair. "He didn't. I killed 'im."

She stiffened. "What?"

"You heard me. I killed my Uncle Crux and to be fuckin' honest with you, Lou, not crazy about you jumpin' to conclusions 'fore I can explain myself. You knew I was a killer."

She swiveled to sit cross-legged on my stomach and crossed her arms under her tits. "I knew it. I did *not* know you'd killed your own uncle."

"You expect me to explain myself you do it askin' fuckin' nicely, Lou. I may be the man in your bed but I'm still Prez of The fuckin' Fallen," I growled.

"Fine, pretty please with a fucking cherry on top, can you tell me what went down with your uncle?" she sassed.

I threw an arm over my eyes and pressed my head back into the pillow. "There goes a great fuckin' orgasm high."

She hit my chest.

I lifted the arm to peer at her then scowled as I propped it behind my head. "Fine, you wanna know? I killed my Uncle Crux by puttin' a bullet through his brain. I put a bullet through his brain 'cause there'd been disappearances happenin' for a while. Brothers just there one day and gone the next. They didn't have much in common, first glance, 'til Bat and I noticed a pattern. They'd all talked back or dissented to Crux. One day Bat pretended to go at the old coot just to bait 'im. The next day he invited Bat to have a 'chat' with 'im somewhere private. Bat got him to confess to killin' brothers and the bastard stabbed 'im in the stomach and threw him into the backa one of our trucks to take him somewhere in the forest to bleed out and die. He didn't know I'd come with Bat. Didn't know 'til Bat and I showed up in Chapel next mornin' as if nothin' had happened. He asked for a meetin' somewhere public, his half of the club versus mine. He chose First Light Church.

I'da put a bullet in his brain just for the stuff he'd done 'fore but he sealed his fate and he did it quick when he put a bullet through a fuckin' kid to get to me. So, I killed 'im right there in front of the fuckin' cops 'cause the bastard deserved more than jail. He deserved hell.

Half the old guys left, angry and confused or just fuckin' done with the life. The rest voted me in as Prez, youngest in history."

"And Ace Munford was one of those brothers who left?" she asked 'cause she was a smart girl and she was puttin' the pieces together.

I nodded, watchin' her eyes for any signs her devotion to me had slipped and smashed like a religious idol to the floor of our church.

She blinked, those ocean-blue eyes settled and there she was.

My girl.

She pressed her hand to my cheek and then kissed me, soft, slowly without tongue and fuckin' sweeter than sugar pie.

"You're a good man, Z," she told me.

I laughed.

"I'm serious, you may live by your own code but you do

the right thing at the end of the day and you adhere to your rules and loyalties like a knight would."

"Told you to stop romanticizin' it."

"Won't ever stop," she promised. "Now, swear to me you won't keep shit like that from me again."

She offered me her little pinky like she had as a kid. I took it solemnly in mine and shook her thumb with my own.

"Deal," I said even though there were a ton of skeletons in my closet and I had no plans to share 'em all with Lou.

CHAPTER THIRTY

Loulou

I WAS DOING A MATH EQUATION IN MY FIFTH PERIOD BIOLOGY class at the whiteboard when dizziness slammed into me like a hand to the back of the head. I stumbled then steadied myself against the wall.

"Louise?" Reece's voice came at me through my sudden fog.

I tried to lift the red dry erase pen to the white surface, but my hand wouldn't lift. Frowning, I looked down at it where it lay limply by my side.

"Louise?" Reece's voice was closer to me then. "Mr. Warren, call the hospital."

"Don't need the..." I tried to say with my heavy tongue

then gave up because I was falling then crashing into blackness.

When I woke up, I didn't open my eyes because I could hear the familiar beeps of whirs of the hospital all around me and I hated the hospital.

My first thought was of Zeus.

I didn't know what time it was, and I'd had plans to meet him after a few hours with Sammy at the Autism Centre that day. If he didn't know where I was, he'd flip.

My eyes shot open as I sat up and then closed again when the dizziness hit.

When I was orientated again, I looked around the room and gasped because Zeus Garro was sitting beside my bed.

He stared at me angrier than I'd ever seen him, his harshly constructed face gone granite with wrath.

"Zeus," I tried but he cut me off immediately by lifting a hand in the air.

He leaned forward, his lips pulled back over his teeth like a wolf about to snap. "Didn't know where you were for hours. No one did. Mute went fuckin' crazy, tore up the inside of Hephaestus Auto in one of his rages when he realized we didn't know where the *fuck* you were. I sent boys out to every fuckin' place I could think of to find you."

He paused and his eyes sharpened to the colour of shrapnel. "Didn't think to look at the hospital 'til H.R. told me she'd heard you'd left school in a fuckin' ambulance."

I flinched but he wasn't done.

"Not once since I took you as my woman have I regretted it or had to face how young you still are. This is the first time I'm hit and hit hard with both'a those things."

Fuck.

"Z, please let me explain. I know I waited too long to tell you but if I'd told you right away then you *wouldn't have wanted me.*" Tears came and they did it like a tropical storm, tearing up mucus and heavy sobs, whipping my chest into a painful frenzy. "If you'd known that you were attracted to a seventeen-year-old girl with cancer and then that you were fucking and fucking *hard* a woman with Hodgkin's Lymphoma, we wouldn't have what we have now."

Zeus blinked at my crying face and for a brief second, I thought I might have gotten through to him.

Wishful thinking.

He stood up with a rough shriek of his plastic chair across the floor.

"Not sure what it is we have, the love of my life doesn't tell me shit about her health."

With that final punch to my gut, Zeus shook his head, turned on his booted heel and stormed out of the room.

I hit my head back against the mattress and let the sob that had been bubbling up in my throat free.

I didn't want to die for a lot of reasons, but none seemed so essential as my desire to stay with Zeus.

There were too many things we still had to do.

Too many rides to take on the back of his bike with his big body between my thighs and the dual rumble of the bike and his laughter vibrating through my core.

Too many nights spent at The Wet Lotus, eye-fucking across velvet booths and scantily clad dancers.

Too many battles to win. Too many people to kill. The Nightstalkers most of all.

I wanted time with him, I needed it more than I needed my next breath and even those were limited.

There wasn't time and there wasn't much of a choice but whatever was left of both, I wanted to use to be with Zeus Garro.

It had never occurred to me that he might not want to spend that time with me.

CHAPTER THIRTY-ONE

Zeus

THE LIGHT COMIN' IN THROUGH THE SLATTED CURTAINS FELL IN fat grey fragments across the hospital bed, highlightin' the gold of Lou's hair but shadowin' the beauty of her face. I leaned back in the chair with my broad back pressed uncomfortably to the rigid plastic contours and raked a hand through my hair.

It was hard to look at her as she was, curled up and frail in a white room stripped of all personality. It was embarrassin', avoiding a bedridden face, like racism or sexism, any-ism. But I couldn't wrap my mind 'round the fact that my girl had cancer.

Again.

And that she hadn't told me about it in the fuckin' first place.

It had taken five hours of ridin' my bike through coastal back roads to figure out where she'd been comin' from.

'Cause she had a point.

If she'd told me about the cancer from the get-go, there's no way I woulda let myself go there with her. I wouldn't'a kissed, fucked or held her like she was my woman.

I woulda coddled her, told her to take care of herself and maybe watched from afar, like I'd done the first four months after seein' her again at that party.

And then Lou wouldn't be mine.

That was somethin' even harder to wrap my head 'round.

Because that girl lying in that bed was mine the way a sculpture created by an artist was his. I'd formed her soft clay shape with my words then cast it in copper with my hands and finally she'd settled in her current shape. A little warrior rebel with the soul of an angel in the body of a sinner.

A contradiction and the most beautiful one ever born in nature.

A nurse came in with a soft, nervous smile at the huge biker sittin' in his leather cut beside the bed of a teenager. She checked the machines and glanced at me like she wanted to ask for a minute alone to do something to Lou a man shouldn't see.

The plastic chair screeched as I pushed it back.

The woman watched me as I dipped down to place my hand across Lou's damp forehead and press a kiss to her cheek. "Be back."

I walked the white corridors with my hands shoved deep in my pockets and my shoulders at my ears.

To occupy myself, I went to the vending machine 'cause I'd forgotten lunch in my quest to find Lou.

Took the side staircase and found it had that stale dead and dyin' smell.

Counted the stairs as I took 'em two by two.

Lingered over my choice of drink—tea or coffee, milk or sugar—when I only ever drank coffee black.

Kicked my boot against the vending machine while it poured my drink then thrummed my fingers against my thigh when it took too long.

Anything to keep myself from thinkin' about my little Lou up in that hospital bed sick and wrong with somethin' I was helpless to fight.

I grabbed the coffee and took the stairs back up at a clip, reachin' her room with a head fulla panic like somethin' could've gone wrong in the three minutes I wasn't by her side.

The nurse was still there. Her startled expression collapsed with empathy when she caught the fear in me.

"She's good for now. Just got a little dehydrated. We're giving her fluids and after some rest, she should be just fine."

"Thanks," I grunted, movin' around to sit in that fuckin' orange chair again.

I pulled it right up to her bed and took her hand.

The nurse left quiet.

I was lucky Betsy had been on staff that day or else I wouldn't'a been allowed in when I found out Lou was even there. I'd spent two hours thinkin' worse, that the Nightstalkers had got 'er or she'd been hit by a car or some shit.

It'd been her ex-boyfriend of all fuckin' people who called H.R. to tell her that Lou'd been taken away from school in an ambulance. No surprise that the kid knew 'bout us at that point—everyone in Entrance fuckin' did—but I had to give the kid some grudging respect for pickin' up the phone for his ex like that.

It'd been Betsy who'd had to deal with me when I started yellin' at the bitches in reception who wouldn't tell me where my girl was.

It was Bets who'd told me that Lou had Hodgkin's Lymphoma again.

Loulou stirred slightly, unpeelin' her heavy eyes to reveal those true blue eyes I loved so fuckin' much.

"You're here," she croaked.

I nodded, pulling our tangled hands against my mouth to give hers a kiss. "Wouldn't be anywhere else."

Tears wet those eyes and made my heart clench.

"Even though I seriously suck?"

I grinned despite the turmoil in my fuckin' gut. "Yeah, Lou, even when you seriously suck."

She closed her eyes and dragged in a shaky breath. "Thank God."

"Told ya you were stuck with me," I reminded her.

She grinned like that was the best thing she'd ever heard. "Can you get up here with me?"

I eyed the little bed skeptically, which had her laughin'.

"I'll lean up and you can sit behind me? Please, I'm cold and all I want is you all around me."

Immediately, I let go of her hand and gently helped her scoot forward so I could settle myself against the raised back of the bed and pull her against my chest. She rearranged the blankets against us and carefully pulled the tubes in her hands out from underneath them.

"Sorry I didn't tell you," she whispered as she tucked my arms tighter around her body.

I pressed my lips to her hair. "Forget about it. I know now."

"What does this mean for us?" she asked, her voice girlish with fear.

That fear wrapped cold fingers around my heart and squeezed like a motherfucker.

"Nothin'. You're still my girl and I'm still your man. You need anythin', I'm here for you. That includes puke clean up, pickin' up drugs at the pharmacy, all that kinda shit. It also means you need someone to sit in the hospital with ya and your parents are too fuckin' selfish to do it themselves, all the better for me 'cause I'm gonna be here every fuckin' time."

She sighed into me, settling warm and contented as a cat when I stroked a hand over her hair.

"I might lose it, you know," she muttered.

My hand stilled on the masses of gold silk. "Fuck, baby."

"You might not want me. Cancer isn't a pretty illness, Z."

I gripped her chin and tilted it up 'til I could look into those scared eyes. Pressed a warm kiss to her lips and said, "Don't be a fuckin' dumbass."

"I might die," she whispered even softer.

"You might," I agreed 'cause I wanted to be honest with her but the thought had daggers shootin' between each of my ribs, all angled at my heart.

"Do you think I'll go to heaven?" she asked me.

"Fuck yeah, which sucks for me."

She shifted between my legs, tippin' her head up so she could look past my bearded jaw and into my eyes. "You going to explain that to me?"

I reached out to rub one callused thumb along the plump curve of her lower lip, my concentration so intense it felt like my eyes burned. "You asked me any day 'fore I met you, I woulda said there was no fuckin' chance I'd get into heaven. A man like me havin' done the things I did, things I needed to do? Fuck no."

When she tried to protest, I pressed my thumb harder against her lush mouth and felt my face turn to fuckin' stone. "Now, I ain't makin' you any promises here, little warrior, but if your fine ass is going to heaven—and it fuckin' well is—I'll find a way to get there too. If I gotta move into that fuckin' church and pay penance every goddamn hour, I'll do it. If I gotta give up boozin', guns and drug runnin', I'll fuckin' well do it and I'd do it *now* if it meant I got a place beside my girl behind those pearly gates."

She bit her lip to keep from cryin' because she knew I didn't like her tears and then she valiantly tried to lighten the mood. "You'd probably have to give up cursing too. I think that's a pretty tall order."

"Fuck yeah, it is," I agreed before jerking her even closer to me until we were fused together, until I could feel the reassurin' beat of her heart against my chest. A heartbeat so much more important than my own. "Do it for you, Lou. Do anythin' for you."

CHAPTER THIRTY-TWO

Loulou

MY HOUSE DIDN'T FEEL LIKE MY HOME ANYMORE.

Not that it ever really had.

But the curving arms of the double-sided grand staircase, the plush carpets under the heavy antique furniture, the window hangings dripping with tassels and threads of gold and the crystal lights all seemed too opulent to me now, bright in a way my eyes couldn't handle. I'd grown used to the dark and neon lights of The Lotus and Eugene's Bar, of the cool natural light that spilled through the wide windows of Zeus's rustic house on the beach and cabin in the woods. I craved his lived-in furniture, the cluster of family photos hung haphazardly on the wall leading from the entryway to the kitchen. The sounds of laughter and instant feel of warmth the second you opened the door to that home.

Instead, I sat in my habitual spot at the grand dining table in my father's house wearing a thick brocade white and gold dress that itched my sensitive skin and did its best to collapse the shape of my curves. My hair was up in a swirl, my pearls were in my ears and I was ready for battle.

It was the kind of battle I'd grown up taking part in so I was ready for the role I'd given myself to play. There was something going on with my dad and his companions—the Danners, Venturas, and Mr. Warren—and I was fairly certain it had something to do with The Fallen.

It was the MC who was my family now, so I made it my business to dig a little deeper.

"You look radiant this evening, Louise," my mother praised me.

"I told her the other day how happy I was that her hair wasn't falling out," Mr. Warren shared with her. "It's such pretty hair."

My mother tittered and touched her own artificially blond hair. "Of course, she gets it from me so I'll take that as a compliment."

"You should," he said with a wink that set my mother to blushing.

Yuck.

Was there no one Mr. Warren wouldn't flirt with?

"How're you feeling?" Lionel asked quietly, leaning forward in his seat across from me to make the question more intimate.

Not for the first time, I surprised myself by liking Lionel Danner.

I shrugged. "As they said, not much hair loss yet so I'm a happy camper."

"Louise," my sister Bea chided me.

She'd been forced to attend the dinner because my parents had forgotten to find something else for her to do that night. She looked immensely uncomfortable in her shapeless black dress with her hair done up in a tight bun.

I winked at her just to see the warmth flood her eyes.

"You've been busy lately, *zorra*," Javier said from my side.

I blinked at him. "Have I? No more than usual."

"I suppose for a smart young lady like yourself juggling academics, cheerleading, ballet, chemotherapy, friendships and serving is an easy task," he agreed with a flippant wave of his hand.

I shot a glance at Benjamin but happily he was talking to Irina on his other side.

"As anyone in Entrance will tell you, I'm a talented girl," I said with a sharp smile that cut painfully into my cheeks.

"Yes, with so many interests, one might almost say you're two very different people at the end of the day," Javier said as he swirled that deep red wine in his glass.

I could tell he got off on it, on being a villain. He was like a little kid with a shiny new toy, so eager to play with it that he didn't realize if he wasn't careful, it would break.

"You know so much about me, Javier. I have to say, I'm flattered."

He inclined his head. "I intend to bed down in Entrance for a very long time, Louise. It's good to know the players."

"And what business is that?" I asked innocently. "Maybe I could intern with you one summer."

He laughed. "Maybe. I specialize in pharmaceuticals. Are you interested in that field?"

"Recreationally." I winked.

His laugh was delighted as he leaned forward intimately. "You are a treasure. I can understand why The Fallen MC enjoys your company so much."

I didn't deny that I knew them because it was obvious that he knew everything about Loulou Fox. "What do you know about them?"

"I know that there's a new MC in town and they seem to have The Fallen's every move written down by an oracle before they even make it. And I know, personally, that they are a *very* well-funded organization."

"Doesn't seem you know much more than speculation," I said as I casually cut into my bloody steak and brought a morsel to my mouth.

Javier didn't like my lack of interest. He leaned closer and divulged. "What do I care about a gang but to use it for a greater means. No, I'm not after The Fallen MC in particular so I don't care what they stand for, what they're really about. I only need to know the basic facts to make my moves."

"So you must know Zeus Garro," I said in a low voice as I served him more wine, watching the red liquid bleed into his glass.

"Not as well as you do, but yes."

My smile was sharper than a shard of broken glass as I accidently slopped wine over his hand and then turned to him. "Then you'll know it's fucking hilarious that you think you're so scary because, Javier, I've seen scary. I've fucked scary and I stared him right in the eyes as I did it so let me tell you, you don't have his smile."

The chime of the doorbell sounded throughout the house, stilling conversation because who called during dinnertime?

My parents stared at each other before my dad excused himself to answer the door.

A shiver of foreboding ripped up my spine as I watched him go and then again when I turned back to Javier to see him grinning at me.

"I may not have his smile, *zorra*, but trust me, real evil doesn't need a face, it just needs a presence."

My dad walked back into the room frowning down at a brown manila folder.

"What is it, Ben?" my mother asked.

"Someone left this on the doorstep," he murmured as he unwound the string holding the folder closed and dozens of glossy eight-by-ten photos spilled out.

I was too far away to see what the images depicted but I knew from talking to Zeus that those were the kind of pictures that had been left at the scenes of the fires started at The Fallen properties.

And now they were in my home.

I was on my feet and moving toward my dad before I was even aware of it.

It was too late though. My mother was closer and my father was already there staring down at the puddle of images like he was submerged in sinking sands.

I fell to my knees in the pile and scooped one up in my hands.

It was me, blond hair streaming in the air as I rode behind Zeus on his great black-and-silver beast down the Sea to Sky Highway with my arms tight around him and my face broke up in a wild grin.

Another one showed Zeus, his big body mostly

concealing my own as he caught me from a flying leap into his arms.

Another. His bearded lips on mine outside his house two days ago, a big hand down the back of my jeans palming my bare ass as we made out.

There were so many of them, at least twenty, all depicting my illicit relationship with the thirty-six-year-old outlaw motorcycle President.

I looked up just in time to see my dad's face contort with black rage and then see the closed fist come flying at my face.

It connected with my cheek and sent me reeling backward across the slippery pictures. I blinked up at the chandelier, stunned. My left cheekbone throbbed with blinding pain.

"Benjamin!" my mum cried as she fell down beside me. "What are you doing?"

"She's sleeping with that fucking thug," he roared, pointing his finger at me.

Lionel Danner was suddenly in his face, holding him back and snarling, "You touch her again, I'm taking you into the station, Ben."

"My daughter is a fucking slut!" Dad shouted in his face.

I blinked back tears as I lay on the floor and tried to find my breath.

My dad had just hit me.

Oh my *God*.

With one simple act, the vestiges of my youth fell away and the girl who'd once been Louise Lafayette died. I lay on the ground blinking up at a life that was no longer mine.

There was glitter and money all around me, the dinner party a frozen tableau of class that felt like a false front over something much darker.

My mum helped me to my knees but then grew distracted by the pictures all around us and shakily picked one up in her hand.

It was a bad one for her to have chosen.

In it, I was naked but for one of Zeus's massive tees and I was straddling his lap as he sat on a chair on his front porch. His jeans were clearly undone and my head was thrown back in ecstasy as I ground down on him.

My mum turned to me with wide, horrified eyes and breathed, "Who are you?"

"Your daughter," I reminded her, and only then realized I was crying.

"Not anymore," she said, getting to her feet quickly like I had an infectious disease and she'd already spent too long in my presence.

"Mum," I tried again, but she was already scuttling toward my dad who was still ranting at Lionel.

I sat there on my knees for a second looking at the table where Mr. Warren sat stupefied, staff sergeant Danner looked disgusted, Irina bored and Javier, fucking Javier, was smiling like the Cheshire Cat.

My dad broke through Lionel's hold and stormed over to me. I backed away on my knees and fell onto my ass, hands in front of my face to shield me as he lifted his hand to backhand me. It occurred to me in a strangely manic way that I'd spent my life comparing Zeus to a monster when it was my father who was the true beast, a man dipped in civilized veneer with an empty center where his heart should have been.

"Stop," Bea shouted as she fell in front of me and wrapped her arms around my body like a shield. "Daddy, please, *stop* this."

He leaned down, pried her sobbing body off me and held her away. "Don't touch her, Beatrice."

"I'm not infected with anything, Dad," I tried to explain, my stomach so nauseated I thought I might vomit all over the photos at my knees.

"You sleep with filthy animals, Louise, you're bound to pick something up. Now get up and get the hell out of my house. I will not have a wanton slut living under my roof, let alone one who associates with the likes of Zeus fucking Garro."

The dry, malnourished part of my heart that I'd tried for years to nurture for my family kindled and went up in flames at the mention of Zeus. I surged to my feet, caught my balance with a hand on the table and stared down my dad.

"Fuck you, Benjamin. Maybe if you'd bothered to parent me *at all* the last seventeen years, things would have been different. But they aren't because you're a selfish fucking bastard who only cares about himself and his career. You want me gone, *fine*, I'm fucking out of here."

"Don't you dare fucking come back and you can kiss your education goodbye. There isn't a chance in hell I'm sending you to university now. When that thug leaves you for someone younger don't come crawling back to me for money." He kicked at the photos and sent them flying through the air. "My daughter, a biker slut."

"My father, a daughter abuser," I retorted through the

snot and tears that streamed down my face and into the hem of my ugly brocade dress.

Then with the limited dignity I could muster, I ran to my room to grab what I could before I left the Lafayette mansion for good.

CHAPTER THIRTY-THREE

Loulou

I KNEW MY FACE WAS ALREADY SWELLING AND DISCOLOURING when Harleigh Rose opened the door for me and covered her dropped-open mouth with both hands.

She was a biker's daughter so I figured she'd seen worse but maybe not on a woman.

"Hi," I said.

There were three big Louis Vuitton suitcases at my feet and two more duffels slung over my shoulders. I had a lot of stuff I didn't want to leave behind, including the wooden box in one of the duffels that contained my letters from Z.

"Ohmigawd," Harleigh Rose breathed, stepping forward with a lifted hand to flutter her fingers along the goose egg forming on my cheekbone. "What happened to you?"

A second later a big shadow loomed behind H.R. and

Zeus was in the doorway, pushing her gently aside even as his face darkened with fury.

"My dad knows about us," I said calmly.

Then, because I'd finally made it to safety and a pair of arms that would close around me if I fell, I burst into tears.

Gently, Zeus hefted me into his arms so I could wrap my legs around his waist and bury my face in his hair. He walked me in the house straight to the left where the family room opened up into the kitchen and sat down with me in one of the big wooden chairs at the dining room table.

Cress and King sat at the table with their half-eaten dinners in front of them, frozen in the act of eating because they were both staring at me with horror.

Zeus's hand stroked down my hair as he ordered King, "Get 'er bags and put 'em in my room. Then get your ass back down 'ere 'cause the second Lou stops cryin' long enough to tell me why the motherfuckin' fuck did this to her, we're rollin' out."

King shoved back from his chair, already pulling his phone from his pocket. Cressida got up too and went to the stove to put on the kettle and grab a bottle of tequila from the freezer.

Zeus peeled my wet face out of his neck and held my head like I was breakable as an eggshell in his ham like hands. A low growl started up in his chest as two fingers gently brushed the aching skin of my cheek.

I placed my hand over his heart, dipping a finger into the divot of his gunshot scar. "Sorry I interrupted you in the middle of dinner."

Zeus shook his head at me but I'd successfully broken the seal on his bottled-up fury and let a little air escape.

Cress and H.R. laughed at me. Then to my surprise, the latter came over to place a gentle hand on my shoulder and asked, "Want me to make you up a plate?"

"Smells good."

H.R. grinned. "I made it, my famous chili. Dad's a shit cook, which you probably know already, but I make some serious magic in the kitchen."

"Looking forward to tasting it," I said with a small smile as I wearily rested my head back on Z's hard chest.

H.R. nodded then looked up at the rage in her father's face and hers transformed into a mirror of that fury. Evidently, no Garro liked a man who hit women and Z's girl wanted to see him ruin my dad nearly as much as he did.

"What the fuck happened?" he asked me.

I sighed deeply. "If I tell you will you promise not to kill him?"

"Fuck no."

I sighed even deeper. "Didn't think so."

"You're still gonna fuckin' tell me," he warned me.

"Someone sent my dad photos of us like you've been getting at the fire sites. There was a whole dossier of them so clearly someone's been watching us."

"Fuck," he roared over my shoulder but I didn't flinch, because I'd known he'd react this way and part of me yearned for it. I wanted to pit my guardian monster against my beast of a father and see Zeus tear him apart with his bare hands.

"I'm goin' to have a word with the fuckin' mayor."

"He might be expecting that, Z," I warned him because even though my dad seemed relatively oblivious, it was clear Javier had a part in the unveiling.

"Good." He grinned down at me then captured my mouth in a toe-curling kiss.

"What was that for?" I panted slightly when he was done, my hand fisted into his tee.

"Can't have my girl in my lap and not kiss 'er," he said like it was obvious.

"Thank you for being my safe place," I whispered, aware of his daughter and Cressida in the room but not caring because my heart was going to implode if I didn't share some of what I was feeling.

"I got you, little girl," he reminded me of the words he'd said when I was seven years old and running toward him through a hail of gunfire.

Even then, I knew the kind of man he was and knew he'd take care of me.

I brushed my lips against his, so silky smooth compared to the roughness of his beard. "I love you, ya know?"

He smiled under my questing mouth. "Love you like it's my religion, little Lou." Then he pressed his forehead to mine and said, "Just in case there was any fuckin' doubt, this is your house now and my bed is your bed. Wanted you here anyway, sorry it happened this way, little warrior, so fuckin' sorry, but glad you're here all the fuckin' same."

"Tequila?" Cressida asked, coming to the table with a full bottle of Patrón Gold, a bowl of fresh cut limes and a salt-shaker. "I only learned how to do a shooter last year but I'm freaking *hooked*. I think it solves everything."

"Not hangovers," H.R. said drily.

"No tequila for Lou," Zeus said over my laughter. "She can't drink doin' chemo. That tea you put on would be good. Somethin' herbal."

Cress, H.R. and I all turned our heads to stare at Zeus with the same shocked expression.

He shrugged. "Did some research when I found out Lou was sick."

"You did?" I asked, moved beyond belief and also a little amused that my badass biker had spent the time looking up medical information.

"Fuck yeah. Gotta know how to take care of my little warrior. Now, get off me so I can handle your fuckin' father."

He slipped me out of his lap and onto the chair then jerked his chin at King as he came back into the kitchen shrugging on his leather jacket and looking like something out of a James Dean movie.

"Aim to maim not kill," Harleigh Rose called out helpfully as they headed out the front door.

I laughed at her and curled up into an even tighter ball, wincing at the pain in my eye now that Zeus wasn't around to distract me. H.R. noticed and went to get a pack of frozen peas from the fridge. She wrapped the package in a dishcloth and gently pressed it to my cheek.

I hissed.

"Sorry, can you hold this here?" Harleigh Rose asked. "I'll make you a plate of food and then we can watch a movie. I know you've had a rough night and I should let you choose the film but I'm really big into old Westerns right now, so how about we compromise. I choose the genre, you choose the film?"

"She's only into Westerns because she has a huge crush on Officer Danner," Cressida explained as she prepared my pot of tea.

I laughed before I realized that she was serious because Harleigh Rose sent her a withering glare.

"Sorry, just, a biker's kid with a cop? Isn't that like *wrong*?"

She tossed her wild mane of streaky blond hair over her shoulder and fisted her hands on her hips as she leveled me with a look. "Sorry, but isn't the mayor's kid with a MC Prez the same fuckin' thing?"

"Touché," I said with a wince then winced again because the expression put pressure on my cheek.

Cressida laughed as she came to the table with the tea and poured us our cups like a perfect little lady. "I shacked up with my eighteen-year-old student a week after we started dating, so I don't think any of us are in a position to judge the other."

"I still can't believe you did that," I said, shaking my head. "Did you guys do it at school?"

"Um, *ew*!" Harleigh Rose put her fingers in her ears. "Disgusting much?"

Cress winked at me. "The better question would be, when *didn't* we do it at school? My King has a thing for public sex."

"Mmm, I know what you mean, Z and I did it under the bleachers at a basketball game."

"No," Cress covered her laughing mouth and propped her pretty face in her hands. "In your cheerleading outfit? King would *love* something like that...Do you think I could borrow that?"

"Okay, hold up," H.R. demanded on a shout. "If we're all going to be one big modern fuckin' family we need to make a rule about sex talk. I don't think my brain can handle knowing what my dad and brother do in bed."

"Fair." I nodded slowly. "My brain can barely handle it either and I'm the one *doing* it."

"Okay, see, that's what I'm talking about, waaay gross."

Cressida and I laughed, or at least, I tried to, but my cheek was too swollen to allow much movement and the frozen peas had made my face numb.

A key rattled in the front door and a second later, Mute appeared in the front hall. He didn't look over at us startled women. Instead, he calmly relocked the door and put his keys on the catch-all table beside the stairs. He watched his booted feet move across the wood floorboards as he crossed into the kitchen and came to a stop unerringly at my side.

Only then did he look up at me and when he did a strange garbled groan emerged from his chest.

"Foxy," he said, dropping to his knees and taking the peas from my hand so he could look at the split flesh. "No."

"I'm okay, Mute," I said softly.

"Wasn't there," he grunted.

There was heartbreak in his dark eyes as he stared up at me. It echoed in my chest.

"Not your fault, Mute. My dad's an asshole."

"Shoulda been there," he said again.

"Can't be there all the time," I pointed out reasonably.

His heavy brow fell into a glower. "Me or Zeus."

"Mute..."

He held out his hand with his pinky extended like he'd seen me do with Zeus.

The gesture warmed my heart but more, I knew this behavior from the Autism Centre. If I didn't agree with Mute on something he felt this strongly about, I knew he would throw a tantrum like Sammy would have. My silent hero was still smarting from not knowing about the cancer and I knew this was the final straw.

Mute would stalk me if he had to, in order to keep me safe.

So, I linked my pinky finger with his and we shook thumbs.

"We're going to watch a movie," I told him. "A Western."

"John Wayne," he said instantly, getting to his feet.

He went to a long cupboard beside the fridge, reached in and came out with a huge bag full of salted nuts and another with HealthWise popcorn. Even his snack food was always healthy. The three of us watched him as he walked out of the kitchen and the sound of the TV floated in from the other room.

"Come on," he called.

I turned to Cress and H.R. and grinned. "I think John Wayne awaits."

CHAPTER THIRTY-FOUR

Zeus

THE NIGHT WAS MINE.

It always had been.

I'd never been scared of monsters in the dark or things that went bump in the night. I was part of that world, been born into it and grown up with intrinsic knowledge of how to tame those beasts and corral those demons toward my ends.

The shadows embraced me as I stalked across the Lafayette yard 'round to the back door where I'd broken in before, using the same lock picks and the same alarm code Curtains and Lou had confirmed for me beforehand.

The house was quiet.

But I could smell the fear and shame waftin' through the

house like the scent of some baked thing, this one cookin' deep in the gut of the man I'd come to scare.

It was just me.

King had wanted a part, Mute too, and Bat, Nova and Buck had been so fuckin' enraged I was sure there'd be a drive-by shootin' on tomorrow's front page of the paper.

But I was Prez and what I said fuckin' went.

So, it was just me. Wearin' all black beneath my cut, leather gloves on my hands and steel toes in my boots.

I had a message to send like the angel fuckin' Gabriel.

Warm yellow light spilled out the door of Benjamin Lafayette's study and the quiet rustle of papers sounded within.

Alone and workin'.

A normal night.

Not one where he'd beaten and verbally abused a seventeen-year-old girl with cancer.

Just a normal fuckin' night in the Lafayette Mansion on Entrance Hill.

Fuckin' dickbag.

I debated stormin' into the room like an avengin' angel but decided that my wrath couldn't be settled with bluster. It sat cold and vibrant, complex like a multifaceted diamond. That hatred had sat like a lump in my gut through the years of writin' Lou, hearin' about the neglect her father shoveled out and the pressure to be perfect he shoveled in. But now it'd been condensed by the monumental weight of his latest fuckin' transgression.

He'd beaten his fuckin' daughter.

Hit her right in the face.

It burned in me that I'd been at the root'a that action, but I knew with clarity that this was not my fuckin' fault.

I wasn't the man bringin' her a lifetime of pain.

I was the man healin' her, from the inside out.

So, instead of dramatics, I slipped around the door and took advantage of his fuckin' self-absorption and walked through the shadows clingin' to the wall until I was just behind him.

He was older than me, not by a lot, but there was grey in his hair and thinnin' at the back of his head that had to have made him self-conscious. He reached back to rub at the spot like he unconsciously felt something behind him puttin' pressure there.

I grinned as I stepped forward, my 9mm in one hand.

Quick as I flash, I took his thin neck in a headlock and pressed the cold butt of the gun to his temple. He let out a shrill kinda garble, the sound a man makes just before he pisses himself.

Loved knowing he was such a pussy that the first sign of a threat put the fear of God into him.

"Shh," I hushed him and tightened my grip so he'd stop his struggle. "Just here to have a chat, Benny Boy. Father to father. Man to man. See, I got my girl at home with a black fuckin' eye and she tells me it was *you* who did it."

I laughed in his ear and felt him shudder.

"Hard to believe though, ain't it? A man throwin' a punch at the face of his own daughter, a young woman with half of his fuckin' DNA and all of his fuckin' love inside 'er? Honest to Christ, Benny, it's hard to wrap my fuckin' mind around. So, I thought I'd come here and ask you straight up, you hit Lou tonight?"

His Adam's apple scraped against my forearm as he swallowed hard.

"I'm her father. This is between me and my daughter." He tried to say it strong, like the mayor he was, only he didn't have shit to stand on and he knew it.

"See, that's where you're just fuckin' *wrong*. That girl you hit tonight, she mighta been your daughter once and she might still have your fuckin' genes, but she's not your daughter now. And to be honest with you, Benny Boy, she started bein' *my* fuckin' girl the first time you left her down in a colossal fuckin' way, when there were bullets flyin' everywhere and you ducked down to save yourself 'fore your kid. She became my girl the second she saw me 'cross the lot and knew in her soul she'd found someone to take care of 'er true.

She was right about that. I take care of my brothers and unlike you, Benny, I put my kids 'fore my every fuckin' breath. And now I have Lou? Now, you've gifted her to me on a fuckin' platter? I'm gonna keep 'er. She'll be warm in my bed, safe in my house and protected from anything that might fuckin' hurt her, *includin' you,* for the rest of her goddamn life."

I tightened my hold on his neck 'til he gasped for breath and then I shoved the barrel of my gun into his mouth until he choked on it.

My voice was low, almost too low and rough to understand but I spoke close to his ear so he wouldn't miss a fuckin' word'a it.

"I'm not gonna hurt you like I wanna, Benny. I'm not gonna string you up from your balls, rip off your pathetic little dick and shove it down your throat or skin you alive and dip you in fuckin' acid. Hush," I ordered when he let out a scared little whimper. "I'm not gonna do any of that 'cause I got a beautiful fuckin' girl to get home to, but I am gonna share somethin' with you. The next time you touch Lou, the next time you degrade 'er or fuckin' *breathe* on 'er the wrong way, I'm gonna end your life and I'm gonna do it with my bare hands around your neck so that I can have the satis-fuckin'-faction of feelin' your pathetic life leave your body. You get me, Benny Boy?"

He nodded as enthusiastically as he could with my arm wrapped around his throat.

I shoved the gun a little farther down his gullet just to hear him choke and then removed it so I could hit the moth-erfucker hard over that thinnin' spot on his fuckin' head so he passed out.

He'd given Lou bad nightmares with his shit that night.

It was only fair I gave him some in return.

And I was only too fuckin' happy to be the monster that starred in that show.

CHAPTER THIRTY-FIVE

Loulou

I MOVED INTO THE GARRO HOUSE JUST IN TIME FOR Christmas. It was strange to live in a house filled with a close but busy family. Harleigh Rose went to Entrance Public school, which started fifteen minutes later and ended half an hour earlier than EBA and at first, she spent most of her time out of the house hanging out with her boyfriend, but as the month progressed and the Christmas spirit deepened, she spent more and more time at home with the family.

King and Cress were home for winter vacation from university and splitting their time between Zeus's house and the clubhouse because Cress's cabin on Back Bay Rd. was undergoing serious renovations. This meant that I walked in on them making out a lot. As in all over the house at all hours of the day. They were two university students without a whole lot to do over break so they mostly just holed up in King's room in the basement or made out when they surfaced for air.

It was strange living with Zeus. I'd never lived by myself, let alone with a lover before so I'd never experienced tripping over men's clothes strewn across the floor because he never picked up after himself or falling into the toilet because he never put the goddamn toilet seat down. He was also the Prez of a highly successful, highly illegal MC that turned wicked profits growing top quality BC Bud and selling to distributors, as well as several lucrative lawful businesses that needed minding. On top of all that, his life was his club, which meant that I didn't see Z as much as I would have thought.

He didn't have a schedule. He was a biker so he did what he wanted when he wanted and most of the time, he wanted to hang out in the morning fucking me in his bed, eating breakfast with his kids and working his big, hulking body in the gym attached to his garage. In exchange, he wasn't around much in the evenings so I ended up spending a lot of time with H.R. and Mute, watching TV, playing poker and cooking. Zeus refused to eat the healthy meals Mute made whenever he was in charge of dinner but I was learning to make things he liked, massive platters of lasagna, homemade deep-dish pizza and a meatloaf that was actually *good*.

I'd even made Christmas dinner with H.R., Cress and Mute and it'd been really fucking good. We'd all eaten at the clubhouse so that we had space for any of the brothers and their families to join us and a lot of them did. When we were done eating, before the serious drinking began, Axe-Man, King and Bat had taken H.R., Cress and me out back to teach us how to use our Christmas presents (identical Sig Sauer hand guns) on bottles they lined up outside. We hadn't had a Christmas tree or decorations because bikers didn't go in for that stuff and I didn't have any money to get presents for anyone so I'd made do with writing them letters, but it was the best Christmas I'd ever spent. Not least of all, because Zeus had surprised me with a new car because Benjamin had mine repossessed the week before.

It was a Camaro and it was kickass in the extreme, silver-and-matte-black just like Z's Harley.

The past two weeks had been rough because the chemo was hitting me harder now but our New Years Eve party at the clubhouse had been epic.

I didn't drink or smoke, but I fucked Z in his room in the middle of the chaos because he couldn't take the sight of me in my fishnet thigh highs and little black skater dress anymore. I'd played pool with Nova, Axe-Man and Boner and laughed with everyone else when Boner lost and was made to drink a pint of toilet water. I danced until I felt dizzy with Lila, let Buck teach me how to play darts even though I already knew how, and had a silent argument with Mute over what playlist to put over the surround speakers until he'd given up with an expressive blink and retreated to the bar for more booze.

It was one of the best nights *ever*.

But the first day of the New Year was even better because I'd woken up beside my man and I was in the mood to worship at the altar of my god.

I wanted to lick the veins that stood out against his bulging muscles, trace the lattice of roots up to his heart and press my tongue there to taste his heartbeat. I wanted to use my tongue, teeth, lips and fingers to explore every inch of his giant's body and I'd taken my time doing so, stroking over the coarse hairs on his thick arms and licking over the steep wedges of muscle cutting up his torso into defined lines. I'd done everything but touch his cock for so long that he was growling and shaking like a grumpy bear, his taste gone to salt with sweat under my tongue.

He was laid out for me, his huge body taking up most of our king-sized bed, his thick thighs parted and bent at the knees to make room for my body.

It was only then I'd set my lips to his flushed cock and worked him over with my mouth.

I looked up from my place on my knees into Zeus's lightning-bright eyes to say, "Happy New Year, Z."

Then I opened my mouth wide and sucked his entire length down my throat and hummed in triumph as his legs shook, his hands tightened in my hair and his cock jumped in my mouth.

"Fuck yeah," he growled long and low as he started to cum in my mouth. "Take my cum, little girl."

A shiver rippled up my spine as his taste filled my mouth, warm and salty, so delicious it made my pussy pulse so close to orgasm all I needed to do was grind my clit against his hair roughened leg to come. So, I did. Gyrating on him like a dirty, wanton girl desperate to get off. He spanked my ass lazily as I climbed up his body to collapse on his chest. He'd wrapped his fist in my hair and taken my mouth, not caring about the taste of himself on my tongue. In fact, loving it because he was a dirty old man and having me young and forbidden in his bed made him want to enact his dirtiest fantasies.

Needless to say, I was loving my life at Zeus's side, in his house and in his bed.

I'd never smiled so much in my life as I had in the last month of living with him.

I was still smiling when I dragged myself out of his unmade bed to clean up a little in the bathroom. My body felt loose and limber as it only ever did rarely now and always with him. Even my face, gaunt from the chemo, glowed with post-coital satisfaction as I braced my hands on the sink and looked at myself in the mirror. My blond hair was tousled all around my face in such aggressive bedhead it made me laugh. I lifted my hands to rake them through my locks and my heart stopped.

Carefully, I continued to pull my fingers to the ends of my hair and brought them down to the sink basin. Thick ribbons of gold silk lay across my palms like an offering to a lover.

No.

No.

I knew this. I remembered it from the first time it had happened ten years ago when my nanny was brushing my hair and it had all started raining down around us like spilled thread.

It was happening again.

I was losing my hair.

A sob bubbled up my throat and burst open in the air.

No.

It was such a stupid, vain thing but I couldn't stand to lose my hair, not again. Not when I was dating the most gorgeous man I'd ever set eyes on and he looked at me like I was the most gorgeous woman he'd ever dreamt of.

"No," I choked out on another loud sob that echoed through the big bathroom.

I bent over the sink with my discarded hair in my hands and cried into the porcelain.

Thirty seconds later, Zeus's rough hands were wrapping around my hips and he was folding his big body over mine.

"Little Lou, babe, what's wrong with my girl?"

I cried harder.

I hated that he had to go through this with me. He'd already held my hair back while I puked into the toilet until all that was left was bile, putrid and green. He'd taken time out of his busy days to sit with me while the poison therapy churned through my veins, playing poker with me even though he always won and entertaining me with stories about his brothers and his youth. He drove me to every checkup and sat with his arms crossed and his brow furrowed as if he could intimidate the doctors into giving us better news.

And now this.

Now, I was subjecting him to a potentially bald girlfriend.

When I didn't answer him, he gently pulled my body upright and into his then even more tenderly unfurled my fists. A low sound of sadness rumbled through his chest as he traced a finger over the lost hair in my hands.

"My girl loves her hair," he muttered.

I nodded, too overcome to trust my voice.

He pressed his nose into the hair above my ear, ducking down slightly so he could do so. Then he started talking in a low voice I felt in my blood, his eyes burnished steel on mine as he traced over my face with two calloused fingertips. "You know what I love, Lou? Love the shape of your face like a heart in my hands, the way your lips look swollen and so fuckin' lush even 'fore I kiss 'em. Love the way your ribs narrow and your hips curve so there's this space for my big hand right at your waist. Love the skin behind your knees and ears, at the base of your throat and between your plump tits 'cause it's so fuckin' sensitive and it flushes such a pretty pink."

He spun me away from the mirror and lifted me onto the sink then stepped between my thighs. I tipped my head back to look up into his solemn face because he had such a fierce grip on my heart, I was worried it would rip in two if I disengaged before he let me.

"You lose your moonbeam hair, your bombshell shape and your sexual appetite, I don't give a fuck. 'Cause I love your soul better than I love anythin' else and that includes the fan-fuckin-tastic package it comes in. You got me, Lou?"

I couldn't breathe because he held my breath, couldn't think because he'd rewritten my thoughts into ones of his own making. He controlled me but only to love me, to make me understand how I could love myself better than I already did.

Suddenly, I understood that I'd insulted him by being heartbroken about my hair. Of course, Z would never care if I were bald or pink-haired or blonde.

"Sorry," I whispered.

He cupped his hands around my face and pressed a kiss to the tip of my nose. "Love you even when you don't."

Another sob catapulted out of my mouth.

He caught it in his as he kissed me, our tongues salty from my tears.

"My girl loves her hair," he muttered again, scouring my face when he pulled back from me. "Listen, want you to do somethin' for me."

"Anything," I said immediately.

He looked hard into my eyes then nodded and opened the drawer to the left of my hip, pulling out his electric shaver and plugging it into the wall behind me. He never used it unless it was to give his beard a quick trim. My man had a lot of hair, thick gorgeous waves of it that fell to his shoulders like gold-dipped mahogany. It was one of my favourite things to run my hands through the windswept tangles, to tug it while he feasted between my thighs and hold it tight while he kissed me.

I looked up with confusion in my eyes.

"Want you to cut it for me, Lou," he explained.

"No!" I said immediately.

"Yeah, little warrior. See, it's important to me you get that I'm in this with you. Can't suffer what you suffer, can't take that pain from ya like I want to more than fuckin' anythin'. But I can stand with you. Don't know if you'll lose all that hair but if you do, I wanna do it with you."

Tears burned in my throat as I tangled my fingers in the ends of his shoulder-length hair. "But I love your hair."

"You love yours. Mine'll grow back just like yours."

My body felt saturated with love, water-logged with gratitude so great that I felt I would drown in it. "What could I have ever done in a past life to deserve a man like you?"

His eyes flashed as he leaned close. "This isn't about that shit. We deserve each other 'cause we get each other. I know the heart of ya and you know the heart of me. Deservin' or not deservin' has nothin' to do with it and it fuckin' can't 'cause if I get to thinkin' 'bout that question, I lose every time."

"Z," I breathed, wrapping my legs around his hips and diving my hands deep into his hair. "Don't let anyone tell you that you aren't what you are."

He grinned at me, amused and feeling indulgent. "And what's that?"

"A true fallen angel, too bad for heaven, too good for hell, stuck on earth like a living divinity."

"I think I'll stick to bein' a monster," he teased.

But I was serious, and I let him know it by sticking my tongue out at him.

He chuckled. "You're the fallen angel here, Lou, and I'm never fuckin' givin' ya back to Heaven."

"I'm good with that."

"Good, now come on. Take this fuckin' mess off my head," he ordered.

I watched him from my perch as he stepped back and turned on the bath. His glutes were round, powerful half moons at the base of his strong back and his thick thighs were dusted with dark hair that condensed at his groin and tapered off just above his wide, brown feet.

He was a god, something from ancient times when gods roamed the earth beside mortals and acted wicked and strong just because they fucking well could.

Just like my man.

He turned to me when the bath was set to running and declared, "You can wash my hair first. Like it when you do that for me."

I liked it too. It was one of the little rituals we'd developed when I'd moved in and we had the opportunity to develop routines. We showered together whenever we could because Zeus liked my curves and he loved them slippery. He also liked my cunt and his fingers slipping among my folds, ostensibly cleaning but really getting me ready to fuck pressed up against the wall or bent over with my hands pressed against.

I'd miss washing that glorious head of hair more than I'd miss washing my own if it all fell out.

But I got where he was coming from because if the situation were reserved, I'd want to do it for him too.

So, I watched as he lowered himself into the tub, his body so big that his limbs barely fit in the big well of it. He hooked his arms and legs over the sides and sank back into the steaming water looking just as ridiculous and strangely charming as a giant taking a bubble bath would.

I giggled through my drying tears and went to sit on the side of the tub, settling his big head in my lap. He hummed like some great beast under my petting hands as I squirted shampoo into them and stroked them through his locks, using my thumbs hard on his skull. Then because I couldn't help myself, I dragged my sudsy hands down his strong brown throat, rubbing at the corded muscles there and then down farther still, to circle my palms over his marble pectorals and flat, brown nipples. He didn't have any tattoos on his chest and when I'd asked him about it, he'd told me that there'd never been anything important enough to wear near his heart. He already wore the name of his children on either pulse point at the underside of his wrists. The fact that he was such a good, loving dad turned my crank harder than it should have, given I was only seventeen.

When I was done rinsing his hair with the handheld

showerhead, I leaned down to pull the drain and Zeus caught my hands in a firm grip.

We caught eyes.

"Don't you fucking dare," I warned him.

Of course, he fucking dared.

I screeched as I went tumbling into the bath on top of him.

He laughed so loud it seemed to shake the walls and the water sloshed all around us, over the lip of the tub.

I hit him in the chest.

"Like the look'a ya wet," he grinned, ducking his chin so he could see my nipples against his chest.

I shook my head at him but didn't resist the urge to lean down to kiss his full lips. Then because he was Zeus and even though we'd had sex three times in the past twelve hours, we made out until the bathwater was cold.

I drained the water and dried off my man with a towel because the opportunity to do so was any girl's wet dream. Then I dragged a chair into the bathroom and sat him down with his head resting over the sink and turned on the electric shaver.

I stared at it vibrating in my hand and felt the tears clog my throat again. Zeus opened his eyes from his comfortable laze and grabbed my hand with one of his, totally engulfing it.

He held my eyes as he brought it awkwardly down to the middle front of his hairline and pressed down into his crown of hair.

I sobbed as we cut off an inch from the root in one long, thick strip.

Then I sobbed even harder as we worked together all

over his broad scalp until a thick pile of sun-kissed hair lay in the sink and all that was left on his head was a short pelt of mink. I turned off the buzzing shaver and fell into his open arms, straddling his waist and kneeling up so that I could press my palms to each side of his bearded face and kiss all over his newly shaved hair. My tears watered the shorn tresses until they gleamed and then Zeus had had enough and he pulled me down into his arms so he could seal my crying mouth with a hard kiss.

"I got you," he murmured into my hair. "I got you."

THE GARROS and I were going for breakfast at Stella's Diner to kick the rest of their hangovers. I was holding Z's big hand even though everyone on Main Street stopped to stare at good girl Louise Lafayette walking beside the notorious Zeus Garro. It made my spirits lift to be able to offend their sensibilities like that so I stopped my man often to plant a big kiss on him just to hear the gasps of offended townsfolk.

Cress was trying to convince me that Satan was the hottest character in the history of the written word.

"Seriously, you should read it. Honestly, I'm thinking of

making it a mandatory family read," she declared with a confidence that moved me.

There was no doubt in her mind that we were all a family. King was her man, I was Zeus's and therefore we were part of the Garro clan.

The thought warmed me the way being a Lafayette never had.

"I don't read," H.R. declared. "Unless it's magazines."

Cress gasped and held an agonized hand to her heart.

H.R. giggled.

"Satan kicks ass," Mute decided to say.

We all stared at him for a second, surprised he'd spoken and even more surprised he'd read such a difficult book.

To my infinite joy, he blushed and looked at me to explain, "King liked it so I read it."

His best friend slung an arm around his shoulders because that was how he operated, close and casual, even with a man who didn't like to be touched. "I fuckin' agree. Satan's the shit. And hey, if Mute's read it then H.R., you gotta too."

She rolled her eyes. "Unlike you, I'm not trying to get into Cress's pants so I'm gonna pass."

All of us, even Mute, laughed.

King smiled smugly and tucked Cress under his other arm. "Who said I was still tryin'?"

It was Cress's turn to roll her eyes. "The second you stop trying is the second I'm gone."

King winked at me, completely unperturbed by the threat. "She's fulla shit. Got my fuckin' words tattooed on her skin. She knows she's my Queen for fuckin' life."

I laughed at their banter as I always did and started to

unwrap a cherry lollipop. I noticed with feminine satisfaction that Zeus's burning gaze immediately landed on my mouth. I pretended not to notice him as I rolled the round red treat between my lips then sucked it hard into my mouth.

He groaned softly and the hand in mine pulled away so he could tuck it into the back pocket of my jeans and squeeze my ass.

I was so distracted by his wicked grin that I didn't notice when we all pulled up in front of Bones Barber Shop. It was only when the bells chimed over the door as we entered the old-fashioned wood-paneled space that I stopped to take in my surroundings.

There were brothers everywhere. Men in leather cuts with long hair and long beards looking hungover as shit because it was the first day of the New Year and they'd partied hard in only the way true rebels know how to party the night before.

I frowned at them all.

"Stella's is down the street," I informed them.

"Nothin' funny," Nova declared, wincingly holding his handsome head from where he was sprawled half in and half out of a chair. "In fact, no fuckin' talkin' 'less it's absolutely necessary."

"Hit the bottle too hard last night?" Cress laughed at him.

He grinned. "Two bottles of Patrón and a pair of twins up from Vancouver. Was fuckin' worth it."

"Seriously, what are we all doing here?" I asked, turning to Zeus because he was being conspicuously silent.

He stared at me with his arms crossed, his booted feet spread apart like a general about to issues orders for war.

"Told the brothers why I cut off my hair. They're here to do the same."

I blinked at him and in that time, the tears came.

Fuck but I hated to cry but fuck if this wasn't the time to do it.

I brought my fist to my mouth to stop the sobs and turned slowly again to face the twenty odd bikers coalesced in the room. They all stared at me with varying degrees of solemnity.

"Don't try an' talk us outta it, Foxy," Buck grumbled from his chair. He had coarse grey hair he wore in a short queue at the back of his red neck. "Not askin' your permission. Just figured you'd wanna be a part of it."

I took a deep breath, in and out as I felt the Garros surround my back and H.R. came up beside me to take my hand.

"Cress and I are cuttin' ours too. Just to our shoulders but we got long hair and we're gonna donate the clippings to the cancer foundation that makes wigs for chemo patients," she explained in a sweet voice I only heard from her rarely, usually when she was speaking to her dad, brother or Cress.

And she was using it with me. While holding my hand. And telling me that she was going to cut off half of her thick, crazy-beautiful hair for me.

"This is way too much," I whispered because my voice wouldn't work properly past the lump in my throat.

Zeus's heat hit my back a second before his arms wrapped around me and his voice moved through my body as he said, "Nothin's ever too much for family."

I deep breathed as I stood in the circle of Z's arms, in the circle of his blood family and within the greater circle of his chosen one and I knew then if I'd ever doubted it before, that I had made the right choice in choosing Z, and more, in believing enough in myself to have made that choice at all.

He waited a beat to let me collect myself then stepped forward, rolling up the sleeves of the black Henley he wore under his cut and saying, "Let's get this show on the fuckin' road so we can hit Stella's for some fuckin' grease and pancakes. Someone hand me one of those fuckin' shavers. I'm doin' Nova's hair. That pretty boy's always had it comin' to 'im."

CHAPTER THIRTY-SIX

Loulou

I WAS SICKER THAN A DOG RUN OVER TWICE BY A SIXTEEN-wheeler.

It was late January and the latest round of chemotherapy was kicking my ass worse than it ever had before. Logically, I knew it was because they were targeting the cancer more aggressively than they had before, that this was a new technique that had proven very successful with women my age in my condition.

I was young and fit, it had seemed like a good idea to my parents and my doctors at the time to knock me around for three rounds of chemo in the depths of dreary winter to see if they couldn't beat the cancer out of me. My mother was the only one who kept in touch with the doctors now and made sure the insurance papers were signed, but I hadn't seen her or my dad since the incident at the dinner party before Christmas.

I sure as hell felt beaten but I didn't feel cured. Not even close.

The only things I was grateful for in all of it was that I didn't have to go to school sick as I was, and Zeus was gone on a run with The Fallen, so he didn't have to see me like this.

He hadn't wanted to go but things were going badly for the club. The second round of fires had revealed that there was definitely another snitch in their ranks, and Z didn't feel comfortable leaving the San Diego run to anyone else, not even his most trusted brothers. After all, back in the day, Zeus had earned his presidency by backstabbing his President and he didn't want history repeating itself.

When he'd left, I hadn't been that bad but the past two weeks had been rough. I'd barely left the house and I hated getting out of bed because my entire body ached like a livid bruise. Zeus called every day to check in and I was never without at least two brothers in the house, lounging around shooting the shit with me as if they actually wanted to hang out with an invalid, and watch marathon sessions of *Game of Thrones*. I knew they reported back to him that I was getting worse, so I wasn't surprised when Z called to tell me he was coming home early and leaving Bat in charge on the run to California. I'd tried to downplay things because I didn't want to cause an issue for club business, but I was thrilled my guardian monster was coming home.

Without him, Mute, Harleigh Rose, and Bea were my angels.

H.R. and Bea helped me in the shower, which was

embarrassing but necessary and they brushed and braided my hair away from my face. H.R. helped me get dressed in new pajamas each day so that the old ones didn't smell like sick sweat and puke, and she made me countless pots of tea that I could barely bring myself to drink. Bea visited nearly every day and she always brought teen magazines, outside world gossip and endless optimism. Apparently, Mum knew she visited but Dad didn't. I didn't know what to think about it until Phillipa gave Bea my old Hephaestus Auto toque one day and told her to give it to me. It was a nice gesture, nowhere near enough, but nice.

Mute didn't do much and yet he did everything. He was there when I woke up in the morning and he was there when I went to bed at night. Most of the time, I think he slept in the old tree house in the backyard for a few hours before coming back to hang out with me. We watched cult classics because we both loved them; *The Godfather* trilogy, *Star Wars*, Quentin Tarantino and Alfred Hitchcock collections. We played board games and card games but spoke as little as we could because Mute, obviously, preferred it and I found it tiring.

My entire body ached, but it was my feet and lungs that faired the worst. By week three, I needed a respirator because my oxygen levels were so low. The bottoms of my feet were deeply bruised and even though I was used to a lifetime of pain in them from ballet and pointe shoes, this was worse. I whimpered at any contact against them so poor Mute had to piggyback me around the house if Bea demanded I get out of bed more often.

I was too sick to see Sammy at the Autism Centre so Mute or Margie brought him to me at home. He was curious about my illness and wanted to know how to fix me. But I didn't have the answers to give him and he'd twice had a tantrum because of it and the fact that when he'd last visited, I'd been too weak and pained to cuddle him as he liked.

I was tired of being sick and I was sick and fucking tired of Zeus's house even though it'd only been my home for two months.

So, when another Friday rolled around, I begged Mute to take us all up to Z's cabin outside Whistler. I missed my man so much it made my heart palpitate just to think of him and the cabin was *our* place. Mute wanted to refuse me, I knew, but he couldn't deny me anything, especially not when I was like this. We couldn't go on his bike obviously but he borrowed a truck from Hephaestus and the four of us loaded it with all the yummy health food we could find and about twenty cherry lollipops because they were still my weakness and we headed up into the mountains.

It was exactly what I needed. I felt like a teenage girl having a slumber party with her friends as we all got into our jammies—even Mute who wore, hilariously, sleep pants that looked exactly like his normal blue jeans and one of his standard black tees—and made a mound of pillows in front of the TV so we could sprawl out comfortably to watch our *Banshee* marathon on HBO.

I was lying diagonally with my head on Mute's stomach, his hands in my gold hair he loved so much, and my legs over H.R. who had Bea curled into her side when Zeus called.

"Little warrior." His rumble came over the phone and pierced my heart like an arrow. "How's my girl?"

"Better," I said, because even though I had the portable respirator beside me and my body ached like it was decomposing, my mind was happy and that was enough for me. "We're watching a super violent show."

He laughed and I could picture him leaning against his bike in the open air outside a bar while he talked to me, rolling a cigarette in his hands by habit but not smoking it because he'd made a promise to me to quit.

"Glad to hear it."

"Tell Dad I say hi," H.R. called out with popcorn in her mouth and more in the fist she was ready to shovel in just as soon as she had the space.

"Tell my other girl I love 'er, yeah?" Zeus said, hearing her over the phone.

"I will but just saying, you never told this girl you love her," I pointed out.

"Love you, little girl. Loved you for ten years and love you for ten decades more," he told me as if it was the simplest thing to do, to declare your undying love for a person like it was nothing special.

To Zeus, it wasn't the miracle it was to me. To him, it just *was*.

There was a beauty in the simplicity of that that I knew I'd never cease to appreciate.

A low rumble sounded through the cabin and at first, I thought it was the TV show but Mute had turned the volume down low when I picked up the phone.

Immediately, my protector slid my head off his lap and went prowling to the window. I watched frozen but electric with static as his posture slammed ramrod straight.

"What is it?" I asked even though I knew whatever it was

couldn't be good and I knew it even before Mute reached into his boot for his knife and ducked down beside the couch to grab his gun.

"What's goin' on?" Zeus asked me, somehow sensing my fear through the radio waves.

"Mute," I whispered as he took up his spot beside the front window and used a single finger to push aside the curtain slightly.

He looked out the pane then turned his head until our eyes locked. His dark gaze was filled with muted horror.

I was on my feet in a second, wincing at the tender pain in them but so far past caring I barely noticed.

"H.R., I need you to take Bea into the back, hide in the closet or under the bed or something, okay?" I asked, already hobbling over to the duffle bag I'd packed for the trip.

Ever since he'd given it to me for Christmas, I'd carried the gun Zeus gave me everywhere I went.

"Lou, what the fuck is goin' on over there?" Zeus barked into the phone.

I was startled to find myself still holding it loosely in one hand. I tucked it against my ear as I searched for my gun and watched as H.R. kicked into gear like the biker girl she was and raced to the kitchen to grab a knife. Bea sat in the middle of the sea of pillows looking so young and so afraid it made my heart ache.

"Loulou," Zeus snapped again.

"Sorry, sorry. I don't know what's happening but Mute is standing at the window looking out at the front yard of the cabin like someone really bad is outside."

"Hand 'im the phone now," he ordered.

I half crawled across the floor below the open window to put the cell in Mute's outstretched hand.

"Three guys," Mute said immediately, his eyes still on the action outside.

Vaguely, I heard the opening and shutting of doors.

Bea whimpered.

I went over to her and wrapped her up in my arms, keeping my gun ready in my right hand.

"Recognize two of 'em, Lysander Garrison and Ace Munford."

Shit, Lysander was Cressida's brother. The guy had been blackmailed into working for the Nightstalkers and spying on The Fallen. His actions had nearly gotten Cress killed and as far as she or I knew, Zeus and King had beaten him close to death then told him never to come back to town on fear of death.

He was back and clearly, he was back with the rival MC.

"Don't know. They're all carryin' far as I can see but that's it. They look calm. Someone told 'em we were here," Mute continued.

My stomach clenched and before I could help it, I was sick all over the pillows behind Bea's shoulder. She stroked my back with a shaking hand.

"Only got my Glock and blade, Foxy and H.R. got theirs and a coupla kitchen knives. 'S not enough," Mute admitted quietly.

Not quietly enough for a room gone thick with silence.

Bea pressed her face into my breasts and burst into tears. H.R. returned from the kitchen and knelt beside me on the other side of the puke.

"We need to figure out what to do with her," she said, tipping her chin at my little sister.

I couldn't think of anything. There was no space inside the house, it was just the rustic three rooms, no basement, only one closet and...

"You can get up on the roof," I said, prying Bea's face out of my breasts. My thumbs rubbed at her tears as I held her tight and drilled my eyes into hers. "Harleigh Rose is going to lift you up so you can get into the crawl space in the closet and then you're going to climb onto the roof. You have to be really fucking careful and don't make one single noise, okay?"

She shook her head manically, her tears spraying out onto my own cheeks as she did. "I can't, I can't."

"Listen to me," I ordered her so harshly, she stopped shaking and blinked at me. "You're a Lafayette and they might not have given us a fuckuva lot but they gave us a cool head, okay? You can do this. I need you to do this because we can't concentrate if we know you might get hurt."

"One's comin' to the door," Mute muttered into the phone he still held to his ear.

My heart thudded in my throat and bile churned volcanic hot in my belly. "Bea, please baby, you've got to go with H.R. now, okay?"

"I don't want to leave you," she whispered brokenly, her huge blue eyes glazed with tears. "You're the one who's sick. You should go up there."

"It's a small roof, honey," I tried to explain with a tight smile. "And you're right, I'm already sick so if only one of us gets through this, I want it to be the one with better odds."

Bea burst into tears again but I'd done my part and when

H.R. took her shoulders to lead her to the closet in the bedroom, Bea went willingly.

As soon as she was out of the room, I got to my feet and walked gingerly over to Mute.

"What do you think they want?" I whispered to him.

Someone knocked forcibly on the door.

I looked up at Mute and tried to suppress the fear I felt like an electric current running through my blood. I saw it mimicked in his own eyes and we shared a moment of pure terror. He broke the moment by pressing an awkward hand in the middle of my chest and saying in the clearest voice I'd ever heard him say, "Something bad is gonna happen. Need you to promise me you'll get yourself safe."

"Mute," I breathed. "We'll be fine."

"If not, you gotta promise me," he ordered.

Another knock came at the door. This one louder, longer.

Mute held out a hand, pinky extended and thumb already hooked to shake mine. He'd seen me do it with Zeus and he wanted me to swear on the same sacred ground I made all my promises on with the love of my life.

My heart burned as I reached out to lock my pinky with his and shake his thumb.

As soon as I let go, he was striding to the door.

"We didn't order pizza," Mute yelled through it.

It was a strange time to be funny but it was so utterly Mute to act against the norm that it nearly made me laugh and then it nearly made me cry.

The person on the other side of the door laughed. "Listen, kid. We just want the girls, yeah? Nothin' bad needs to happen to anyone."

"No girls," Mute said.

"Know they're here, brother. A little birdy told me Garro's sweet teen lover and daughter would be here and looky look, the lover's bodyguard is here so she must not be far behind. Now, open up before I kick this fuckin' door down."

I didn't recognize the voice but Harleigh Rose seemed to as she came back into the room because she froze in the hallway entryway.

"Who?" I mouthed at her.

"Blackjack's dad, Ace," she whispered as she came toward me and peered carefully out the curtains.

There was one man in the front yard, a Mexican man by the look of him, wearing a Nightstalkers cut with the laughing demon face on the back. He sat on the hood of a black van picking under his nails with a huge, curved blade.

"Lysander's here," I whispered.

"Why do you want 'em?" Mute demanded.

Ace laughed. "Zeus Garro killed my best fuckin' friend, think he deserves to know some pain 'fore we take back an operation he never shoulda been Prez of in the first fuckin' place."

"I'll bring 'em out," Mute said after a long pause. "Back away from the door and I'll get them sorted for ya."

"No fuckin' funny business. You got nowhere to go and you know it," Ace said, ending on a maniacal laugh.

I heard his boots stomp across the small wooden porch and down the stairs.

"Stuff in front of the doors," Mute snapped immediately, turning around himself to drag the kitchen table over.

I went over to help him, sweat breaking out across my

skin at the effort to walk and then push the heavy oak table over the wood floors.

"You're going to pass out, sit the fuck down," H.R. hissed.

"I do, we die," I said because it may have been dramatic but I had this awful, gut-wrenching feeling that it was true.

Mute didn't say anything. Once the table was in front of the door, he went to the huge armchair and hefted it into the air before slamming it down over the table, barricading the door entirely.

"Close all the curtains. I've got the back door," Harleigh Rose whispered as she dashed down the hall.

Mute held out my phone to me again. "Call him."

My fingers slipped with sweat against the screen as I pressed in the number. Zeus answered immediately, "Update me."

"It's me," I told him as lazy male laughter floated into the house from outside.

The bastards weren't even nervous about what Mute could do to them. They thought we were easy pickings, most of The Fallen's senior officers out on a run and the President's women alone in a remote cabin.

Fuck, we were dumb.

"Lou, baby, got guys comin'. You just have to hold out for as long as you can, yeah?" Zeus's voice was strong and sure as always.

"I'm so fucking scared," I admitted as I watched Mute grab another knife from the kitchen and add it to his arsenal.

"Nah, not my little warrior. It's gonna be fine, Lou. I'm on my way home right fuckin' now and by this time tomorrow, this'll all be a nightmare and you'll be safe in my arms in our bed."

"You don't have nightmares," I told him inanely because I was so terrified I could barely remember my own name.

At least Bea was safe on the roof.

But Mute was at the front line and my lover's daughter, a daughter who strangely enough had become one of my best friends as well, was right there with me.

"Even the devil's got nightmares, Lou, and mine is losin' ya so you take care, you hear? No fuckin' rebel schemes or heroics. You get outta there safe."

"Comin' back," Mute muttered from beside the window.

"Come out, come fuckin' out," Ace yelled at the house. He sounded high and he probably was. "No? Eh, we figured as much. Fuckin' pussies. Don't worry, we got a cure for that."

"Fuck," Mute swore and dove at me.

We slammed to the ground away from the window a second before the glass smashed and something heavy landed amid the glass.

A Molotov Cocktail, a nearly empty bottle of booze with a gas-soaked rag stuck in it, burnin' bright like a white flag in flames.

Two more crashes followed as more of them were launched through the windows of the house.

"We wanted 'em alive to reason with the fuckin' Prez but if you wanna do this the hard way, we figure killin' 'em will work to shake things up just as well," Ace shouted into the house.

Mute hauled me to my feet and quickly checked me over for bruises and scrapes I didn't feel. I couldn't feel anything except for sheer terror. He grabbed my hand and ran down the hall to the back door only to find it hanging open on its hinges.

Harleigh Rose.

Mute shoved me against the wall beside the door and carefully rounded it with his gun up and out.

"Fuck," he swore a second later as he backed up into the house slowly.

Lysander Garrison appeared in the doorway, Harleigh Rose dwarfed in his big arms, the huge barrel of a sawed-off shotgun to her temple.

"Put the gun down, Mute," Lysander ordered softly. "I'm not gonna hurt anyone, okay? I'm just doing this because you've got to listen to me. The police are on their way but they won't be here quick enough to save the girls. You have to trust me here, brother. I can help you guys."

Mute snarled. "Not your brother. Lou, get here."

I immediately obeyed, racing to him and sliding behind his back. He braced in a slight squat so I could—painfully—climb up onto his back. I wrapped myself tight around him so he wouldn't have to waste a hand supporting me.

Smoke started to billow hot and black at our feet as the flames in the front room grew stronger.

"Fine but we don't have time to argue. I'm workin' with Lionel Danner on this. You gotta trust me here, if not 'cause you want to, then 'cause you know I'm the best chance for you here," Lysander tried again.

The two men stared at each other for a long moment.

Sweat beaded on my back. It wasn't a big house and it was only a matter of time before the fire spread, eating up all the wood like a starving, feral creature.

Lysander sighed then slowly lowered his gun from H.R.'s

temple before taking a step back and lifting his arms in the air. Immediately, she ran to us and stood at our side, her hand finding my back and pressing in for comfort.

"No harm," Lysander said, putting his gun slowly over his shoulder so it lay across his back by a thick bit of rope. "Now, if you're willin' to take a chance, I'm leaving now. They think I'm back here to catch you if you think of runnin' but I'm helpin', okay? There's a car waiting just through the trees to the left of the estate, thirty meters tops. You run fast and hard, you can make it before they figure out what's happening."

"Mute, let's do it," H.R. whispered.

"Agreed," I seconded then louder I said, "My sister is on the roof. You need to get her down."

Something flared behind his eyes as he thought about my little sister on the roof of a flaming building and I immediately warmed to him for it.

"Let's go, Mute," I urged him.

He didn't move.

The smoke was thick now and the snap, crackle and pop of wood tearing, burning and crumbling to ash was loud all around us.

I could barely breathe from the smoke in my already weak lungs when I begged. "Promised to stay alive for you, Mute. Need you to get me there and that way is through this guy."

I don't know if it was the hoarseness of my voice and my resulting body jerking coughing fit or if it was my words, but Mute jolted forward as if he'd been jump-started.

"You get her hurt, I kill you," he threatened even as he started running to the door and out it.

Harleigh Rose followed us but Mute put her in front, as we followed Lysander around the side of the house and stopped just out of sight of the front driveway.

"Thirty meters through the trees straight ahead," Lysander said when we came to a stop. "I'll get Bea and you worry about gettin' out of here alive."

I whimpered at the thought of leaving my sister but the shouts from the front of the house alerted us that our time had run out.

There was about ten meters between the forest and us, with twenty meters still more after that.

"Doable," H.R. said, her soot-streaked face set with determination. She still held a knife in one hand and her gun in the other, both held up to her face as if being able to see them made her more confident.

"Got this," Mute agreed.

"Good, now go," Lysander ordered.

Mute took off like a shot, Harleigh Rose on the other side of us, farther away from the driveway. I clung tight to him as he thundered across the grass, his breath and pulse thumping away in my ear as I pressed my face into his neck.

Pop.

The familiar sound of gunshots followed close behind us.

Pop. Pop.

"Let me down, I can run and you'll be faster without me," I shouted in Mute's ear but he only hefted me higher on his back and ran harder.

Pop.

Harleigh Rose screamed.

And in that second that Mute stopped slightly to turn his

head and check on her, I saw a fourth man, one we hadn't known was there, one that looked so familiar, at first, I thought he was there to help us.

He had pale hair and wore a leather vest like brothers of any MC would. He was too far away for me to see clearly but through my haze of adrenaline, I felt sure I knew him. He stood by the trees we were running to, a gun in his hand leveled high and steady at Mute and me.

It felt as though I caught eyes with him in that second and saw a wealth of things in that corrupted gaze: anger and greed, vengeance and fury. He was a man on a mission and that mission was to end me.

I screamed before I even heard the *pop*.

Mute grunted a second later, faltering in his steps and almost falling to the ground. He collapsed to a knee briefly before pushing up with a hand and taking off again.

"You're okay?" I screamed into his ear.

He grunted.

Harleigh Rose limped beside us, running fast even though I could see the blood at her calf where a bullet had gone clear through the muscle.

We made it to the edge of the trees three seconds later without any more gunfire but I could still hear the shouts back at the house and see the dark plumage of smoke wafting over the cabin through the forest. Harleigh Rose had darted ahead into the brush to get the car started.

"Keys in the ignition," she shouted from somewhere in front of us.

"Thank God," I said, about to ask Mute to put me down when my world tilted and we both went to the earthen floor *hard*.

"Mute," I cried out before I'd even landed, then as soon as I regained my breath I was scrambling over the cold, wet soil to his side.

He lay on his back, blinking up at the sky like he couldn't understand what was wrong with him.

What was wrong with him was that there was a bullet hole through his neck. A sob exploded in my throat and tore out my mouth as I fell on the wound with both hands, pressing hard into the blood spilling through his throat. My fingers slipped in the mess and I worried frantically that I was making it harder for him to breathe.

"Help!" I called out, not caring that there were more gunmen in the vicinity. "Harleigh Rose!"

"Fucking fuck," she said, tumbling to a stop beside me in the mud. "Ohmygod, ohmygod, ohmygod... *fuck*."

"Mute, just wait a second, okay?" I told him, leaning down so I could look into his eyes.

They were wide and eerily knowing on mine as he blinked, gurgled through a deep breath, and blinked again.

"Loulou!" Bea's voice came to me, pulling my gaze from Mute for a second to see her running toward me with Lysander just behind her.

"You have to help me get him in the car," I told Lysander. "Quick, please, God, help me get him in the car. He needs an ambulance."

Lysander crouched down without missing a beat and cursed as he smoothly hefted Mute's dead weight into his arms. "Get in the fuckin' car. Now."

I pushed Bea toward the car with my bloody hands then sprinted forward so I could brace against the backseat and carefully accept Mute's head on my lap. Bea crawled into the front seat and H.R. kneeled in the trunk.

Lysander jumped into the front seat and immediately peeled out of the muddy clearing just as there was a great bomb as the cabin imploded.

"Mute, Mute, I'm right here and we're going to be in the hospital in just two seconds, I promise, it's going to be alright... just hold on, okay?" I ranted as I pressed the bunched edge of his tee into the gushing wound and ran a hand over his head, too fast and hard to be truly comforting.

I could see the blood under his skin thinning, watched as his flesh turned bright red then paler and paler like spilled milk. He couldn't talk, couldn't move and couldn't even really breathe.

"No, no, no," I sobbed as one of his heavy hands tried to lift to comfort me and fell back weakly to the seat.

There was blood everywhere, pooling warm in my lap, the metallic scent of it stuffed up my nostrils.

He was dying.

God, I knew he was dying.

"Is he okay?" Bea whimpered from the front seat as we drove off the edge of a dirt hill and onto pavement with a rough crash that jerked me and made more of Mute's blood spurt out over my hand.

"No," I whispered as my tears rained down on Mute's face.

There was so much in his eyes as they watched me; pain and stunning acceptance of his fate, pride that he'd saved me and love, so much love it overflowed from him and filled me up to the brim.

I couldn't breathe, my weak lungs were filled with smoke

and too damaged to deal with the added stress but I focused all my energy into staying clear headed so I could hold my silent hero in my arms and look into his eyes as he died for me.

"Love you, love you, love you," I croaked through my tears, through my lack of breath.

He blinked slowly and opened his mouth, maybe to say something, but instead a thick trickle of blood spilled out.

My sobs ricocheted through the car like the gunshots in the clearing.

"Love you," I said again as I bent double and pressed my lips to his face, kissing his heavy brow, his broad forehead, his blood-speckled cheeks and nose.

His breathing was faint, so faint I couldn't even hear him struggle for it anymore. I pulled back just enough to see his face and watched as those beautiful brown eyes, more eloquent than his lips had ever been, sparked one last time and then went out.

I cried out like a wounded animal, so long and low and loud that black spots dotted my vision and my tired lungs gave out. I passed out over Mute's still warm, dead body with my cheek on his cheek.

CHAPTER THIRTY-SEVEN

Zeus

THANK FUCK IT WAS RAININ'.

Yeah, it fit the mood, which was good. Loulou woulda liked that.

But even better, it hid the fact that my grown ass son was cryin' beside me as he comforted his woman and his sister. I didn't blame him for cryin'. How could I when I'd spent the past forty-eight hours leaking tears like a broken fuckin' faucet?

Besides, I was fuckin' thankful that he had it in him to take care of Cress and H.R.

I was barely keepin' myself together.

The crater in the middle of my chest kept yawning open like the jaws of a monster to swallow up every ounce of strength I mighta had under other circumstances. I was no father, no Prez. I was barely a man, held together by three bottles of Canadian whiskey and a serious prayer.

That's right, Zeus fuckin' Garro, President of the maddest, baddest, fuckin' richest MC in the country was praying.

And he was praying with every atom of his crumblin' black soul that God would send Lou back to him.

She wasn't gone yet, I reminded myself for the thirteen-thousandth time. She was hanging on tight to life, fighting like only my little warrior could.

The docs said she had inhalation injury made worse by the preexistin' condition of her lungs 'cause of the chemo. There was a thick tube stuck down her throat and they'd put her in a medical coma so her body could have a chance of healin'.

Wasn't allowed to see her for the first five hours I sat there in the hospital reception, yellin' and demandin' to be let in to see my girl.

They refused.

She was seventeen and technically, still under the guardianship of her parents.

So, I'd had to wait five hours while the cops contacted the Lafayettes then visited with Lou. The mayor had glared at me as he came and went but there was genuine fuckin' panic and sorrow in his face when he left after an hour of visitin'.

It was the panic, I was stuck on most.

I'd been railin' at the fuckin' nurses and doctors for the eighth time about lettin' me in to see Lou when Phillipa Lafayette appeared beside me.

She'd been wearing a pink suit with a pink band in her

hair. It struck me in the throat that she looked like an older, sadder Loulou. Phillipa tried to hide it behind her conservative, ugly clothes and a shit-ton of pearls, but she was almost just as much a bombshell as her daughter.

Thank fuck, I'd gotten to Lou in time to stop her from becomin' her frigid bitch of a mother.

The woman had stared at me for a long minute. Watched my chest heave with the force of my fury, my fists tight at my sides and my eyes, I knew it, were crazy. I was a beast at the end of his rope, threatening to go green as the Hulk in about two seconds fuckin' flat if someone didn't let me see Lou.

"You can come in," she'd said in such a soft voice I'd had to lean forward to hear it and she'd flinched as I'd done it.

"Come a-fuckin'-gain?"

Her lips pursed and she held her purse to her chest like a shield. "I said, you can come in and see her. She'd want that."

I blinked at her for a sec before decidin' not to give a fuck about the reasons for her change of heart.

"Put my fuckin' name on the approved list," I snarled as I stormed across the hall and into the white room housin' my fallen angel.

Since then, this was the third time I'd been forced to leave her bedside and the only time it was worth it.

My brother Mute deserved a funeral befitting of the gods.

And we were givin' it to him.

Every single brother from every chapter of The Fallen on the west coast of North America and our neighborin' province of Alberta was in First Light Church Graveyard. They spread nearly as far as the eye could see like a murder of ravens and when we'd done the funeral procession through town, seemed every citizen in Entrance had come out to watch The Fallen flood Main Street on a tide of rolling thunder.

Only family was close to the deep wound in the earth where the casket was bein' lowered, a circle of people linked by choice insteada blood that would always and had before, bled for each other.

Cops ran like a loose chain-link fence around the perimeter, hemmin' us in and watchful of so many outlaws in one space. It was standard procedure for an MC funeral to have the cops up our ass but I fuckin' hated that they were there today watchin' like they always did instead of *doin'*. The only thing they were fuckin' good for was keepin' the press at bay.

"Zeus Garro, I understand you would like to say a few words." Pastor Lafayette was doin' the ceremony. It was fucked as shit but I respected the guy. He didn't like my way of life, didn't like that his granddaughter was livin' that same life beside me, but he supported me anyway because it was what she wanted.

So, he was doin' the ceremony for a biker and not carin' that it was unconventional as fuck.

I stomped through the mud to the microphone beside the pastor and pulled my presidency all around me like a fuckin' shroud. The sound of tears underscored the rain, could see the tracks of 'em on the cheeks of women and brothers alike. This was not a happy time for the club. The loss of a brother hadn't happened to the main charter of the MC since I'd killed Crux and inadvertently started this whole mess.

It was up to me to be strong, to be Atlas bended on one

knee with the world on my shoulders, holdin' up my family for as long as they needed that from me.

I took a deep breath, thought of Lou to give me strength, and started.

"Wonder if those motherfuckers who ended Mute woulda done it if they'd seen a movie of his life. They woulda seen a neglected, abused kid with huge brown eyes wiser an' more soulful than ten grown men. They woulda seen his character grow with the struggle of bein' different, how he found acceptance with a brotherhood that nurtured 'im and how he threw himself body and fuckin' soul into givin' that back and more." The sobs were louder now, in my ears with more in my throat. Fuck, if I was gonna cry but fuck me if I'd ever had a better reason to.

"Yeah, I wonder if they woulda killed a man like that if they'd known him; if they'd known his quiet fuckin' wit, how he could play us all like fuckin' pawns without even sayin' a word. He lived by a simple mandate like the rest of us, brotherhood, loyalty, livin' free and even in the end, dyin' hard. Brings me some small degree of comfort to know my brother died how he woulda wanted to, defendin' his and my girl. Whatever place he's in where fallen angels go, I know he's livin' a dead man's dream 'cause a soul like his woulda bought him first class seats to paradise."

I nodded out at the sea of my people, catchin' eyes with Nova as he held Lila, with Buck as he cranked the mechanism that lowered Mute's black coffin into the cold, wet earth.

"And while Mute finds peace in the Underworld, we'll be busy up here findin' justice for 'im," I declared, hand over the microphone so only the force of my lungs carried the promise of vengeances to the eager ears of my brothers.

A shout swelled in the air like a punctuation mark.

I nodded, tipped my chin at the pastor, and stepped down.

King was the first to step forward when the coffin was finally bedded down, a silver coin in his hand, probably a nickel. His face was gaunt like a fuckin' skeleton's, his lips held tight against the force of his misery. I wanted to go forward and wrap my kid in my arms like I'd done when he was a boy, but he was a man now and it was man's walk to the edge of the grave to pay last respects.

"Go easy, brother, knowin' you touched our lives like the hand of God 'imself." He flipped the coin into the grave, payment for the ferryman or the pearly gates, wherever death mighta taken him.

The Fallen always pay their debts, even in death.

So one by one, my brothers stepped up to toss a coin onto the coffin and pay Mute's way to Eden.

It took half an hour just for the Entrance brothers and when I stepped up last, we were all soaked through past the skin to the fuckin' bone.

But I took my time 'cause I had two coins, one for me and one for Lou.

My heart burned like a torch in my chest, never fuckin' goin' out, not since I'd rode into Entrance straight to the fuckin' hospital and found Lou with tubes in her mouth and so many damn needles in her arms she looked like a pin cushion. Fuck but she shoulda been there beside me. I coulda been strong for her the way I didn't feel strong for anyone else.

Instead, she was fightin' for her life in a fuckin' hospital bed and her brother, my brother, was in the cold ground.

"Rest in peace, Walker Nixon," I said, usin' his full name for the last time. "Deserve more than this for the guardin' you gave my girl. Wish you could know I'd sell my fuckin' soul to get you back. For you, for me, for the club and for our girl."

I tossed the coins into the ground but couldn't see 'em through the wet in my eyes.

Fuck me.

A small hand went to my back and I jerked around to see H.R. starin' up at me with red-stained eyes.

"Dad," she whispered through her tear-swollen throat.

I lashed my arms around her and carted her up against my chest, tryin' to breathe through the knife in my heart as I held my sobbin' girl in a group of mostly grown men who wanted desperately to sob too.

"NEED TO TALK TO YOU."

The party was windin' up, not down.

It was the way of biker funerals. First came the procession markin' "Mute's Last Ride", then the ceremony, then the reveling. No one could celebrate a life well lived like my MC brethren.

The clubhouse was overfilled and spillin' out into the complex, the big industrial lights on across the lot so that everything was coated in yellow. People were shitfaced, high off their rockers and drunk as Irishmen. Families had left when the food the old ladies had put out disappeared and now it was just the brothers, partying hard to forget and celebrate.

I wasn't.

I didn't want to be with my fuckin' brothers drinkin' beer and doin' shots.

I wanted to be by my girl's bedside just in case she woke even though the docs told me that wouldn't be for days yet even if she did wake up.

She would.

She would wake up 'cause no God was cruel enough to give her to me only to rip her from my hands months later. No God would take away the idol of a man's religion just when he needed it most.

She'd wake up.

And I needed to be at the clubhouse with my brothers. They needed their Prez. I loved Lou more than most grown men are capable of ever lovin' anythin'. Loved her enough to kill and die for her 'cause only the finality of death could match the finality of my kinda love for that girl.

But it was my brothers who had taught me how to love like that. To do it eternally with loyalty and pride.

So, I was leanin' against the wall beside the front door of

the clubhouse, sippin' a beer gone warm and listenin' to Bat, Buck, Blackjack, and Priest shoot the shit.

Then, Bat said, "Need to talk to you."

"So, talk."

He rubbed his head and I noticed his hair was longer, that all our hair was longer now. It'd been nearly two months since we'd shaved our heads for my girl.

"Hate to say this, 'specially right now, but we don't got shit to go on 'ere. The cops have been fuckin' assholes about not sharin' their intel and the only thing we know is that Ace Munford is leadin' the Nightstalkers and the man's got a helluva a bone to pick with you. We don't know where their fuckin' base is or how they knew about Lou and H.R. bein' up at the cabin unless we have a rat in our ranks."

"'Course we have a fuckin' rat," I growled. "I need to know who the *fuck* it is so I can gut the bastard with a chainsaw."

Blackjack laughed. "What makes you so sure there's a rat? They coulda been followin' Lou or H.R. knowin' they're your weak spot and then just struck when the chance came."

Buck thumped him on the back with a meaty fist. "Don't be a fucktard, B.J."

B.J. ran a hand over his pale buzzed head and peered up at me. "She's your weakness, boss. Just sayin' you should be careful with who knows that. Shame somethin' happened to her 'cause of ya."

I took a step forward, the fury that lay at the heart of me ignited with one fuckin' little match. Trouble was I was fuckin' furious with myself. "You wanna say that again, brother?"

He laughed nervously. "Nah, listen, I just meant, she's a

good girl. Maybe, maybe this is a sign that this ain't the life for 'er."

His words fucked me dry. They were the same words been goin' 'round my head for the last four days since the fire.

She was too good for this life.

Too good for murder, wrath and greed, too good for all the vices I lived and breathed.

My girl was an angel and I'd taken her to the dark side like she had a hope in hell of thrivin' there.

I did it 'cause I was a selfish fuckin' bastard and once a man's tasted the kinda sweet ambrosia Lou'd given me, there was no goin' back.

So I didn't pray to God that I'd leave her to a better life if —no *when*—she pulled through.

I knew myself and I knew I wasn't capable of that level of self-sacrifice.

But I did pray.

I went every goddamn day to First Light Church and sat in the same front pew Lou'd spent almost every Sunday mornin' of her life in 'til she found me again, and I fuckin' prayed to God for her life. Pastor fuckin' Lafayette had seen me the first day and sat with me each time, sayin' nothin' just lendin' me his goodness so I could use it to amplify my own and make my prayers shine brighter.

If God'd give her back to me, I'd never let 'er go. Not to violence, wrath or greed. Not to vice or virtue. Not even to death.

I'd keep her safe, I promised the Almighty, and I'd do it keeping 'er at my side and guardin' her 'til my last fuckin' breath.

Still, I didn't need fuckin' B.J. remindin' me of the dark voices in my head sayin' I was no good for her and where the fuck did he get off thinkin' that shit himself?

"You got a problem with me, Blackjack?" I asked low.

Somethin' dark flashed in his eyes then fled like prey. "Sorry, brother, you don't need my shit."

"Damn right, he doesn't." Buck hit him again, this time *hard* in the shoulder. "Shut your mouth 'til I tell you to fuckin' open it again."

"Prez, there's someone here you need to see," Axe-Man said as he came up the steps.

"Who?"

"Lysander Garrison."

Immediately, I was tearin' down the steps to the front gates. The fuck stood there talkin' to a mean lookin' Nova.

"What the *fuck* are you doin' here? It better be to fuckin' explain why you were with those fuckers who killed my brother and got my girl wastin' away in the hospital," I roared as I picked the six-foot-two motherfucker up by the neck and shoulder and shoved him into the chain-link fence.

He blinked at me, calm as could fuckin' be. "It is."

"Start talkin' then."

"After you let me go and told me to get lost forever, Officer Danner picked me up as I was hightailin' it outta town. Told me he needed my help puttin' the Nightstalkers down for good."

Buck snorted behind me. "Like the cops could take down an operation like that. Fuckin' pigs."

Blackjack laughed his nervous, yippy laugh.

I turned to glare at him and found him sweatin', lookin'

back and forth between Lysander and me like we were puttin' on a tennis match.

He was high as a fuckin' kite and somethin' about havin' a high brother involved with club business had always seemed like a bad fuckin' idea.

"Get him in a cold fuckin' shower 'fore he keels over and dies," I ordered Priest who immediately acted, his face twisted with disgust as he dragged the tweaker away.

"You gonna tell me where those motherfucking Nightstalkers are hidin'?" I asked, turnin' back to Lysander.

"No," he said. "But mostly 'cause they don't have a base of operations here. They have a clubhouse down in Vancouver right now, but they won't relocate 'til they flush you out. Like I said, I'm workin' with Danner and even the cops can't get a location on 'em."

"Why the fuck would you help Danner? You think I was lyin' when I told you I'd put you in the ground if you showed your face again in Entrance?"

"Wanted to be able to look my sister in the eye again and tell 'er I'd made things right."

"And how are you makin' things right? Far as I can tell, my brother is dead 'cause of you," I snarled in his face.

"I know. I'm so fuckin' sorry. But Ace is a maniac and no matter how long I ride with him, I can't predict what that high motherfucker is gonna do. Someone told him your girls were up at that cabin. One of The Fallen."

"Fuck," I roared into his face and squeezed his neck tighter. "Who!?"

"Don't know. All I came 'ere to tell you was that Danner's a good cop and between the two of us we're *this* fuckin' close to nailin' 'em."

"And what the fuck do you want me to do about it?"

I stared at his neck to center the anger threatenin' to overwhelm me. I stared at the pulse in his throat thumping up against my thumb and I thought about how easy it would be to snap his neck. I'd done it before; it wasn't as hard as you'd think.

"One of the players, Warren, he has a thing for Louise—" His voice cut off with a garble because I now had my hand pressed to his windpipe.

"You dare to fuckin' mention her name when she's barely fuckin' breathin'?" I said quiet. "Don't think you understand that I'm a fuckin' monster, Sander, and I ain't afraid to kill a man. Not even one that's kin to my son's woman or one in bed with the fuckin' police. I'll snap your neck and have you with the pigs in record time. You know it takes pigs eight minutes to eat a full-grown body?"

Finally, there was fear in his eyes and his body stank of it, of sweat and somethin' more metallic.

"You go back to Danner and you tell him to get his glory on his fuckin' own. The Fallen is not helpin' anyone but their own," I growled then shoved off him before I throttled 'im and stalked off to take my frustrations out on a fuckin' punchin' bag instead of Garrison's motherfuckin' face.

CHAPTER THIRTY-EIGHT

Loulou

I woke up crying.

There was no gap between unconsciousness and waking.

I knew the second I opened my eyes that Mute wouldn't be there because Mute was dead.

I couldn't remember any other details of that night, which the doctors would later inform me was normal after a traumatic event, but I remembered immediately and brutally that Mute was dead.

The tears fell hotly down my face, burning so badly I thought they'd leave scars. A part of me wanted them to. I felt mutilated by the pain of his loss.

It took me a few minutes of deep, thready breathing to open my eyes and take in the hospital room around me.

Everyone was there.

My entire family.

Harleigh Rose was curled up on a sofa with her bandaged calf in King's lap and her head in Cressida's.

Bea sat in the cradle of Nova's arms against the wall in a long line of bikers—Cy, Lab-Rat, Curtains, Bat, Priest and Boner—that extended out the open door and into the corridor.

Ruby lay on the ground beside my bed wrapped in a thin hospital blanket with Lila curled up behind her for warmth and comfort. Maja was curled up in Buck's lap in a huge chair someone had dragged in from another room, and Hannah, Cleo and Tayline lay curled up liked kittens against the sofa at King's feet.

They were all asleep.

Even my guardian monster.

He sat in chair that was too small for his enormous frame, the upper half of his torso collapsed on the bed at my side with one of his big hands curled around my thigh and the other tangled tightly with one of my own.

Even in sleep, his handsome face was tense with worry. I pressed my fingers to the crease between his thick brows and over the fan of wrinkles beside his eyes but he didn't wake up.

I wondered how long they'd been there.

"You've been out for days, honey," a familiar voice said from the doorway.

I couldn't have been more shocked to see my mother standing there, not only because she was *there* but because she wasn't wearing makeup—something I couldn't *ever* remember happening—and she was wearing a tracksuit. It was a designer one but still, my mother didn't wear anything more casual than slacks on her worst day.

"Mum?" I croaked through a painfully dry throat.

She rushed as quickly as she could pick her way through the sleeping bodies on the ground to my side to pour me a cup of water from the pitcher on the bedside table.

"Here you go, sweetie," she said as she tipped it up to my lips for me.

I had a *déjà vu* moment, remembering her doing the same thing for me when I was first diagnosed with cancer as a kid.

When I was finished, I turned my face away and asked, "What are you doing here?"

Pain slashed across her features like a blade but she recovered admirably. Her hand shook slightly as she put the cup on the table and perched on the side of my bed without the mammoth man half on it.

"It kills me that my daughter has to ask why I would visit her in the hospital," she admitted.

"It's not something you've done much of before," I reminded her. "And you recently told me that you'd never talk to me again."

Her lips rolled under her teeth, a habit I realized with surprise, that we shared.

"I'm so sorry. I...The truth is I never knew what to do with you. You were born this beautiful, vibrant little girl with a personality that developed *very* quickly and it was one I didn't understand. Then you got cancer and..." She brought her hand to her mouth and pressed at it as if that would stop the tears that coated her words. "I didn't know what to do with a little girl with cancer. I was afraid to get close to you because you were so close to dying and then what would I do?"

I tried to remain unmoved by her speech and mostly it was easy because my heart was preoccupied with mourning Mute, but I decided to give her the benefit of the doubt because honestly, I didn't really want to lose another person close to me.

"You're supposed to love them anyway."

She nodded empathetically. "I know, I know, and there's no excuse but you can't understand what it's like to have a daughter who's so sick. It feels like *your* fault. Maybe if I hadn't eaten starch when I was pregnant with you or if I hadn't let you get so close to the microwave when we cooked together or—"

I interrupted her with a snort. "We never cooked together, Phillipa."

She flinched again at my use of her first name instead of "Mum". "We did, sweetheart, and I'm so sorry you were too young to remember because I do and they were some of my favourite times. You always wanted to put candy in everything, gummies in the cookies and sour cherries in cakes. They were truly awful, but you loved them, so we made them."

Something flickered at the back of my mind but I clamped down on it. "When did they stop?"

She knew that I knew the answer. "When you were seven, after you got shot in the horrible accident."

I pulled Zeus's hand closer onto my belly and stared at it, loving the coarse brown hairs on his arm and the way the feathers merged with his skin like they were part of him. My big, bad fallen angel had saved me back then and he'd saved me every day since just by existing.

"I don't want to hear this, Mum. I want to wake up Zeus and the rest of my family and mourn my fallen friend with them," I told her honestly.

She sucked in a breath but nodded. "I know. I'm so sorry, honey. He was... a sweet boy and I'm sorry I couldn't move passed my own worries to see that and get to know him better."

Sorrow slammed into my throat and brought tears rushing to my eyes. They spilled over as I stared at her and shook my head. "I don't get what you're doing here. I'm sorry but I don't have it in me to comfort you or make you one of your martinis."

"I deserve that." She nodded even though her voice was bruised from my words. "I just wanted to see you well and whole with my own eyes. They wouldn't let me in at first but I'm your mother so I just waited in the main reception until it was late enough they were all asleep each night. Only a few of them have come and gone, honey. Most of them have been *living* here the eight days you've been unconscious."

Her words were filled with wonder as she stared around the room at the scattered bikers, their rough faces and scraggly beards, their cuts and the weapons visible if you looked hard enough at the opening of their boots and the backs of their pockets.

She saw disgusting outlaws.

I saw brave knights in rebel colours.

"I just wanted to tell you that I love you," my mum tried

again and when I looked back at her face, I saw it was damp and crumpled like a used napkin. "I just wanted to say it with a small hope that you'd see I was being honest. I just wanted to tell you that if you're willing, I'd like to be in your life again."

"I don't think so," I said immediately and then regretted it.

She looked down at my hand where it rested on the bed and gently reached out to run the back of her pinky on the needle scars there. "So beautiful and so brave. I never deserved a daughter like you."

My throat burned but I didn't say anything as she stood up and hesitated.

"Even if you don't want to have a relationship with me moving forward, I need you to know that there's something... Very wrong with your father. I thought maybe I could talk to your, er, gentleman friend about it."

My heart clenched. "You know something?"

She bit her lip. "He left some files on his desk when he left after I told him you'd been injured in a shooting again. I haven't seen him since but I was curious so I read the papers."

"Bring them here," I told her instantly, struggling to sit up further so I could properly relay my intensity. "Go home and come straight back with them."

"Okay," she said with wide eyes. "Take care of your sister while I'm gone."

"I always do," I snapped and winced when my mum ducked her head and scurried out of the room.

I tipped my head back into the pillow and tried to take deep breaths.

Mute was dead.

Mum wanted reconciliation.

The world had gone fucked.

Zeus stirred beside me, his hand flexing in mine as he rolled out of his bend and into awareness. The second he hit upright, he opened his eyes and found mine staring at him.

"Loulou," he rasped, and there was so much emotion in that one word that I'd thought I'd die from it.

Just my chosen name on the lips of the man fate had chosen for me at seven years old. It was the most beautiful and poignant thing I'd ever heard.

"Zeus," I breathed back.

We stared at each other, his eyes devoting every inch of my face to memory. There was a panic to the way he searched me as if he couldn't believe I was whole and real before him. It made my heart ache to think of what he must have gone through when he thought I might not wake up.

I was staring into his silver eyes, counting the rings of deeper grey radiating through the iris like rings in a tree so I watched as they went shiny then wet then as one tear welled up in the wedge of his lower lashes and spilled down his cheek into his beard.

He was crying.

"Lou," he croaked, tears falling. "Fuck me, I thought you were gonna leave me. I really fuckin' did."

"I'd never leave you," I promised turning our hands so I could link our pinkies and shake my thumb with his. "Fucking swear it."

He smiled through his tears and leaned into my hands when I touched my fingertips to the wetness on his cheeks.

"Come here," I told him. "Get on this bed and hug me."

He laughed and it sounded like a sob. "Not yet. You're awake and I'm fuckin' doin' this 'fore anythin' gets in our way."

"Doin' what?" I asked, absorbed with the sight of those tears on my badass biker's face.

Zeus Garro, big bad Prez of a notorious outlaw motorcycle club, was crying for me.

I watched as he pushed his chair back with a loud screech that had most of the sleepers in the room jerking awake and then dropped to his knees with a hard thud. He was so tall, even kneeling beside the bed, his face was nearly at the level of mine.

"What are you doing?" I asked.

One of his big hands pushed back the hair on my head and cupped my face. "Couldn't see you for five fuckin' hours when I first got 'ere, Lou."

"God," I said as my heart bled for him.

I couldn't imagine not being able to see him when he was injured.

He nodded, anger a brief flare in his eyes. "Fuckin' right. And that's never happenin' again. I will not be parted from you, ya get me? I'm your guardian monster, your fuckin' lover and your fuckin' man. That's not ever gonna change."

"Fuck no," I agreed.

His smile split his face in two. "Fuck no." He reached into his back pocket, palmed something then reached for my hand as he said, "Left your side three times in ten days. First, to talk to the fuckin' pigs and identify Mute's body, then for his funeral—which was epic, little warrior, don't you worry and I'm sorry you missed it—then to get this."

He slid something cool onto my finger, but I was so fascinated by the expression on his face, the ferocity of his passion and determination like war paint on his features, that I didn't notice.

"It's you and me, Lou. Has been since you were seven years old, so even though you're young, I figure it was gonna happen sooner rather than later and I decided that it better happen right fuckin' now."

I frowned at him, slipping my hand out of his to cup his face. "You aren't making sense, Z."

There were a few teary giggles and deep chuckles from our sleepy audience but it was Zeus who laughed from his belly.

"We're gettin' married."

My ruined lungs seized and then seemed to collapse because I couldn't breathe properly. I stared at him, wondering if I was hallucinating or still asleep but as I stared I noticed the twinkle of something big and shiny on his face, on *my* hand on his face.

A ring.

It was big; one huge round black diamond surrounded in a halo of small green stones on a band of white gold.

The Fallen MC colours on my hand.

And their President, my guardian angel, my childhood dream man had put it on my finger.

"You're fucking me," I breathed.

He laughed uproariously again, manic with relief that I was alive and sassing him. "Not yet," he said like he had the night he'd first touched me at The Lotus, "but I fuckin' well plan to. For the rest of our fuckin' lives."

As far as proposals went, it wasn't the most flowery or the most well-thought out.

It was simple and honest.

So true to us, I felt like I was living in a fairy tale. One of the horrible ones, Grimm brothers fairy tales where the wrong people die and the good guys don't always win, but a fairy tale nonetheless.

I burst into tears as I shouted, "Fuck yes."

Zeus laughed with me and finally, *fucking finally* wrapped me up in his arms and hugged me. Our audience erupted, the men into shouting revelry and the women into sobbing congratulations.

"Now," Zeus said. "Was serious, Loulou. We're doin' it right fuckin' now."

I pulled away slightly and looked down at my white-and-blue polka dot hospital gown, knowing I looked like shit and, honestly, still felt like it too.

He laughed at my expression and pressed his forehead to mine. "You want a big party, we'll have one when you get better but for now, let's get this thing tied up tight, yeah?"

"Okay," I agreed, not daunted by the idea of getting married in a hospital room without a pretty dress or flowers. I'd given up that version of my future a long time ago anyways. "But um, I'm seventeen so I don't think I can even legally marry you."

"Can't," Z said with a strange, twisted smile.

"I told him I'd sign off on it for you," my mum said from where she stood in the doorway, dwarfed by Axe-Man and Boner on either side of her.

My mouth fell open. "Seriously?"

"I, um, I went to Ben's office to get special dispensation for a license when Zeus asked me about it and, well, your grandfather is waiting outside to see you and, if you want, perform the ceremony."

I blinked at her. "What? Grandfather approves?"

"He said something about God having different paths for everyone and then something about some princesses needing dragons to protect them instead of Prince Charmings to save them."

Despite my shock, I laughed because that was totally something my grandpa would say.

Phillipa smiled shakily. "I don't fully understand how you ended up this way or why this lifestyle appeals to you so much but it would be clear to a deaf, dumb and blind person that that man loves you more than anything so, if you really want to, I'll sign off on it. He's been a better guardian to you than I've been anyways," she admitted with a self-deprecating smile.

"Damn straight," Harleigh Rose muttered.

King elbowed her in the gut. "Shut *up*."

"Hey, I got shot too, you know? You should be nicer to me," she told him, fisting her hands on her hips and tossing her hair.

"Shot in the fuckin' calf, H.R., and it was barely a nick. Stop milkin' it."

She glared at him. "Thanks for the sympathy, bro."

"Children," Cress chided on a wary sigh. "You're ruining a perfectly romantic scene with your bickering."

King laughed and slung an arm around his woman. "Right, sorry, Dad keep goin', you're on a real roll 'ere."

"Glad you approve," Zeus said dryly over his shoulder before he turned back to me and said, "Well, you ready to commit yourself to the dark side?"

I stared at the man that had been mine in one way or another for over a decade. The man that had raised me more than my parents had, who was my father and my best friend and my lover all tied into one complicated but beautiful knot.

I beamed at him. "Bring it on."

CHAPTER THIRTY-NINE

Loulou

FIVE MONTHS LATER.

"MRS. GARRO, I'm happy to be the one to tell you that you are officially in remission."

I blinked hard at Dr. Radcliffe but Zeus was already up out of his chair and pulling me into his arms to crush me in a hug.

"Seriously?" I squeaked as Zeus squeezed the breath out of me.

Dr. Radcliffe laughed delightedly. "Seriously, Louise. I'm so happy to be able to give you the good news."

"Not happier than fuckin' me," Zeus practically shouted.

I laughed even as I said, "I think I'm in shock."

"Why? You've been doing really well since the incident in January," he said, referring to the fire that had so brutalized my lungs. "The chemo worked beautifully on the cancer and we'll obviously keep an eye on your lungs, but this has been a while coming."

He was right. I'd been feeling like myself again since April but I hadn't wanted to get my hopes up too high even though each checkup, I'd received good news about my prognosis.

Zeus's hopes had been high and stayed high the entire time.

And now, he was so happy he looked like an overgrown kid on Christmas morning.

I watched him as he talked to Dr. Radcliffe about follow-up appointments and what I was and was still not allowed to do.

His hair had grown out in the last six and a half months since he'd shaved it for me and it was a wavy, kinking mass to just below his jaw. The gold was coming out in it again now that summer was here and his perpetual tan had caramelized to an even darker tan. He was even bigger now than he had been at the beginning of the year, so broad and quilted with muscle he was a physical threat just standing there. I'd needed to get back into the swing of exercising after the chemo ended and Zeus had taken it upon himself to work out with me each morning before I went to school and he went to work. Most of the time, especially at first, we'd just ended up fucking on the exercise equipment but the rewards of our new early morning routine were especially obvious in him. I'd mapped the growing muscles like a mountain explorer with my teeth, lips and tongue with wifely delight.

My fascination with him only grew deeper each day I spent by his side.

He turned back to look at me as he spoke to the doctor, reaching for my hand to tug me to his side. Even though I was well, and it'd been months since the incident, Zeus never liked to be in a room I was in without being able to touch me.

"Perfect, thanks, Doc," Z said, offering his rough hand for the medical man to shake.

Dr. Radcliffe was used to us now, his teenage patient and her nineteen years older biker husband, so he didn't hesitate to grasp that hand and do it with a smile.

"Congratulations, you two. Take the opportunity to celebrate."

"Oh, we will," Zeus said on a grin as he scooped me up in his arms and threw me over his shoulder in a fireman's carry.

"Zeus," I yelled through my laughter as I beat against his back. "Put me down, you monster."

"Yeah, your monster," he agreed, practically running out of the doctor's office and down the stairs to the parking lot. "Your monster who's gonna celebrate by fuckin' you right goddamn now."

I caught my breath when he dropped me onto my little seat on the back of his bike and swung on. Before I could question his intentions, he revved the engine and shot us out of the parking lot.

I screamed in delight as he gunned the engine and took us zooming out onto the highway. We only drove for ten minutes before hitting The Lotus and pulling to the narrow side alley. I was surprised he would have brought us there for the celebration until he grunted, "Closest place to the hospital."

I laughed at his impatience as he swung off the bike but when I went to get off too, he shook his head. "Gonna fuck you on my bike."

Sweet Jesus.

He knelt down to pull off my boots and strip off my tank, jeans and panties then gruffly ordered, "Straddle the seat, ass tipped back and hands on the bars."

"Zeus," I said like I was going to protest when I really was *not*.

"Need to take my girl on my Harley," he muttered, distracted by my naked body as I arched it just to his liking.

He ran his rough fingers down each notch of my spine then dipped them into the shadowed crease between my ass cheeks.

"Already wet," he hummed with approval. "You like being played with, don't you, little girl?"

I threw my head back and panted as he sank three thick fingers inside me and circled his thumb at my ass.

"Yes, Z, I fucking love it when you play with me."

We'd gone two long months without sex at the height of my illness but since then, we'd been fucking like rabbits. I couldn't get enough of him even though we were having so much sex, I was perpetually sore and swollen between my thighs.

"Wanna take my cock in this sweet little cunt?" he asked darkly, moving around the back of the bike with his fingers churning inside me so that he could straddle the seat as well and grind his jeans clad cock against my ass.

I ground back on it and moaned shamelessly. The cool air of the breeze in the alley pebbled my nipples and I loved knowing that anyone could walk by and see the huge man fucking his little girl on a great big Harley.

I shuddered and creamed all over his fingers.

"That's it, get this pussy nice and wet for me," he praised as I heard the telltale clack and release of his belt buckle and then felt his hot flesh against my ass cheeks.

The hand in my pussy disappeared but I could hear him moan as he spread my juices on his cock and gave it a few long pumps with his fist.

"Use me, not your fist," I complained, canting my hips higher for him.

He jerked off faster. "What if I want to come all over this sweet ass and watch you touch your cunt until you come all over the leather?"

"God, yes, but please next time. I need to come on your cock," I begged.

"Right answer, little girl," he growled then planted a hand on my hip and rooted his big cock balls-deep inside of me.

I threw my head back onto his shoulder and tried to grind down on him, but I was too precariously perched on the handlebars with my feet on the foot pegs.

I didn't need to work because Zeus lifted my ass higher with one hand then started to fuck up into me ruthlessly, his legs long enough to brace himself on the ground as he fucked me into his bike. My tits swung over the handlebars, the peaks catching on the cold metal and pulling them tight.

I moaned and swore and bucked against him.

The hand not on my hips curled around my torso to cup

my throat, his thumb at my pulse. "Love hearing my girl moan for me, love feelin' you alive and burnin' against me."

"Fuck," I cursed as my womb coiled painfully, ready to spring into orgasm. "Zeus, I'm going to come."

"Do it. Come all over my cock so hard it christens my fuckin' bike with your juices," he growled and squeezed slightly at my throat.

The coil released and I came undone, bones rattling under loose muscles as I fucked down against him and clenched him hard with my cunt.

Zeus roared like a triumphant beast as he came a second later, biting down into the junction of my neck and shoulder the way a wild cat would do to still his mate as he bred her.

A shiver rippled down my spine as I collapsed against the bike and Zeus slid his wet cock out of my sex. He cupped me gently in one hand and leaned down to press a kiss to the back of my neck.

Without words, he carefully peeled me off the leather seat and dressed me, his touches reverent as a worshipper attending Madonna. I pressed my hand to his bearded cheek as he knelt before me in a quiet gesture of love.

"Feel alive, little wife?" he asked me.

"Whenever I'm with you," I told him.

He beamed. "Glad to fuckin' hear it. Now, we're late, which is your fault 'cause you're so fuckin' edible but we've got to hightail it or we'll miss our appointment and Axe-Man will be fuckin' pissed."

"Our appointment?" I echoed as he swung back onto the bike.

He ignored me as he reversed out of the alley and took us back onto the highway and onto the Main Street of Entrance.

We stopped in front of a revamped Street Ink Tattoo Parlor, brand-new without a sign of the Nightstalkers trauma.

Zeus got off the bike then plucked me off and put me down on the pavement.

"You wanted a tat for a while now, this is as good a time as any seein' as mine'll take 'bout three hours. Just cleared it with the Doc and you're good to get one now, if you want one," he explained.

I blinked at him.

I'd wanted a tattoo since Mute died.

He'd come to me in a dream, as he often did, silently standing off to the side of my adventure packed dreams like a sentry. And one time, he'd shown me what he wanted me to get inked on my skin to remember him by.

But, "What are you getting done?"

He grinned at me and for the first time, I thought he looked like his son in all his boyishness. "You'll see."

And I did. Because two hours after Nova finished giving me a Mute symbol on the inside of my left wrist, Zeus appeared bare-chested in the main room of the shop and I got my first look at his tattoo.

It was an angel, one inked right over his heart. Her small, detailed face was mine and her hands were raised to cup the scar of the bullet wound Zeus had taken for me nearly eleven years earlier.

"Z," I breathed as tears compressed my chest.

He wrapped an arm around my waist and brought me into his right side. "My fallen angel."

"My guardian monster," I breathed into his mouth as he lowered it onto mine for a kiss.

CHAPTER FORTY

Zeus

I NEEDED TO TELL 'ER.

In fact, I'd needed to tell her for fuckin' weeks but she was so goddamn happy and healthy for the first time in over a year so fuck me if I wanted to be the one to ruin it.

But I knew Danner wouldn't wait for much longer.

My girl was eighteen years old now, celebrated her birthday in the hospital with an ice cream cake from Dairy Queen that she couldn't eat because she was avoidin' sugar so the dozen of brothers and their families had indulged while we pumped AC/DC into her hospital room.

Shit birthday but she'd told me she loved it anyway 'cause it was her first with me.

Girl still gave me a fuckin' toothache, she was so sweet.

And now she was mine in a way that was permanent.

I watched her black diamond ring glint in the light as she waved it in the air to punctuate her story about what Sammy had done at the Autism Centre the other day. She was gearin' up to work there full-time after graduation after decidin' against university. I'd pushed for it. Lou was smart and if things had gone a different way—as in I wasn't in her life—she woulda gone for sure. Told her I had enough money to send her to the best university for twenty fuckin' degrees if she wanted.

She didn't.

My girl didn't want to commute to Vancouver or be away from the club and me for any length of time. She liked her new family too much to let 'em go.

I loved that so I'd shut up about school.

Besides, she'd be happy as fuck at The Autism Centre and the club had just done a charity run down the coast to raise money for it. Raised enough to add an after-school special needs tutorin' program, one that my girl was going to set up.

H.R. was leanin' toward her, captivated and nearly as in love with her as I was. It was weird as shit that my daughter's stepmum was her age but we made it work and the way we did that was through lovin' each other like we'd never be given another chance to love again.

Fuckin' cheesy shit but we'd embraced it after Mute's death and Lou's long battle with cancer.

The only shadow over our fuckin' heads was the Night-stalkers.

There'd been no vengeance for Mute's death.

No opportunity to extinguish the fucker MC for good.

Until now.

And that opportunity was hangin' on Lou.

"You're quiet, old man," Loulou said as she leaned over her stool to nip my chin. "Please God, tell me I'm not boring you already? We've got a long marriage yet to go."

I grinned at her but my heart wasn't in it 'cause the door was openin' and two men I'd rather not have seen walked into Eugene's.

Seemed my time was up.

"Evenin' Garro, Loulou," Danner hesitated when he noticed my kid sitting on her stool in little shorts that made her look practically naked and a deep cut tank. His eyes darkened in a way only another man could understand. I let a low growl work in my throat and watched the officer swallow. "Harleigh Rose."

My girl nodded at him in a cool way she'd learned bein' raised by biker babes.

Lou grinned at him. "Lionel, how are ya?"

The cop's face softened. My wife had that effect on people. "Better question is, how're you?"

Lou grinned at me and placed a palm over my heart where her tattoo was still bandaged. "Cancer free and ready to graduate."

"Married and in high school," Danner mumbled. "Never a dull moment with the Garros."

I raised my brows at him and stuck a toothpick in my mouth wishin' it was a cigarette. "You'd be outta a job if there was."

He laughed. "Touché. Speaking of, I was hopin' you'd had time to talk to your wife about the situation."

Lou's head spun to me.

I glared at the cop. "No."

Danner frowned over his shoulder at his partner Gibson who crossed his arms over his chest and scowled at me.

I scowled back harder.

"Talk to me about what?" Lou asked.

Danner looked to me, which was the only reason I wasn't fuckin' stranglin' him. I tipped my chin at him 'cause the damage was already done.

Once Lou knew she had the power to help bring down the Nightstalkers, there would be no talkin' her outta it even if it meant puttin' her life on the line. A-fuckin'-gain.

"We got a lead on the Nightstalkers," Danner explained.

Immediately, Lou sat up straighter and the glimmer of vengeance I saw in my own face every mornin' when I brushed my teeth appeared on hers in full force.

"We got the opportunity to smoke them out. Thing is, we need your help," he continued.

"How can I help?"

"We have reason to believe that Mitch Warren is involved with the Nightstalkers. We'd like it if you could get close to him. We'd outfit you with a wire and hope to get a confession out of him," Gibson explained.

I snorted. "Like I said, this fuckin' plan is held together with a hope and a fuckin' prayer."

Danner's eyes flashed and his voice was low like a man at the end of his rope and seekin' retribution. Finally, he was talkin' like a man I could understand.

"It's as good as we got, Garro. I know you want justice even more than I do and you give the okay for your woman to do this, I may just see it in me to let you overhear a conversation that lets slip where the Nightstalkers have been holding up."

"Oh, yeah?" I asked casually, leanin' back in my seat to play with the ends of Lou's hair. "Not sure why I'd care about somethin' like that."

"Yeah, me either," Danner played, his eyes shrewd.

"Let's do it," Loulou said like I knew she would and then added, "Can I bring my gun?"

CHAPTER FORTY-ONE

Loulou

THE TAPE BETWEEN MY BREASTS ITCHED BUT I TRIED NOT TO wiggle as I sat in McClellan's Bar waiting for Mr. Warren to show up.

He was the "Mitch" my dad and Danner had spoken about in the parking lot of EBA after the basketball tournament. We still didn't know who Jack was but it was clear that everyone else at my parent's frequent dinner parties were in on the plot to take down The Fallen using the Nightstalkers to do it.

Mitch Warren. It was stupid of me to have forgotten his first name but everyone, even his friends, called him Warren.

When I'd called him to ask him to meet with me and discuss my options for a future after EBA, to say that I was feeling hemmed in by my relationship with Zeus and that I wanted an out, he'd been thrilled.

Mr. Warren liked young girls and I was a young girl with a biker mentality. Catnip to pervs and rebels alike. Mr. Warren was the former.

When he showed up, he was wearing one of his stylish suits, this one navy blue over a blue, red and white plaid shirt with his signature bow tie, this one yellow, at his neck. His thick brown hair was pushed away from his forehead and he could have been handsome if his chin wasn't so weak and his eyes weren't filled with false pride.

"Wow, what a vision," he said with an approving grin as I slipped off my stool to greet him and he got a full look at me in my short black dress, tight at the hips, thighs and ass but blousy up top to hide the lines of the wire beneath it.

I shook my curled hair over my back to give him a clean shot as he leaned forward to kiss my cheek.

He smelled like expensive deodorant but also a little bit like a teenage boy trying too hard.

"Warren, thank you so much for agreeing to meet with me," I gushed as his hand found my lower back and escorted me to one of the more intimate booths at the back of the bar.

I spotted Nova dressed in civilian clothes at one of the tables talking up a pretty waitress even as his eyes tracked us across the room. There was a man with a stern face and too-good posture sitting alone at the bar nursing something that could have been a gin and tonic but was probably just Sprite. Watchful eyes surrounded me, but I still hated Warren's hands on my body.

"So," he started as we settled in, "already tired of your

walk on the bad side, eh? The filth getting to be too much for you?"

I smiled at him even as I thought he was a complete dumbass for hitting on the well-known wife of The Fallen MC President. He was either incredibly cocky or incredibly dumb. My money was on both.

"Honestly, Warren, I don't know what I was thinking. He's so..." I struggled to find something bad to say about Z. "Big, just like this big oaf, you know?"

He nodded sagely. "I could have told you that, Louise. I understand that he got to you at a vulnerable time but I thought I'd made it clear to you that I would always be here to help."

He opened his hands on the table for me to place mine into.

I did so with a bright smile, calling on all my years as the dutiful daughter of Benjamin and Phillipa Lafayette in order to pull it off.

"If it was a matter of money, I know I'm a high school biology teacher but you should know, I'm a man of means," he continued.

"Oh?"

He smiled slyly. "You obviously don't care if it's dirty as long as it's money if you're with Garro so yes, Louise I'm a man of means. I can keep you in the lifestyle you've become accustomed to with your parents. Richer even, if things go right and my investments keep turning a profit."

A server appeared without being asked with a bottle of champagne. We were quiet as the woman uncorked it then served us each a glass. He watched me the whole time with a small smile of self-satisfaction as if he had always known I would cave for him and it had only been a matter of time.

His thumb rubbed back and forth over my engagement ring and wedding band.

"What are we celebrating?" I asked as he handed me my glass.

"A return to the rightful order," he cheered, clinking our glasses together.

I took a small sip and then put the glass down because I hated the sweet, bubbles enough that the taste made me want to gag.

"Did Garro even give you a proper wedding?" he asked me sorrowfully. "A girl like you deserves a big day, Louise."

He was lecturing me about what I did or did not deserve, about what kind of girl I was. It was exactly this kind of pedantic condescension that I hated most about polite society.

I thought about my perfect wedding. Remembered the plastic tiara I'd worn that proclaimed *Bride* with a short veil that Harleigh Rose and Cress had found at the dollar store in town. The bouquet of beautiful red roses that Nova had splurged on from the hospital shop and the enormous red velvet cake in the shape of Clifford the Big Red Dog that Maja had bought off some baker who'd had a last-minute cancellation. Zeus had the rings because he'd sent King out to buy them, two black titanium bands that Hannah had just stoked at Revved & Ready.

My grandfather had done the service and it was beautiful in the way that forgiveness is beautiful because I knew my family would never really understand my love for Zeus and his world but it felt right that they should pass me over to him, to someone who always had and always would under-stand me better.

Afterward, after Zeus had kissed me as long as my grieving lungs would allow, someone put on old school rock music and everyone cracked open Coke and Sprite because there wasn't any alcohol allowed in the hospital and we'd all eaten cake with our hands and laughed with each other until I was too tired to socialize. And then even though it was our wedding night, Zeus hadn't copped even a feel. He'd just held me all night, stroking my hair and whispering to me about all the things we were going to do when I was well.

I looked up at Warren and tried to strip my voice of the sheer joy the memory held for me. "He tried his best."

"And his best wasn't good enough. Honestly, I give the brute props for even thinking he stood a chance with someone like you."

"Someone like me?" I asked, leaning forward and tucking my hair behind my ear.

His eyes tracked the movement hungrily. "A princess."

I fought the urge to roll my eyes and tried to get us back on topic. "So, say I did leave him. Say I did want to be with you—what would that mean?"

His eyes flared and his grip on my hands tightened. "It would mean I'd treat you right. Lavish you with money and attention."

I pouted, flipping his hand over in mine to draw circles on the palm in a way that had him shivering. "What about those other girls?"

He frowned distractedly. "Other girls?"

"I've seen you with Lily and Talia. If we're together, I don't want to share and..." I leaned deep over the table to press my lips right beside his ear to say, "I think you'll find I can keep you satisfied."

He groaned. "You really are a minx, aren't you?"

"I prefer fox, but yes, I really am," I agreed with a winning smile.

"Well, no need to worry there. Lily and Talia are just two cogs in the machine of my alternative means of income."

My pout deepened and I was glad I'd worn red lipstick when his eyes landed on them and stuck. "What does that even mean?"

"It means, pretty girl, that Talia and Lily are a means to an end. They deal product for me."

I gasped in faux shock, hand flying to my heart only so I could define the shape of my breast beneath the fabric for him. My heart beat fast but it wasn't with modest surprise, it was with adrenaline. He was staring at the catalyst of his demise and he was literally handing himself over to it.

I could have clapped, I was so happy.

Instead, I kept up the act by saying, "You deal drugs? Warren, I never knew you had such a dark side."

He preened under my compliment and looked around the way a spy in a movie would to see if anyone was listening.

People were listening but they weren't dumb enough to do it obviously.

"I wouldn't say I'm a dealer, but I buy wholesale from a distributor and resell to the kids at EBA and Entrance Public. You'd be surprised by what a cash-cow partying teens can be," he caught my eye and then laughed, "Or maybe you wouldn't."

"No, I wouldn't," I admitted. "But I don't understand. You can't just go to Costco for drugs."

"No, sweetie," he agreed with a patronizing smile. "You go to the cartel or the MC."

"Cartel?" I asked because something was sliding into place, something obvious and dangerous, the barrel of a shotgun clicking into place.

"Javier Ventura's come up from Mexico to establish a base in Canada and he's doing it from Entrance."

Tell me more, you fool. Dig your own grave.

"Oh, that nice man who's friends with my parents?"

"Looks can be deceiving. He's really a poor piece of shit risen in the ranks, but yeah." Warren spewed his cruel words with the casualness of an arrogant man born white, rich and oblivious.

"So you buy it, use the students to deal it and then you split the proceeds with the cartel?"

There must have been something in my question that alerted him to my eagerness for information more than any eagerness for *him*. He frowned at me over the rim of his champagne glass.

"Why don't we get out of here and continue this conversation at my place? We can get to know each other a little more comfortably there."

I really didn't want to but I wasn't sure they had enough information on everyone to make the necessary arrests and there was no way in hell I was going to back off this before I bought vengeance for Mute.

So, I smiled at him. "That sounds wonderful. Just give me a moment to use the washroom?"

He tugged my hand in order to give me a brief kiss on the

lips, his tongue touching my lips like a promise. I fought the urge to rub at my mouth when he pulled away and let me go with a smug tilt of his chin.

I rolled my hips side to side as I walked calmly to the bathroom, feeling his eyes on my ass. When I made it to the short hallway with the bathrooms, I unlocked my phone screen to text Zeus.

"Hey, Foxy," someone said over my shoulder.

I startled as I whipped around then laughed when I saw Blackjack standing there with his hands in his pockets. "Jesus Christ, B.J. you scared the crap out of me. What are you doing skulking down here?"

He shrugged, his eyes wet and dilated as he looked over my shoulder then back at me. "Zeus and Danner sent me to tell ya that they got enough. They're waitin' for ya at the police station and I'm supposed to give you a ride."

"Oh." I looked down at my phone, at the text conversation with "My Guardian Monster" and pressed the Home screen to close it. "Cool, let's go."

He nodded as he led the way down the hall and opened the door for me. It disconcerted me enough to turn to look at him as I passed and caught his pale brown eyes. Something jolted free from the back of my mind, something that had lain buried in my traumatized consciousness from the night of the incident at Zeus's cabin. The night Mute died.

The night I'd looked into a pair of pale brown eyes and saw the evil intention to kill.

I saw the same thing now as I passed him when he didn't think I'd be looking, his eyes hard with purpose and his mouth twisted with malicious pleasure.

Fear catapulted through me as I froze. "I think I'll just double check—"

"Fuck, what gave me away?" he asked with a nervous laugh then shoved me out the half open door. "I've gotten so good at hidin'."

When I gained my footing, I turned to run only to be caught by Ace Munford who laughed into my hair as he held me against his chest and placed a foul-smelling wad of fabric over my nose and mouth.

"If only you'd come with us in the first place, maybe yer friend wouldn'ta died."

I tried to pry my mouth away from his hold but blackness edged my vision until that was all I could see.

CHAPTER FORTY-TWO

Zeus

THE DOOR OF MCCLELLAN'S SPLINTERED AGAINST THE WALL AS I threw it open and stormed inside with Bat at my back. Warren was still sittin' in the booth, his smug motherfuckin' smile frozen on his face as he saw me comin' for him.

He held up his hands like that would make a fuckin' difference.

I hauled him over the wooden table and then slammed his back against it, my hand at his throat. "Where the *fuck* is Lou?"

His throat worked against my hand. "Bathroom."

"She isn't in the fuckin' bathroom you, piece of shit." I leaned on his neck harder and looked back at Bat and Nova who'd joined us.

Nova shook his head. "Not there, Prez. Fresh tire marks on the street out back. Someone took 'er for fuckin' sure."

I could feel Warren's pulse beat hard under my grip. It called to me like a fuckin' song. If I put just a little more pressure right *there*—he choked—for a little longer, he'd be dead.

Fuck but I wanted to kill him.

"Garro," Danner called from the gapin' front door. "Put him down."

I ignored him.

"You want to take one more breath, it better be to tell me where my goddamn woman is," I growled into Warren's face.

The fucker started crying.

Pathetic.

"Garro, I mean it. Put the man *down*," Danner tried again, from closer this time.

Bat stepped in front of him when he tried to get into my space and held up a hand. "Hold the fuck up."

"Nova, get this fuck somewhere private," I ordered and then gave into my impulse to squeeze the breath outta 'im.

Warren was passed out in thirty seconds under my hand. I wanted it to be longer. I wanted the fucker to never wake the fuck up.

But I needed to know what he knew so I could get my fuckin' wife back.

"Not letting you go with him, Garro. You've got to know that," Danner said.

I waited 'til Nova slung the cunt over his shoulder then led the way out of the bar, aware of the eyes of Entrance at my back. There'd be gossip and news reports. The big bad Fallen had assaulted a teacher at the local watering hole.

I'd make sure there were bigger stories to break before the day was fuckin' done.

Axe-Man and Buck were already waitin' on their bikes in the lot and Curtains was pullin' up with one of the club trucks to transport Warren.

We passed the surveillance van where I'd been sittin' with Danner and Gibson when we'd seen Lou go to the bathroom and not fuckin' come back for ten minutes. I'd torn outta there the second it was obvious she wasn't coming back, clocking Gibson in the temple when he'd tried to stop me. Bet he was still in there passed the fuck out.

A hand closed over my arm from behind me and Danner said, "Zeus, stop and think about this for a fuckin' minute."

The van dented with a metallic groan as I threw Danner into the side of it with my arm at his throat and yelled, "You fuckin' swore you had this shit on fuckin' lock down, motherfucker."

The fuckin' pig looked at me steady as I pressed against his airway.

"This is my fuckin' *wife* you put in the line of fire, my fuckin' reason for bein' who near lost her life fuckin' *twice* already this year. You think to stop me, I'll tear you limb from fuckin' limb, ya hear me? She gets hurt, she fuckin' dies...That. Is. On. You. Danner."

He nodded slowly, his face red as rage but calm as ice. Hated that he was so fuckin' cool in the face of his mistake.

I snarled at him. "You gonna let me do what I need to do to secure my woman?"

"Let me help," he croaked.

I released him so quickly he sagged against the dented metal 'fore he could catch himself.

"This is on the brotherhood now. You had your fuckin' chance." I turned to my brothers and called, "Roll out. Make the calls, every fuckin' brother is ridin' out on this right fuckin' now. Find out where those motherfuckers took my fuckin' girl."

"We're gonna find her, brother," Bat told me.

I knew it. We'd find her if I had to scour the nine levels of fuckin' hell for her. I was just worried as fuck about what I'd find when I did.

"Garro," Danner called out again as I swung my leg over my bike and throttled the engine. "I want to help."

"Like I said, you fucked this once. It's club business now."

His face set. "I've known Loulou her entire life, there isn't a chance in hell I'm not playin' a part in getting her back. You do what you gotta do but I'm goin' in to McClellan's and getting the security tapes. I'll text you if I get plate numbers."

I stared at him for a beat before slidin' on my aviators and givin' him the finger as I rolled out of the lot, my brothers at my back.

BLOOD SPRAYED across my face as my brass knuckles contacted with Warren's nose and busted it open. I wiped it off my mouth with the back of my hand.

"Wanna try again, motherfucker?" I asked him.

We had him tied to a pole in the barn out at Dixon's farm, the dirt gone to red mud beneath his feet. His pretty face was a pile of broken flesh and crumbled bone, prettier than it had been 'fore in my eyes.

He looked the way the inside of his fuckin' soul looked.

Repulsive.

"I told you, I don't know where they took her," Warren sobbed like a motherfuckin' baby. "They never told me shit like that."

I adjusted my stance and hit him hard across the right cheek, listening to the crack of the bone. "What's your fuckin' play in all'a this? And you better fuckin' tell me all that there is to it or I'll do a lot worse than brass knuckles."

Warren closed his eyes, his head hangin' awkward 'cause he was in too much pain to hold it up. "At first, it was just an idea Ben had. We both hated the MC so we thought we'd try to take you down, get the people to hate you enough to cast you out. So, we dealt bad drugs."

Somethin' clicked. "You the one to plant that shit in King's bag?"

There are different kindsa fear. Fear for loved ones and fear of failure or rejection, but nothin' is more powerful than fear for yourself.

Mitch Warren felt that fear lookin' into my eyes 'cause he saw his doom written there. Man fucked with my wife *and* my son?

He was leavin' in a body bag.

"You put that shit in King's bag," I confirmed. "Tried to get my kid expelled and arrested just 'cause he's the son of a biker?"

Lifelong bigotry flared in him. "He shouldn't have been allowed into EBA anyway. He's filth just like you and yours."

My laugh was cold. "Like Lou? 'Cause she's sure as fuck mine."

He paled. "Louise made a mistake but she's not filth."

I snagged out to grab the back of his hair and held him still while I connected my fist to his temple.

"You made a mistake when you thought you could fuck with The Fallen." I crouched down and grabbed his mangled jaw in my hand to hear him whimper. "You think I won't be happy to kill you, you don't give me what I need?"

"Yes, yes, I know, please, God, don't," he whined, blood and mucus slidin' down his face and into his open mouth. "Fuck, I didn't mean it. You're not filth, I just, I was wrong. Please, don't kill me."

"Oh, I won't kill you. I don't have the kinda patience for torture, not really. I like to kill 'em quick and personal, just my hands, ya know, like the good ole days. Nah." I shook my head then jerked my chin at Priest who stood in the corner watchin' avidly. "Priest over there, he'll kill you proper. He likes it, ya get me? Likes to make a man sing when he peels off his skin, piss himself when he cuts off each of his fingers with those garden shears. You want to see how Priest makes an art outta killin' a man, Warren?"

"Oh *God*," he cried, shakin' his wet mess of a face back and forth so blood went flyin'. "No. Listen, okay, I know Javier Ventura is backing them and he's been buying up property in the area. Maybe if you check one of them out, you'll find her. But…"

"But what?" I asked, studying the blood-slicked brass knuckles on my right hand.

Warren whimpered. "But I don't know how you'll find her. Ace and Jack always said they'd kill your entire family and make you watch before they killed you."

"Who the fuck is Jack?" I pressed my thumb into his broken cheekbone and thundered, "Who the *fuck* is Jack?"

"He's one of you," he cried out, breathin' heavy through the gore in his throat. "One of your brothers. The one who killed that disabled kid."

The energy in the room went electric.

"You fuckin' lyin' to me when I've got your damned life in my hands?" I growled low.

We had a snitch. I'd known it, kept shit tight. Only the most trusted brothers were kept in any sorta loop: Buck, Bat, Priest, Nova and on a need-to-know basis, our tech kid Curtains and my old friend, Blackjack.

Black. Jack.

Ace's motherfuckn' son.

I closed my eyes and scrubbed my hand down my face across blood that wasn't mine.

No.

B.J. had been my brother since 'fore we were brothers. I'd known the guy since we were fuckin' kids.

There was no fuckin' way he'd turn after all these years.

'Less he didn't turn on a dime.

'Less he'd been workin' behind my back for fuckin' years, just bidin' his time to stab me in the fuckin' back.

I opened my eyes again and Warren moaned at the look in 'em. "Not lying, not lying, promise."

"Zeus, brother," Buck called from behind me where he leaned against a stack of hay. "Blackjack's MIA. Tried to call 'im into action but he wasn't pickin' up his phone.

"Fuck," I boomed, slammin' my fist into Warren's face just to feel it crunch, just to rid myself of the fuckin' burn in my fuckin' chest.

"Someone find me that fuckin' Judas so I can rip off his fuckin' head," I shouted into the night air.

Behind me, someone left the barn.

"Prez," Nova appeared at my side holdin' out my cell. "Let Priest take over, yeah? Danner's on the line."

I ripped the phone out of his hands and ordered, "Don't fuckin' kill 'im," before I said to Danner, "Talk."

"They took her in a black van with stolen plates. We found it, Garro, outside the fuckin' gates to your house," he said.

A message.

A message, as those goddamn pictures had been.

Not that they were just watchin' me from afar but from up close to.

From B.J.

"Garro?"

If Blackjack hated me enough to sit on that hatred for years and let it burn his ass, what were the fuckin' odds he'd let Lou live?

Fear pierced through me, radiatin' from the bullet scar just above my heart.

"Here. Got a lead, man named Javier Ventura's been backin' the Nightstalkers, check his properties for any activity, will ya? I'm ridin' out now." I swallowed my dislike of the cops even though it felt like fuckin' acid goin' down. Anythin' to save my girl. "Owe ya, you find 'er."

"No," Danner's voice was firm. "No, I owe you for putting her in and getting her taken. I'm on it. But do me a favour. I heard there was a barfight off 99 at Lloyd's Bar. Some guy got beat on really hard. Dispatch is sending out a car to check on it." He paused. "That guy might be Mitch Warren."

I looked over at the miserable fuck that had thought he'd had a chance with an angel like Lou just 'cause he wore a fuckin' suit. I wanted to kill 'im but then, I was in a murderin' mood. I figured so long as I could get my hands around motherfuckin' Ace and motherfuckin' Blackjack's throats, I'd be okay to let Warren rot in jail 'fore a while 'fore he went to hell.

"Heard there were gunshots too. Might need the paramedics," I added.

I hung up and tossed the phone to Nova.

"Priest," I called to the redhead settin' up his medical tray of tools. "Next time. This one's a catch and release."

I stalked up to Warren, grabbed my 9 mil from the waistband of my jeans and drilled a round into both of his hands. "That's for puttin' my boy in prison and havin' a hand in gettin' Cress and my fuckin' woman tied up in this shit as well."

With his wails in my ears, I turned around and stalked out of the buildin' callin' to my brothers as I went.

"First man to find that motherfucker Blackjack gets to be the one to put a bullet through his fuckin' head."

CHAPTER FORTY-THREE

Loulou

I WOKE UP TO THE SOUND OF MY DAD'S VOICE.

This confused me because I hadn't seen or spoken to my dad since the night he punched me in the face and kicked me out of my house.

Briefly, I wondered if I had died and gone to hell for my sins because only there would I find that voice again. Only there would I be punished like Sisyphus or Tantalus with the fruitless repetition of a single horrific act; begging my dad not to hit me over and over again, even as his fist crashed into my cheek.

I decided to open my eyes because anything was better than imagining that horrible possibility.

I opened them and realized that I wasn't dead and, in fact, I wasn't even harmed.

I was curled on my side in an empty room in a house. There was duct tape across my mouth, hands and feet and someone had taken off my dress so I was only in my skimpy black lace underwear. My pain ached but it was nothing I couldn't handle after months of cancer and weeks of chemo. They hadn't hurt me. In fact, I had the feeling they'd only tied me up this way to degrade me.

There were divots in the carpet from displaced furniture and the sharp scent of turpentine in the air like it had been recently painted. When I stood up to look out the window, I had a direct line of sight to Zeus's and my house. I thought back to the drive home on the bike every night and remembered the bright blue beach house that had been on the market for months without any offers because the last owner had died of a heart attack in it.

That's how they'd been watching us.

There was even a tripod in the corner.

I took a deep breath to center myself and remember that Zeus was coming for me. There was no way in heaven or hell that my guardian monster wouldn't find me. He would find me and as was his habit, he would save me.

"This has gotten so far out of hand." My dad's voice was coming closer, up a set of stairs I could just see through the open door. "I can't even comprehend how you fucking idiots could have let it come to this."

"Javier told us we could have the girl." Ace's voice followed behind him and a second later they both appeared on the landing. "That was the deal."

My dad wasn't listening. Instead, his eyes were riveted on the sight of me bound up in the fetal position with silver duct tape at my wrists and feet where he'd normally placed only the most expensive bracelets, the most famous brands of shoes.

"Look at you," he breathed.

I didn't know what he meant by that. If he was horrified by how far his society princess had fallen or by the way his criminal associates had treated me, or if hope of hopes, he was disgusted with himself for his part in my situation.

I knew the answer a second later when my Armani suit-clad father rushed Ace and thrust him into a wall.

"What the *fuck* have you done to my daughter?" he shouted.

"Dude, chill, you know she's Garro's whore. She deserves worse." Ace laughed with his hands in the air.

"She's a Lafayette," my dad said as if that meant everything.

And to him it did.

If my mouth hadn't been taped shut, I would have told him I was a Garro now.

"She's a Lafayette and she will *not* be hurt in this. Do you understand me?"

Ace blinked and from one second to the next his affability was gone. His face was rough and pockmarked like the face of a cliff, worn and creased from hard living. It grew jagged edged as he snarled, "You don't got much say in things now, Mayor. Javier runs this show."

"Javier runs this show because I let him. Don't mistake that. Now let Louise go."

Blackjack appeared in the doorway, pale and slim as a beam of light in the already sun-drenched room. The thin blade in his right hand sparkled as he stalked toward my dad with it.

I tried to shout behind my gag but the sound was muffled and ineffective.

Still, my dad heard it and turned to look at me just in time to see Blackjack clock him on the head with the butt of the knife.

Ace kicked Dad in the face *hard* with his motorcycle boot and spat on his prone body. "Tie this motherfucker up."

My stomach clenched into a hard fist as I watched Blackjack strip him down and tape him up just as he'd done me.

Ace paced the room, running his fingers over his thinning, grease-smeared hair like a man who'd been high every day of his life.

And he ranted.

"Gonna get that fuckin' prick. Gonna get 'im, gonna get 'im, gonna get 'im and string 'im up like a great old bear and skin 'im alive. Yeah, gonna skin 'im alive and take it slow so he can watch his pretty little bitch die slowly first. He's gonna suffer, yeah, finally he's gonna suffer."

I'd never had any experience with craziness. I'd been sheltered until a few months ago and then what I had been exposed to was violence, sex and greed, but never full-blown whacked-out craziness.

That's what Ace was.

Pure crazy.

I was so distracted by the two Munfords that I didn't notice the dark man in the beautifully styled suit come up the stairs and into the doorway until he said my name.

"Louise."

Javier Ventura stood in the doorframe flanked by two enormous bodyguards. He looked so incongruent in the modest home with two junky bikers before him that at first, I wondered if my mind was playing tricks on me.

He walked toward me on his beautiful hand-tooled Italian leather loafers and pinched his slacks at the thighs so that he could settle into a comfortable crouch before me.

"Such a shame, *zorra*, to see such a pretty woman in such an ugly place. I wish I could help you out of this situation but alas, we make our beds and we must lie in them. It was your decision to lie in that bed with Zeus Garro and so it was your decision to die for him too, if it came to that."

I tried to say something but the tape at my mouth muffled it.

Javier sighed and indicated for one of his hovering body-guards to rip the tape off even though he could have done it easily himself. I was beginning to understand that Javier was the kind of man that did nothing if he could get someone else to do it for him first.

The tape left my mouth stinging as if I suffered third degree burn.

"What is it you were trying to say?" he asked me with mild curiosity, as if we were having one of our dinner party conversations.

"Any bed would be better than one you were in," I repeated with a beatific smile.

He blinked at me before a lazy smile spread over his dark face like spilled molasses. "Such fire. I can see why you would appeal to a dark man like Garro. Such a burning flame you are, even in the darkest of times."

He carefully replaced the tape over my mouth, drawing the shape of my lips through the material after he did so.

My father started to rouse as Blackjack finished his

ministrations and pushed him up against the wall beside me.

"Ah," Javier said, turning his attention from me to him. "I'm so happy he learned of you being here, Louise. Mr. Mayor has become a rather large pain in my side."

My dad blinked open his eyes, saw Javier and immediately began to struggle.

Javier laughed, stood up and went to loom over him as he explained to me, "Did you know your daddy was involved in my plans, sweet Louise? He was so angry with Zeus Garro and the MC for ruining his town and ruining you. It made him *so* blind and ridiculously easy to manipulate." He reached out to run a finger down Benjamin's anger-reddened cheek. "I needed him to set me up with the right people, to help me get all those lovely legal problems out of the way so I could set up shop right here in pretty little coastal Entrance. And he did it so beautifully. I honestly thought I'd keep him around but"— he frowned and shook a finger in his face—"when you were hurt in that fire, he got so...*protective.* It was almost like he'd started to care for someone other than himself."

Javier laughed gently, like the idea greatly amused him.

It was obvious he knew my father well.

Benjamin Lafayette cared for no one more than himself.

Dad turned his head to look at me, his eyes the exact same shade of blue as my own. They were filled with worry, fear and loathing. One for me, one for him and one for Javier.

"It's such a shame but you have to understand from a business perceptive, I can't have liabilities," Javier said. "And Benjamin has outlived both his usefulness and his loyalty."

He smiled kindly at my dad as he crouched down before him and leaned close. Benjamin shook his head frantically and then whimpered when Javier produced a gun and pressed it to his temple.

My breath froze in my lungs, crystallizing into an acute burn.

No.

"It's nice this way," Javier mused. "You two can go together."

My dad stared at me with huge eyes, my eyes, as they filled with tears and spilled over. I struggled to yell under the tape, to wriggle out of my bonds but the tape only cut into my flesh and burned.

No.

I may have hated him, but no one wanted their father to die.

Javier leaned forward to press a chaste kiss to my dad's forehead and murmured, "Be well on the other side."

And then he pulled the trigger.

I screamed, long and rough in my throat as I squeezed my eyes shut against the flying blood and brain matter that sprayed across the wall, across me.

Dad's blood dripped down my face, stuck in my eyelashes. I screamed again, when his dead body slumped over and into my side.

Oh my God.

My thoughts arrested in my head, suspended in shock. This couldn't be happening. Numb and reeling, I watched with blind eyes as Javier handed the gun to one of his lackeys then turned to smile blandly at me, grab my bloodied face in his hands and press a gentle kiss to my duct-taped mouth.

"I won't see you again, *zorra*, as I promised these gentlemen they could kill you for sport, but I hope you know that I enjoyed our time together immensely. You were a worthy player."

I blinked at him because all I had left was minimal body functions.

My mind was on lockdown.

There was no dead Dad pressed to my shoulder.

None of his blood dripping from my chin to my shoulder.

No more death.

No more anything.

I blinked and I breathed and I *did not think*.

Javier spoke with Ace and Blackjack then left with his lackeys.

Ace ranted some more about retribution, but Blackjack was surprisingly quiet, doing a few lines of coke off the windowsill then retreating to the corner. There were other bikers from the Nightstalkers in the house. They came into the room sometimes to check in with Ace, knives in their boots and guns tucked into pockets and waistbands.

The sun sank so low in the sky that long shadows shaped like ghouls floated through the room.

I didn't know what they were waiting for, why they'd even taken me, and obviously, Ace was growing impatient because at one point, he came to kneel before me and poked at my forehead.

"You said she was pretty," Ace accused as he kept poking me. "She looks like a dumb Barbie to me. Look, no life in her at all. Probably lies there while Garro plows 'er and pretends she likes it."

"She's a class act," Blackjack said quietly from his corner, his head tipped back against the wall. "And she's a real beaut under all that blood, trust me. Stops a man in his tracks, she does."

"Huh," Ace said, bringing up the gun he kept in his hand to scratch at his stubble with it. "Should I fuck 'er, you think, before he gets here?"

Blackjack straightened from the wall. "Fuck off, Dad. He'll be here soon and we can get this shit rollin'. We're after Zeus, not his fuckin' woman."

Ace turned his head to stare at him as he sucked his teeth. "You like 'er, that it?"

"Fuck off."

"That's why you don't want to kill 'er—you like the slut! What, did she give you a piece of her sweet cherry pie?"

Blackjack was off the wall and in front of his father in a second. "I said, fuck off, old man. I'm in this for Garro just like you are. He fucked with the club, he killed your fuckin' best friend and he's taken all the *fuckin'* glory from me. Won't promote me to fuckin' shit in the club, won't tell me nothin' of his plans. He gets the kids, he gets the shit hot wife and he deserves fuckin' none of it."

I watched detached as Blackjack flipped out, spittle flying as he yelled into the face of his father and I thought, okay, he's whacked too.

The next minute, there was the all-too-familiar sound of gunshots.

Pop.

I wondered if I'd ever get used to the sound or stop

thinking that it sounded so innocuously like a giant chewing bubblegum.

Pop. Pop.

Ace and Blackjack immediately went into action.

I watched from my strange third person perspective as Ace knelt behind the open door with a gun and knife in his hand and as Blackjack crouched in the corner with a bigger gun trained on the door. Three more bikers settled in, guns trained on the door.

We all watched the stairs.

The gunshots outside moved closer then echoed throughout the main level. There were shouts and thuds as violence swept through the house.

Then it was quiet.

The men in the room looked at each other but Blackjack held up a hand for stillness and we waited.

Then there was a roar at the base of the stairs and thunder as men ran up them. A crash sounded from a window on the landing and someone landed with a knife in his teeth amid the Nightstalkers set up outside the door.

Bat.

The three men turned to him but the ex-military man was already moving, dropping down to a lunge then coming up with his knife, slicing clean through the belly of one of the men.

His guts spilled out and he followed them with a thud to the floor.

A shot went off as they tried to get Bat in their sights, but he shifted at the last second like a dancer and the shot hit the Nightstalker behind him.

Another down.

The commotion on the stairs grew even louder but everyone in the room with me was focused on Bat as the remaining man leveled his gun at his face and fired.

A bullet grazed the outside edge of his arm but Bat was undeterred as he slammed the gun out of the man's hands then slipped his big knife effortlessly between his ribs and up into his heart.

Third man down.

One of the men in the room with me hesitantly moved forward to engage him.

Before he could get the chance, a body flew through the air from the stairs and crashed into the wall with a horrific crunch.

Seconds later, Zeus appeared in the doorway.

From deep within my cocoon of shock, my heart began to thaw and my mind began to whir.

Zeus was there.

I tried to scream because there were about four guns trained on him the second he stalked through the door with Bat at his back.

Zeus didn't care.

He plucked a dead body from the ground and used it as a shield as he walked into the room then roared like some great angry beast as he threw it into two of the Nightstalkers kneeling closest to him.

They fell back and before they could get up, Bat and Axe-Man, who had appeared out of thin air, were on them with knifes sinking through their butter-soft flesh.

Zeus took a step toward Blackjack, utter rage in every line of his enormous frame but before he could get there,

Ace emerged from behind the door and jumped on his back, sinking the edge of his blade into Zeus's trapezius.

Zeus bellowed so loudly, the room shook with it. I watched without breathing as he reached back with one of those mighty man-killing-hands I loved so much, grabbed the smaller man and flipped him over his shoulder. Then before he could land, Z picked him up by the throat and flung him against the wall.

There was a sickening snap as Ace's spine broke on impact.

Vaguely, I noted that Nova had his knife at Blackjack's throat and that Axe-Man was beside me, gently cutting through the tape at my ankles and wrists.

"Don't have to watch this," he mumbled.

I watched on as Zeus stalked over to the crumpled man, pinned him against the wall with a knee to the gut and cupped his face. Then with a quick, almost casual flick of his wrists, he broke Ace's neck.

The man dropped to the ground like a broken toy, but Zeus wasn't done. He prowled over to where Nova held Blackjack and smashed his head into the wall behind him.

"What the fuck is wrong with you?" Zeus shouted. "You betray your brothers like this?"

"You aren't my brother," Blackjack spat. "You never gave a shit about me or my problems. You fuckin' promoted that Irish fuck Priest over me. There's no fuckin' brotherhood under a Prez who'd kill his own brothers."

Zeus's laugh was hard. "That what your dad told you, that I killed Crux for kicks? He was fuckin' killin' brothers, you motherfuckin' idiot. He was killin' brothers just like you killed Mute, for no goddamn reason other than that you're fuckin' sick."

My system rebooted like it'd been jumpstarted and suddenly I was on my feet, so powered by rage my body vibrated with it as I moved toward the group huddled in the corner. I didn't notice the blood drying my clothes to my skin or the fact that my dad's body dropped to floor when I got up.

All I noticed was Blackjack and the words Zeus had just uttered.

The words I'd been thinking already.

Blackjack killed Mute.

Before Zeus or Nova or Axe-Man or even I understood what was happening, I was grabbing Zeus's gun from the back of his waistband, lifting it with a steady hand and popping off a shot into Blackjack's throat.

He watched me in shocked horror as the shot slammed him back into the wall and blood spurted like a geyser from the wound.

I watched him without remorse as he fell to the ground and slumped over, bleeding out like a stuck pig.

The Fallen men looked at me and they did it carefully.

"Lou, give me the gun," Zeus grumbled.

I didn't.

Instead, I flipped the safety, threw it to the ground and wrapped my arms around Zeus's blood-drenched back.

A second later, I burst into tears.

My guardian monster's arms came around me, his lips pressed to the clean side of my hair. "I got you, little girl," he said in a voice as rough and deep as any monsters, while he held me like a guardian angel. "I got you."

Loulou

I was graduating. Somehow, the year was finally ending and I was graduating. I still had my hair, something I never would have thought at the beginning of the year but then again, I never could have predicted where these months had taken me. My dad was dead, entombed in the Lafayette Mausoleum at First Light Church that no one ever visited. Warren was dead too, found floating in Entrance Bay just weeks after he'd been involved in a bar fight that left him with an ugly, broken face. Only Javier remained standing, an impenetrable pillar of Entrance society, stepping into the vast vacuum left by the Lafayette's abdication from the societal throne. There was nothing to pin on him, no evidence stating he'd funded the Night-stalkers, no witness to his cold-blooded murder of my father but for me. He lived free and well but with an itch at the back of his neck that told him The Fallen would never forget.

I'd beaten cancer for the second time, watched two men integral to my life die right in front of me, and married a thirty-six-year-old MC biker Prez. Graduating seemed like small peanuts compared to all of that but I was the only one who thought so.

Everyone in my family was in the crowd watching for me to walk across the stage. King and Cress were up from UBC where they were taking summer classes, Harleigh Rose sat beside my sister Bea and beside her, somewhat miraculously, my mother and my grandpa, and the rest of The Fallen brothers filled out the three rows around them. They all sat in their cuts, some of them hungover as fuck, some of them looking bored to tears, but they were all there to see their Fox graduate.

It made me want to cry but I was doing a lot of that these days.

I wasn't over Mute's death and I knew I never would be.

He'd been in my life only half a year but he'd given me what only one other person ever had, unconditional love right from the start.

I felt his absence like partial deafness, as if my ears were always straining for the quiet sounds of him in my life, the steady whoosh of his deep breaths as he piggy backed me, the gentle huff of his exhale when he thought something was funny. He'd been such a quiet man that I'd learned to listen harder to the silence and find treasures of sound in it.

And now he was gone and that awareness remained as a constant reminder of his nonexistence.

"Louise Lafayette Garro," Headmaster Adams called out from the podium.

I swallowed hard, tossed my hair over my shoulder and strode across the stage in my gold gown and combat boots.

"Congratulations, Louise," Headmaster Adams said with a sour smile. "I'm surprised you actually made it to graduation given the company you keep."

I smiled back. "I made it to graduation *because* of the company I keep, but thank you."

Then with my rolled-up diploma in one hand and my stupid graduation cap in the other, I faced the audience, lifted my arms and shouted, "Fuck yeah!"

The audience's nervous giggles were drowned out by the roar of The Fallen brothers yelling, "Fuck yeah!" right back at me.

"Way to go, Mrs. Garro!" Zeus yelled loudest of all, standing so tall above everyone else, his hand up in the "rock on" symbol as he yelled for me.

I shed my gown as I ran down the stairs, revealing the little denim skirt and green tube top I wore, which was totally *not* appropriate graduation wear. I didn't give a fuck. My family was celebrating at the clubhouse and I was beyond ready to blow this popsicle stand.

I didn't stop running until I hit Zeus's chest and he yanked me up into his arms. He planted a deep wet kiss on me, doing it so long and so well I was dizzy by the time we broke apart. There was a smattering of awed, nervous applause but I didn't notice it because Zeus Garro was looking at me with pride in his silver-grey gaze.

"My wife is a high school graduate now."
I threw my head back and laughed.

Zeus

THREE YEARS LATER.

IT WAS A BRUTALLY COLD DAY, SNOWIN' like it never did in Entrance, but Lou wouldn't be fuckin' deterred. So, we'd bundled up and headed out to First Light Church graveyard to visit Mute as we did every year on the anniversary of his passin'.

We stood in front of his gravestone, starin' at the epitaph I'd had carved into the black stone.

> *Mute Garro (Walker Michael Nixon) 1999-2018*
> *Cherished Brother, Silent Hero, Eternal Friend*
> *The Fallen remembers.*
> *R.I.P.*

Lou was cryin' but she always cried when we visited and I'd grown as used to it as any man whose mission in life was to kill off any reason for his wife's tears could be with it. That was to say, I curled her under my arm and tried not to give in to the crater of tears in my chest too.

When she was done, she placed the model Empire State Building beside the other Lego buildings we'd left on other visits. Sammy made them for Lou whenever she visited.

"Ready to go?" I asked her, wantin' out of the cemetery 'cause it gave me bad vibes though I'd never say it out loud.

Besides, it was Sunday and we were havin' family dinner in a few hours, which gave me just enough time to bed my hot young wife 'fore they arrived.

"Not quite yet," she surprised me by sayin', then bizarrely she added, "If it's a boy, I want to name him Walker."

I blinked at her. "You want a dog or somethin'?"

She smiled through her tears and the weak grey light shone down on her face like a haloed fuckin' spotlight. "A dog would be nice but we might be busy for a while so a dog's not the best idea."

"Fuck, we're busy enough as is," I said and it was true.

The Autism Centre took up a shit-ton of my girl's time. Not so much she couldn't find the odd afternoon to come hang out with her man, suckin' on a cherry lollipop while she watched me work on a bike, but enough that I didn't see her for precious hours every day. The club was fuckin' thrivin' now that King was prospectin' and lendin' his business expertise to our operations. We'd expanded our product to fuckin' China just last month.

I had enough money so I was thinkin' of handin' over

more of that side of things to King when the time came 'cause what I didn't have enough of was time.

I'd never have enough fuckin' time with Lou.

"I think you'll like this kind of busy," Lou said, smilin' like a fuckin' loon.

"Fuckin' tell me already, little girl. What are you playin' at?"

Her little hand reached out to thread through mine and press to her belly. "When the baby comes, if he's a boy, I want to name him Walker after Mute."

I blinked.

Lou was pregnant.

It wasn't like we were tryin'. She didn't like goin' on the pill after the cancer and the contraceptive shot she'd been takin' lapsed more often than any two people tryin' *not* to have a baby woulda liked.

But I'd never thought of it, not in real life, not in anything but my deepest fuckin' fantasies.

"You've got my kid in you?"

She pressed our hands tighter to her womb. "I got your kid in me," she confirmed.

"Well then, let's hope it's a fuckin' boy," I said with a grin as I hauled my girl into my arms nearly up over my head so I could kiss the slim belly holdin' my future kin.

She tipped her long hair back and laughed into the sky and I looked up to watch her thinkin' for the millionth fuckin' time that somehow I'd been blessed with a fuckin' angel.

Baby Monster and Baby Angel,

Fuck me, there's gonna be two of ya.

Lou won't like it that I'm cursin' in a letter to my kids 'fore they're even born but we ain't givin' you these letters 'til you're eighteen years old, an' I figure by then you'll 'ave already lived a decade under a roof with me so you'll know your curse words from a-to-fuckin'-z.

And this is worth cursin' about.

Always knew I was an unholy man, figured I got as blessed as a man could get when Heaven gave me my King and Harleigh Rose then knew it for sure when Lou fell from grace right into my dark world and decided to stay there with me forever.

So, blessed. Fuck me, but I've been truly fuckin'

BLESSED IN THIS LIFE AND NOW, SOMEHOW, I GOT EVEN LUCKIER 'CAUSE GOD OR SOMETHIN' LIKE THAT HAS GIVEN ME MORE KIN IN THE FORM OF YOU TWO.

I GOTTA SAY, THERE AIN'T NOTHIN' IN THIS WORLD I LOVE SO MUCH AS I LOVE YOUR MAMA AND HONEST TO CHRIST, DIDN'T THINK I COULD LOVE THAT GIRL MORE THAN I ALREADY DO. BUT STANDIN' 'SIDE HER WITH A HAND TO HER SWOLLEN BELLY WHILE THE DOC SHOWED US YOU TWO ON THE SCREEN FOR THE FIRST TIME, CURLED UP TOGETHER LIKE YIN AND YANG, MY HEART 'BOUT BURST OUTTA MY FUCKIN' CHEST.

LOU'S GIVEN ME EVERYTHIN' AND SHE'S STILL FOUND A WAY TO GIVE ME MORE.

ONE'A YOU'S A BOY. LOU ALREADY CALLS YOU HER BABY MONSTER AND SHE LAUGHED THROUGH HER TEARS WHEN THE DOC POINTED OUT THE WAY YOU WERE BOWED OVER YOUR SISTER, PROTECTIN' HER EVEN IN THE WOMB. ALREADY THE PERFECT NAMESAKE FOR YOUR LOST UNCLE, MUTE. YOU CARRY THE NAME OF A MAN THAT GAVE HIS LIFE FOR YOUR MAMA, A MAN THAT WAS LOYAL AND SO PURE OF FUCKIN' HEART, SON, HE SEEMED TO GLOW WITH IT. KILLS ME HE WON'T HAVE THE CHANCE TO TAKE YOU AND YOUR SISTER ON HIS BACK AND SHIELD YOU THE WAY HE WOULDA LOVED TO, BUT I GOT NO DOUBT HE'S WATCHIN' OVER THE BOTH OF YA FROM THE AFTER-LIFE AND THAT HE'S SMILIN' EACH TIME YOU GIVE YOUR SISTER THE PROTECTION AND PIGGYBACKIN' HE CAN'T. KNOW IT WITHOUT NEEDIN' TO SEE IT PLAY OUT THAT YOU'RE GOIN' BE THE BEST OF MEN, WALKER GARRO, ALL THE GOOD BITS'A ME AND MY FALLEN BROTHERS AND KING. YOU'RE GONNA BE GOOD LIKE THAT 'CAUSE LOVE DOES MAGIC TO A PERSON AND YOU'LL BE THE MOST LOVED BOY THERE EVER FUCKIN' WAS WITH A FAMILY LIKE OURS TO GIVE THAT TO YA.

My baby Angel. Lou doesn't want to name you that, somethin' 'bout the name bein' to much of a burden to carry. Named my firstborn son, King, and he wears that shit like the crown it is. You'll wear Angel too, like white wings behind your back. Nothin' but the sweetest thing of beauty could be born of the love I got for your Mama and the beauty she's got shinin' golden at the heart of 'er. You're my Angel and I'm gonna show ya how precious that is to me every single day from now when you're cradled in your Mama's sweet body until the day I die. I did wrong by your big sis, Harleigh Rose, and I didn't let her into the brotherhood the way I shoulda, but not you. Gonna have my girl on her Dad's knee while I tinker with the engine so you grow up with the skills. Gonna teach ya to ride a bike with flames painted on the handle bars and how to shoot a gun on your sixteenth birthday just like your brother 'cause your Mama's taught me that girls are badasses too, and that's a fuckin' thing'a beauty.

Can't wait to meet ya, kids. Can't wait to hold you in my arms and see what gifts my Lou's given ya, which ones you've taken from me and all the ways you're just straight up, uniquely yourselves. Never written a love letter to my kids 'fore but I got no shame in tellin' ya this won't be the last one I write to you, not when I can feel all the love I got for you already burin' up a hole in my chest just blazin' to get out.

Just gotta say one more thing right outta the gate here, my first lesson to ya both as your father. You treat your Mama like gold, ya hear? That woman has been to hell and back in her life and she's the strongest

WOMAN ANY OF US'LL EVER KNOW. SHE'S GONNA TREAT YOU SO GOOD, TRUST ME, YOU WON'T KNOW WHAT TO DO TO PAY 'ER BACK FOR IT. YOU KNOW WHAT YOU GOTTA DO, MY BABIES? YOU GOTTA LET HER LOVE YA AND THEN YOU'VE GOTTA MOVE THE MOON TO MAKE SURE SHE KNOWS YOU LOVE 'ER TOO. TRUST ME, SHE'LL DESERVE THAT FROM YA AND YOU'LL WANNA GIVE IT. I'LL TEACH YOU HOW TO TAKE CARE OF 'ER, DON'T YOU WORRY, BUT IT'S THE FIRST LESSON I WANTED TO GIVE YOU TWO. YOUR MAMA IS AN ANGEL, AND SOMEHOW, SOME FUCKIN' WAY, SHE CHOSE A MONSTER AS HER SOULMATE, AND TOGETHER WE CREATED YOU. IT'S HER YOU GOT TO THANK FOR THAT MAGIC. LORD FUCKIN' KNOWS, I'LL SPEND THE REST OF MY DAYS THANKIN' HER TOO, FOR THE GIFT OF GIVIN' A MAN LIKE ME HER BUT EVEN MORE, GIVEN ME THE BLESSIN' OF THE BOTH OF YOU.

CAN'T WAIT TO FUCKIN' MEET YA,
YOUR DAD,
Z.

Thank you so much for reading *WELCOME TO THE DARK SIDE*!

After the Fall (The Fallen Men, #4) *is LIVE now!*

Inked in Lies (The Fallen Men, #5) is coming next!

Not ready to say goodbye to Zeus and Loulou?
Pick up the short story *Fallen Son* (A Fallen Men Christmas Short Story)!

If you love Daddy Zeus and his little warrior's forbidden love story, you will love his daughter, Harleigh Rose's romance with the good cop, Lionel Danner! Discover what happens when Harleigh Rose is forced into a life or death situation and Danner arrives to save the day... or complicated it further.

"TOP FAV of Forever! Good Gone Bad is Giana's newest masterpiece. Addictive, gut-wrenching, and beautiful. I could not PUT THIS BOOK DOWN! Danner and his Rose stole my heart and I cannot wait for what Giana does next!"
—Author R. Scarlett

One-Click GOOD GONE BAD now!

Or discover where it all began with the first Fallen Men book, LESSONS IN CORRUPTION! If you love forbidden romance, you will swoon over my eighteen-year-old biker poet, King Kyle Garro, and his prim and proper teacher Cressida Irons!

Sexy, forbidden, and a touch of sweet! Lessons in Corruption by Giana Darling hits all the marks when it comes to a taboo relationship, a badass biker, and a yummy love story! This book draws you in and tethers you to the Fallen Men MC world. Once

you're in, you're never getting out! Five KING & QUEENIE stars!
—**K Webster,** *USA Today* Bestselling Author

One-Click LESSONS IN CORRUPTION now!
Turn the page for an excerpt...

(The Fallen Men Series, Book 1)
Excerpt

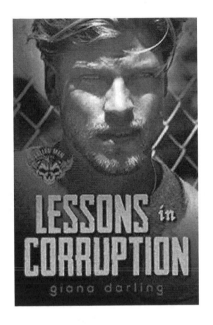

He was eighteen.
The heir to a notorious, criminal MC.
And my student.

There was no way I could get involved.
No way I could stay involved.
Then, no way I could get out alive.

Book One in The Fallen Men Series. A standalone.

One.

Lessons in Corruption

I saw him in a parking lot when I was picking up groceries. Not the most romantic place to fall in love at first sight but I guess you can't choose these things.

He had grease on his face. My eyes zoomed in on the smear of motor oil, the aggressive slash of his cheekbones protruding almost brutally under his tanned skin so that they created a hollow in his cheeks. His features were so striking they were almost gaunt, nearly too severe as to be unattractive, mean even. Instead, the softness of his full, surprisingly pink mouth and the honeyed-coloured hair that fell in a touchable mess of curls and waves to his broad shoulders and the way his head was currently tipped back, corded throat exposed and deliciously brown, to laugh at the sky as if he was actually born to laugh and only laugh...none of that was mean.

I stood in the parking lot looking at him through the heat waves in the unusual late summer heat. My plastic grocery bags were probably melted to the asphalt, the ice cream long gone to soup.

I'd been there a while already, watching him.

He was across the lot beside a row of intimidating and gorgeous motorcycles, talking to another biker. His narrow hips leaned sideways across the seat of one, one booted foot propped up. He wore old jeans, also with grease on them, and a white t-shirt, somehow clean, that fit his wide shoulders and small waist indecently well. He looked young, maybe even a few years younger than me, but I only guessed that because while his structure was large, his muscles hung on him slightly like he hadn't quite grown into his bones.

Idly, I wondered if he was *too* young.

Not so idly, I decided that I didn't care.

His attention was drawn to the group of college-aged kids who pulled up in a shiny convertible, their brightly coloured polo shirts and wrinkled khakis dead giveaways even if their gelled hair and studied swagger hadn't given them away already. They were chuckling as they reached the two motorcycle men I'd been watching and it struck me that compared to the newcomers, there was no way the sexy blond I'd been lusting after was young. He carried himself well, regally even, like a king. A king at home in a grocery store parking lot, his throne the worn seat of an enormous Harley.

I watched without blinking as he greeted the crew, his expression neutral and his body relaxed and casual in a way that tried to veil the strength of his build and failed.

There was something about his pose that was predatory, a hunter inviting his prey closer. A couple of the college kids fidgeted, suddenly uneasy, but their leader strode forward after a brief hesitation and extended his hand.

The blond king stared at the hand but didn't take it. Instead, he said something that made the fidgeting increase.

I wished I were close enough to hear what he said. Not just the words but also the tone of his voice. I wondered if it was deep and smooth, an outpouring of honey, or the gravel of a man who spoke from his diaphragm, from the bottomless well of confidence and testosterone at the base of him.

The kids were more than nervous now. The leader, one step ahead of the others, visibly shrank as his explanation, accompanied by increasingly more agitated hand gestures, seemed to fall on deaf ears.

After a long minute of his babbling, he stopped and was met with silence.

The quiet weighed so heavily, I felt it from across the lot where I lurked by my car.

The blond king's sidekick, or rather henchman seemed like a more fitting word for the frankly colossal, dark-haired friend beside him, stepped forward.

Just one step.

Not even a large one. But I could see how that one movement hit the college crew like a nuclear blast wave. They reeled back as a unit; even their leader took a huge step backwards, his mouth fluid with rushed words of apology.

They had obviously fucked up.

I didn't know how.

And for the first time in my life, watching a potentially dangerous situation unfold, I wanted to know.

I wanted to be a part of it.

To stand beside the blond king and be his rough and tumble queen.

I shivered as I watched the men before him cower, his loyal friend at his back. Slowly, because he was clearly a man who knew the impact of his physique and how to wield the sharp edge of power like a literal dagger, the blond king rolled out of his slouched position on his bike and into his full height.

The sight of him unraveling like that made my mouth go dry and other, private, places go wet.

It had a different effect on the college kids. They listened to what he had to say like men being read their last rites, clinging to any hope he could give them, desperate for salvation.

He gave it to them. Not much, but a shred of something to hold on to because as one they practically genuflected before sprint-walking back to their fancy silver car parked on the street.

Blond king and henchman remained frozen in position until the car was out of sight before they clicked back into movement. Simultaneously they turned, staring at each other for a few long seconds before the laughter started.

He laughed and the sound carried perfectly to my ear. It was a clear, bright noise. Not a chuckle, a guffaw or a mumbled *hahah*. Each vibration erupted from his throat like a pure note, round and loud and defined by unblemished joy.

It was the best thing I had ever heard.

I gasped lightly as his joy burned through me and, as if he heard it, his head turned my way. We were too far away to truly lock eyes but it felt like we did. His friend said something to him but the blond object of my instant obsession ignored him. For the first time since I noticed him, his face fell into somberness and his jaw tightened.

I may have loved him from the moment I saw him but he clearly did not feel the same.

In fact, if the way he abruptly cut away from me was any indication, throwing one long leg over the seat of a huge chrome bike and revving the engine before I could even think to tear my eyes away, he may have even hated me on first sight.

Paralyzed, I watched him peel out of the lot with his buddy. It hurt. Which was insane because I didn't even know the man and more importantly, I refused to be taken in by a pretty face.

The last time that had happened, someone had died.

I pulled myself together, collecting the grocery detritus that spilled out of some of the melted bags and moved to my car. It was hot as hell in the compact sedan, the leather seats nearly burned the skin off my bottom when I sat down. I got back out of the car and manually cranked open all of the windows before I started the drive home.

Home was a sweet white-shingled house in the quiet residential area of Dunbar in Vancouver where real estate prices were crazy and desperate housewives were a real thing. My husband had grown up in the ritzy grove about eighteen years before I'd been born and grown up in the house next to his. Everyone *oh*ed and *ah*ed over our little love story, the older neighbor falling for the quiet girl next door.

Once, I'd done the same.

Now, as I rolled up the asphalt drive and saw William's car parked in the garage, I felt only dread.

"I'm home," I called when I opened the door.

I didn't want to say the words, but William liked the ritual. He liked it more when he came home to me already in the house, dinner on the stove and a smile on my face, but I'd gone back to work this year after three years of staying at home waiting for kids to come when none ever did. I loved working at Entrance Bay Academy, one of the most prestigious schools in the province, but William thought it was unnecessary. We had enough money, he said, and things around the house grew neglected in my absence, especially when you added on my hour-long commute there and back to the small town north of Vancouver that harbored the school. We had no children and no pets, a housekeeper with a more than mild form of OCD who came to the house once a week. I didn't notice much of a difference but I didn't say anything. This was because William wasn't a fighter in the traditional sense. He didn't yell or accuse, bruise with his actions or words. Instead, he disappeared.

His office became a black hole, a great devourer of not only my husband but our potential conflict and our possible resolution. Every fight we could have had lingered in the spaces between his leather-bound law books, under the edges of the Persian carpet. Sometimes, when he was late returning home, I would sit in his big wingback leather chair deep in the heart of his office and I would close my eyes. Only then could I find relief in my imaginations, yell at him the way I wanted to so many days and so many nights across so many years.

We'd married when I was eighteen and he was thirty-six. I was head over heels in love with the curl in his mostly black, slightly graying hair, his incredible *manliness* next to the boys that hung around me in school. I was infatuated with him, with how I looked beside him in pictures, so young and pretty under his distinguished arm. I'd known him my whole life so he was safe but also, I thought, *not safe*, older and worldlier and, I hoped, dirtier than me. There were so many things an older man could teach a naive girl. I used to touch myself at night imagining the things he would do to me, the ways he could make me pleasure him.

Sadly, I still did.

"Beautiful," William said, smiling at me warmly from where he read in a deep armchair in the sitting area off the kitchen.

He presented me with a cheek to kiss, which I did diligently.

Every time I did, I wished he would grab me, haul me over his lap and lay into my ass with the flat off his palm.

I had these aggressive sexual fantasies often. Wishing that his sweet gesture smoothing back my hair was his fingers digging deep into the strands to puppeteer my head back and forth over his erection. Switching out our separate showers before bed with a shared one, where I bent double with my hands around my ankles as he pounded into me and the water pounded against us both.

I'd tried at first, a long time ago, to make these fantasies realities, but William wasn't interested.

I knew this, I did, but I was more than a little hot from the blond guy in the parking lot, the way he had commanded those men without even lifting a finger. It was only too easy to imagine the way he might command me if given the chance.

It was him that I had to blame for my actions.

I dumped my messenger bag beside William's chair and dropped to my knees between his legs.

"Cressida..." he warned softly.

He couldn't even scold me properly.

I ignored him.

My hands slid up his stiffly held legs until they found his belt and made quick work of undoing it. His cock was soft in its nest of hair but I pulled it into the light as if it was a revelation. It was silky in my mouth and easy to swallow.

William's hand hit the top of my head but didn't grab me, didn't even push me away.

"Cressida, really..." he protested again.

He didn't like oral sex. He liked vaginal sex: missionary, me on top or sometimes, if I forced him, doggy style.

I sucked him hard until basic biology took over and he grew in my mouth. I slammed my head down his shaft, taking him into my throat and loving the way it made me want to gag.

"Damn it," William said, not because it felt good, though it did, or because he liked it but because he didn't *want* to like it.

I didn't care. I squeezed my eyes shut tightly as I jacked the base of him and imagined the way the blond king may have held my head down until I groaned and gagged around him. How he might have praised me for taking him so deep and pleasuring him so well.

Instead, I got, "I'm going to come and I don't want to do it in your mouth."

"Please?" I panted against his dick, my tongue trailing out to lick over his crown.

It was his turn to squeeze his eyes shut. His legs shook as he orgasmed, his semen landing in my open mouth and over my cheeks. It took him harshly, wrung him up dry and useless afterwards like a used napkin in his chair.

I leaned back on my haunches and wiped my mouth clean with my tongue and then the back of my hand. My pussy throbbed but I knew he wouldn't touch it so I didn't try to make him. Sex was for the dark hours and I was already in violation of his unspoken code of sexual conduct.

I knew what his reaction would be but, since I was a glutton for punishment, I waited patiently on my knees for him to recuperate. To open his eyes and pierce me with their disappointed, confused condemnation. He reached forward to touch my cheek softly as he asked me, "Why do you degrade yourself like that, Cressie? I don't need *that*."

I closed my eyes against the hot prickle of tears that threatened to elucidate my shame and leaned into his hand so that he would think I was sorry. In a way, I was, because I knew he didn't need *that* to love me. William loved me in a beautiful way, the way one might love a perfectly formed rose, a sentimental trinket. But he didn't love me in the way I needed, the way I'd wanted secretly since I was old enough to feel a heartbeat in my groin, the way one animal loved another.

"I'll make dinner," I said quietly, unfolding from my knees and going into the kitchen.

"That sounds nice," William agreed, easily forgiving me for my exploitation.

He efficiently did up his pants and went back to the book

he was reading while I uncovered the Shepherd's Pie I'd already prepped the morning.

Our night continued from there in a normal way— happy, trivial conversation about our days over mashed potato-topped meat and veg, an hour or so of reading side by side in front of the fire because we didn't own a TV and then our nightly, separate showers before going to bed. We didn't have sex. We rarely did anymore because the doctors had said that the odds of William having children were slim and my husband was of the mind that sex was for a purpose, not recreation.

So, I lay next to him in our beautiful house long into the night until it was the darkest of the evening hours. Only then did I quietly turn onto my back, lift my nightgown and sink my fingers into my burning hot pussy. I came in under two minutes with my clit pinched between my fingers and another two shoved deep inside, thinking of the sexy young blond king and how he would rule me if I were his queen. It was the hardest I had come in years, maybe ever, and right on its heels came the tears. I cried silently and long into my pillow until it was steeped in salty wet and I was steeped deeply in shame. It was in all two hundred and six of my bones, so entangled with my molecules it was an essential strand of my DNA. I'd been living with it since I was pubescent teenage girl and I was so tired of it.

I was tired of boredom. The monotony of my loving husband and our life together, the hamster wheel of our social life with shallow suburban moneyed folk and the irrefutable fact that I was not attracted to my husband.

I lay in the dark for what seemed like an eternity,

dissecting my thoughts like an academic at a conference. Slowly, with no discernable evolution, I was furious.

I was a twenty-six-year-old woman acting like a depressed middle-aged housewife. I had decades ahead of me still to live, to live a life where excitement, spontaneity and change could be a constant. Why was I lying in the dark like a victim? Because I was ashamed that my perfect life and husband didn't make me happy?

Pathetic.

Then, I wondered if I really was. William loved me because I was beautiful and obedient, because he had trained me to be this way since I was an impressionable girl. He did not love the side of me that was scratching and wailing to break free of the social constraints he'd bound me in so beautifully for years. It was the part of me that wanted to lie, steal and cheat; to sin a little every day and gorge myself on a steady diet of thrills. That side would bring the Irons name shame and the most important thing to William was his wealth and reputation.

It was his wealth that gave me pause. I had no real money of my own unless I counted the few thousand dollars my grandpa put into a small trust for me. I didn't know if it would be enough to start a new life. I didn't even know if I was savvy enough or strong enough to strike out on my own, not after an entire life of obedience to my father, and then my husband.

I didn't know, but as I lay there cradled in the dark night, I decided that I didn't care about the certainty. That, in fact, it was part of the thrill.

I rolled over to look at William lying beside me, his face slack and peaceful in slumber. Reverently, I traced his thick eyebrows, the slightly jagged edge of his hairline down to the winged ear that I liked to kiss. I peeled the covers away from his body carefully so that I could run my eyes over the entirety of my husband for the last time.

The finality settled in me like a bright thing, something light that made the heaviness in my bones fizzle and pop into nothingness.

"William," I whispered, pressing a thumb to the corner of his lips. "Wake up. I have to tell you something."

Now FREE on Kindle Unlimited!

THANKS ETC.

Welcome to the Dark Side came to me one day when I was doing The Lean outside a liquor store. I was raised by a conservative mother in a well-established family in a smallish city but my father was a rebel. He was the kind of man who happily flouted societal rules, doing whatever he wanted and doing it with a charming smile. There was always that dichotomy of spirit inside me as a result, the same duality that Louise/Loulou found in herself in the book. I believe that everyone has a kernel of rebellion in their hearts. Sometimes, people live their whole lives without anything to water and feed that seed into something more, something substantial and beautiful like a rose with thorns. Zeus does that for Loulou. He does it by being supportive and totally accepting of every facet of her so that she doesn't feel the need to hide and even more, she wants to expose every nook and cranny of her soul to him so that he might love all of her. Their story is about love and acceptance, about being who you want to be regardless of perceptions because as Zeus would say, livin' free is the only way to die.

I have so many people to thank for loving and supporting my own rose with thorns and this book.

To Becca at Hello Lovely Box for featuring Daddy Zeus and Loulou! It has been a dream of mine to have a limited edition in one of your magnificent boxes and I am so honoured to participate now!

To Emily Wittig Designs for crafting a beyond stunning cover for this edition!

To my darling, PA, Annette who brings light and support to my life every single day. I will love you and be grateful for you forever.

To Michelle Clay for her gentle spirit, enduring support and 24/7 advice about everything from cover photos to plot details. In her, I have found utter acceptance and a beautiful friendship. She rearranged her days in order to proof and edit this manuscript's rough draft and there aren't enough thanks in the world for me to bestow upon her for that.

My darling Cassie Chapman has been one of my best friends in this wonderful book words for ages but I will never cease to appreciate her. I'm sorry, ladies, but Daddy Zeus is HERS. Thank you, my darling Cass, for the gorgeous teasers and last-minute graphics I asked you to make, for beta-reading Daddy and for loving me. Love you more than tacos.

There are some people that you meet online and instantly forge a connection with over HTML pages and Facebook posts. Rebecca Scarlett, my gorgeous fellow Canadian, is one such person that happened with. I feel overwhelmed by her support and genuine friendship. Thank you for the shout-outs, beta-reading WTTDS and just being my friend. I can't wait to meet you and bake pies!

When I first started reading indie romance, K Webster was one of my ultimate favorite authors and she still is to this day. It still blows my mind that I can also call her my *friend* (cue fan-girling) and that she proofed Daddy's book for me. Daddies for life, Kristi!! I'm so jazzed to know you haha.

Lylah James, you Canadian beauty, thank you for all our chats and for beta-reading Daddy and going easy on me.

Najla Qambar is my cover designer and all-round graphics magician. She brings my delicious Fallen MC men to life so beautifully it's as if she lives in my imagination (remind me to wear a tinfoil hat if we ever meet in person!).

To Marjorie Lord for her proofreading expertise, I'd be a mess of errors without you.

Olive Teagan, my darling, thank you for taking your keen eye to the book! It astounds me how error-ridden this book would be without you. But most of all, thank you for giving me your beautiful friendship!

To Stacey from Champagne Formatting, THANK YOU for making this book a gorgeous, polished gem!

Every day that I interact with my readers in Giana's Darlings, I feel so blessed. Thank you to my loyal Darlings for assuaging my doubts, reading my works and sharing your passion with me. You make every single day feel like a girls' night and I couldn't love that more!

The biggest shout out has to go to the readers and book bloggers in Daddy Zeus's ARC Team! I love you for your enthusiasm and willingness to share Daddy with others. Your support is essential to me <3

I believe that you create your own family and I am so blessed to have so many friendships with beautiful women and authors in this community. For the authors who participated in my Release Party—K.J. Lewis, Carian Cole, Saffron A. Kent, Kennedy Ryan, Shanora Williams, Mara White, Dani Rene, M. Never, K.K. Allen, Sierra Simone, Leigh Lennon, Dylan Allen, Rebecca Scarlett, Auden Dar, Marley Valentine, Meagan Brady, Ava Harrison, C.L. Matthews, Ella Fields, Jane Anthony, Fiona Cole, Kathryn Nolan, Lucia Franco, L.B. Dunbar, Lizzie Hart Stevens, Ella Fox, L.J. Shen, K Webster and Charleigh Rose! Also, to my girls, Olive Teagan and Lee Piper—your support is one of the best gifts I have ever been given in this life.

I can't even begin to express my gratitude for Sierra Simone. You are such a goddess and the fact that you take time out of your busy, beautiful life to help and encourage me humbles me. Your friendship means so much to me.

Kristie Lewis, my darling Southern girl, I love you so much. I love that we are on this crazy journey together, loving and supporting each other. Thank you for holding my hand.

Sunny, gorgeous, thank you for letting me bug you with all my newbie author questions and endless need for advice. Love your face.

Ella Fox, I love that you read *The Evolution of Sin* without me even realizing it and I love that you are one of the most supportive friends I have but make absolute zero deal out of it. You rock.

Ella Fields, your gentle Australian voice in my ear each time you leave me a voicemail makes my day. I love your words, both in your books and to me over Facebook messenger.

I can't list all of the book bloggers who make my day with their reviews and teasers but special thanks goes out to Sarah at Musings of a Book Belle, Ella at Honeyed Pages, Keri at Keri Loves Books, and the girls at Kinky Girls Book Obsessions.

Whenever I write about men, especially from a male perceptive, I draw on my decade long friendship with my boys: Chris, Devo, Jeff, Colin, Kevin and Alex. Thank you for teaching me how to love myself, for telling me that men love a body full of curves and a personality filled with edges. You have been my fathers, my brothers, and my best friends for over a decade and I am never afraid of the future knowing that you will be there for me for another seven decades at least.

Armie, my love sponge, thank you for putting up with me writing in the car while you drove, in the kitchen while you cooked and in bed at night when you were trying to sleep. I've spent the last six months nearly 24/7 with you and I couldn't imagine anyone else willingly putting up with me for that long. Your friendship is the pillow I rest my head on at night, the strength in my spine and the convection in the sails of my dreams.

And last but never least, to the Love of My Life. Every single one of my love stories pales in comparison to the love you have given me the last ten years of our lives. Thank you for loving me and supporting me through everything we've been through. I promise I will never stop appreciating you.

OTHER BOOKS BY GIANA DARLING

The Fallen Men Series

The Fallen Men are a series of interconnected, standalone, erotic MC romances that each feature age gap love stories between dirty-talking, Alpha males and the strong, sassy women who win their hearts.

Lessons in Corruption

Welcome to the Dark Side

Good Gone Bad

Fallen Son (A Short Story)

After the Fall

Inked in Lies

Fallen King (A Short Story)

Dead Man Walking

A Fallen Men Companion Book of Poetry:

King of Iron Hearts

The Evolution of Sin Trilogy

Giselle Moore is running away from her past in France for a new life in America, but before she moves to New York City, she takes a holiday on the beaches of Mexico and meets a sinful, enigmatic French businessman, Sinclair, who awakens submissive desires and changes her life forever.

The Affair

The Secret

The Consequence

The Evolution Of Sin Trilogy Boxset

The Enslaved Duet

The Enslaved Duet is a dark romance duology about an eighteen-year old Italian fashion model, Cosima Lombardi, who is sold by her indebted father to a British Earl who's nefarious plans for her include more than just sexual slavery... Their epic tale spans across Italy, England, Scotland, and the USA across a five-year period that sees them endure murder, separation, and a web of infinite lies.

Enthralled (The Enslaved Duet #1)

Enamoured (The Enslaved Duet, #2)

Anti-Heroes in Love Duet

Elena Lombardi is an ice cold, broken-hearted criminal lawyer with a distaste for anything untoward, but when her sister begs her to represent New York City's most infamous mafioso on trial for murder, she can't refuse and soon, she finds herself unable to resist the dangerous charms of Dante Salvatore.

When Heroes Fall

When Villains Rise

The Dark Dream Duet

The Dark Dream duology is a guardian/ward, enemies to lovers romance about the dangerous, scarred black sheep of the Morelli family, Tiernan, and the innocent Bianca Belcante. After Bianca's mother dies, Tiernan becomes the guardian to both her and her little brother. But Tiernan doesn't do anything out of the goodness of his heart, and soon Bianca is thrust into the wealthy elite of Bishop's Landing and the dark secrets that lurk beneath its glittering surface.

Bad Dream (Dark Dream Duet, #0.5) is FREE

Dangerous Temptation (Dark Dream Duet, #1)

Beautiful Nightmare (Dark Dream Duet, #2)

The Elite Seven Series

Sloth (The Elite Seven Series, #7)

Coming Soon

Caution to the Wind (The Fallen Men, #7)

ABOUT GIANA DARLING

Giana Darling is a USA Today, Wall Street Journal, Top 40 Best Selling Canadian romance writer who specializes in the taboo and angsty side of love and romance. She currently lives in beautiful British Columbia where she spends time riding on the back of her man's bike, baking pies, and reading snuggled up with her cat, Persephone.

Join my Reader's Group
Subscribe to my Newsletter
Follow me on IG
Like me on Facebook
Follow me on Goodreads
Follow me on BookBub
Follow me on Pinterest

Made in the USA
Columbia, SC
21 March 2023